# *The* House *at* Silvermoor

## TRACY REES

Quercus

First published in Great Britain in 2020 by Quercus
This paperback edition published in 2020 by

Quercus Editions Ltd
Carmelite House
50 Victoria Embankment
London EC4Y 0DZ

An Hachette UK company

A CIP catalogue record for this book is available
from the British Library

PB ISBN 978 1 78648 670 7
EB ISBN 978 1 78648 672 1

10 9 8 7 6 5 4 3 2 1

Typeset by CC Book Production
Printed and bound in Great Britain by Clays Ltd, Elcograf S.p.A.

MIX
Paper from
responsible sources
FSC® C104740

Papers used by Quercus are from well-managed forests and other responsible sources.

Praise for *The House at Silvermoor*

'A tenderly evoked and compelling read ...
*The House at Silvermoor* deserves to be a huge success'
Rachel Hore, author of *The Love Child*

'I loved *The House at Silvermoor*. Tracy's writing is
always so warm and convincing ... the story is both
romantic and compelling'
Rosanna Ley, author of *The Lemon Tree Hotel*

'Tracy Rees has a rare gift for making us care about her
characters from the very first pages ... a compassionate and
compelling novel, with a heart-warming love story at its core'
Gill Paul, author of *The Lost Daughter*

'*The House at Silvermoor* is a sweeping saga full of
likeable characters. What a joy to read'
Lorna Cook, author of *The Forbidden Promise*

'A rich, riveting and romantic read'
Joanna Courtney, author of *Blood Queen*

**Tracy Rees** was born in South Wales. A Cambridge graduate, she had a successful eight-year career in non-fiction publishing and a second career practising and teaching humanistic counselling. She was the winner of the Richard and Judy Search for a Bestseller Competition and the 2015 LoveStories 'Best Historical Read' award.

## Also by Tracy Rees

*Amy Snow*
*Florence Grace*
*The Hourglass*
*The Love Note* (originally published as *Darling Blue*)

For Phil,

For my parents

and

In memory of my grandfather, Leonard Rees,
who was a coal miner in South Wales

# Part One

# Chapter 1

～c～

# Tommy

*Summer 1897*

''Scuse me, Schoolmaster.'

The bell had just rung to mark the end of our last day of school. The other boys had fled in an instant; a proud stampede. For them, finishing school meant a new stage of life; the chance to bring a wage to their families. Stepping into the shoes of generations, rising to the challenges of our heritage: that's what becoming a man meant on the coalfields. But I lingered.

I watched as Mr Latimer tidied his desk and shook out the jacket that hung on his chair while he delivered his lessons. White chalk dust had settled on top of the coal dust that we all wore and breathed. We swallowed it when we licked our lips. The mingled black and white always gave Latimer a curiously grey and muted appearance.

He looked up. 'Tommy Green. Still here, lad? Do you want something?'

'I'd value a word, sir, just a moment of tha time.'

Latimer continued to shake his jacket and line up his chalks. I fidgeted, unsure what to do with my hands. I didn't even know what enquiry to make. I knew of nothing but coal mining and earls. What should I ask?

'Thank you, sir. It's just, you see, sir . . .' I took a deep breath. 'Tha's always been good enough to say I'm fair at school, sir.'

I hoped he might help me then. Perhaps chime in with, 'You certainly are, Tommy! In all my years' teaching I've never seen such a promising lad. You'll be wasted in the mines . . .'

But he said nothing. He dusted off the blackboard, erasing the proverbs and verses from which we had drawn our final instruction in spelling and morality. I saw my hopes swept off with them.

Over the years, I'd worked hard in school, drawn praise from Schoolmaster. I'd won prizes, three years in a row, and had them presented to me by the smiling earl at Sunday school, with my ma in a bonnet clapping wearily along. It was the closest most of us had ever been to the earl and each time he shook my hand and called me a bright boy. The second time I was prepared to greet him like an old acquaintance but he showed no sign of recognising that I was the same bright boy as before.

The third time, he was accompanied by his six-year-old son.

4

Young Lord Walter Sedgewick's christening had been held on my fifth birthday and all the villagers had been invited to Silvermoor for the celebrations, which had culminated in fireworks. The fact had always made me fancy an affinity between us. We shook hands too, he as solemn as a little judge. I stared fiercely into his eyes. *Don't you know me?* I pleaded silently. *You were christened on my birthday, we are linked.* But he only looked a little frightened. When I released him, he brushed off a smudge of coal that I'd left on his cuff.

It wasn't only in school that I'd proved myself. I'd also satisfied my father in a dozen small challenges of manhood. I'd shot rabbits – and he clipped me when I cried. I'd stayed locked in the coal house all night when I was nine – to get me used to facing darkness alone, he said. I'd stood over corpses and gazed into their wide eyes – there was death aplenty before me, he said.

I'd dreamed – oh, how I'd dreamed – of leaving Grindley and going far away. I dreamed of meeting people who did and talked of other things besides mining. I dreamed of rooms full of books. But whenever these hopes spilled unwitting from my boyish lips, I'd earn a lashing from my father. So I learned to stay quiet.

When I was very young, my favourite daydream was that one day the earl would come to our cottage and claim me as his own long-lost son and brother to Walter. I would go to live at Silvermoor and ride ponies every day. But when I was older, and came to understand such matters, I realised that this fantasy could only come about through my mother's disgrace – and *that* could not be unless she were a very different sort of person.

Despite all my efforts to grow up right, life had shown me the same number of avenues that it showed us all – one. To work at the mine. So here I stood, aged twelve, desperately hoping to avert my destiny.

Latimer turned to his next task, the repositioning of books in the wooden cupboard we called a library.

'I just wondered, sir, if there might be . . . if I might . . . ?' I'd never so badly needed to go to the toilet but I steeled myself. 'Is there more schoolin' to be done, sir? And can I do it? Is there summat I can do in life other than the mines? Canst tha help me, Schoolmaster? Please.'

'So there it is,' he said at last, putting on his jacket. 'Fair at book learning, perhaps, but the important lessons have clearly passed you by. Humility, acceptance, duty. You're a coal miner's son, Tommy, a coal miner's grandson. Do you disrespect them and what they do?'

'No, no!' I hastened. 'It's nowt like that, sir . . . But I know there's a world out there, beyond Grindley. I know there are those as *don't* work underground and I only wondered if there's a way for me to be one of them. I disrespect no one, sir.'

'I see.' He sat down and steepled his hands on the desk in front of him. Years I had sat and watched Mr Latimer at that desk. 'I'm grieved, Green, if I have given you false pride. It's true that you have come top in class numerous times, but this merely reflects the sad lack of basic intelligence possessed by the majority of Grindley children. It isn't their fault, it's breeding. Someone has to come top, Tommy. In a tiny village school where only the dullest of intellects grasp for a basic understanding, that someone was you.'

I felt a rush fill my head but I did not cry, another thing I had conquered for my father.

'But, but, sir . . . the earl . . .'

He looked at me sharply then. 'What about the earl?'

'He . . . he called us a bright boy. When he give us me prize.'

He snorted. 'He'd hardly call you a dunce at a prize-giving. Merely good manners, Green, not something to take to heart. It's all relative, you understand. Relative.'

I didn't understand, but I struggled to, as was my habit when something was new to me, or difficult. 'Does tha mean I'm *not* bright, Schoolmaster, that I only seem that way compared to some?'

His face lost some of its anger. 'Green, lad. You must understand, the world out there is more complex and difficult than you could ever imagine. Its realms and reaches are not for the likes of you. Here, you may be the star pupil. Out there, you would be nothing. You would be crushed in an instant, as surely as those men were crushed in White Arrow Drift Mine years ago. Does the minister not tell us that we are born into our right place on this earth? Do you doubt God's plan?'

I was tongue-tied. In quite real terms, my tongue had lodged in my throat in a glutinous lump, and I could neither swallow nor speak. I hung my head and I stood there and burned.

'I should think not,' he concluded, as if I had agreed with him. 'Off with you now, lad, and in recognition of your efforts in this classroom I'll not tell your father of this. Mention it again and I'll see to it he gives you a sound thrashing to rid you of your notions.'

It would be the thrashing of my life, I knew. I whispered, 'Then there's really . . . nothing? For me?'

'Nothing,' he agreed.

I turned and left the schoolroom for the last time. At the door no sense or wisdom could prevent me from turning and asking one last question. 'What were *your* father, sir? Was he a schoolmaster too?'

The board duster came hurtling through the air with a wicked accuracy. '*Out*, Green!'

# Chapter 2

## Tommy

I wended my way home greatly dispirited. Hearing that I wasn't sufficiently bright to make a good fist of aught but this life was as great a loss to me as when my brother Dan died in the pit last year. But I knew I must shake it off before Da got home. He'd often told us that back in the old days, before the law had changed, children were sent to work in the mines at the age of five. His tone suggested a certain nostalgia for that time.

I arrived home to find my brother John sloshing in the tin bath in the yard. 'All right, our Tom?' he asked.

His clothes had been whipped away by Mercy, my eldest sister, who was at the laundry tub, and a pair of clean long johns was slung over the wall. Needless to say, those of us who worked were utterly barred from the house before washing.

I stepped into the back room through the only door we ever used, where Ma was cooking something with bacon. The housing was better in Grindley than in many a pit village. We had two rooms downstairs and decent sizes at that. Twelve by twelve, one of them. Ernest and Alfie sat on the floor, playing jacks. My middle sister Mary was in a corner, sewing and sulking. She was always sulky since our Jimmy, who was her twin, had started down the pit last year, and she'd never been the smiliest lass to begin with. Grandma was peeling potatoes by the stove. Year round she sat there – she felt the cold.

'Where's our Con?' I asked Ma, giving her a kiss and tearing a piece of bread from the loaf that was cooling on the side. Connie was the little one, my favourite.

'I don't know,' Ma answered, flustered. 'I can't keep track of you all any more. My head's not what it used to be since our Dan went.'

It was true that my formerly calm, clever mother had gone to pieces since we lost Dan. Not in any way that a neighbour would recognise – she continued to cook and clean and sew our buttons and organise us all. But inside our cottage we saw the changes in her. She was often distracted, quick to tears. She forgot things she would never have forgotten before and we all knew that a piece of her was away with Dan.

He'd been the handsomest of us brothers. Only seventeen when he died. No big disaster, no astonishing accident. Just that Ned Vale, the timberer working behind him that day, hadn't shored up the ceiling sufficiently. Or he had, depending who you spoke to. It had never happened before with Ned's props so maybe it was just one of those things. Down came the ceiling, crushing our Dan. Ned was inconsolable. It was the only time I'd ever seen Da cry.

No report reached the newspapers – that only happened when many lives were lost. The more the better, from the point of view of the papers, who wanted sensational reading. For the miners, too, those stories made greater leverage to campaign for better conditions. But no newspaper could have altered the horror of what happened to him, three hundred feet below ground, alone in the dark . . . the sudden drop of rock . . . Had it been quick – Dan snuffed out in an instant – or had he lain there a long while, knowing death was coming?

The door burst open and John came in from his bath, followed by Mercy, looking red-faced and hot, followed soon after by Grandpa and Connie, who was clutching a small bucket and chuckling with glee.

'I done it, Mamma!' she piped. 'I catched a fish!' She beamed when she saw me, and threw her arms around me, her bucket clonking my leg.

'Ouch!'

'Sorry! Look at my fish, Tommy!' I peered in to see one very small silver minnow dead at the bottom.

'I took her to the stream,' Grandpa explained. 'She wanted to have a hand in the supper.'

'I said thank you to the fish for being caught,' Connie explained, slapping the minnow triumphantly onto the table.

'And to the fish's ma and da for letting me have their bairn. And to the stream for letting me fish in it.'

'Where *does* she get these notions?' marvelled my mother, moving the fish to one side.

After dinner, when the little ones had climbed the ladder to bed and Grandma and Grandpa were tucked into their folding bed under the stairs in the corner of the kitchen, the rest of us sat in the front room, Ma playing the harmonium softly: 'His Mercy Shall Raise Me Up'. Mercy was crocheting. Mary rested her head on Jimmy's shoulder, her face more content now that her twin was home. George and John were playing cards. These short intervals of peace in the evenings meant a great deal to me.

Then my father caught my eye and jerked his head towards the door, lifting a finger to pursed lips.

'Time for a smoke then,' he said, taking up his pipe and heading out.

I waited a convincing moment or two then sauntered after him. He was sitting on the wall, tapping his pipe bowl. Away down the row other neighbours were doing the same. He had swung his legs over to face the street and other people's houses, set in a parallel row to ours. I sat beside him, facing our house.

'I'm takin' you tonight,' he said without preamble. 'I won't take Jimmy now he's down pit. Food's scarce and I need a hand.'

I stayed silent, digesting it.

'Say nowt to tha mother,' Da said unnecessarily. Ma regularly berated Da for taking her sons poaching. Our deaths couldn't come fast enough for him, she accused him each time a new one of us did it. We'd all be shot or hanged, she railed, but there, at least we'd be saved from the mines. Da took no notice but I don't think he liked it.

'I'll not,' I assured him. 'What time, Da?'

'Midnight. There's a good moon tonight. Mind you learn the ways whilst you can see. Now go on. Leave us finish me pipe.'

At midnight I stole from the bed. Ernest's feet were lodged under my chin, an arm of John's was thrown over me and my own left leg was trapped beneath a snoring George. Never mind the hazards of poaching, getting out without waking everyone was my first challenge.

Da was waiting in the yard, grim-faced as usual, and we set off without a word. Even so, it felt like high adventure. It would take a worse father than mine for a boy not to feel the thrill of venturing out in the moonlight with him.

Poaching was illegal, of course, and risky, but I was excited to set foot on the Silvermoor estate again. The glorious memory of my fifth birthday had never faded and my secret fascination with the gentry had not waned. But when we reached the turning for Silvermoor my father kept walking.

'Where are we going, Da?'

'Can't go to Silvermoor a while. I had a run-in last week.'

'Then . . . ?'

He didn't answer. Man of few words, my father.

We walked a couple of miles in the direction of Arden, the next village over. It dawned on me that the next big estate we would reach was Heston Manor and fear stilled my blood. Heston belonged to the Barridges, the other coal-owning family in our area. They owned three mines and worked their men harder than dogs. When we in Grindley told ourselves we were lucky to work for the Sedgewicks of Silvermoor, since there were others far worse, it was the Barridges we meant.

Twenty years ago, there had been an explosion in one of the Barridge pits, caused by firedamp, one of the noxious gases that made life underground so very hazardous. The deputy, a very experienced man, had raised concerns about that stretch of tunnel with Winthrop Barridge, who told him to carry on. Hundreds of men were killed. I could scarcely believe a man could be so uncaring. All those deaths, so unnecessary.

And Winthrop Barridge paid not one penny of compensation to the widows. The very next day they were ordered to leave. So many grieving women and children with nowhere to live and no means at all. It was said that he had a lump of coal for a heart.

The women protested, camping at the edge of the Heston estate. Barridge set his dogs on them. They went to a local newspaper, which made much, for a time, of the greedy and merciless mine owners. Barridge paid them off and the story died. Those widows and bairns disappeared to who knew what fate, while Winthrop Barridge brought in new men to work his Hepzibah mine and toasted the birth of twin sons with champagne.

The story summed up everything we knew about the Barridge clan. And now we were going to poach on their land.

Heston was empty now. Perhaps God had punished old Barridge for his coal-heartedness, for six years ago his eldest son, the Barridge heir, had met a tragic end. A keen horseman, he'd been thrown from a new mount. Soon afterwards, the Barridges had moved to their other Yorkshire home, which was smaller than Heston but free of bad memories. In our families we could not indulge our losses in such a way.

Heston Manor was a chilling place, fenced, walled, chained and in all other ways forbidden. The woods were thick with game but it was common knowledge that although the Barridges weren't around to roast their rabbits, they didn't want anyone else to get them either. Paulson, their groundsman, was a violent man with a zeal for catching poachers. I'd heard the place was trapped and patrolled nightlong by Paulson, with his henchmen and three great black hounds. Since my father was taking me there, I could only assume that these rumours were greatly exaggerated.

'Now, lad,' said Da, coming to a halt in the shadows. 'Tha's heard the stories of this place? Aye, well, they're all true. There's only so far we dare go, a corner or two that seem to slip old

Paulson's notice. Stick with me and do as I say, you hear me? That man will string you up by the ankles if he catches you.'

I nodded, numb with disbelief that we were about to cross such an inviolable boundary. A tall, thick hedge, bristling with nettle and briar, barred our way like something from a tale. It seemed positively alive with ill intent. But Da showed me a small area where it was sparser. Leaves and more pliable branches had been pulled across, but the moonlight showed it up like the bald patch on Preacher Tawney's head. He combed his hair across it, but it was there nonetheless. Da parted the branches and nodded for me to slip through. He followed and put his hand on my shoulder for a minute while I looked around. We were surrounded by trees.

'Don't be deceived,' murmured Da, close in my ear. 'We're not safe, keep a sharp eye at all times. If you see anyone, even far off, run and get out. They've got dogs like you've never seen. Fastest bastards I ever knew. We've got two paths we can use. I'll show you.'

I nodded, nervous, but probably not as nervous as I should have been. It all felt like a dream. We walked less than half a mile along a very thin path that threaded through the brambles. In Da's traps we found two rabbits and a pheasant. In the weird white light his face wore a look of determined victory. We slung the game in a bag and he showed me how to reset the traps.

'See that pine tree,' he said then. 'The tall, thin one next to

16

the fat bushes? That's our limit. Go no further, never ever, if you value your life. Understand me, son?'

'I understand,' I whispered. He rarely called any of us that so I knew he was deadly serious.

'I'll show you why,' he said, leading me to the thin pine. The moon had vanished for a moment behind a cloud. When it sailed out again, he pointed. I could see nothing and frowned but he clipped the side of my head and I looked again. Then I saw it. A thin, thin line, like a hair, across the path. I looked at Da in shock.

'That's not . . . ?'

He nodded. 'Shotgun's in t'bushes. That string'll trigger it. They've been illegal eighty years now, but Paulson still uses them. Traps too – this place is crackling with them. So where do you stop, lad?'

'At the thin pine by the fat bushes.'

He nodded. 'Back we go then. You lead, show me you've remembered the way.'

I had a good memory for the countryside and the moon was bright. I only threatened to veer off the path once and Da slapped the side of my head again so the right way was lodged in there good and proper.

The other path took us an even shorter distance; Da was playing it safe, staying well within the boundaries of peril. His traps yielded nothing but a squirrel this time. Da cursed softly and threw the small, broken body into the bracken. He showed me how important it was to pull the foliage back over the traps, to keep them concealed. 'We don't want Paulson on the lookout in our patch.'

Then he pointed. 'That tump there? That funny hillock just off the path? That's where you stop.' He marched me up to it. I didn't even want to wonder how he had found all this out. Da took up a stout stick and threw it just ahead. I hadn't seen the trap, veiled as it was by ferns, but I saw its grey glint as it sprang shut. It wasn't a small trap like Da's; it was intended for poachers, not game. There was a loud snap and the stick was cracked in two, bits of wood flying up. I swallowed.

'Could be yer leg,' Da said briefly. Then, with our small, hard-won booty, we went home again.

# Chapter 3

## Josie

*April 1898*

There was always a sense of rivalry between Arden, which was our village, and Grindley, three miles over. I took quite some foolish pride in coming from Arden because it had the prettier name; as a girl I required nothing more from my place of origin. Looking back, I marvel at my complacency. A miner's daughter I was, a miner's wife I would one day be and Arden was where I lived. All that changed the day I met Tommy Green.

My sister Alice was getting married. I'd been charged with fetching violets for her to wind in her hair, to bring out the colour of her cornflower-blue eyes. Alice and her perfect colouring and angelic face! Why should *she* care about bringing out her eyes? She was only marrying Fred Deacon. He was squat and swarthy and I wouldn't have married him if you'd paid me five whole pounds. She said she loved him but I think she loved the overwinder's job that would be his when his father died. I think she especially loved the large cottage that came with it.

It was late April. Didn't think of that when they sent me out for violets, did they? The flowers were gone from the lanes by then but I knew where they still grew. I set off to my secret place, a small corner of the old Barridge estate, Heston. They'd have killed me if they'd known I went there, for a fact.

The Barridges were the landowners, our gentry. Our homes, our labours, all belonged to them. Our souls too, some said. Once, the Barridges had lived at Heston Manor, and held balls and dinners and taken part in the usual customs of the wildly rich. But now Heston was empty and abandoned and *forbidden*.

That was one thing I envied the Grindley lot. *They* had gentry they could see and tug their caps to and chatter about. Ours were too far off now for all that. I'd never seen a lord or lady, never glimpsed a shiny carriage. Only the men ever saw a Barridge, for, despite the distance, despite his age and whatever the weather, Winthrop Barridge visited his mines *every single day*. That was not a good thing, they said.

It was known across the county that he was a hard master. Back then I didn't fully understand what that meant. All I knew was that the family wasn't liked, but what was that to me? It wasn't as though I would ever cross paths with any of them.

I sauntered through the lanes, enjoying the weather, until I came to a rocky incline that rose to an old stone wall. Behind it was a copse of trees, pressing to get out. In one place the wall had crumbled and the gap had been stopped up with a wooden fence but the boards had rotted and it was easy enough to squeeze through. I doubted the gamekeeper ever bothered with this dense tangle; there was estate aplenty to patrol and nothing here but wildflowers and bramble. All I did, once I was in, was look out. I would peer through the wooden boards, observing the sweep of countryside from a landowner's perspective. I would enjoy the peace, which I never got at home, and after a while I would leave.

The woods were full of bluebells and violets this time of year and they were bluer, brighter than elsewhere because the thick trees protected them from the coal dust in the air. It was rare to see pure colour, unclouded by grey. I gathered a coronet's worth of violets for Alice and an armload of bluebells for me then headed home. It should have been such an uneventful morning.

But then I met the gamekeeper coming the other way. I'd never seen him before but I knew him at once, by his gaiters and boots, and his hat bristling with pheasant feathers. And by the shotgun hanging at his side. And the swing of his stride, tramping the lanes as if he owned them. I thanked God that I was back where I had a perfect right to be.

'Good morning, sir,' I said, a little perky.

'Where did you get those flowers, girl?' he demanded.

I flushed. I know I did. With my complexion you can't get away with anything. I hate my red hair and my white skin. Never mind vanity, they're impractical. Now Alice, *she* could tell a barefaced lie and stay just the colour of ripened corn. But what concern could he have with a twelve-year-old girl carrying wildflowers?

He had concern aplenty.

'Did you steal them from Heston?' he boomed. I was suddenly aware of the wide, silent countryside spreading in every direction around me. 'Have you been trespassing, girl? Answer me!'

'They're for my sister's wedding, sir!' I was gabbling. 'Our Alice. She's getting married at one. I'd best get back or me mam will kill me. Nice to meet you, sir. Good day.'

'Not so fast!' He yanked my arm and the bluebells scattered in the lane. The violets were tucked into my pinny pocket so at least they were safe.

'No!' I cried, shocked at the waste, the petty black and white of it all.

'How did you get in?' he roared in my face, still holding my arm. 'Can't you read the signs, girl? Perhaps you can't read. They say, *Trespassers will be prosecuted*. What do you say to that?'

'I weren't trespassin'!' I wailed. 'I swear!'

'Then where did you pick them? Not a great many bluebells in the hedge, are there?'

'Sir, they're nowt but flowers!'

'To Heston flowers you have no right and no entitlement. I ask you again: how did you get in?'

'I were at Grindley, sir! There's bluebells in the lanes at Grindley, only go and see 'em.'

He looked at me disbelievingly. 'You walked all the way to Grindley, to fetch flowers for your sister?'

'I did! For her wedding, sir. A special day.'

He let go of my arm. 'What's your father's name?'

Everything inside me stilled. We all knew the trouble that men like this, men who had the ear of the family, could cause for the likes of my father. I couldn't tell him the truth. 'Broad, sir, Thomas Broad.'

'And your name, girl?'

'Lizzie.'

'Well, Lizzie Broad, you'd best go on back to Grindley, hadn't you, and pick more flowers for your sister? These are all quite spoiled now,' he said, pacing back and forth over my bluebells, crushing their stems and grinding their lovely heads into the ground.

'Aye, sir. I'd best. If that's all, sir.'

'Don't let me catch you this close to Heston again.'

I turned tail and fled towards Grindley, which was in the opposite direction from where I needed to go. After a while I looked back over my shoulder. He wasn't following. He'd turned off the lane and was cresting the hill towards Heston. Even so, I must have run half a mile before I let myself stop and think about turning back. And when I did I found myself crying. I'd been so cocky and now I felt scared and stupid. God, I hoped that man didn't go to Arden and ask about for a Thomas or a Lizzie Broad, for no such folk existed.

I'd never had anything I'd wanted snatched away from me before, and the reason for that, I realised, was that I never wanted anything. When something as small as wildflowers was denied you, well, there was some sort of shame in that.

The next minute I heard whistling and a lad about my own age strode into view. I gasped in annoyance and dragged my sleeve over my wet face. Was no one at home this Sunday, or in church? Must they all tramp the lanes between Arden and Grindley and get in my way?

'How do?' said the boy, tugging his cap.

'Good day,' I said, giving myself airs because he was a Grindley lad, I'm not sure why. I took my cue from the adults, I suppose. The men always swore that Grindley men were soft, that the Sedgewicks, the family for whom they worked, were soft, that a Grindley lass should count herself lucky to marry an Arden man. (Despite the fact that had never happened in living memory.) In time I came to learn that Grindley folk were as proud to be them as we were to be us, a discovery which astonished me at first.

He smiled as if I'd said something funny, which made me puff myself up all the more. I was especially irritated because I really needed to turn around and start for home. If I did it now, I'd look as if I were following this young fellow-me-lad. I was quite sure he rated himself enough to think it. He was all down at heel and covered in coal dust, as we all were, but he was good-looking. His pond-green eyes were ever so slightly bulbous – not enough to look strange, just enough to be striking. Froggy eyes, I thought at once; they gave him an open and enquiring look. He was tall – that wouldn't help him down the pit – with dark curly hair and an air about him. That's all I could think then, that he had an air. I hesitated, because I didn't know which way to walk and because I was curious.

'Fine day,' he remarked and his striking eyes still danced on me as if I were a delight – or a great source of amusement.

'Look,' I said. 'I'll be honest. I have to turn around and go home. I need to get back for me sister's wedding and me ma will kill us I've been out that long. But now tha's happened along and I don't want you to think I'm following you. I'm sure the girls in Grindley consider you very fine and all but I'm an Arden lass and we stick to our own. So don't think owt.' And I turned round and marched ahead of him, though I don't know how I thought I'd maintain my lead. He was tall, as I've said, and I was ever so medium-sized.

'Would you like me to turn round so you don't think I'm following you neither?' he called after me, cheekily I thought.

I sniffed. 'I'm sure it makes no difference to me where you go. Enjoy your walk, why don't you.'

He laughed aloud, a surprising burst of sound on that hushed

Sunday morning. 'I'll carry on then, seeing as it's all the same to you,' he informed me and fell into step at my side. 'As we're companions of the road, introductions seem proper,' he said. 'I'm Tommy Green of Grindley.'

I looked at him sideways, getting a little puffed but not wanting to slow my pace. Truth be told, I didn't want him to keep up his same long stride and pull away from me. 'Josie Westgate of Arden.'

'Pleased to meet you. If your sister's getting' married, and your ma wants you home, why were you racing as fast as your little legs could carry you away from Arden?'

'I do *not* have little legs!' I said indignantly, stopping dead, gasping for breath. 'I have perfectly normal legs for a lass my age.'

'A lass of . . . ?'

'I'm twelve year old, Tommy Green, though it's nowt of your business. And I was heading to Grindley, if you must know, because I had a run-in with the old gamekeeper and I had to get away. And are you always so full of questions?'

He stopped too and sighed. 'Aye. I am. Everyone tells me so. Old Paulson do you mean? Him as wears the feathers an' blots out the sun?'

I couldn't help but giggle. 'Aye, him.'

'What's he doing picking on a young girl then?'

'I had bluebells . . .' I hesitated; I hadn't told a soul about my excursions to the forbidden estate so why would I tell a complete stranger? Yet somehow I wanted to. We came to the place in the lane where my beautiful flowers were spilled and trampled. I gestured at them sadly. 'He thought I'd stolen them from Heston. He were that angry. I told him I'd got them from Grindley lanes to get out of trouble and he said I'd best go back and get some more. So I had to go that way.'

He stared at me. 'And did you? Get them from Heston?' He looked intrigued and admiring and worried all at once.

'See up there?' I pointed and he followed my gaze. 'There's a gap in't wall. I don't go far, only into the woods, but it's quiet and the flowers are beautiful.'

'They *were* beautiful,' he murmured, picking up two or three stems from the ground but discarding them again when he saw how damaged they were.

'Only he called it stealing,' I went on, glad to have someone to confide in. 'And he asked me da's name, so I made it up, and now I'm that scared he'll go to Arden demanding to see Thomas Broad and there's no such man. An' now I'll have to spend the rest of me life in hiding. There's no mistaking me with this hair.' I pulled a long strand of it away from my face and inspected it. As red as it had been that morning. And every morning. 'Oh, well done, Josie Westgate,' I concluded bitterly. 'A nice pickle tha's made of this one.' We were walking again now, matching each other stride for stride and comfortable, as if the differences in our legs didn't matter after all.

'Well, I think you were brave,' he said. 'Don't worry. I reckon he just wanted to put the fear of God into you so you wouldn't go back to Heston. You shouldn't, by the way, he's a nasty man with a crew of nasty men working for him. They're no company you'd want to keep.'

'And how do *you* know?'

'I've been poaching there for months,' he said. 'Me da's told me stories that'd make your hair curl.'

I was horrified and impressed by his daring and astonished at his honesty. 'How old are you then?' I asked.

'Almost thirteen.'

'At surface?' Boys around here left school at twelve, did surface work until they were fourteen, and then they went underground.

'Aye. Crooked Ash.'

'Does tha like it?'

He snorted. 'Like it? Nay, I've no liking for any of it. It's better than it'll be when I go underground, I know that, but if the best you can say about something is, "I probably won't die today," then it's not saying much, is it?'

Now that he said it, I had to agree that it wasn't. His logic was clear but I'd never heard my father or my brother Bert say such a thing. 'But . . . it's our *lives* . . .' I breathed, wondering at his audacity. 'I mean, it's what we *do*, isn't it?'

'Aye, it is,' he conceded. 'But we don't have to like it.'

'Don't we?'

'Coal mining,' he said, adopting the tone of a schoolteacher addressing a class, 'is a mighty industry. For a hundred years now it's been making money, *lots* of money, for our lords and masters. Not so much for us, it must be said,' he added. 'It's dangerous, it's difficult, but the masters don't concern themselves with that bit of it. The dangers and the difficulties, they're for the likes of us. *We* can't expect better, simple folk like us who wouldn't know what to do with a better life if we had it. It's what we're bred for, to risk our lives for them. It's our path to glory.'

I gawped. He had quite the lyrical flight, did Tommy Green of Grindley. I hadn't heard anyone else talk this way, but I did recognise a degree of sarcasm when I heard it.

'Most say it's a fine system, as God ordered it, and perfect in its simplicity,' he went on. 'I say it's a fool of a system and the masters could stand to think a lot more than they do about the men they work to death and what they might want or be capable of. Some masters are better than others, and yours are the worst of all.'

I opened my mouth automatically to defend Arden but something stopped me. I wanted to know. 'If it's so bad,' I interrupted, 'why do so many do it?' In school, when we asked a question, we got a cuff and were told we were stupid. But Tommy didn't make me feel stupid.

'Good question. Because a man must earn a wage. He must be able to support his family. And he's grown up being told that this is the only way he can do it. So he never wonders what other capabilities he might have.'

I saw him clearly then. 'But you wonder, don't you, Tommy Green?'

'I have wondered, aye. But it's been carefully explained to me that there's nothing to me but arms for hewing and legs for carrying and a head for cracking on a deep stone ceiling. So underground I go when the time comes.'

'And you're scared.'

'Course I am.'

No Arden lad would ever admit to being afraid. But Tommy said it like it was the most natural thing in the world. And now I came to think of it, it was.

I put my hand on his arm, not knowing why. 'Why, Tommy Green,' I said at last, 'are you a . . . a . . . ?' I'd always tried to ignore talk of politics at home. What young girl is interested in that? And I preferred to think that our lives were not so very bad. But now I struggled to remember a word I'd heard the men use, a word I thought referred to the sorts of sentiments Tommy was expressing. 'Are you a . . . revolution?' I knew I was a couple of syllables short, but I couldn't call it exactly to mind.

He laughed again. Not scornful, like my brother, but good-natured as if, despite all his anger, there was something untouched in him. 'Aye, that's me, Josie. A walking, talking one-man, revolution. Change the world I would, if I could.'

'And will you?'

'Nay. I'm nowt but a lad. There's a whole system in place, a century of history behind us. I'll change nothing. I'll go about my work, same as all of us, accepting my lot. Only I did wish I might . . . ah, never mind.'

'What?' I asked. I, who had never wished or dreamed or questioned, badly wanted to know what his wishes were.

'I'll tell you another time. Look, there's Arden. Go and see your sister wed, and stay away from Heston. I mean it. That place is more deadly than you could ever imagine.'

He was right: we were looking down the last slope before Arden and could see the cottages and the schoolhouse and the church tower. The wedding bells were ringing. I would be skinned.

'Well,' I said, sticking out my hand. 'Thanks for the lesson and good luck with your wishes, whatever they may be. Ta-ra, Grindley lad.'

He shook my hand and grinned. 'Ta-ra, Arden lass.' I picked up my skirts and ran. 'I like your hair,' he called after me. It was wriggling around my face like so many red snakes. Cheeky bugger. Like my hair indeed! Alice was the one with the flaxen braids, fair as a princess. If he'd said my eyes, I might have believed him. They were dark as sloes and rather handsome I thought. But no one ever called me the girl with beautiful dark eyes. I was always just 'the red-head'.

The violets were limp in my apron pocket when I got back,

their delicate petals so dark and damp they looked as though they were crying. I found my family already on the march to the church. I flung the violets at my mother, who gave me a sharp slap then wound them hastily into Alice's hair anyway; always reluctant to change a plan in the face of circumstance was Ma. She ripped off my apron and stowed it in a bush to collect later. She gave an expressive look up and down my person and shook her head in shame. She drew a comb from a pocket and dragged it through my hair, so that I was in tears all the way through the psalms. Alice married Fred and looked a picture.

Afterwards, when I fetched my apron from the bush, it fell open to reveal a bunch of shining, lovely bluebells.

# Chapter 4

## Josie

A week after Alice's wedding I decided, through sheer obstinacy and nosiness, to visit my secret place again, but the weak spot in the fence had been discovered and mended with an excess of boards and nails. So Tommy became my new secret.

We met again, several times, always by accident. (Accident was enhanced by the fact that I knew that Sunday was a likely day for him to walk out and my own walks now always took me in the direction of Grindley.) I didn't see him often; our lives weren't such as allowed for a multitude of leisurely hours. But nevertheless we became friends – were so from that first meeting, I suppose.

I would often hear his whistle travelling the serpentine lanes before I saw him. Then he'd appear before me: clumpy boots, long legs, wide smile, froggy green eyes and mad brown curls. The sight never failed to bring a smile to my face. We would walk and talk and climb Silvermoor Rise, a hill that overlooked both our villages. It watched over us as we lived and worked, its gentle slope turning green, grey and gold by turns.

From our usual spot high on the rise we could look out over the county. We could see the mighty pithead of Crooked Ash, where Tommy worked, behind us and those of Hepzibah and Drammel Depth, both Barridge mines, to our west and north-east. We faced a cleft in the hills where no pithead was visible, but we knew that White Arrow Drift (Barridges) and Horizon Drift (Sedgewicks) lurked unseen under the folds of earth. The air was always veiled and dirty but we were used to that. This was our world.

We talked about all sorts, but mainly where we would go, if we could go anywhere in the world. Tommy was obsessed with foreign places and I learned more of the wider world from him than I did in all my years at school. I never paid attention in class. But when *Tommy* told me facts about Amsterdam or Peru I remembered them without effort. Talking to him opened up a brighter horizon.

'Egypt,' he sighed. 'The pyramids, the Nile. Crocodiles. I should love to see a crocodile, Josie. I imagine they're the most ancient creatures on earth.'

'Strange boy,' I remarked, shivering. 'They'd love to see you too – and crunch you to bits.'

'India,' he murmured. 'India most of all. Elephants, Josie! Rubies as big as eggs.'

His fascination for the distant and exotic was catching. Within a week or two he had me daydreaming too.

'I think I'll go to Africa and tame lions,' I mused one day. 'I'll teach them to pull carts and carry me around. They'll guard my children and let me sleep with my head on them at night like furry golden pillows.' Soon I couldn't imagine how I'd never thought about such things before.

We also talked of our families and village life and of our gentry. They had no idea of our names, yet they held our keeping in their hands – and they fascinated us.

Some days we climbed further up the rise to look down on Heston. Lawns and woodland we saw and just a glimpse of roof, red and pointed, through the trees.

'A brooding, bristling sort of place it is for all that it's worth a king's ransom,' I shivered. 'Why did they leave? I know their son was killed but . . . that happens to *us* all the time. We can't run from our grief, we have to live with it.' I was getting like Tommy, asking questions. They were like weeds. Once they started springing up there was no holding them back.

'Aye,' he sighed. 'That we do.' He stared off into the distance and I knew he was thinking of his brother Dan, dead at seventeen, so I changed the subject.

'What's Silvermoor like, Tommy? Is it beautiful?'

Then he told me about his fifth birthday, the little lord's christening. 'All these years later and it's still the brightest and best of days in me mind. Oh, you'd have loved it, Josie. All the miners had the day off and we were all invited to Silvermoor, the whole village! There were feasting and barrels of ale and games on the lawn . . . pony rides and laughter and music. And then, at the very end, *fireworks*! Showers of silver and rockets of gold.' He laughed. 'Needless to say, it were the best birthday *I* ever had! I were so young, Josie, I couldn't help imagining that it were all for me. I thought, if they chose *my* birthday, it must mean summat. But then it got dark, and we all went home, to the mines and the laundry tubs and the schoolhouse, and the black dust and hard graft . . .' He sighed again. 'Even then, I knew which I preferred.'

I was quiet for a moment, imagining it. 'And what about the family? Did you see Lady Amelia?'

'Aye, a dress like blue cornflowers she wore. You know how the women are around here, Josie, bent and frowning and wrapped in aprons? Well, *she* was tall and graceful, with fair hair and grey eyes. They say the earl's strayed many, many times, but can that be true?'

I shrugged. Who understood men?

'The earl was right splendid,' he went on, 'with a big smile and a huge moustache. Lady Flora's just a few years older than you, Josie, and Lady Elizabeth's just a few years younger.'

I wished the Sedgewicks were *our* family. The Barridges were a very grim rogue's gallery in comparison. A pair of boy twins, who were twenty-one or so, a pair of girl twins who were even older – *boring* – and a dead heir. A cruel master and

36

a mistress I'd never heard described as beautiful. I would never see a lovely gown or a fine carriage.

'I know there's folk as hate the gentry,' said Tommy. 'Folk as hate all they stand for and want to pull it down. But I think it's the wrong way round. I think *we* should have *better* lives. Maybe not just like theirs, but closer to theirs. *We* should see daylight and have choices and celebrate things with fireworks. Everyone should, shouldn't they?'

I'd never thought about fireworks before, but now that he said it, it didn't seem too much to ask for.

'Perhaps you're really the earl's son.' I embarked on another flight of fancy. 'Perhaps one day he'll take you in and you'll be Thomas Sedgewick and be too grand to know me.'

Stranger things happened. It wasn't unheard of for a lord to fancy a bit of village skirt, though he would always vanish back to his big house when there were consequences. People mostly had very little sympathy for the woman; she was expected to get on and deal with the gift he'd left her. She wouldn't be cast out or anything like that – after all, who could say no to one of the masters? What was really frowned upon was if she gave herself airs and graces over it; worst of all if she gave the bairn one of the family's names. I remembered my father holding forth on the subject when I was small, I couldn't remember why. Aristocratic origins had to be hidden behind a simple Joe or Molly. There'd be no little Winthrops or Clementinas in Arden; no Rufuses or Amelias in Grindley.

'I used to daydream that very thing,' Tommy said, 'but no. You haven't met me ma, Josie, but if you had, you'd know it were impossible. Besides, I'm Da's son, right enough. We're that different, but you can see it sometimes in the set of his mouth and the way my hair falls here . . . I do belong in Grindley, Josie, which only makes it all the more frustrating that . . .'

'That you don't,' I finished.

# Chapter 5

## Tommy

The following Sunday I sat in church, smiling to myself at the thought of Josie. She was like a candle, bright and cheering in the grey of my days, days I now spent in the shadow of the gargantuan pithead of Crooked Ash, engaged in the interesting occupation of washing coal. Crooked Ash was the deep mine owned by the Earl of Silvermoor. He had a drift mine too, Horizon Drift, and all us Grindley lads were destined for one or the other. Mostly we followed in our fathers' footsteps; Da worked at Crooked Ash, so I did too.

When my classmates and I started work, there was no need for the overseer to explain to us what needed doing or why. Coal was in our blood; our fathers and brothers talked endlessly about their work, with weariness and passion and pride. The language of gob and rolley-way, of heapstead and slack, was our mother tongue. Our job was to place coal into a tank. Good, clean coal would float and could be passed along for sorting. Coal which sank had to be removed, and crushed to separate out the dirt. All day long we stood under our wooden canopy, washing and sorting, for the appetite for coal was unquenchable. Small wonder that Josie's friendship was so precious to me.

I breathed in the cool, glossy smell of the furniture polish that turned the mahogany pews to sable and idly watched the thin swirls of Preacher Tawney's sandy hair glistening in the sunshine, making the bald patch beneath much clearer. He should just give up, I thought, accept that he was balding. But I felt immediately appalled with myself. If anyone was to understand the need to keep fighting a losing battle, it should be me.

My own dreams lay dormant inside me. I had buried them so deep they would probably turn to coal themselves, but they were there. And I wasn't the only one, I realised that day.

After the service we were stopped by Millicent Tawney, the preacher's wife, a small woman who darted around like a quick little robin. There was to be a county-wide concert of different children's choirs in Rotherham next Easter, she told us in her flighty way. She thought it would be a splendid thing – a joyful thing! – if Grindley sent a choir. She would select the music and undertake the coaching. Might Connie swell the ranks?

Connie let out a deep gurgle of excitement. She was only six, but loved music. Grandma often sang to her in the evenings and Connie would sing back, mimicking the tunes easily. None of the rest of us had an ear for it.

Pa grumbled and groused, of course, worrying about the cost, the disruption, but Mrs Tawney, bitty thing though she was, answered all his objections until Ma said, 'Oh Jim, what harm can it do?'

'I don't want that child gettin' notions,' he said, scowling. 'It'll fill her head with fancy ideas. There's no future in it for her.'

'Of *course* not,' Ma soothed. 'Just a one-time thing, Jim, just for fun. She's nowt but a littl'un.'

He groused a bit more until Grandma, who was usually so quiet we often forgot she was there, poked him hard. 'She should do it,' she said. 'I like hearing her little voice. You've passed on your complete lack of musical talent to every single one of my grandchildren but her, Jim Green, and I'm not best pleased with you. She'll do it, Mrs Tawney.'

In the general excitement I think I was the only one who saw the light in Connie's eyes. I recognised that light. It was the lure of Things Beyond. And if she dreamed of those, I wondered how my little Con would fare, stuck forever here in Grindley.

# Chapter 6

———— ❧❧❦ ————

# Josie

*June 1899*

Weeks crept by and turned into months, melting into summer of the following year. Knowing Tommy had changed me utterly. He had given me the gifts of questions and dreaming and laughter. Yet his fourteenth birthday was looming and he felt that entering the mines would be the end of his life. Not the end of his life *as he knew it*, but simply the end. He was possessed by a dark foreboding that he would die in the mines like his brother Dan.

He was such a sunny soul most of the time that it was hard to see him brooding and glum. And the thought that he might be right, that I might lose him, flew through me like a fluttering bird. My life would be the poorer without him, in unmeasurable ways. We tried to cheer ourselves up, distract each other from what lay ahead.

'What would you do then, if you could do anything?' he asked me one day.

'There's . . . farming,' I mused. 'I could be a dairy maid. There's service. Ummm . . .'

'Groundsman, gamekeeper,' frowned Tommy. 'How does a person get to do *that*, for instance? I can't believe that Paulson's educated. He can't be cleverer than me.'

'Maybe it runs in the family with those jobs, like with ours.'

'Maybe.'

'But we were talking about *me*,' I reminded him. 'Girls can't be gamekeepers. Maybe I should go on the stage!' We dissolved in giggles at the thought. It was as likely a prospect for me as becoming a unicorn. 'Be a chorus girl!' I gasped. 'With ringlets and ribbons . . .'

'And fancy bloomers,' said Tommy.

'What do *you* know about ladies' bloomers?' I demanded, swatting him on the arm.

'Our John's got a card from a cigarette packet. Lillian Sharpell, back in the eighties. Pointing her toe and lifting her skirts. I can see you in frilly bloomers, Josie Westgate, that I can.'

'Disgusting,' I sniffed. 'It's true what they say. Grindley lads are horrible, base creatures.' I said it even though our Bert had a similar card, of Patricia Lamar. It was shocking, of course, but she was so pretty. Prettier even than our Alice.

Our merriment was short-lived; the future was just too close now. 'When is it exactly?' I asked him softly. I had to, while we were together. He knew what I meant.

'Two weeks.'

'Two weeks?' His birthday was very close.

'Aye. Two weeks left of sunlight,' he said. 'Then into the darkness I go. And that'll be it for me.'

I shivered in the summer sunlight and hoped he was wrong.

# Chapter 7

―――∞∞――――

# Tommy

*June 1899*

During my last week of surface work, I started to feel weighted and numb. Sometimes I tested the sensation, just to be sure, the way you poke a wobbly tooth with your tongue. I thought of Silvermoor. I felt nothing. I thought of the little lord and I felt nothing. I thought of sunlight and geography and art and how they would not be part of my life. I felt nothing. Such relief. Maybe like this working in the mines would become possible for me.

Over the past two years I had progressed from washing the coal to screening it for different markets by tipping it through iron sieves, an equally monotonous occupation. By those last days, which were numbered in my mind as surely as if someone had drawn large black figures on them, I could have done it in my sleep. In fact, I often did.

It was from just such a mundane dream that my father woke me one night, angry because I'd slept through midnight. I stumbled out of bed, the heap of my brothers disturbed.

We set off at a punishing pace. My father was forty-five years old but he was as strong as an ox. Within a mile I was puffing.

'Wait,' he said, catching my arm when we reached our secret way in. 'Yer fourteen tomorrow and down pit Monday. This'll be yer last night out, you hear?'

'Aye, Da, all right.' We all started work the first Monday after we turned fourteen. The prospect of my birthday was more a death knell than a celebration.

'I'll take Ernest next week. He's at surface now, almost a man.'

'Oh Da, no,' I protested in a whisper, while the hedges rustled about us. 'Not our Ern. He's that weakly.'

The clip around the ear that he gave me wasn't hard but he only held back so I didn't cry out on that soundless night.

'And who else should I take?' he demanded, quiet but fierce. 'Our Alfie's nowt but a bairn yet. Or should I take our Con?' Connie was now seven and still the light of my eyes. A lovely little creature with an unspoilt spirit like a sunbeam. Her Easter choir concert had come and gone and never been repeated.

'No, Da,' I said wearily. ''Course not. But you know how our Ern is.' Ernest was fragile. Tired easily, caught a cough every month, could hardly lift the coal bucket . . .

'He'll have to step up now. He has to show us he's the makings of a man.'

'He's not weak on purpose, Da. Some are just made that way. I'll go instead of him for a while, till Alfie's older. I don't mind.' Alfie was a robust little thing, as suited for Grindley life as Da was, I think.

He clipped me properly this time, and I did cry out and then he shook me hard for doing it. It had been a while since we'd had one of these conversations, in which what seemed like common sense to me completely incensed my father.

'You, lad,' he growled. 'You and yer fancy ideas. You have *no* idea what the world's about. You won't be *able* to get through a day in the mine and then come out at night. You'll find out when you get there.'

I tried one last time for my brother. 'Ma doesn't like any of us poaching but you know how she is about Ern. She'd skin you, Da, and if going out at night will affect any of us, it's him. She'll notice summat, I'm tellin' you.'

'Oh, *telling* me, are you? Well, I'll tell *you* summat, boy. I'm off. I've no liking to work with you tonight. Seeing as yer such a man, and you can do everything and you know everything, this should be a piece of piss for you, shouldn't it? And don't come back empty-handed.'

He strode off down the lane and fast vanished in the shadows. I sighed. Then I squeezed through the hedge and got on with it. I went down the trap path first: a squirrel and two rabbits. I threw the rabbits in my bag. There'd been a time in my childhood when the sight of a dead rabbit, all tender and velvety and bloodied, had made me cry. Now I was hardened to it. We did need to eat, after all. I made my way back, then started off along the shotgun path and found a pheasant. I was pleased, because Da would be. I reached the tall, thin pine next to the fat bushes.

Then something happened. The night had been dense as dense. But suddenly the moon came out and poured light onto the path. I could see the treacherous silver wire glinting and a mad thought came to me to cross it.

I remembered Da that first night: *That's our limit. Go no further, never ever, if you value yer life.*

But I wasn't sure that I did any more. And I hated that old bastard. I looked up, expecting the cloud to swallow the moon any minute, but it shone steadfast and brilliant, as if saying, *Go on, lad, I won't fail you.*

'Fourteen tomorrow,' I whispered. And, taking care to lift my feet as high as they would go, I stepped over the wire.

# Chapter 8

─◦◦◦─

# Tommy

The path remained narrow, with overhanging bracken on either side, and I walked recklessly, heedless of traps. Trusting to the moon, I followed one bend after another, deeper and deeper into the woods, until I was through them and stood at their edge, gazing down a long sweep of grass dotted with stately oaks. Across it, within plain sight, was Heston Manor. The house built on the deaths of a thousand men.

I should have got myself away from there while my luck held. But something more than a death wish transfixed me. The story of that house was so poignant; it was like a vision of what I had always wished for, except gone badly wrong. And it would be something wonderful to tell Josie.

In the moonlight its red roofs were black and grey. It was gabled and haughty, old-fashioned even to my ignorant eye, and more elaborate than Silvermoor, which was simpler and more classic in style. I'd never seen a Barridge, nor wished to, but gazing upon their abandoned manor brought the drama of it home to me. The eldest son, prized not as the first wage earner, as it was with us, but for reasons of heritage, tradition and pride, killed in his prime. The family fled. How deep their pain must have been.

Seeing the arches and eaves and chimneys and lawns, even imperfectly at night, made it all come alive. The life they must have led here. The balls and banquets and learning and travel . . . all cast aside. The house must have brimmed with life as it now brimmed with shadows. The thought of the empty rooms, populated only by spiders, made me shiver. Most of Grindley would have fitted quite comfortably in there, but we endured cramped quarters only two miles from this ghost house.

The moment that thought crossed my mind, I *saw* a ghost. A white man on a white horse dancing on the lawn. Again, I should have run. But I couldn't. I was like a boy turned to stone. I rubbed my eyes, hoping desperately that I was seeing things. *A dancing horse?*

But when I removed my fists from my eyeballs it was still there. The man wore no hat and his pale hair gleamed in the moonlight. He wore no jacket, only a loose white shirt. His hands were white upon the reins. And the horse! Not only did it dance, it floated, an inch or so above the earth. It was white all over with a white mane that shimmered. It arched its neck and pointed its hooves and looped and swayed in elaborate formations as I watched, as though moving to the music of an invisible orchestra.

Wonder overcame fear. I had never thought a ghost could be so beautiful. What would Josie make of *this*?

Then I heard a sound that curdled my blood. Dogs. Barking in the woods, coming closer. My death wish had passed. I didn't want to be ripped to shreds by those black hounds. That floating apparition had sparked something in me that had been long dormant. Some rekindling of whatever it was in me that was moved by beauty and revered the miraculous. My soul perhaps. I ran.

The guiding moon kept her promise. I had never been so fleet. My long legs stretched and my heart pounded as I heard the dogs grow closer, their massive bodies tearing through the undergrowth, breaking it apart. When I reached the thin pine by the fat bush I didn't dare slow and look for the wire but judged its position as best as I could and cleared it with a bound, my poacher's bag jogging on my back. I threw myself through the gap, stopped a brief instant to ram the branches and tangles of ivy back into place to veil the opening, then took off again. Soon my heartbeat grew louder and the dogs grew fainter and I knew they hadn't followed me through.

I stumbled to a walk. My legs were water and I could hardly hold myself upright. I was glad of the distance to Grindley to gather myself. I thought hard. No one could have seen me to recognise me through those dense trees. It seemed likely that

I would get away with it. But when the men caught up with the dogs and found them nosing around at the place where I'd disappeared, they'd find the gap. They'd seal it up and there'd be no more poaching at Heston. Da would be furious. I couldn't tell him about my part in that.

If Da couldn't go back to Heston, and since he was still wary of going to Silvermoor, there would be no poaching for a while. I realised that the night's events might have saved Ernest. Perhaps that pale horse with his pale rider hadn't been a ghost. Perhaps he had been a silver shining angel.

# Chapter 9

# Josie

*June 1899*

It's funny how sometimes you get to thinking about a certain thing and then life answers your questions. Soon after that gloomy day when Tommy and I puzzled over what a woman might do with her life, an unimaginable thing happened. Old Mr Embry, who ran the village shop in Arden, died. Well, this was not the unimaginable thing; this was the natural outcome of his life. What was extraordinary was that his nearest relation was his niece. Who was, in the way of all nieces, a woman. We saw her at the funeral; over from Leeds she was. We couldn't see much of her face behind her black veil and the handkerchief she kept dabbing at her eyes. But she had a slim, upright figure and a graceful step and when word got around that she had inherited, everyone said the same thing.

'Oooh, what a shame. Such a waste. That shop were his whole life. Couldn't he have rustled up a male relative from *somewhere*? Now it'll have to go to strangers.'

A few years later I came to learn that women very often worked in village shops, and it was nothing so very remarkable. But there in Arden our view of the world, as Tommy so often lamented, was defined by the narrow radius of what we knew, and we had never heard of such a thing. Mr Embry had always been the shopkeeper in Arden, the Grindley shop was run by a Mr Goldsworthy and over in Steepley, the shopkeeper was a Mr Grunt, which I thought very funny.

So that was it. Shopkeepers were men. Everyone felt terribly sorry for the departed Mr Embry, his life's work wiped out in an instant. For clearly a woman couldn't run a business.

Miss Embry, it transpired, had other ideas.

Embry's Emporium was shut for two weeks, out of respect for the old man's passing, and due to the practicalities of his niece needing to pack up her life's possessions and move from the city to the back of yonder. Then it reopened, with the same name and the same goods, but with a very different figure behind the counter.

I made sure to go down there that first day and introduce myself. Miss Embry seemed like a deity to me, coming from the city, unmarried, independent and quite lovely to look at, no less! She had dark brown hair rolled into a smooth coil and lovely creamy skin. She greeted me kindly and said, as I left, that she hoped we could be friends. I floated and shone as I walked down the street after that.

And there it was. Just after I'd wondered what a girl might do in life, other than marry a miner or go into service or work on a farm, a stranger arrived among us and gave the answer: anything at all. I couldn't *wait* to tell Tommy all about her.

I walked out every single Sunday but I didn't bump into him in the lanes. In fact, I wasn't to see him at all for a very long time.

# Chapter 10

### Tommy

*June 1899*

It had arrived. My first day underground. Deep mining it was, at Crooked Ash. Three hundred and fifty feet deep, to be exact. I stood with the others, waiting to step into the cage, dressed in my clogs. My flat cap was stuffed with newspaper, the only protection we had for our poor, breakable heads. I clutched my lunch tin containing its slices of bread and jam. Only that sweetness could be tasted through the coal dust underground; I knew it from everyone who had gone before me. Ma had given it to me when I left and bid me, 'Be careful.' The memory of her voice was hard to bear.

Da wasn't working that shift, nor John nor Georgie. Jimmy was, but we hadn't spoken. I wasn't sure what he made of any of it, he never talked about the mines. He didn't talk much at all, except to Mary.

Around me boys were joshing, trying to cover up nerves; men were muttering grim predictions of strike and starvation, something to do with Hebzibah pit over yonder. I paid no attention to any of it. I simply stared into thin air.

The cage rattled up. I bent low under the grille and stepped inside with nineteen others. Then the grille was pulled down and the cage door shut. We stood shoulder to shoulder and the air was rife with emotion: the fear of the newer boys, wondering if they could endure it, and the world-weary superiority of the experienced men, who'd been enduring for years.

There was a jolt, and we plunged downwards. I kept my head tilted upwards, partly because otherwise my nose was lodged in Sam Kerrell's armpit, and that was not a nice place to be, and partly to keep my gaze fixed on the daylight above until the last possible moment. It was a white-grey rectangle. It shrank to an envelope. A postage stamp. A pinprick of light, and then it was gone.

I wanted to cry for how wrong it seemed. Was I really an oddball for seeing it that way? I glanced at the others – a reflex, to see if other faces reflected something of what I was feeling – but of course, I could not see them.

The cage landed with a clunk. There was a pause. Darkness. A darkness such as you can never imagine if you haven't been down there in the bowels of the earth. A crushing dark it is, fit to grind the very air out of your lungs. I wasn't afraid of the dark above ground, but this was something different. I knew that *this* darkness could – and had – sent men mad.

We were silent for a moment then voices broke out. The door was wrenched open, the grille rattled up and the work-force was released. Someone struck a match and I couldn't help but think of firedamp, of blackdamp, the gases that lurked in the dark like lethal, silent snakes. But of course, this close to the shaft they would not be coiling and collecting; the air flow was strong here. Then the lamps were lit, casting an unsteady glow into the darkness.

The deputy allocated our tasks. Eventually I would be a hewer, like Da, but mostly the new boys started off pony driving, a tried and tested way to learn the ropes. That's what I expected today and there was some comfort in the prospect as I loved animals.

We were all sent off in different directions but Bulford, the deputy, held me back. In the flickering light of our lamps he jerked his head and he took me off, just the two of us. I wondered if I were being given some preferential treatment because I was Jim Green's son, whether I was to start on some greater responsibility right away. All the same, I should have liked to work with the ponies.

The tunnel that we followed sloped downwards. There was no room to stand up straight. In the sheer black, my senses tingled like an animal's, and picked up things they shouldn't rightly have been able to feel. I fancied I could feel the whole weight of a million tons of Yorkshire above me, poised to fall in. I touched the timber props above my head and thought of Dan. I felt that I could sense the sunlight sparkling on the ocean, miles away, even though there was no sun down here and I'd never clapped eyes on the ocean in my life. I could hear Josie's voice, teasing: 'Are yer scared, Tommy Green?'

Oh, I was. Not of any one specific thing for really, the dangers were too great and too many to contemplate so my mind balled them up into one vague menace and set it aside, but of this life. Of being a human being who lived like a burrowing worm. Of having a brain I would never use. Of loving the lanes and the light and the rain and never being allowed to see them during all my long working days. I was like a train that had slipped onto a wrong track and would end up at the wrong destination.

The roof grew lower and I stooped further. Eventually I was bent double and my back burned with the strain of it. I started to wonder if I'd be better off crawling on hands and knees but Bulford kept to a certain pace. I wouldn't be able to crawl as fast as I could walk. And even then, it would only mean my knees would burn, instead of my back. All this before we started our day's work. The walk to the coal seam was not recompensed. There was no pay for those thirty minutes' stooping and groping through the earth. It was our privilege to take that walk just in order to get to the spot where we would eventually be able to start earning our pay.

But the injustices of the system were the least of my worries that first day. A mile and a half from the cage, Bulford stopped by an enormous mound of dust and a row of empty tubs. 'Fill them,' he said. 'I'll fetch thee after tha shift.' And he walked away, or rather crouched and shuffled away like a grotesque insect. I watched him go, the light of his lamp growing fainter and fainter with him until he disappeared altogether.

It had to be some sort of joke. How could I possibly pass nine hours here, all alone, shovelling dust in the silence? What if my lamp went out? Suddenly I was terrified of that eventuality. I knew it happened regularly but had assumed I'd be with other men and that between us, we'd get by. Here, there was nothing to fall back on. That thick darkness would come rushing in and take me over . . . it would crush me as surely as a rockfall.

And what if Bulford didn't come back? What if he forgot, or got killed, or simply left me there from malice? When and how could I leave? I had no way to gauge the length of nine hours. But if I left before my shift was over, there'd be no end of trouble. And how would I find my way? The mine was an under-earth labyrinth. We'd passed countless intersections of tunnels, all exactly the same. The depth and the darkness had already wiped my brain of any sense of direction. I didn't know where the cage was. I didn't know how to get home. I felt this morning's breakfast, lovingly prepared by Ma, come rushing up to empty out of me. I was violently sick for some time.

When my guts were empty, I felt dizzy and weak. The atmosphere was stifling, the silence dense and only interrupted by odd creaks and cracks that had me sincerely believing that the whole roof was about to come down on my head. It seemed impossible that such a huge, hefty entity as the earth could make such sounds if disaster wasn't nigh. Again, I thought of Dan.

They were long hours down there. Longer than hours above ground, that was certain. It was a strange phenomenon which I grew to know well. An hour at home, or outside in the lanes, or running errands in the village, was a quicksilver thing, gone in a flash. An hour underground was a dragging, hissing, relentless sort of a beast.

I shovelled and wept and kept my eyes fixed on my flickering lamp. I dared not stand it on the floor in case I knocked it over. I dared not rest it on a shelf in case it should fall. If I set it far away from me, I felt too distant from its light. I kept moving it in an endless rotation, looking for the perfect solution that didn't exist.

All this for a shilling.

Nine hours later Bulford returned and led me out again. On the way up in the cage I clung to the bars, unable to stand. I was shaking and thought I was already going mad. The other men looked at me knowingly. But on the walk home I realised that I'd survived. It was the one time I was ever grateful to Da for the childhood he'd given me.

I learned later that everyone's first shift was like this. They did it as a form of initiation, to toughen us up. No one ever, ever talked about it; it was the mines' best kept secret. I felt angry about that at first, until I decided I was actually glad I hadn't known in advance. If I had, I don't think I could have gone, and what would have happened then? So in my turn I kept that unspoken vow of silence, never telling the younger boys about that day, because I didn't want to make their dread worse. By the time I reached the house I was able to put a brave face on it for Ma. By the time I arrived at the mine for my second day I was able to wear a tough face, the face they expected from Jim Green's son.

# Chapter 11

# Tommy

Day two, and I was on the ponies. That brutal rite of passage had one thing to recommend it: nothing could ever seem so bad again. Stan Baldwin, who was in charge of the pony team, took us to the stables, a queer place near the bottom of the pit shaft.

Crooked Ash had one hundred and forty ponies who used to run wild in the Welsh hills. Their names were engraved over their stalls and the stables were full of rosettes they had won, as if they were part of a kinder world. To see ponies confined underground, in the dark, was strange and cruel. And yet they were well treated, for they were valuable assets. Our productivity depended on them. Very often, our lives depended on them.

That day I was allocated to a pony called Mint, who had been there six years and who was, I was quite convinced, the smartest being ever to traverse those tunnels. He knew the job did Mint.

Between him and Stan, I learned the ropes: how to drive the ponies by verbal commands, how to get them to manoeuvre in difficult places, how to ask them to trap, as we called it when they opened doors with their heads. The tunnels were full of twists and bends and strewn with debris. They sloped up and they sloped down. The height of the roof varied wildly; a bashed head was a frequent occurrence. Sharp corve rails, two feet apart, ran along their length and they were perilous in the dark, though I would come to know them like the back of my hand in time. Whenever I saw a wooden pit prop sagging with the weight above I thought of Dan and felt nervous.

After three weeks I was allowed to train a pony. I was a natural with them, Stan said. The first pony I trained was a white stallion called Rogue and I apologised to him every day for fitting him for such a dreadful life.

Another week went by, and another, and I knew, somewhere in the back of my mind, that I hadn't seen Josie for a long time. I was always tired and always in pain, but that wasn't the reason. No doubt we would have met between Arden and Grindley in that way of ours, without appointment or plan, and we could have passed at least a short while together. Yet when I walked out after church on a Sunday, I headed in the opposite direction from Arden.

If anyone had asked if I was avoiding Josie, I would have said no. It wasn't a conscious choice to turn south those Sundays. But I suppose I felt I *couldn't* see her, now that my life was like this. She belonged to *before*, when there were patches of pleasure, and even times when I felt carefree. Josie, like hope, or ambition, or sunlight, had no place in the life of a miner. With her bright red hair, dancing dark eyes and wicked sense of fun, I still thought Josie was a candle. I didn't want to snuff her out.

My days were spent in darkness. More often than not I lay horizontal now, wedged right into a seam, underneath an over-hang of crumbling rock while I wielded my pick and chipped and struck at the coal in front of me. After the first half hour or so my neck felt as if it were about to break. By the time I went home my body was no longer familiar to me. After a day twisted into unnatural positions, it ached and burned in ways I had never imagined.

There was no privy down there, of course. When we needed to go we merely took ourselves to the side of the tunnel and did what we needed to do. Urinating was fair enough. There was so much damp down there anyway, so much water sloshing about our ankles, that it really was the least of our discomforts. For more serious business we tried to find a little inset so it wouldn't be underfoot. We stuck a stick in it so that those coming after us knew where to avoid.

We had one fellow on our gang, Mikey Rawlins, who had what *he* termed a grand sense of humour and what the rest of us called a dule's buck, meaning a devil's impudence. He never put a stick in his, and he wasn't beyond shoving the man in front when we passed a spot he'd christened. More than once

I went home with Mikey's offerings plastered on my clogs. At least it wasn't personal. We all tried to avoid walking next to him but every day, someone had to.

Sometimes things did get personal and that was horrible to see, when we were all in it together, or should have been. I was lucky. I was tall and strong and my father was not only respected, he was feared. I came in for a bit of teasing on account of my 'dreaminess' and being a 'scholar', but nothing too bad. But little Benny Larkin, who'd started soon after me, suffered. He was small and looked less of a miner than Josie did. Worse, his grandfather had worked through the strike of 1839 and memories were long around here. Benny hadn't even been born when his grandfather had made his unpopular decision yet he still carried his family's shame.

Bulford, the deputy, took him aside on his first day, lit his lamp so we could all see and pulled Benny's trousers down so we could all have a good laugh at his parts. I didn't laugh. Benny cried.

Then they slathered his little fellow with a mixture of muck and shale called bank, and told him it would make it grow. For months afterwards, every miner in the gang except me felt entitled to comment on his manhood, or the lack of it as they maintained. So the inhumanity in the mines wasn't just confined to the system, it spread into the way we treated one another. It made my blood boil. But if I'd said anything, I'd have made my own life worse and Benny's besides.

Josie was terminally curious. She would want to know every last thing. And what tales of the mines could I carry to my friend, to a young girl? Tales of shadows and shit and shame? Nay. I would not. That's why I walked south every Sabbath.

# Chapter 12

### Josie

*September 1899*

I walked around that September with tears brimming inside of me, but never falling. It had been more than three months since I'd seen Tommy. At first I'd told myself it was the new job, that he was tired, that he didn't have the time. But I didn't really understand it. I was only thirteen and a half and though I'd heard about mining all my life, I couldn't begin to imagine it.

I didn't suppose that Tommy was happy. But then wouldn't you think he'd want cheering up? And wasn't I just the person to do that for him? Surely if he *really* wanted to see me, if our friendship meant as much to him as it did to me, he would have found a way.

I had no one to talk to about it. Although I had three sisters, Alice and I had never seen eye to eye. At six, golden-haired

Tansy was too little. Dark-haired Martha was two years older than me and patient as a saint, but she was too sweet, I didn't want to burden her with woe. The very thought of confiding in Ma was a joke. We had never got on well. I didn't fancy I had any particular intelligence like Tommy and I certainly wasn't a beauty. I *tried* to fit in. Yet somehow there was always this feeling that I was different and Ma didn't like it.

'Think yer special, don't you?' Ma would scoff at regular intervals throughout my youth.

'I *don't*!' I'd exclaim. 'I'm not special, Ma, that's one thing I know!' Only many years later did I realise there was something sad about a daughter trying to placate her mother by assuring her that she was in no way special.

As I grew older, we were together more. Martha was the eldest unmarried daughter, so it was her role to be Ma's shadow in the kitchen and at the hearth. But when it came to having help, Ma liked plenty in reserve. I think she also thought I was the least likely to marry, so I'd be the one she was stuck with.

Anyway, learn I must, how to do the laundry, how to remove all the buttons from the clothes before they went into the mangle so they wouldn't be crushed, then to sew them all back on again afterwards. I hated the mind-numbing repetition of it, the knowledge that whatever you did – buttons on or buttons off – had no lasting value. At least I wasn't in danger from it, like Tommy and Bert, except the danger of going mad.

I learned to bake – barely – and to scrub floors and sweep

the fire, but my abilities were hard-earned and even then I remained 'kaggy-'anded', as Ma put it.

I would have liked to ask Miss Embry what she thought about Tommy's sudden disappearance from my life, but during those early weeks of her time in Arden I was afraid of being a nuisance, so I only went to the shop when I had a genuine reason. I admired and adored her, and dared not hope that her prediction that we would become friends might come true.

One day, as I was about to leave her shop clutching a pound of flour, I caught my first ever glimpse of aristocracy. To say it didn't measure up to my expectations was an understatement. When two gentlemen crowded past me into the shop, I didn't realise who they were. I only thought how unusual it was to see strangers here, and dressed so differently from village folk. My natural curiosity held me in the corner by the door, gazing at their backs, while they approached the counter.

'May I help you, gentlemen?' Miss Embry asked. How I admired her poise, the way she spoke to everyone.

'We haven't come to buy,' said one, 'only to look.'

'You're welcome to browse. Was there anything in particular you wanted to see?'

'*You*, my dear,' said the other. 'We heard rumours that there was a new shopkeeper in Arden, a woman, and that she was pretty. So of course, we came to see.'

It was the only time I had ever heard her lost for words.

It wasn't curiosity that kept me there now but instinct. She shouldn't be alone with those men.

'On the first count, the stories are true,' said one of the men. 'As you see, Willard, quite clearly a woman. What's your opinion of the other report?'

'Hmm,' said Willard. 'Pretty? Yes, I would say so. Dusky hair and eyes, all very Baudelaire. What do *you* think, Jocelyn?'

'I'm afraid I'm unconvinced on that score. Not to my taste.'

The other sniggered. 'We all know your tastes run in a different direction, Joss. Well, have you seen enough? Shall we go?'

'Quite enough for me. A rather disappointing expedition on the whole. Though perhaps not for you.'

'I'm glad I've seen for myself. A pleasing face, I maintain. But not worth the trouble of coming back for.'

'I should say not! Good day, Miss Shopkeeper.'

Still, Miss Embry said nothing.

They turned on their heels, swept towards the door and saw me standing there, clutching my pound of flour. They were tall and slim, with pronounced cheekbones and sharp noses. I hated them, deeply and instinctively. They had dark brown hair swept back from high foreheads and dark brown moustaches carefully trimmed and oiled. They were identical. Now I knew who they were: the eldest surviving sons of the family, of Winthrop Barridge.

'Good Lord!' said Jocelyn Barridge. 'Willard, look at *that*!'

I quailed. If he could speak so disrespectfully of Miss Embry, whatever would he say about *me*? I remembered all the stories of gentry wanting a bit of novelty with a village girl and I felt scared. I didn't flatter myself that I would appeal to them but I had never felt such a sense of badness from anyone as I did from those twins.

Willard looked me up and down with an unreadable expression.

'Do you see it?' persisted his brother.

'Yeeees,' said Willard at last. 'Yes, I do. What a thing. What do you make of it, Joss?'

Jocelyn laughed and shrugged. 'Never mind,' he said. 'Never mind.'

They left. I was so relieved my arms and legs went limp and I dropped the flour. The bag burst and the flour flew up in great white clouds, covering the shop floor.

'Oh, I'm sorry!' I cried. 'I'm so sorry, Miss Embry. I'll clean it for thee. Only fetch me a broom.'

'Nonsense!' she scolded me, hurrying over, her shoes in the flour making the mess much worse. Then she surprised me by folding me in her arms. 'Are you all right, dear?'

I yielded to the embrace. It was so good to be held. I never was! 'Oh,' I said in a shaky voice. 'They were horrible, horrible men.'

'Like father, like son, they do say,' she agreed, turning the sign on the door to *Closed*. 'I'll clean this before I let anyone

else in or they won't thank me for floury shoes and hems.'
She fetched a dustpan, a brush and a mop and while I scooped
the worst of it into the bin, she washed the floor behind me.

'I've never been so relieved to be found wanting,' she
laughed. 'What vile creatures.'

'Oh! How could they *say* such about you, miss? Yer that
handsome. Beautiful, *I* think!'

'Well, thank you, Josie, that's kind. I'm quite happy for *you*
to think so, but them? I believe *their* regard would make my
skin crawl worse than their disdain. If you ever see them again,
you stay right away from them, do you hear?'

'Oh aye, miss, I do. I know that.'

We got the floor clean and she gave me another pound of
flour at no charge, which was kindness beyond believing and
saved me from a hiding from Ma. Then we hugged again and
I went home, shivering whenever I thought of those two cold,
impersonal faces looking at me.

*Good Lord . . . Look at that!*

*Do you see it?*

*What a thing.*

As if I were a curiosity, and not a person at all. Although
I didn't want their admiration, I couldn't help but think: if
they didn't think Miss Embry lovely, then I certainly was not,
and I wondered if perhaps that was why Tommy had stopped
walking out to Arden on Sunday afternoons.

# Chapter 13

---

# Tommy

*September 1899*

One September Sunday I took myself to the stream and walked west until the stream became a river and the grassy way on either side opened out. Trees draped their branches over the water and I thought it must be one of the prettiest spots in South Yorkshire. I meandered along, trying hard to persuade myself that these scant hours of leisure and beauty could be enough to make my life worthwhile.

I was roused by a thin little voice: 'Eee, 'ow do, Tommy? Fine day fer it.'

It was Benny Larkin, down in the shallows with his trews rolled halfway up his skinny legs and a net and a pail.

''Ow do, Ben? Fishin' for supper?'

'Nay, I'm after bugs and such . . .' He paused, accustomed to ridicule, I guessed, then carried on, presumably remembering that I was odd too. 'I like seein' the creatures God put into t'world.'

I made my way down the bank to join him. He took a gauze off the top of the pail, so I could peer in. A bright blue dragonfly shimmered and shivered there, alongside a small frog and a late bumblebee, looking wilted from their captivity. I knew how they felt.

'Bullstang, froggy, bummelkite,' said little Benny with some glee. 'Look at the bullstang, Tommy, eee, that colour!'

I nodded. The dragonfly was of a brilliance that almost hurt the eyes after a week in the mines. I looked at Ben's pinched, excited face, realising something. 'Tha's not fourteen,' I murmured.

Families often sent their boys down the mines a year or two early to get the wages coming in sooner. In Sedgewick's mines they got away with it because the managers didn't know the families well enough to realise. In Barridge's they got away with it because Winthrop Barridge didn't care. He'd have taken their babies if he thought it would get the coal out quicker, so they said.

Ben shook his head. 'Eleven,' he admitted.

'Poor lad,' I said without thinking. I didn't mean to patronise but honestly, grown men taunting an eleven-year-old boy. What kind of a world was this? 'You pay no mind to what they say at the mines,' I told him suddenly. 'Yer a brave kid, Ben Larkin, and out there in the world there are people who don't think like they do around here. Remember that. It's not *you* there's owt wrong with.'

I wished Ben luck with his spotting of insect and animal friends and went on my way. My heart broke a little as I left him there, with his love of natural history and a lifetime of cruelty before him. I walked on until I heard shouts and laughter up ahead of me.

I paused. There was a stone bridge just ahead and boys were jumping off it. I watched from the shade of a broad oak. I recognised young Lord Walter Sedgewick, slight and fair, playing with three older boys who were egging him on to more and more daring stunts, which he never shirked. Like a nimble, darting minnow he was.

One of the fellows was much older, perhaps twenty, and seemed to have the charge of the younger ones. Although he teased and challenged them he stopped them from getting silly. When he ran onto the bridge they all stopped playing to watch him for he could do the most wonderful dives. 'Hurrah! Bravo, Cedric!' they cried.

I smiled, imagining saying, 'Bravo, Da,' or, 'Bravo, Georgie,' for a job well done in the village. This then was Lord Walter's older cousin from York. There were two, and they visited the Sedgewicks often: Cedric Honeycroft and his sister, Clarissa or Camelia or something beginning with C. When I'd told this detail of Silvermoor life to Josie she'd sighed and gone starry-eyed.

'I'd like to marry someone called Cedric,' she'd murmured. 'I'm sure a Cedric couldn't slap his wife or complain about the dinner. And if I was called Camelia . . . well, there couldn't be a thing wrong with my life.' Always put too much store by names did Josie.

The whole scene was such a picture of sunlight and splashing that I couldn't tear myself away. The boys flew from the bridge, turning tipple-tails on their way down. They wore nothing but long johns. Their bodies were pale in the sunlight and looked the way mine used to: slender and quietly muscled. A miner's body was different. We had ropes and strange bunches of muscles like barnacles in odd places from the peculiar tasks we performed. As the boys dropped, the water flew up, the beads in the air crystal-bright and golden. The contrast between their life and ours could not have been greater.

# Chapter 14

———⌘———

# Tommy

*October 1899*

That contrast stayed with me as the weeks went by. In Grindley, we learned from Preacher Tawney that far away in the Transvaal Republic a war had broken out. Snippets of news reached us of a hot, dry country. Africa. Rightly or wrongly, I pictured a landscape of high yellow mountains, sweeping valleys and dark, wide-winged birds circling against a brilliant sky. Meanwhile I trudged to and from the pit in the Yorkshire mists and clinging drizzle.

Autumn was drawing on. The blackberries were dropping from the hedges, those that were left after greedy Grindley lads had crammed great handfuls into purple mouths, and after the lasses went blackberrying for their mothers, filling bowls and buckets for pies.

One evening Georgie came a-visiting. He'd married Agnes

Storr in the summer and lived down the street now. He, Da, John and Jimmy were discussing Wyard Pit over Maltby way, a small mine where the owners had decided to pay each man an extra tuppence a shift. No one could work out why or how they were doing it, when all we ever heard from our masters was how tight their margins were. They pondered and speculated at quite some length.

'Who cares?' I wondered. 'It's not as though any of us'll move to Maltby. We'll none of us go anywhere. Not even for the great fortune of *tuppence*.'

My father disliked sarcasm. 'Well might you sneer,' he snapped, 'but you're not running a household. You're not the one responsible for keeping body and soul together for you and all yer family. Tuppence is a great deal when you add it up day after day. That's twelvepence the week! Think what tha mother could do with that.'

'Aye, Da. I know. Only . . . never mind.'

'Only *what*?'

I shouldn't have said anything. I knew better than anyone that there was no arguing with Da. And yet I couldn't help myself. Since that day at the river, I was surer than I'd ever been that the mines were an affront to human life. And I'd kept quiet a long, long time now.

'Only, doesn't it strike you as pitiful? Tuppence? For a day of a man's life? When he risks his neck, breaks his back, toils like a packhorse . . .'

'Oh, I'm sure tha's far too good for honest toil,' fumed my father. 'But the rest of us have been brought up to take pride in our work. It's skilled work, it's honest, we're the legs the nation stands on!' It was a phrase the earl kept using whenever he addressed the villagers.

'Aye, that's exactly what I'm saying! I'm saying that *as* it's so needed, so honourable, it should be better paid. It's not just *me* is too good to be paid a pittance for all the strength and life I've got to give, it's all of us.'

'Will you listen to your son,' said Da to Ma, disgusted.

'He's your son too,' she replied mildly and returned to her Bible.

'We give up *everything* to go down there!' I insisted. 'All our God-given rights. Daylight, fresh air, the chance to see the world . . .'

'Oh! Seeing the world, is it? And what's wrong with Grindley, might I ask? It's been good enough for all of us, time beyond counting, but *you* need to see the world. I'll listen to no more of this talk from you. Sedition, that's what you'll be preaching next. If you cause trouble for this family, Tommy Green, I'll thrash you to within an inch of your life, that I will, and I don't care what your mother says.' Ma paused her reading and looked up at that.

'It's not sedition to want choices!' I howled. 'Jesus God, why can't you see?'

It was a blazing row. Over the course of it, the girls crept from the room. Then the boys left. Only Ma stayed. She never interfered, but she never deserted us either, neither one of us.

Da leaped to his feet and pulled me to mine. He paused for the sharpest second when I stood an eyelash away from him and he realised I was three inches taller than him now and just as broad. But physical heft had never intimidated my father, not from any man in the mines and certainly not from his own son.

'There's an order to life! This is our tradition, our heritage. *We* may not have fancy headstones and urns in the cemetery, they won't make statues of us for the abbey when we die. But we belong here *just* as much as they do. The coal must be got. The masters must sell the coal for the good of our country. Everything depends on it.'

'Then let *them* go down and fetch it,' I said.

He shook me until my teeth rattled and I didn't fight back because he was my father, and some things went as deep in me as they did in him. I couldn't stop myself talking, though.

'Dan *died* down there, Da! Any of us could, any day! Doesn't it make you question any of it?'

'Don't take tha brother's name in vain,' Da growled in a voice full of menace. 'Your brother never complained, he never questioned. He was the best of lads and you won't even show him the respect of following his example.'

'Dan *was* the best of us, I know that as much as you do. But men spending their lives underground, with that little trouble taken to make us safe, is *wrong*. I know it.'

Da's fist flew at me, a blow I thought had split my cheekbone. I staggered across the room, stumbled over a chair and fell in a heap. Ma shrieked: 'Jim! No!'

It was a proper dark time after that. Da wouldn't speak to me and Ma lamented it every day. All my despair was dredged up to the surface, like coal, and laid out on a conveyer for all to see. There was no burying it any more. Yet what could I do but redouble my efforts? At work I watched my feet, I watched my tongue and I concentrated every nerve upon that gleaming back seam within the rock.

Then came news. The Barridges had leased one of their pits to Tysen's, a corporate coal owner. Such syndicates had existed in South Yorkshire for decades – businessmen who wanted to profit from the mighty coal rush that never seemed to end. But we'd never had one so close to home before. And we'd never heard of a coal-owning family, gentry, going into partnership with a company in this way.

Working for a corporation was even worse than working for a family. At least the gentry felt responsibility and honour towards the land they possessed, which had been handed down through generations. Of course, some families, like the Barridges, neglected that responsibility. But others, like the Sedgewicks, saw their role as one of stewardship. This didn't alter the fact that we were the ones underground doing all the work, but it did mean that our conditions could have been much worse.

The men in charge of a corporation had no sense of history, of mutual dependence. It was all just about exploiting an opportunity. And these were the men who would be wading in, making decisions. We heard that they were going to cut pay, then sink two new shafts within a six-mile radius and wage them at the same low rate. We felt grateful all over again to be Sedgewick's folk. The mine to be leased was Drammel Depth, where Josie's father and brother worked.

# Chapter 15

―❦―

# Josie

*November 1899*

Since the news about Tysen's, I could hardly bear to be at home, such a shower of gloom had fallen over the place. When Da returned from work he sank directly into a chair by the fireplace and did not stir from brooding over those flames till the time came for bed. He even ate his supper there, hunched over his bowl, the spoon lifting and falling rapidly, as though even the act of nourishing himself was a distraction from his reflections. Ma started shredding the skin around her fingernails with her teeth on a constant basis. She would even put down the bread she was kneading to do it, nibbling away regardless of the specks of dough that rubbed off on her face. I'd never seen her distractible before.

The only silver lining was that she watched me less closely. Perhaps with the certainty of harder times ahead, my deficiencies were the least of her troubles. I got off to the emporium two, sometimes three evenings a week after supper. Ma didn't know how much time I spent there. It never would have occurred to her that someone like Miss Embry might welcome me as a social caller. But since that day with the horrible twins, we had become friends indeed. A couple of hours in the evenings, a couple on a Sunday, Miss Embry and I would sit and drink tea and talk.

As the weeks went by she begged me to call her by her Christian name, which was Dulcie, a name I liked very much indeed. Everything seemed interesting when Dulcie talked about it, even mining; she had that gift, like Tommy. Unlike everyone else I'd ever met, she didn't seem to think mining was an incontrovertible fact of life, here to stay forever. The industry was declining, she mused. The best of British coal was already dug up and sold and all the export industries had faced competition from Germany, America and France for decades . . .

'Then how do we carry on?' I wondered.

'Our position is established, we have a great deal of experience and a high-quality product, even now. We're holding our own, Josie, but this life won't last forever.'

I thought my head would explode! If there was no coal industry, then what would the Barridges and the Sedgewicks do? If there was no coal industry, what would be the point of Arden, or Grindley? What would become of *us*? In a flash I had a vision of rows of empty miners' cottages, tin baths rolling empty around the yards and a long tramp of men, women and children leaving their homes. It couldn't be, surely. An alternative future was impossible to imagine.

More enjoyably, Dulcie described for me the wider world, by which I mean parts of Yorkshire outside the grasp of the Barridge family. Leeds, of course, her home town, with its huge art gallery. The gaping mouth of the silver Humber. Hoyland Lowe, an old huntsman's lodge from which, on a clear day, you could see all the way to York Minster.

'You should *see* the Minster!' she rhapsodised. 'It's beautiful beyond believing and it rolls out a glory of bells to summon the folk to evensong! Josie, you would *love* York. There are city walls all around it and the whole place is so ancient that there are ghosts of every description – Vikings and Romans and who knows what?' How I longed to see it!

Best of all she read me stories; not the dull parables we'd heard in school, in which wicked children went to the devil and good children went to the angels, but stories like the *Arabian Nights* and the fairy tales of the brothers Grimm, like *Alice in Wonderland* (which I enjoyed despite the heroine having my insufferable sister's name) and *Little Women* (which I loved for reasons beyond the heroine having my own).

Then *I* began to read the stories while Dulcie listened and helped me when I stumbled. One such evening we were interrupted by a scuffle and bump in the yard outside. Dulcie sighed and went to the window. 'Foxes again,' she grumbled, pulling back the drapes. Then she shrieked, which set my heart clattering like a pony.

'There's someone out there!' Dulcie exclaimed. 'Oh! What can he want?'

I couldn't resist joining her at the window, even though I was afraid. I'd never seen a villain before, unless you counted Ma.

There was indeed a shabby figure by the wall, who, seeing the alarm he caused, stepped forward from the shadows. To my utter astonishment, I beheld Tommy.

'Don't be frightened!' I exclaimed. 'It's only Tommy. I don't rightly know why he's here, but you've nowt to fear.'

'Tommy?' asked Dulcie, recovering herself. 'He must come in, perhaps he's in trouble.' She opened the window to issue her invitation. Then she hurried to the shop door while he sloped off round the side and I fidgeted in excitement. A moment later he was standing before me in Dulcie's lovely parlour.

I could hardly believe I was looking at him again, it had been so long. His face was thinner, his body thicker, his curls cropped close to his head. He looked like a man, even though he was still only fourteen and just a few months into his new life. The biggest change was the expression in his green eyes. Before, they had been clear skies, with occasional clouds when a dark thought troubled him. Now they were a storm coming in; the skies were set and dark.

'Oh Tommy,' I said, 'I'm that glad to see thee. Is owt wrong?'

'Nothing's wrong. I just came because . . . it was time to see thee.'

'*High* time to see me, I should say. Long *past* the time to see me, I should say!' I was indignant, but not too much. I could see the reasons in his face before he explained them.

'I know,' he sighed. 'I do know, Josie.'

'Tommy,' said Dulcie, 'please sit. Would you like something to eat or drink?'

His jaw lengthened in disbelief. He was all wrong-footed, one minute skulking around outside, waiting for me to leave, the next being offered refreshment.

'I'll not put thee to trouble, miss. I'm right sorry to turn up like this. Only I needed to see Josie, and I didn't want to go to her house; I thought her parents wouldn't like that. I saw her come here, so I waited . . .'

'You'd have waited a long while,' she told him in her dancing way, 'for Josie and I are great friends and talk many a long hour. I hope that we will too, Tommy. Let me fetch you tea and toast.'

His big eyes widened at that. Food. She hurried off and he took a chair, looking awkward. 'There's that much to be said,' he sighed.

'And nobody's fault but thine,' I said archly. 'But yes, I don't rightly know where to start.'

'Is this really all right?' He gestured around at the room, a stranger's home.

'Oh aye! Miss Embry, Dulcie *I* call her, is the nicest soul. Ma doesn't like me coming here but they're all that taken up with changes at t'pit, I don't reckon they'd notice if I got married and left home. You've heard, I suppose?'

He nodded. 'That's partly why I came. That and ... I've got summat exciting to tell thee. I know I've left it too long but ...'

'But it's hard,' I supplied.

'Aye. Going underground is like going underwater. You take a deep breath and down you go. I don't breathe again till I next come up. There's so much to say, but nowt I'd want to place on your skinny shoulders. It's as bad as I thought, Josie, and then it's worse.'

'I can see it. And I'm sorrier than I can say, Tommy Green. But you can't go on avoiding me like this. We don't have to talk about any of it ever if you don't want. Or we can, and you'll soon learn my shoulders are stronger than they look. But we can't just stop being friends because you're in t'pit, else you lose more even than you need to.'

'I know it. Aye, we'll meet up again, Josie, go back to havin' our Sundays when we can.' He grinned, a flash of the old Tommy. 'If yer not too busy coming here and seeing a finer friend than me, that is.'

'Daft bugger. A girl can have two friends, you know.'

The thought of spending time with Tommy again lit up my life brighter than Miss Embry's gas lights with their fancy tasselled shades. Miss Embry's company had saved my sanity over the last months, and I valued it more than I could ever tell her, but Tommy was part of me, I suppose. Being parted from him was like walking around with a shadow lodged within, the approximate shape and size of my ribcage. The solid sight of him sent light into that cavity. I breathed easier for it.

Miss Embry took a long while over that toast. I think she was giving us time to talk alone before she joined us. Only facts, not feelings, we shared. For now it was enough just to see each other again.

Dulcie returned and Tommy wolfed down that toast as if he'd never see bread again. He got over his shyness with her very quickly. They started discussing the mines and the changes that were coming to Arden and before long he was as animated as I'd ever seen him.

All too soon we had to disband. There was my mother to think of and Tommy had a long walk home, then a hard day's work ahead. We thanked Dulcie and took her hands as we made our regretful farewells. Then we walked back through the quiet village together, pausing at the end of my street.

'I nearly forgot!' he whispered. 'Part of why I came.'

'Oh aye, you said summat exciting. What then?'

'The Sedgewicks are holding a New Year's Eve party at Silvermoor for the Grindley folk. I've told thee about last time, the christening?'

'Only about a dozen times.'

'Well, I don't know much about this one yet but I just know it'll be . . .' — he paused to search for a word we didn't use very often — 'magnificent.' He nodded. 'I thought . . . if you wanted . . .' he said casually, 'I could probably sneak in one small extra person. It's not as though the family know us all so well they'd know the difference.'

A grin stretched my face from the top of one of my bright red braids across to the other. A party to celebrate the new century! With Tommy! In a grand house, with all the gentry in their fine dresses! Oh, it was too much excitement to be contained.

'Pass as a Grindley lass?' I teased. 'Eee, I don't know as I can. Won't the Sedgewicks be able to see my superior quality?'

'Oh, at a glance,' he laughed, 'but I'll take the risk if you can lower yourself to mix with us for just one night.'

'Go on then,' I giggled, then threw my arms around him. We held tight to each other for a long while, making up for the last months, then I pushed him away. 'Thank you, Tommy.' I looked at him seriously when I said it. 'I'm that glad you've come.'

# Chapter 16

# Tommy

Before the New Year celebrations at Silvermoor, Josie and I met several times in the lanes on a Sunday. Sometimes, when the weather was bad, we went to sit with Miss Embry in the parlour at the back of her shop.

And once Josie came to Grindley to visit me. She'd never been before. The odds of seeing me weren't high enough to be worth it; my shifts were unpredictable and it was a way from Arden to Grindley, though she'd never have liked to admit it. 'Only three mile betwixt 'em at their straggliest parts,' she always said. Still, it was a fair walk and she didn't have much time to spare, with all the chores her mother gave her.

But that morning she'd had a row with her mother. She'd finally told her about me – sneaking off on a Sunday afternoon was one thing but if she wanted to disappear for a whole evening on New Year's Eve and stay out past midnight, she had to give some sort of explanation. Mrs Westgate had been furious to learn that Josie was consorting with a boy – and one from Grindley at that. She forbade her to go. Josie refused to be forbidden, and Mrs Westgate banished Josie from the house. 'I don't want to see thee again the rest of this day,' she warned.

'Fine by me,' retorted Josie, who stormed all the way to Grindley. She asked about a bit and learned that I was underground but expected up soon. Anyroad, up I came, gulping the air as I always did, bone-weary and longing for my bath, to be greeted by the sight of a bright red head and some swinging boots on the wall nearby. I couldn't have been more surprised if it was Queen Victoria.

'Josie! What's wrong?'

She jumped down, grinning. 'Nowt wrong, Tommy Green, except our ma's a witch and I'm not to go home today. So I've come over here instead!'

Our John came up from underground. 'Oh aye, our Tommy, a lady friend?' he teased, jostling me. 'Kept her quiet, didn't you? *Dark horse!*'

'Don't be daft. John, this is Josie Westgate, a friend of mine, over from Arden. Josie, this big lummock is my brother John.'

They shook hands. 'I'll keep her entertained whilst you take a bath,' offered John. 'You can't take her around like that.'

I wasn't especially keen to leave her with John, who'd come to fancy himself something of a charmer. Not that I thought of Josie *like that*, of course. But he was right, I was filthy. They strolled up and down the street while I took the hastiest bath of my life. It wasn't easy to shift the coal dust. I didn't even understand how it got into some of the places it reached. When I finished I tipped all the black water away and fetched fresh.

'Hurry up, our John,' I shouted, running into the street. 'Water's ready!'

He winked at Josie. 'Proper keen to have you to himself, isn't he? I'd watch him if I were you, Miss Westgate.'

Miss Westgate indeed!

Josie grinned. 'Now, our Tommy, will you show me the splendour of Grindley?'

'Every brick and cranny,' I promised.

We were brought to a halt in the main street by a crowd; every local who wasn't actually underground seemed to be crowded around Goldsworthy's.

'What's up?' I asked Aggie Bradstock, a friend of my mother's.

'They're all in there!' she explained, excited as a girl. 'The family! *And* the cousins, them from York! They say that young Mr Honeycroft takes a great interest in the mines!'

Josie gasped. She didn't count her unpleasant encounter with the Barridge twins as a proper gentry sighting and now she would see all of ours at a sitting! On cue, the shop door jingled open and out walked Lord and Lady Sedgewick followed by a line of children like ducklings. 'That's his little lordship,' I told her, pointing to golden-haired Walter, who fronted the line. 'That's Lady Flora and Lady Elizabeth and the youngest, Lord Humphrey.'

'They say as his lordship's a proper ladies' man,' Aggie murmured. 'Not above a tumble with a village lass. Well, if a woman like that can't keep a man close to home, then I don't know who can.'

It was true that Lady Amelia was every bit as blonde and beautiful as I remembered her. Her grey eyes were grave and she wore a burgundy gown. Her deportment was as elegant as a statue. *Was* it true that the earl went elsewhere for his pleasures?

Josie's eyes were like saucers and I knew she was taking in every detail of their costumes. I couldn't help feeling sorry for the boys, all buttoned up in waistcoats and jackets and every sort of whatnot, but I could tell that Josie was coveting Miss Flora's dark pink dress and fine brown jacket. What a doll of a girl Miss Flora was, a beauty like her mother. Miss Elizabeth reminded me a little of Connie, with her straight brown hair and pert nose. Only Connie could never have looked so prim and timid. Little Humphrey's legs were so short he could only toddle, yet he too was dressed like the great *I am*. Of course, it was Walter who fascinated me the most.

He walked with extraordinary dignity for a nine-year-old. Our children were still running around screaming at that age, making the most of every short year before they went to work. And when they did, they became men overnight. The little lord was quite different, something between a child and a man, something we didn't have the chance to become. Clearly he was used to being gawped at by crowds of people, unlike his little brother who was close to tears under all the sooty stares. Walter was dignified, but he still had the light, unburdened walk of boyhood. He was fair and slender, the opposite of me in every particular.

The earl stopped and his clan stopped behind him. 'Good afternoon,' he said to us all, tipping his hat. We murmured a greeting, tugging our caps and gawping. The women dipped a curtsey. 'It's good to be back in Grindley,' he went on. 'I'm very pleased to see you all. Good day.' Again, we murmured and tugged and dipped.

They went on their way and a moment later the shop door jingled again and out came the cousins, Cedric, who I had seen at the river that day, and his sister beginning-with-C. Josie gasped. For Miss Honeycroft had hair as red as her own. Bright, flaming red it was and she didn't wear it in apologetic plaits, she wore it curled and poofed enormously with the smallest imaginable hat perched at an angle on top. Her dress was bright red too. It clashed remarkably with her hair yet the effect was undeniably handsome. She was bold and vivid and Josie almost dribbled with adoration. Miss Honeycroft walked arm in arm with her brother, leaning against him as though there were a real affection between them.

Mr Honeycroft didn't make a formal greeting like the earl. He stepped over to the edge of the little crowd, towing his exceptional sister, and began talking to the people at the front. We tried to jostle forward but everyone else was doing the same and we could only watch and try to catch his words.

'How is it *really* to work at Crooked Ash?' I think I heard him say. 'Are you happy in your employment?' I couldn't see who he was addressing or hear the reply. When they went, Miss Honeycroft raised a gloved hand and smiled.

We watched them go. They were a mirage of colour and light and gracious good manners. Grindley seemed even greyer when they'd gone. Then daily life reasserted itself and we shook ourselves, before all going back to what we'd been doing.

Later, Josie and I found a quiet spot on the outskirts of the village where we could sit and talk in peace, even though it was getting cold during these last days of the century.

'Oh, to see them like that,' she sighed. 'And they *talked* to us! Weren't they splendid, Tommy? It's right set me to dreaming. Oh, what I wouldn't give to be that Miss Honeycroft. Or Lady Flora. Imagine . . .'

She waxed lyrical for a while, then I remembered that in all our catching up over the last weeks, I hadn't told her about the ghostly vision I'd seen on my last visit to Heston Manor.

'It really floated? Above the ground? How do yer mean, *dancing*?' she demanded. When I reached the part where the dogs had chased me through the woods, she listened in horror. When she'd finally digested my tale in its entirety she was quiet a long while.

Eventually she said, 'I'll tell you what *that* means, Tommy Green. It means you're not to stay down t'pit.'

'How d'you reckon that then?' I wished it were true.

'Because no one *I* know sees spooks or angels. *No one* comes that close to Paulson's hounds and gets away wi'out so much as an ankle nipped. There *is* something special about you, Tommy. I've always seen it. You were right all those years ago at school. There is another road for you, though I don't know what or where. You'll see. One day.'

# Chapter 17

———— ❧ ————

# Tommy

*31st December 1899*

It was the end of the year and the end of a hundred years and we walked up the long drive to Silvermoor on the eve of the twentieth century like two children under a spell. My recently acquired world-weariness and even my miner's strength seemed to fall away somewhere along the way, leaving me weak-kneed and drenched in wonder as we arrived at the great hall.

It was built of Portland stone and shone pearly white in the fading afternoon. The sky was grey behind it, the trees a dark mass beyond. Wet snow fell, more rain than crystal. An owl glided before our eyes, then vanished into the woods.

All the Grindley miners and their families were there. Crowds and crowds of us. My own family were somewhere in the throng, but Josie and I had allowed ourselves to get separated from them. My sisters raised their eyebrows at meeting her and my mother looked rather askance at my scrawny, flame-haired friend; I knew she was sizing her up as a daughter-in-law. No point explaining that it wasn't like that. They wouldn't understand. As for Josie's parents, they still weren't happy at her coming out with me, to Silvermoor of all places. But Miss Embry had intervened, assuring them that our friendship was innocent and that no harm could come of it. Neither of us were thinking about the Westgates tonight.

Despite the slanting, northerly sleet that fell in smatters and splatters against our faces, the main doors to Silvermoor stood wide open. All we could see inside was a blaze of light. A housekeeper and a butler waited to welcome us, wearing their smart house uniforms; they must have been cold. Perhaps that's why they looked so peevish! They scrutinised us minutely as we stepped over the threshold, vigilant against thievery and destruction.

'This is even better than last time!' I muttered to Josie as we entered a vast hallway. 'We never went in the house before.'

The ceilings were so high. I was used to working in spaces that weren't as tall as I was. Here there was so much air between the top of my head and the enormous chandelier that it was dizzying! Colourful, ornate designs of flowers and fruit and cherubs decorated each square, corniced panel of ceiling; I had never seen paintings on a ceiling before. Josie poked me and I realised I'd been gawping so long my neck had stuck. I righted it painfully.

And then I saw the most splendid sight my eyes had ever beheld, apart from the dancing silver horse at Heston. A Christmas tree, thirty feet tall if it was an inch, and not one needle of it uncovered by shining glass balls and glitter and candles. An angel with trumpet and wings and every other perfection graced the top. Every child in the place gravitated towards it as though magnets compelled them. Soon you couldn't get in touching distance of the tree for all the little people sitting and kneeling around the lovely thing.

'Phah, that's a grand waste o' money,' grumbled Neil Smisby, our next-door neighbour. 'Fancy showing that to us as 'ave nowt. Us could feed us whole family on 'alf what that cost. Fancy havin' that much money they can throw it away on summat useless like that. I ask thee. Better they give us all food than show us that.'

But I didn't agree. On one level you couldn't argue his logic. Food *was* more useful than a decorated tree. And yet I would not have swapped that vision for all the bread I could ever need. I already knew that the picture would get stored away in my head along with the ghost horse, the christening day, the rich boys splashing in the sunlit river and Josie's red hair. Another thing to torture me and make me long for transcendence when I was underground. But I would pay that price just to know that there *was* more to life, even if I couldn't have it.

Several maids stood by to take our coats and lay them out on trestle tables that had been arranged along one wall. We'd have the devil's job finding them again later from the great ragged array, but it was warm inside and our feelings of being out of place made us still warmer. The girl who took our jackets was friendly.

'Oh, I like your hair,' she said when Josie pulled off her hat, some alarming knitted thing several sizes too big. Josie glared at her suspiciously but the girl went on: 'It's just like Miss Coralie's.'

'Miss . . . ?' asked Josie.

'Miss Coralie Honeycroft, her as is a cousin of the family.'

Josie looked at me speechless. I knew what she was thinking. *What a perfect name!* I grinned.

'Go through,' said the girl. She probably thought us very strange. 'There's drinks through there and his lordship will welcome you when everyone's settled.'

The festivities took place in the great hallway and three large rooms that opened off them – I wasn't even sure what to call them; I didn't understand about drawing rooms or dining rooms, or the distinctions between them. There was ale in one room, food in another and gifts for all the children in yet another. There was a great deal of swapping and bargaining as they traded hair ribbons for balls or hankies for hoops. Lady Flora was there, overseeing it all with a great deal of humour. I couldn't see Walter, whom I persisted in thinking of as my long-lost brother, in some childish, irrational part of my heart.

The earl welcomed us from halfway up the staircase and soon there was dancing; Miss Elizabeth and Master Humphrey partook. Miss Elizabeth was a fair dancer and took a turn with many a village lad. Master Humphrey was too little yet to do aught but toddle between our legs and trip us up but he added to the merriment with his round, beaming face and infectious chuckle. I saw my sisters in the crowd, radiant with the novelty. Josie and I considered ourselves no dancers but to our immense surprise, we found we could follow the steps and cut a nimble pair on that great polished floor.

Hours passed. I had been guzzling ale and lemonade by turns and eventually needed a privy – an embarrassing predicament in a house like that. Josie glowered when I refused to dance any more but bouncing around with a full bladder was worse than uncomfortable.

'Well, just *ask* someone,' she said, with a woman's pragmatism. Honestly, women!

I shook Josie off and hurried outside. The snow was falling in earnest now. Little clusters of folk stood around, escaping the heat and noise of the party, watching the snow and the moon. I growled, and hurried along the side of the house. It took a while, the house being so very long. I finally rounded a corner but it still didn't seem right to go just there. I slipped through a gate leading into a walled garden. It was a kitchen garden and I didn't like to think of watering their crops in that particular way. I kept going, my teeth chattering with cold and frustration. Through another gate I spied a compost heap at last. I sighed in relief. That was the spot.

Afterwards, as I hurried out from the kitchen garden I ran slap into a fair, slender boy: young Lord Walter.

'Good lord!' he cried, stumbling backwards. He was accompanied by two dogs, though I only saw one at first, an enormous, shaggy liver and white beast. I *heard* the other, however; the frantic high-pitched yapping of something too small to be easily glimpsed. I didn't know where it was until it attached itself to my ankle.

I cried out, alarmed by the death grip of the little creature. I lifted my foot and took the dog with it. It dangled from my thick leather boot, paws scrabbling, tail wagging for all it was worth; obviously the felling of a foe was what it was born for. When it realised the boot wasn't going to yield it started running round me in tiny circles, barking wildly, determined to bring me to justice. The large dog, meanwhile, maintained a low but constant growling.

I stood like a dunce, appalled to have slammed one of the family, mortified to be seen leaving a garden where I had no business to be. 'Beg pardon, m'lord,' I stammered at last. 'I just needed some air is all. I didn't see thee. I'm sorry for bumping thee.'

'Teacup!' he shouted to my surprise. 'Teacup, hush now! Stop it, I tell you, he won't hurt us. Stop that noise! Teacup!'

I couldn't help smiling. To be menaced by something named Teacup struck me as terribly funny.

'Empress, you too,' he commanded. 'I can hardly hear the lad speak. Teacup, here!' He scooped the little dog up in his arms. Teacup contented himself with showing me tiny white teeth while Empress sniffed me carefully and fell silent.

'No harm done,' said the boy to me. 'That is, assuming you haven't demolished the kitchen garden, or stolen a marrow.'

'Oh no, my lord, no, I wanted a look is all. I shouldn't have gone in, I know, but I've done no harm, I promise . . .'

'No, no!' he said. 'I was only teasing. Of course you haven't stolen a marrow. Who would? They're detestable vegetables. *I* don't mind you looking around, though I can't answer for my father. I take it you're from the village?'

'Aye, m'lord. I am. Thank you, sir.' I started to walk off but he called after me.

'What's your name?'

'Tommy Green, m'lord.'

'And you work at the mines, Tommy?'

'I do that, at Crooked Ash.'

He nodded and kept looking at me, smiling.

'Will that be all, sir?'

'Yes. No. Will you walk with me a while, Tommy? Or are you too cold?'

'*Walk* with you, sir?' I couldn't have been more surprised if he'd asked me to turn a cartwheel.

'If you're willing. I don't think I've ever met a village boy before.'

'You've met *me*, m'lord!' It came out before I could think. He looked startled and I wished I hadn't said it. 'Beg pardon. It were a few year ago now, m'lord, at the school prize-giving. But you were only a little lad and couldn't be expected to remember.'

'No, I don't. At least, I remember the occasion of it. I remember going to the schoolhouse with my father and a lot of people staring. Were you one of the prize-winners?'

'I was, sir. Three year in a row.'

'I see. And do you study now? Come, walk a little.'

In a strange, dreamlike turn of events, we fell into step. It was as if I had willed this moment into being, the culmination of a lifetime of wishful thinking.

'Not now. We leave school at twelve, m'lord, and go to work. There's no chance to study then. But we're grateful for the work, o' course,' I added because that's what we always said if we were asked.

'Of course. And I suppose you were glad to be rid of tiresome lessons? Mining must be very exciting, I imagine. I do frightfully admire you all.'

I was speechless for a little minute. 'Ah, no, m'lord. If I'm to be honest wi' yer lordship, I weren't glad to be rid of school at all. I loved learning. I dislike being ignorant. I hope I don't speak out of turn.'

'I see.' He looked puzzled, so I fell silent. 'This is Empress and this is Teacup,' he said, lifting the latter, who was still wriggling and gnashing in his arms while Empress followed us like a stately guard.

'Tha's picked right proper names for them. I couldn't have found better names if I'd thought for a year.'

'I love dogs. Do you, Tommy?'

'I don't know any well enough to say, m'lord.'

'Your family has no pets?'

'No, m'lord. We have thirteen mouths to feed in our house as it is.'

'Yes,' he nodded wisely. 'My father always says my sisters eat enough to bankrupt us.'

I dared not speak. I wondered if there was one particular of my life that he might imagine rightly.

Lord Walter set Teacup down. 'Teacup!' he admonished, wagging a finger at her while she gazed up at him, bright-eyed. 'If I put you down, you are to *behave*, do you understand? No biting the miner!'

I had to laugh, again. 'Thank you, m'lord,' I said. I could imagine what Neil Smisby would say, or the other men in the village, if they heard a young boy, a fledgling, talk about them in such a way. But he did not *mean* to be condescending, I could tell. He was just from a different world.

'Why aren't you at the party, m'lord?' I wondered. 'Your brother and sisters are there and having a merry dance.'

'I didn't feel like company tonight, Tommy,' he explained with a world-weary air. 'I have matters on my mind.'

'Oh.' I daren't ask. Up close, he seemed much younger. He was still poised and spoke beautifully, but he seemed so innocent.

'Yes,' he went on. 'My father won't let me have a new pony and Merrylegs is quite old and slow now. I want to learn to jump, but Papa says I must content myself with trotting Merrylegs until I am older. Can you credit it?' He leaned in, as if I would relate easily to his concerns. 'Is not Papa *quite* the worst stuck-in-the-mud?'

'Perhaps he won't make you wait long,' I murmured. 'Perhaps it'll be no more than a year.'

'A year. Do you think, Tommy? I'll be ten then, do you think that's the right age to start jumping?'

'I'm no horseman, m'lord.' He continued to brood.

'You'll be ten in June,' I ventured. 'I'll always remember the date, m'lord, because your christening was held on my birthday. So it's stuck in my memory.'

'I suppose it would. I hope my christening didn't take you away from your own celebrations.'

I laughed again. 'Nay! We hold no celebration for turning a year older, m'lord. Your christening were the best day o' me life! I loved every minute of it.'

'Oh, I'm glad of that. Tommy? Pardon me if I seem impudent, but it seems to me that you're not well suited to being a miner. I mean, I'm sure you do a good job, but you enjoy education and parties and exploring kitchen gardens by moonlight. I was not aware that miners valued such things. I'm not partial to education myself, though I shall have a glut of it, until I'm eighteen at least. My sister Flora is the real scholar in our brood and *that's* a waste, since she's a girl. *Do* miners enjoy lessons, in general?'

'Some do and some don't, m'lord. Though . . . I'm often different than the rest.'

'Could you not do something else with your life?'

'Nay, I've got no means. No money and only that basic schooling. And my da would kill me. He needs my wage coming into the house.'

'So are you . . . unhappy, Tommy?'

I paused. There were so many reasons to be diplomatic. But I wanted to tell the truth; I couldn't do it with my own people.

'Yes, m'lord, I am really.'

'I'm sorry for it, truly. But what can *I* do? I'm only nine,' he sighed weightily. 'I suppose we should go back now. Papa won't be pleased if I miss his speech and the midnight bells.'

'Nor will Josie.'

'Is Josie your sweetheart?'

'Nay, we've none of that. She's my good friend is all.'

'Is she pretty?'

'Aye, to me.'

'Then I bet she'll be your sweetheart one day,' he grinned,

a little boy for sure in that moment. 'Tommy, I've enjoyed our talk.'

'And I, sir.'

'Would you visit me again sometime?'

It was what I had always wanted: a bond between me and his little lordship. But I was older now and I knew that the way you *wanted* things to be, even the way things *should* be, wasn't always how they were.

'I'd like that very much indeed, m'lord. I should enjoy it so very much. But I should probably say thee nay. Your family wouldn't like it, I'm sure. Tonight's different because of this special holiday for the new century. But usually the only time I'm not at work is of an evening, when you must be in bed, or a Sunday, when I see Josie and do chores.'

'Chores on a Sunday?' He wrinkled his nose. 'I don't much like the sound of your life, Tommy.'

'I'm not sure you would like it, no.'

'But perhaps one Sunday? You could bring Josie. I should like to meet her.'

'I truly want to oblige, it would be the greatest pleasure. But I think you should ask your father first. We may see nowt wrong with it, but that doesn't mean that others won't. Ask him, and if he says yes, I'd be very glad to come.'

He sighed. 'Then I hope Father says yes. My friends, the Craymill boys, have moved to London and Cedric – he's my cousin, you know – isn't much fun now that he's grown up.

That is, he's still an awfully decent chap. But he's very much taken up with his work now, always worrying about the mines and writing letters to change them.'

'He is? How?'

'I don't know. And he used to be a regular whizz at climbing trees.' He was despondent all the way back to the house, musing on this sorry development in Cedric's character.

At the front door I hung back and watched the great laughing throng swallow him up. I glimpsed Josie, her face bright with excitement, talking to my little sister Connie; perhaps young Walter Sedgewick was right about us. But I shoved the thought from my mind at once; I was too young to think of such things.

Even so, when the earl's speech ended and every villager held a glass of champagne and the bells struck to herald the dawn of a new era of human history with all its hopes and intentions, I did kiss Josie. Just a quick one.

# Chapter 18

# Josie

*January 1901*

Life in the new century was a sorry anti-climax. Tommy had been right when he'd warned me that we wouldn't wake up on the first day of 1900 magically liberated. Now yet another year had passed and the new century wasn't quite so shiny new any more. The queen had died and Edward VII had come to the throne; this made no difference to us either. I started to doubt the truth of what I'd told Tommy. Perhaps there *was* no other destiny for him, nor for any of us.

In Arden, spirits were still low. The first of the new pits was sunk and new housing had been hastily slung up to service it. They just joined it onto Arden, more or less; didn't even give it a new name. So the newcomers said they lived in Arden even though the houses they occupied were no part of the Arden that had stood for over a hundred years. They had to say they lived somewhere, I suppose.

Our little population had more than doubled, seemingly overnight. I think the worst of it was how powerless we all felt. It was a dramatic demonstration that we had no control over our circumstances at all. Our household economics could change, our village could change, and all at the decision of other folk, not ours.

There wasn't too much trouble between us and the new ones. We were all too exhausted to fight. But neither was there warmth or welcome. We could not help but bristle at their presence, disturbing everything we'd always known, and they could not help but be guarded around us when we had such cause to resent them. We tried to live as two separate communities, even though we were right on top of each other. I was happy for Dulcie, though; her shop was busier and she was glad of the extra income.

Bert was married now, to Franny May. She didn't, it had to be said, look much like Patricia Lamar. Alice had twins, both girls — a blow. I can't say I wasn't pleased she'd failed at *something*. Lovely Martha was courting. Tansy was still a bright spirit in the gloom of my home life, slender and fair, blowing about our grim world like a dandelion seed. If I was ever greeted, when I returned from my walks or my errands, it would be Tansy who did it. If anyone ever kissed me, it was Tansy, puckering up her pink cherub lips and planting them on my cheek. I hoped that life would be kinder to her than it was to the rest of us. I couldn't bear to think of her turning out like Ma.

In February I turned fifteen and I didn't know what life had in store for me either. No Arden lad showed any interest in me so it didn't seem likely that I would marry and have the grand opportunity of recreating our life in an identical house down the street. I would probably live with Ma forever.

One Sunday in April, I set off Grindley way after lunch but I didn't see Tommy that day. I did, however, see something quite unexpected. There was a stretch of the road which rose up gradually, then plunged more sharply. It was fun to run down it on the way, not so much fun to toil up it on the way back. From the top of this rise I saw an unusual splash of colour down by the stream: a carmine pink so bright it seemed to glow. A dress. And then I saw a thing that made my blood boil. Two loutish boys, chasing none other than Miss Coralie Honeycroft. It had to be her. Who else would wear such a gown?

I ran. I ran as fast as my little legs, as Tommy still called them, would carry me. New lads, they had to be. Not that Arden boys were incapable of fault, but they all knew local gentry when they saw it and they'd know the consequences of misbehaviour. I reached the stream but couldn't see them anywhere. Just along the grassy pathway was a stone bridge, tucked underneath the hill. Just grey stone it was, nothing special, but pretty in its way because of its position. That must be where they'd disappeared to.

Sure enough I heard voices: Miss Honeycroft shrieking, 'No, please no!' and male voices jeering. I dreaded what I would see. But when I got there, it wasn't as bad as I'd feared. Intent on robbing and taunting her they were.

'Such a pretty little chicken,' one was saying. 'Why so far from the hen coop, chicken?' And the other made chicken noises: '*Boc, boc, boc* . . .' I rolled my eyes. Honestly!

The first was swinging her bonnet by its ribbons, the chicken one had grabbed her bag. In her terror she was unfastening her earrings with shaking hands, obviously willing to give them anything if it would save her person. I knew something of rough lads, though, and I didn't think they were bent on that sort of mischief; they just didn't know our ways around here. They might have been from Ireland or Northumberland or over the sea for all I knew of accents.

'What else will you take off for us, eh?' they demanded and burst into raucous laughter. I don't think they even knew what they were suggesting, fools. The thing was to make them leave, if possible without being seen, for I liked to wander around alone and I didn't want to fear two New Arden idiots taking revenge. Much though I felt I could slay an army in that moment, I was a fifteen-year-old girl and still no more than medium-sized at best.

I took up a stone and aimed it, narrowing my eyes into

the shadows under the bridge. I'd always been a good shot; growing up in Arden with bright red hair, it was a useful skill to have. I'd had many a song sung to torment me over the years and I'd always been short on patience. I hit one lad square on the forehead and down he dropped like a shot pheasant. His companion turned in alarm but facing into the daylight, he squinted blindly. I pelted him with four or five stones, one after another, and he turned tail and ran. He dropped the bonnet and left his friend lying there, dead for all he knew, though I hoped not for my sake.

I hurried to Miss Coralie's side. She was huddled against the damp wall; a heartbreak it was to see that vibrant young woman reduced to cringing fear. 'There, there, miss,' I said. 'They've gone now. You're safe.'

'Oh!' she gasped. 'Thank you, thank you! I thought . . . I was so afraid that . . .'

'Don't think on't,' I advised. 'Wait until tha's home and with your own folk. Can you walk, miss? We should get out of this tunnel and get thee home. I'll come with you if you like.'

'Oh, would you? Would you really? How kind! And how brave you are. Was it you who threw the stones?'

'Aye, miss. Look, here's tha bag . . .' The chicken lout had dropped it when I felled him.

'Is he . . . ?' she asked.

I bent closer, my righteous anger ebbing away all of a sudden. I was afraid, in hindsight, of what I had done. But he was breathing, ugly brute that he was. A big lump was already coming up on his temple but he groaned when I poked him and his eyelids fluttered a bit.

'He'll live,' I judged.

I handed her the bonnet and hurried her towards the lane. It was the main thoroughfare between Arden and Grindley and I doubted we would come to harm here.

'Oh wait!' she exclaimed. 'I almost forgot! My pony's just along the track there. The shock drove it straight from my mind.'

I didn't know horses, but it looked a pretty enough beast, dark brown with white socks, merry eyes and a tuft of grass sticking out of its rubbery mouth.

'Oh Maverick!' she exclaimed, throwing her arms around his neck. 'I've had *such* a time. I thought I'd never see you again, my darling, darling boy.' And she started sobbing heartily.

'Miss, please.' I touched her arm gently. 'We should go, truly. Anyroad, *you* should.'

'And leave *you*?' she demanded, lifting her face from the horsehair to look at me. Her eyes were red and her face was livid and mottled. I couldn't help feeling comforted that she looked exactly like me when she cried. 'As if I ever would! Come up behind me, and we'll go home together.'

'Oh, I don't know, miss.' I stepped back. Horses had always seemed too big and too flighty to me. 'I've never ridden a horse, miss.'

'You don't have to! I shall do the riding and you shall simply sit behind. Come now, you have promised to accompany me.' She swung herself into the saddle and seemed immediately more composed, as though that were where she felt most sure of herself. She pointed to the stirrup. 'You'll have to hitch your skirts up, I'm afraid, and sit astride. Sideways is almost impossible without a saddle. Put your foot in there . . . no, no, your left foot. That's it. Now spring up and down a couple of times and jump, throwing your leg over his back.'

By the time Maverick trotted up the great avenue of royal oaks at Silvermoor, I was enjoying bouncing around on his hindquarters. What an adventure to tell Tommy.

A groom came to take the pony and a servant came rushing out. 'Miss, wherever have you been all this time? His lordship's that worried about you and I'm to tell him the minute you're back. Who's *this*?'

'Thank you, Dorcas. You may tell Uncle that I'm back at last and have someone I wish him to meet. This is Josie. She has saved my life from desperate rogues today.'

The expression on Dorcas's face very plainly said, *Well, I never*. 'Shall I bring you some tea in the library, miss?'

'Please. And some of Cook's marvellous scones. Josie deserves a treat and adventure gives me a fine appetite, apparently.'

I followed Miss Honeycroft into the house, remembering that a year ago I had been there with Tommy. How I wished he'd been with me today. Then he could have shared this experience. This *marvellous* experience, I thought, using my idol's word. But then, boys *were* altogether annoying.

She led me through the grand hall that I remembered so well. We entered a room that I hadn't seen before. Brown walls were lined with books and there was a great deal of wooden furniture: gleaming tables, serious-looking chairs, bookcases and a wide desk near a window. Miss Honeycroft went straight to a small, round table laden with crystal glasses and decanters.

'Tea and scones are all very well,' she said. 'But we have had a fright and I deem this medicinal.' She handed me a tumbler of a golden liquid which I sniffed doubtfully. I'd never drunk alcohol, except for the ale at the party, and that I could live without. But Miss Honeycroft clinked her glass against mine then threw hers back, her cheeks glowing pink. I took a sip and dissolved into a long coughing fit. I was still spluttering and streaming when the earl strode in.

'Good God, Coralie, where have you been? You said you'd be back for lunch, we've been worried.' He seized her in a warm embrace, holding on to her hand even when he released her. When I was late home, Ma gave me a slap.

'Dorcas is babbling something about you being set upon by villains . . .' He turned to me and I rued my watering eyes and runny nose. I curtseyed and hung my head for vanity, rather than servility.

Coralie quickly told him the story and laid the entire credit for her life at my feet.

'Good heavens! Miss . . . Westgate, was it? What an extraor-
dinarily brave young lady you are. Please, take a seat. Ah, here's
Dorcas.'

Dorcas set down a tray and unloaded silver pots, china
cups, flowered plates, a platter of scones and little silver dishes
holding cream and jam and horns of butter. There were dinky
little spoons and knives, the likes of which I had never seen
before. I had never taken an interest in housekeeping – I was
never more bored than when Ma and Alice took to discussing
bed coverings or cutting up newspaper to make doilies – but I
thought then that I might take an interest if I could have things
as beautiful as these!

Miss Honeycroft poured my tea and slathered my scones
with butter and jam and cream, perhaps guessing that I would
not know what to do with the array before me, and the earl
asked me for my story. I felt so shy. It had been one thing
talking to Miss Coralie on the ride home when crisis had levelled the ground between us. It was quite another to hold forth
to the earl, in his home, surrounded by bewildering grandeur. I
was aware for the first time of how imperfectly I spoke, compared with them.

'I were out for a stroll,' I said carefully, 'hoping to meet up
with a friend of mine. We meet most Sundays if he can spare
the time.'

'Oh!' cried Coralie. 'I've kept you from your sweetheart.
You must send my apologies to him. He'll be worried.'

'Nay, miss. It's not a fixed plan we keep. We both wander out if we can is all. And he's not my sweetheart, just a friend.'

'Even so, I've put you to a lot of trouble today.'

'It's nowt o' t'sort,' I murmured. 'I were that happy to help. Anyroad, I were coming down the hill over Arden way when I saw Miss Honeycroft, sir. I knew it were her by the bright dress and her hair . . . I saw her once before and I always remember because . . . well . . .' I lifted a lock of my own hair and they both smiled.

'I could see she were being chased and I ran hell for leather – pardon me, sir, for the language. I ran fast as I could anyroad . . .' I recounted my rather unladylike stone-throwing and how I'd been in such a haste to get her to safety that we almost forgot her pony.

'Who were these boys?' demanded the earl. 'Not Grindley boys, surely?'

'Nay, m'lord. And not Arden lads either, but from New Arden, as we call it. That as was built onto our village for the new pit.'

'Of course. Typical Barridge to be so expedient. So you are from Arden?'

'Aye, sir.'

'And the new housing, the new mine . . . Is it considered a positive development, by your people?'

'Nay, m'lord. The very opposite. Wages have dropped and our village is twice its size. We live cheek to cheek with all manner of new folk who don't know our ways. I'm sure they're not all bad but it's not . . . easy between us all.'

'Barridge,' said Miss Honeycroft. 'He's the one Cedric says has a seam of coal for a heart, isn't he, Uncle?'

He nodded thoughtfully. 'Many people say it, though perhaps we should not speak so before young Josie of her master.'

'Indeed, I do beg your pardon, Josie.'

'No need, miss. I don't know him, I've never seen the man. I wouldn't speak against him for that very reason, but in general we've no affection for him, master or not. Less than ever this past year. But I'm sure he does his best.'

'An intelligent young lady. A thoughtful young lady,' said the earl. He sounded surprised, whether because I was a villager, or a girl, or young, I don't know.

'And I must tell the truth, your lordship. Miss Honeycroft said I saved her life but I think I saved her from robbery and unkindness, not worse.'

'I won't hear of it,' said Coralie stoutly. 'Even if what she says is true, Uncle, her aid was quite valuable enough to render me in her debt forever. And I'm not convinced she *is* correct. She wasn't standing before them looking into their boorish faces and seeing the darkness in their eyes. I shall never stop thanking you in my heart, Josie.'

I hung my head again. No one had ever declared me to be a person of such value before. It was an experience altogether too new and wonderful for me to be quite comfortable.

'I entirely agree,' said the earl. 'Miss Westgate, you must accept a reward.' He went to a desk to fetch something and handed me a note. 'Ten pounds is inadequate compensation for my niece's life, or her welfare as you would have it, but perhaps it will help your family through this difficult time. For I doubt they'll receive a penny of aid from Barridge,' he muttered. That was true enough. Even so, I didn't want to take it.

'No, no,' I cried, pushing it away from me. 'Please don't, sir. All I did was help. We *should* help one another, shouldn't we? I'm sure you would've helped me if you'd seen *me* being set upon?'

'Well yes, of course. But I am a man, in a position of power. You helped my niece at very great risk, Miss Westgate.'

'But I were happy to do it, sir! I only came to see Miss Cor . . . Miss Honeycroft safely home. Only then she bid me come for scones and I thought that was how she wanted to thank me. And I did so want to try a scone . . .'

'Bless you, child,' said Miss Honeycroft, even though she was only three or four years older than I. 'A scone as reward? You must take Uncle's money, indeed you must, for times are hard in Arden – I've often heard my brother say it. And we cannot help there, for it is not our land, nor our business . . .'

'As Barridge likes to remind me,' added the earl.

'I insist you take it or I shall go out and put myself in danger again directly. And what's more, I have a plan. Uncle, might I speak to you? Josie, would you excuse us for just a moment?'

They withdrew, leaving me alone in the opulent room. I looked all around, storing it up to tell Tommy and to remember forever. A funny sort of feeling started creeping over me. I told myself I was overwrought but it was more than that. It was the beginning of another change in me. I didn't need to be an earl's niece, I didn't need land or servants or an excess of jewels. But for the first time I realised that I did need to feel valued and safe and given a little luxury from time to time.

I looked at the ten pounds on the table before me and sighed. I should take it, I knew. It could do so much for my family. But I had spoken true when I said that I didn't want money for helping Miss Honeycroft. And . . . that it must go to my family caused me an internal sigh. It wasn't that I didn't want to share it, it was that it would all get swallowed up on food and drudgery. It was a special reward for a special day and if I took it, I would have loved to save part of it for something special. But my family would never agree to that.

The earl and Miss Honeycroft returned and resumed their seats. She looked at him and he looked at her. 'Your idea, my dear. Your offer to make.'

She nodded. 'Well then. Josie, I have a proposal for you. My lady's maid, Sheila, is leaving me. She's getting married and I'm very happy for her but not for me. I don't know how I shall go on without her. I haven't even advertised the post yet because I don't have the spirit for it. I'm sure I shall receive fine applications from excellent girls but they will be strangers and

I don't like the thought of that. Would you consider coming to live with me in York, and working for me in that capacity? I already feel we are friends and I know most people don't look for that in a servant, but I *do*. *Will* you, Josie? Would you?'

I couldn't speak. I could not get out one word. I just stared, and my mouth was open all the while.

'I know it would be a big change for you,' she hurried on, 'and of course, I don't expect you to give me your answer right away. But you know nothing about the post! How foolish of me. Well, the house in York is nothing like as large and splendid as Silvermoor, you mustn't imagine that. It's a modest home a good twenty-minute walk from York Minster. It's near the racecourse . . . but that means little to you if you don't know the city. Anyway, it's thought to be a good position . . .

'The household currently comprises my father, my brother, my aunt Catherine. My mother passed away many years ago. We have four servants, including Sheila. You see, we are very modest. But I am a *paragon* of an employer, if Sheila is honest with me, and the remuneration would be fair. You needn't worry about lacking experience. Our other maid would teach you and I would be very patient. Cedric and I visit Silvermoor often, you know, and so your time would be divided between the two households . . . Perhaps we could arrange for some time for you to visit your family when we are here . . .'

How she ran on. As if she needed to persuade me. As if I might not like the idea! Every fact she laid before me demonstrated further that the life she was suggesting for me was my perfect dream come true. And in York, of all places, the city I had dreamed of ever since Dulcie Embry had described it to me. I wanted to go more than anything. I wanted it so much it hurt. And yet I let her words fade into the distance for I could not stand to hear more. I did not want to refuse but I knew I must. And so I started to cry.

'Good heavens. Poor child.' The earl got to his feet. 'I shall leave you ladies to your negotiations.' He shot out as though hounds were on him.

'Gracious, Josie, whatever is wrong?' Miss Coralie buttered me up another scone. 'I'm sorry if I've upset you. Perhaps you do not wish to leave home. I assure you, there's no obligation. If your answer is no, I completely understand.'

'Oh miss,' I wailed, raising my head from my hands and looking at her in anguish. 'Oh miss, if you only knew how much I want to come with you.'

'Truly? But that's tremendous! Then do, by all means!'

'But I can't. Oh miss, what you've just offered me . . . I can't even begin to explain. I wouldn't mind leaving Arden, miss, or my family. In fact, I'd be *glad* to. And I would see York! It's a place I've dreamed of. And the chance to *learn*, miss! New skills, new people . . .'

'If learning is what you crave, I could certainly help you there,' she put in eagerly. 'You could borrow books, attend concerts in the town, for there's a great deal of music in York and they put on performances for the community at very affordable prices . . .'

'Oh stop, miss, please!' I cried. 'It's too much, it's too perfect, but I can't leave Tommy. There. I've said it. I can't, I can't, I can't. My answer must be no, Miss Honeycroft, though I thank you with all my heart for offering me the chance. You'll never know the value of it to me.'

'I see. Tommy is the friend you mentioned earlier? But surely he wouldn't expect you to pass up a chance that means as much to you as you say?'

'He never would, but if anyone should have a chance, if anyone should get to leave here and learn things, it should be him. You see, he came here when he were five for young Lord Walter's christening and he's dreamed all his life of . . . of bettering himself. But he's been told there's no other way for him. He's been down pit nigh on two year now and it wears at him. He does his duty, miss, he's a good worker, but his spirit doesn't belong there. I can't go before him. It were his dream long before it were mine.' I nodded decisively and took a savage bite of scone to fortify me against the loss of my perfect life, gone before it had even begun.

A thought struck me. 'Oh! Miss Honeycroft! Could Tommy come too? I'm sorry, I'm proper forward for asking, only you'd never regret it. He's a good person, miss, and that clever. He got all the prizes in school – I didn't! He's strong and honest and you'd like him ever so much. He'd be ever so grateful.

He'd do any work at all that needed doing, miss,' I promised rashly on his behalf.

'Oh Josie, I should *love* to help, truly,' she said, 'but we are, as I told you, a modest household. Our few servants have specific functions. We have no vacancy for a manservant. I can hardly ask my father to take in a stranger and keep him to no purpose.'

'Nay, miss,' I agreed, subdued, 'and Tommy wouldn't want that.'

Miss Honeycroft bit her lip. 'But are you sure this is the right decision, Josie? It seems a quite extravagant sacrifice. How does your missing out help Tommy?'

'It doesn't. Only, I *can't*, Miss Honeycroft. He's had to give up all his dreams. I never even *had* dreams before I met him. I can't just *leave* him there in his wrong life. He must have a dream come true first, before I do.'

Miss Honeycroft sighed and got to her feet. She went to one of the desks and wrote something. I watched her, admiring her grace, the way her carmine dress fell. Then she handed me a piece of paper. 'My address in York, Josie,' she said in the tone of one defeated, who did not like defeat. 'I will never forget the debt of gratitude I owe to you. If you're ever in need, I implore you to call on me, or of course, you may send word via Silvermoor.'

'Thank you, Miss Honeycroft,' I said in a small voice. I tucked it into my bodice next to my heart. A symbol. A lifeline.

# Chapter 19

## Josie

The earl insisted on sending me home in the Sedgewick carriage, driven by a servant called Matthias. I asked him to drop me outside the village; I could not so soon face returning to the life I had sentenced myself to. Instead I climbed the rise and sat where Tommy and I had so often sat, and looked over the landscape, the gentle rolls and folds of green and grey. The sky was watery pale, narrow bands of lemon sunlight streaking the grey. It would have been quite beautiful if not for the pitheads standing black and unnatural against it all, intrusive as a foot jammed in a door.

I wrapped my arms around my knees and rested my head on them. So often we had sat here and discussed the fact that people like us weren't *given* a choice. Today I'd been given a choice and I'd thrown it away. I knew I'd done wrong. My only consolation was that taking it would have felt equally wrong – because of Tommy. Every excitement of the journey to York, of settling into a new life, would be marred by the knowledge of Tommy trapped back in Grindley, working underground. It wasn't within my power to ease his daily life but I was the one person in our two communities who understood how he felt. How could I take that away from him? And worse, what if he had an accident? In Arden I'd hear of it soon enough – all us mining folk kept an ear cocked for disaster. Nothing would stop me flying out the door and running to Grindley to be at his side. If I was in York, how would I ever hear? If I was pledged to look after Miss Coralie, how could I leave?

The breeze blew cold about my shoulders and I stirred. I was already so much later than I'd planned to be. I hoped my unlikely explanation and the earl's ten pounds would placate them at home.

I'd never had such a sinking feeling in my life as I did when I stepped over the threshold of our cottage. Only Martha and Tansy looked relieved to see me. My parents' faces darkened. I remembered the earl rushing to Coralie's side, embracing her.

'I'm sorry,' I said before they could start. Ma's mouth was already open. 'A thing happened today. I saved someone and I've been rewarded . . .' I sank into a chair, the drama of it all catching up with me at last. 'Here,' I said, holding out the money. 'My reward. I want you to have it, to help.'

It was out of my outstretched hand before my lips closed on the final 'p'. Pa snatched it, turning it over, checking it was real. He was a man close to desperate, I saw clearly, and this should have comforted me that I'd done the right thing, but it didn't. For one thing there was something ugly in the way he examined it. And I had a bad feeling as he stared at it. I understood in that moment that when someone was that desperate, they couldn't properly be trusted.

It was my mother's reaction, delayed though it was, that was the most shocking. She finally flew out of her chair and clipped me across the face. 'You wicked, wicked girl!' she cried. 'You filthy little hussy! *Saved* someone, my life! You've sold thissen. Some fine gent fancied a bit of mining skirt and up yours went. Yer no good, I've always known yer no good.'

She lifted her hand to strike me again but I flung myself out of the way. It was Martha, bless her, who caught Ma's arm and held her back. Pa was still gazing at the money, in ecstasy and suspicion.

'Ma, stop!' said Martha in her quiet, strong voice. 'You're all wrong. Josie would never do owt o' that sort and you know it. Stop now and let's listen to her.'

'I won't tell them now,' I raged, my legs trembling, staring at my parents. I had never felt more unhappy. 'Not after she's accused me like that! Me own ma! You don't know me at *all*!' I ran from the house, accompanied by the sound of Tansy crying.

Martha followed. I ran to Miss Embry's, of course, and she took us both in, and it was to them that I told my story.

A week later I had to tell Tommy. Oh, what he had to say to me!

He seized me by both arms and for a moment I thought he was going to shake me, though I should have known better. The hurt and bewilderment I saw in his eyes made me regret my decision all over again.

'Oh Josie,' he sighed. 'Don't you know you're the most precious person in the world to me? I'd give *everything* for your happiness. And you've thrown it all away for me! Just because I haven't got out doesn't mean you shouldn't.'

'I'm happy!' I protested, then relented. 'Aye, well, I have thrown it away, that's true. But I made a choice, Tommy. I chose you. There'll come a time when you'll get out and that's when I'll leave too.' But in my secret heart, I was starting to wonder.

'But Josie! You would have met new folk, you might have heard of an opening for me! Friends of the Honeycrofts, perhaps, or neighbours. You might have been my eyes and ears in a better world. We could still have seen each other when the Honeycrofts come to Silvermoor. Oh Josie, won't you write to her? Tell her you've changed your mind and go? Please! I'm afraid you'll resent me otherwise!'

I was crying and he was pleading and in the high emotion of it all, he forgot himself and bent his lips to mine. It was the sweetest kiss. Soft and warm and somehow full of everything we wanted for ourselves and couldn't have.

It seemed to me that time stopped and I only pulled away because we were standing in the street in broad daylight. If it got back to Ma, she would take it as proof that I was what she thought me. And *why* she should think that I couldn't say! I'd never had the boys after me, like Alice, I'd never taken a fancy to one myself. Anyway, now was not the time for thinking about Ma, now was the time for gazing at my lovely, wonderful Tommy and for grinning, so it seemed, like a fool. But I wouldn't write to Miss Coralie. With that kiss Tommy had done the very opposite of what he'd intended. There was less chance than ever that I would leave him now.

# Chapter 20

## Tommy

I spent at least two months reeling from Josie's news. An opportunity like that – and she'd turned it down. *Because of me.* I brooded on it through my days underground. I could picture it all so easily, Josie learning the tasks of her new situation, wandering the cobbled streets, breathing the chocolate-scented air, hearing the Minster bells. It was what she deserved. It would have changed her life. Because I had not found a way out for myself, I was a millstone around her neck. More than once I felt tempted to send word to Miss Honeycroft myself, to beg her to take Josie on whether Josie agreed or not – to kidnap her if necessary! But I had no reason to believe a missive from me would meet with a favourable reception with the earl's niece.

The previous year, just a week after the New Year's Eve party at Silvermoor, a parcel came for me from Silvermoor. I had never received a parcel before. At the sight of the crest stamped on the paper, my heart lifted. Inside were three books that appeared to be about a boy called Gerard Appleby, living in the court of King Arthur. They looked rather young for someone my age but I loved them no less for that. There was a letter too and I unfolded it eagerly.

*Dear Tommy (if I may),*
*Please accept these books as a gift, with my compliments. They are my favourites and I am sure you will like them. I did as you said and asked my father if you might call on me but he said that you are not a suitable friend for me. I must say I am disappointed and I do wish you hadn't encouraged me to ask. And he still makes me ride Merrylegs. Anyway, perhaps I am too young for you to wish to be friends with me and you will not be much disappointed. I wanted to write and explain. I hope you enjoy the books.*
  *Yours in annoyance,*
  *Walter Sedgewick*

I had known the earl would feel that way. Yet to have it set out so baldly, in a child's open communication, was dreadful. I felt hot and tumultuous. *I'm not suitable*. What did the earl know? He knew nothing *about* me! I couldn't help but feel ashamed, offended, and for a moment I understood why the men resented the gentry so much, why they said they wanted none of their fancy ways. For a moment I was tempted to fling the lovely books into the fire, but that was not my way. It meant a great deal that the child had taken the trouble to write, and send me a gift. It meant that though our society was flawed, which I already knew, Walter had felt true friendship towards me, even though his father could not.

A strange thing happened a while after that. I was on my way home from the pit one day when I ran into Schoolmaster. I hadn't seen him for a long time. I expected no conversation but to my surprise, he hailed me. I blinked out from the thick layer of coal covering my face; he still wore his chalky grey coating. 'Evening, Mr Latimer. How do?'

'Well, thank you, and yourself? How go your visits to Silvermoor?'

'My what, sir?'

'I hear you've become friendly with young Lord Walter.'

I frowned. 'I make no visits to Silvermoor, more's the pity. You've been misinformed.'

He made a face of surprise, but it was a deliberate one, like the one our Alfie made when he was accused of stealing and eating food that he had, in fact, stolen and eaten. 'Oh indeed? You do surprise me. My mistake. Good evening, Tommy.'

I wondered how he had come to know about any of it. But now another year had passed and I rarely thought of it any more until I remembered it now, in the wake of Josie's news. I didn't think that *I* would do her any favours by pleading her case with the gentry. She had made her decision, though I did not like it. Not one bit.

# Part Two

# Chapter 21

———◊———

# Josie

*March 1902*

In the business of Miss Honeycroft's offer of employment and my noble refusal, my regrets, as I have said, were numberless. But I never had so much cause to regret it as I did the following year, in the spring of 1902.

It was a Sunday in March. I didn't go looking for Tommy as his old grandfather was poorly. The doctor had been sent for and he was much caught up in family things. So, after church and the usual Sunday chores, I spent a pleasant time with Dulcie, chatting and helping her choose bits and pieces for the shop from a fat haberdashery catalogue. I would have stayed but that she had family from Leeds calling in on their way home from somewhere, and I didn't want to be in the way.

When I walked into the house, Ma and Pa were sitting in

front of the fire talking hard. They both started at my arrival. I knew I hadn't interrupted a romantic interlude; in Arden we didn't have time for those. They were looking at me strangely, almost as if they were afraid of me, which was very odd.

'What's wrong?' I asked. 'Is Tansy ill?' Our little angel Tansy had been coughing non-stop through the winter. Every bark she gave shuddered right through me. I would have given anything to protect her, but what could I do in a world of hunger and coal dust and toil?

'Nay, she's right,' said Ma.

'What then? Martha?'

'Everyone's well, Josie. It's time we must do something about our situation is all.'

'You mean . . . money?'

'Aye, money,' said Ma. She stopped, disinclined to expand.

I looked at Pa. 'What does she mean, Pa?' My stomach was curling in a most unpleasant way. My skin prickled. Something bad was coming. The air was thick with it.

'It has to be you, lass,' he said, as though carrying on a conversation I'd been party to all along. 'Tha's strong and sharp. Martha's gentler and she's courting besides. I'll not risk the chance to get another one wed.'

'*What* has to be me?'

He glanced at my mother, who stood with her arms folded across her chest, lips compressed, glaring at me.

'There's no other way,' he went on helplessly. 'We need

that cough medicine for littl'un and there's not enough food on table as it is.'

'So what will we *do*?' I cried.

Ma threw Pa a glance so scornful it could have rotted fruit off trees. 'Tha's going down pit,' she spat out. 'There it is. We need another wage.'

'The *pit*?' I said slowly. 'But . . . I'm a *girl*!'

'Aye, I know that. I birthed thee. If we had a son, *he'd* be going. But we don't. So don't start carrying on and bleating about this and that. I know that Grindley lad's been filling your head wi' fancy nonsense. But you'll do your bit for this family, Josie Westgate, or so help me I'll skin thee alive.'

A million thoughts all at once. I was a girl and it was against the law, but I didn't expect to dissuade them. I heard Tommy's voice in my head, all the stories he'd gradually revealed to me over the last years. The completeness of the dark, the physical pain, the coal dust that you swallowed with your bread. The need to relieve yourself in the tunnel with all the other men just a footstep away. How could that work for me? What about during my monthly courses? How would I manage? The jeering men, the tests of manhood, the physical strength needed to hew and hoist and endure the long, hot hours . . .

Somehow, mixed up in all this, I could see that it suited Ma to have me out of the way, to have tonnes of earth and rock between us. It was more than just my failure to live up to her expectations of a daughter. There was something between us that I'd never known. I couldn't think what.

But never mind that now. The pressing thing was to avert this. At once, two escape routes occurred to me. 'I'm happy to work,' I said, my voice breathy, my words rapid and ragged. 'I want to bring in a wage, I do. But there's other ways, and probably better money with them. I didn't tell you this but a while ago I was offered a job as a lady's maid. You remember when I had that ten pounds for helping Miss Honeycroft? Well, she asked me then. I'm sure if I went to her now—'

'Don't talk soft,' Ma cut in, more withering than ever. 'As if a lady would want the likes of *you*, you lying little toad.'

'It's true!' My voice rose and rose. 'I swear it's true! Let me go to Silvermoor tomorrow and send word to her and you'll see. I'll earn more than I will in the pit and we'll be better off!'

'As if you would ever have said no!' she laughed, as if I hadn't spoken. 'Tell me something, fine miss, if your Miss Honeycroft had offered you the chance of a lifetime, why didn't you take it? Nowt to keep you here, I know that. I don't flatter myself that you've so much love for us you'd stay.'

'Well, that goes both ways!' I cried. 'I could die underground for all you'd care. Even so, it's true, and it's a better way. Let me write to her.'

'Oh, you'll *write* to her, will you? You'll *send word*, will you?' Her voice was nothing but a sneer. 'My my, yer fancy. You'd go and never look back. We'd never see a penny from you and that's for sure.'

I gasped with the unfairness of it. 'Ma! I gave you the whole ten pounds! I would send you half my wages, I promise! Won't you at least let me try?'

'Every week counts now, Josie love,' said Pa. 'Even if what you say is right, by time you've wrote to her and she's wrote back, it'll be a week and now that Bert's married we need a second wage to start coming in. Richardson expects you tomorrow.'

'He *expects* me?' I started, backing away from them slowly, hardly realising I was doing it. 'Are you *mad*?' No time to prepare myself. No time to tell Tommy or Dulcie. Richardson was the deputy. If he was expecting me, Pa had been arranging this for days and said not a word.

'Dulcie then! She'll give me a job in the shop. Let me ask her now. I could start tomorrow, I know I could, she'd never have me work down the mine. She'd want to keep me from it!'

'Oh, she'd *want to keep you from it*, would she? So *she* wants what's best for our daughter, while we're cruel and heartless, is that it?'

'Well, yes! It seems so.'

'Oh, how my heart wails for poor little Josie. All those good people wanting what's right for her, while her cruel parents treat her summat awful.'

'Well, if the cap fits, Ma,' I muttered.

The slap across my cheek was immediate and burning. She yanked me away from the doorway I'd been sidling towards. I started kicking and screaming but Ma was strong, oh yes, our Ma was strong. She forced me into the chair by the fire and sat on me to keep me there. She held my arms at my sides and nodded at Pa.

He stood wearily and fetched the kitchen scissors. I couldn't make sense of what was happening. Were they going to *stab* me?

'Pa!' I shrieked. 'Why are you so set on this when I have choices? There's other ways!'

'Josie, love,' he said. 'If Miss Embry could afford to pay a shop assistant, she'd have one. It's a village shop. We all know she's just getting by. And we won't take charity.'

'Then Miss Honeycroft . . . If you'd only let me——'

'That were a *year* ago. She'll have a new maid by now.'

'You'll not work for that family, and that's flat,' said Ma in a granite voice. 'I'll not have it. Giving you ideas, setting you up above myself. *Lady's maid*, my eye. I don't suppose you told her you're the clumsiest clod this side of Sheffield! You'd have torn her dresses and burned her hair and lost her trinkets before a week was out. You've no grace to you, girl. The mines will do just right for you. Come on now, Sam. Don't drag it out.'

And my father lifted my braids and cut them off, sharp at the top, in two decisive snips. Ma stood up. She took the scissors and trimmed for a brief minute, while I was limp with shock. She looked at me and nodded. 'Just in case Barridge should see you,' she said. 'Not that he'd even care, most like.'

I leaped up and ran from the house, sobbing.

# Chapter 22

Tommy

*March 1902*

One Sunday in March, as dusk crept into our home, sadness came with it. Grandpa was near the end. We were all gathered, not around his death bed or anything like that – we had a little while yet. But family time was more precious to all of us just now. We didn't do anything different, just treasured our usual evenings, with Da sloping out every so often to smoke a pipe, the girls working at some sort of stitchery and Ma playing the harmonium, Connie singing softly along.

Into this melancholy tranquillity came a disturbance. An urgent knocking at the front door, which we never used. Da scowled and wrenched it open.

'Who are you? What's tha want?' he demanded.

I looked up to see Miss Dulcie Embry. She had no coat or hat. She looked as if she had one minute been entertaining in her parlour and the next found herself on our doorstep. I later learned this was exactly the case.

I hurried outside. My family were unlikely to be welcoming at the best of times and this was not the best of times. 'What's happened?' I asked when the door was shut behind us.

'Oh Tommy, you must come! They've cut her hair! They're sending her down Drammel Depth in the morning, dressed as a boy!'

I ran inside. I threw on my coat and cap and left with no other word than, 'I'll be back,' and a kiss on the forehead for Grandpa.

Miss Embry had borrowed the messenger trap from the deputy at Hepzibah. We rattled through the shadowy lanes while she told me more of the drama.

'Wait!' I cried when we passed the turning for Silvermoor.

She reigned in and we paused at the broad stone pillars that marked the beginning of Sedgewick land. The pony blew air and stamped.

'She's safe tonight?' I checked. 'She can't go down pit till tomorrow and she'll do nowt foolish in the next half hour?'

'She won't get the chance! She'd only been with me two minutes when her father dragged her off, swearing he'd lock her up. I begged him to leave her with me but he was like stone. Josie was hysterical. She just kept shouting, "Tell Tommy, tell Tommy," over and over. It was pitiful, Tommy. I didn't even stop to think what you could do, but it was what she asked of me.'

'You did right, miss. I'm that grateful. I'm just thinking it might be wise to let Miss Honeycroft know. She told Josie to come to her if she was ever in need. Well, this is need all right.'

'It certainly is.'

'Let's go to the big house. She may be there. If not, we can send word and go on to Arden not much delayed.'

She turned the trap and we rolled up the broad avenue. It was an ill time for a social call, even among equals. For a village lad to call on the masters uninvited at such an hour was the height of bad behaviour. I was glad of Miss Embry; I fancied she lent me an air of respectability.

We rang the bell and waited on the great stone steps. The butler, when he saw us, was the very portrait of horrified dismay. Miss Embry quickly apologised and explained that it was a matter of urgency that we speak with Miss Honeycroft at once.

'Miss Honeycroft and Mr Honeycroft are not here,' he told us. 'They are currently in York. Good evening.'

'Wait! Please! Do you expect her to return soon?'

'Not within the month, ma'am,' he said, all but shutting the door in our faces.

'Then may we send a message? Please, it is a matter of life and death, concerning a . . . a friend of hers.'

'Indeed?' His tone dripped with disbelief. I said nothing, knowing it wouldn't help our cause to inflict my village vowels and miner's manners on him.

'Yes, *indeed*!' Miss Embry insisted in a bristling tone I had not heard her use before. 'If you please, Mr Portis, we require paper and pencil to write a note and then you must send it to York first thing in the morning.'

His eyebrows travelled upwards. 'I beg your pardon, miss, but if the village shopkeeper is indeed connected with a good *friend* of Miss Honeycroft, I would have thought that *friend* would have her address and could avail herself of the postal service in the usual way.'

Then I heard a voice in the hall behind Portis. A pair of dogs, one very large and one very small, scuffled to the butler's side, growling suspiciously.

Portis looked over his shoulder and explained the matter, taking care to let his disbelief drip through his words and paint us in the worst possible light. Miss Embry was rallying herself to explain again when Teacup recognised me and dashed out of the house. She launched herself at me and I caught her, whereupon she applied herself to licking my face lavishly and with the same urgency with which she had previously wanted to shred the flesh from my bones. A dog of passionate conviction was Teacup.

Lord Walter came to the door, curious to see what had distracted his tiny hound. 'Why, isn't that . . . aren't you . . . ?' he said, peering from the light into the darkness.

I stepped forward and doffed my cap, which Teacup began to gnaw. 'Good evening, your lordship. We're that sorry to disturb the house, only as Miss Embry has explained, it's a matter of life and death for a very dear friend, and a friend of Miss Honeycroft. We only want to send her word, then we'll be away.'

'It's Tommy Green, isn't it?'

'Aye, sir.'

'Well, how very good to see you again.' He stepped outside and shook my hand. My astonishment was nothing compared with the butler's. Lord Walter was eleven now and on his way to being a man, in manners and dignity at least. His face was still open and good-natured and I knew that we should have been friends in a different world.

'Portis, when is my father expected back?'

'Not before midnight, Lord Walter.'

'Then I will see to these people's needs myself. Thank you, Portis, I shall take them into the library. They won't stay long.'

Portis melted away with a face like a wet Sunday. Within moments Miss Embry had written a note and stuffed it into an envelope and the little lord swore it would go by the morning's post. He saw us to the cart, flanked by Empress and Teacup.

'Tommy, the friend in need . . . is it Josie, by any chance?'

'Aye, my lord, it is.'

'Well, whatever the matter is, I hope Coralie can help. Good evening, Tommy. Miss Embry.'

When we arrived back in Arden, it was properly dark. The

streets were empty. Like Grindley, it was a place where Sunday nights were a time of rest around the hearth.

'What now then?' I asked.

'I need to return this cart to the pit or Hawkins will never trust me again,' said Miss Embry. 'Will you come with me? We can try to conjure a plan together.'

'Thank you, miss, you've done enough. I'd best see what I can do.'

'Well, you know where I am if you need me. I admit I'm not keen to interfere further tonight. Her father looked fit to slay something and his wife is always far angrier than he. It's a devil's business, Tommy. I said I'd give her a job, that she could stay with me and her wage go to the family, but they wouldn't hear of it! If I'm here a hundred years, I'll never understand that thinking.'

I understood it. I'd grown up all my life with it. 'They see it as offence, to have a stranger offering help, as though you can do better for their daughter than her own parents.'

'But I can!'

'Aye, and there's the shame, though they'll never admit it, for a miner's pride is everything. He has nothing else, you see.'

'Short-sighted and selfish.' She shook her head decisively. 'But Tommy, what will you do? I fear if you try to speak to her parents tonight, you'll get nowhere.'

'It's true they've no love for me,' I agreed ruefully. 'But don't worry about me, miss. I'll think of summat.'

I climbed down and she gasped. 'God! I have *visitors* at home! I completely forgot! What a night, what a night . . .' She drove off, muttering.

I walked down the quiet length of Josie's street. Men were out smoking pipes here and there, and they favoured me with suspicious glances. I walked to the end of the street and turned the corner. I couldn't very well loiter outside Josie's house and I certainly wasn't ready to go in. In fact, as I pondered Miss Embry's advice, I wasn't sure it was the right thing to do at all. I leaned against a wall in a side alley and waited. They'd all go in soon.

Sure enough, another ten minutes saw the street deserted and I crept over to the house. Through the window I could see Josie and her parents, arguing. Josie was on her feet. Her mother sat in a chair, pretending to knit, but the needles were idle in her hands. Every so often she jumped up and slapped her daughter hard. Josie never backed down. Her father was pacing the length of the room, up and down, putting in his brief tuppence worth against Josie's tirade. The other girls were nowhere to be seen; banished to the upstairs room, I presumed.

It was hard to see Josie crying and hurt, her hair hacked off at the roots, making her look like a scrawny, ginger-headed boy. It was hard to see the lack of love in her parents' faces. My da was a man of granite but my family was happier than this. It was all I could do not to rush in and tear her from those blows, that unlovingness. But I would do her more harm with rash

152

action. I was a miner. I knew a critical situation, an impending disaster, when I saw it.

She was theirs – that was the mentality of everyone around here. It went deep, even in me. Each family was breeding their own little workforce and the Westgates had been unlucky in their ratio of boys to girls. When that happened, it was sometimes unfortunate for the girls. I had *no* right to tell them to treat her differently and certainly not to take her away. Even so, I would.

Eventually, Martha came downstairs, the only calm one of the lot. I couldn't hear her words but I knew she was pleading. The mother dragged both girls upstairs and came down again looking like a woman who'd been attacked by a mighty wind. A moment later, a window above my head creaked open and when I looked up I saw a familiar boot, a skinny white leg poking out of it.

*Not yet, Josie, it's too soon!* I willed her to hear my thoughts, but of course, her urge to get away was more compelling than sense. As the other leg came through and her boots scrabbled against the wall, her father hurried outside. I darted behind the coal shed, a cramped, dark, spidery place. He was too focused on his wayward daughter to notice.

'I can see thee, tha' stupid girl!' he shouted. A couple of windows over the way cranked open. 'Get back inside this instant or you'll catch the back of my hand and then some!'

I couldn't see, but I assumed the boots went back inside for

I heard the front door slam. A moment later it opened again. 'Right then,' said Sam Westgate. 'I'm locking you in t'coal house. You'll not get out of there, thou devil child, don't think you can.'

I heard her shriek then a faint tumble of coal and limbs from inside, muffled by the brick walls. I heard bolts being sent home, one, two, three. I heard something heavy being dragged across the yard and shoved up against the door. I heard him go back inside, and Josie screaming.

Above me, the windows across the street were still open. After a while I heard neighbours' voices, hushed.

'What a crying shame, to have to send a daughter down Drammel Depth.'

'To have a daughter that disobedient, you mean! By 'eck, if our Nancy ever raised her voice like that to me, I'd have her hide. No wonder Maggie Westgate's always got a face on her.'

'Hush, you don't mean that, Mary? Such a happy little thing that girl is, such a bright way about her. To face spending years underground? No wonder the poor mite's kicking and screaming.'

'You've a soft heart and no mistake. She has to do her bit. Airs and graces she's got, but it's no better than she deserves, her an' her *bright way*.'

'Goodnight, Mary.'

I heard one window close, then the other. I straightened my cramping legs and went to the coal house door. It was too

154

early by far to think about opening it but I wanted Josie to know I was there. Her kicking had subsided and her screams had reduced to a steady, audible sob. *Hush*, I told her in my mind. I began to whistle softly.

At first the sobs continued and I stopped, frustrated. She'd have to cry herself out first. When the crying became more of a low-pitched grizzle, I started to whistle again: 'Hey Bonny May', a tune she'd heard me whistle a hundred times before. At once the grizzling stopped. She knew I was there. Good. Two hours I waited in the darkness. And she didn't make another sound.

Other than wanting Josie's ordeal to end as soon as possible, it was no hardship for me. If I held my hand out six inches in front of my nose, I could see it. The air blowing down off the rise was cool. No darkness, no cramped quarter could ever match that first shift down Crooked Ash. Sometimes I wondered if I'd ever fully recover from the memory.

I watched as the lamp was blown out in the girls' room, and as the curtain was pulled across the window downstairs. I watched as the crack of yellow light around the edge was extinguished and then I waited some more. I heard a loud cough in the street and the noise of someone spitting. Footsteps. Then silence. And at last, when I judged all to be safe, I moved the tin bath away from the door.

I winced every time it rasped a cobble, only moving it far enough for a skinny girl to squeeze through. I glanced at the house every few seconds but it stayed dark and still. The bolts were harder; they were rusty with disuse and scraped and groaned as I jiggled them. In the quiet night the noise sounded like the alarm at the pit to me. It was slow, slow work. And the longer I took, the more chance there was that the noise would wake the Westgates.

When I reached the last bolt I worked more quickly. Once it was done all we had to do was run. I glanced at the house yet again and my heart nearly failed when I saw the upstairs curtain drawn back, a face at the window watching. But it was only Martha, and she waved. Would it fall to her to earn the third wage? I wondered briefly. I thought not. They were fonder of her than of Josie and she'd be wed in a year, I guessed.

The last bolt relented with a rasp and a clunk. I almost flung the spiteful thing on the ground but I placed it quietly. I opened the door a few inches and peered inside.

'Tommy?' A whisper from within.

'Yes.' I reached my hand in and felt her take it. She stumbled out, and stood in the yard blinking. She was tear-stained, shorn and covered in black. It was a vision of what her every day would be like if we didn't somehow stop it and I knew this was worth whatever trouble lay ahead.

I pointed to Martha at the window. Josie blew a kiss and Martha laid a hand over her heart, then made a shooing motion. We ran. We didn't slow or speak until we were a fair way along the lanes. Then she stopped and hugged me.

'Thank you, Tommy, thank you, thank you, thank you, thank you,' she whispered and burst into tears.

I'd never seen her cry like this. This was honest, unguarded heartbreak and I held her tight. And still I didn't know where to take her. They would go to Miss Embry first of all. My parents would never take her in, both for the extra mouth to feed and the trouble it would cause. My only idea was to take her to Silvermoor and in the morning, plead with the Sedgewicks to keep her until Coralie came. But it seemed a far-fetched plan to me.

While I held her, hoping for a better one, I heard an all too familiar sound. A dog was in those lanes, none too far away, and I knew exactly which dog it was, or at least, it was one of three. One of Paulson's burly, vengeful familiars.

I put my finger to Josie's lips. 'Paulson,' I mouthed. She stared at me in horror. If Paulson found two young village folk out at this time of night, he would think that we were out to poach on Barridge land; his mind would conceive of no other possibility. It was said that he never forgot a face, and although Josie's hair had been cut, it was as red as it had ever been. It was a desperate situation, the very worst possible stroke of luck.

Another bark. They were coming closer. They might be around the very next bend! If we started running, the dogs would hear us. Of one accord we crept closer to the hedge and snuggled into it. The branches gave way a little. A moment later and Josie was through. It took more doing for me, with my broader shoulders and longer legs, but then I was through too. We looked at each other, wide-eyed. In our haste to stay out of trouble with Paulson, we had found our way onto Barridge land. Now we really *were* trespassing.

Then we heard him. 'What's tha bother, Fang?' A rattle of chain told us that he'd yanked the dog by the lead. The dog was growling and whimpering. He knew something was amiss. We dared not move or breathe.

'Well then? Where is he, if there's someone out? Nowt but a rabbit, I'll wager. Come on, you great brute, let's get us gone.'

We heard his footsteps move off down the lane. I stood up and took Josie's hand again. 'Stay quiet and stay behind me,' I whispered. We weren't much more than half a mile from Da's old entry point. If we could wriggle around those new boards, we'd be out and over halfway to Silvermoor. My biggest concern now was the traps for which Heston was famous. If we stayed right at the very edge, we might be lucky. Even so, I wouldn't let Josie come beside me. I found a stick and prodded the ground ahead of me, every step, like a blind man.

It was slow going but we made it at last. However, the new boards were firm and as I examined them for a means of escape, Josie stared into the woods. 'Tommy, can we see the house?' she whispered.

'Are you mad?'

'I want to see it. We're here anyway. I want to see the dancing horse you told us about.'

'Haven't you had enough trouble for one night?'

She shrugged. 'In for a penny . . .'

I sighed. There was no getting out this way. Best I could think of now was to retrace our steps, go out the way we had come in, and then retrace them all *again*, on the lane this time . . . We'd be tramping South Yorkshire all the cursed night at this rate! A detour wouldn't make much of a difference at this point. And I was *curious*. I could hardly believe the silver rider would be there again, and this wasn't a magical, moon-flooded night like the last time. But still . . .

I opened my mouth but Josie spoke first. 'I know, I know, I'll stay behind thee.'

When we reached the tripwire I pointed and pointed and made sure she'd seen it. I exaggerated the movement of lifting my leg over it. She followed. We wound our way through the woods, the trees whispering, a hare pausing to size us up before loping on its way. I thought of Da. At last we came to the top of the slope from which I'd seen the house, the horse. The house was still there, of course. The night was darker but its massive shape, the crest and swoop of its elaborate roof, could still be seen quite clearly. I looked at Josie; her face was grey from dirt but full of wonder. In vain we stared for ghosts and angels but the night just rustled softly and kept its secrets.

And then, the most hideous déjà vu I have ever experienced. Dogs, baying and snarling in the night. And not deep in the woods this time, but emerging from the trees only a short distance away. One man, two dogs, staring straight at us. The man bent. It wasn't Paulson. He unleashed the dogs. We ran.

We darted into the woods but Paulson and Fang blocked the way. We zigzagged blindly and I thought of the traps but there was nothing to be done. One moment we burst out of the trees onto the grassy incline again, the next we were back in the woods. I lost all sense of direction. There was no attempt at stealth or outwitting the hunters. Undergrowth crashing, heart pounding, breath pumping . . . We ran crazily. Now we were flying towards the house, which surely couldn't be a good thing. The woodland was thin; saplings waved slender branches and the leafy canopy was light. Josie was just ahead of me . . . and then she wasn't. She just vanished, into thin air.

# Chapter 23

## Josie

Like Mr Carroll's Alice, I dropped through the earth. Was it a giant rabbit hole? Anything seemed possible here in this queer, unlikely place. I landed on an earthen floor with a hard thunk and felt a sharp agony in my ankle. I heard a rustling and cracking above and the next instant Tommy came crashing through to land beside me.

He scrambled up at once. 'Josie, are you hurt?'

I shook my head, though the pain in my ankle was searing. 'Where *are* we?' We both looked up. We heard the groundsmen stamping overhead. I was sure they would send the dogs down after us, but perhaps they didn't know about this hidden place, for after a moment's confusion, hounds baying, fat paws circling, they set off again and all was quiet. Tommy raised his eyebrows at me and I shrugged. What did I know? Heston was a stranger place even than they said.

Reluctantly I got to my feet and winced. 'My ankle,' I

explained and staggered against him. I knew what he was thinking: *This night will never end.* I had never loved Tommy so much as I did in that moment when my ankle tore with pain and our situation was quite, quite desperate, and all he did was nod, hold out his hand and set off again, moving at my pace. I understood then that he would never give up on me, never leave me, and that few people on this earth had someone like that. In the year since he'd kissed me there had been no further budding of romance and I'd often wondered if he thought about that kiss as much as I did.

The going was painfully slow, literally, and I felt terrible about that, but my ankle was quite wrenched. The tunnel ran gently downwards; one way or another life seemed determined to get us under this earth.

Had we fallen through a crack between worlds? How did Paulson's men not know to follow us here? The earth underfoot was soft and the ceiling grew higher and lower by turns. Then the ground started to rise again.

'We've been walking away from the house,' murmured Tommy. 'If this keeps climbing, we should come out soon. Probably still on the estate, but maybe out on the lanes with a bit of luck, over towards Skelton way . . .'

Up ahead was a light, a gentle glimmer. It shaped itself into an oval just above our heads and the tunnel came to an end. It was easy to pull ourselves up through the opening and into a . . .

. . . place where stalls built of brick with bolted wooden doors stood in a row. Mounds of straw, heaped like Rumpelstiltskin's hoard, gleamed gold in the light of the brazier. We heard the unmistakeable sound of a horse harrumphing and the clop of a hoof on stone. We were in a *stable*?

There was a shout outside and we looked at each other in despair. *Again?*

Tommy unbolted a door and pulled me inside. A large black horse looked at us in surprise and our surprise was equal. Why was a beautiful horse stabled in a deserted manor? What if the Barridges used the place secretly after all? Imagine being found and brought before a Barridge! It couldn't get much worse than that. I shuddered at the thought of those hard-faced twins with their cold smiles and appraising eyes. We dived into the straw banked in the corner. We heard footsteps walking up and down between the stalls and a voice.

'Well, he told us to check it and we've checked. I want to get home. There's no one here.'

A second voice said something in agreement. Footsteps receded and a door closed. Silence wrapped itself around us and we waited a good while before dusting ourselves off and leaving the stall. We tiptoed out, hearts racing, hand in hand. And came nose to nose with a gentleman leaving the stall directly opposite.

# Chapter 24

## Tommy

'Please don't tell anyone I'm here,' he whispered.

Confusion rippled through me. Surely that was what *we* should be saying to *him*! A moment ago, I had only perceived a gentleman, a master. I was convinced it was a Barridge and we were about to hang. Now I really saw the individual who stood before us on the cobbled floor. He was gaunt and his face was very white. His long hair was old-fashioned and he was dressed in breeches and a white shirt with flowing sleeves. Most peculiar of all was his expression: plaintive, timid. I'd never seen gentry look at one of us that way.

A large white head appeared over the stable door behind him and nudged at his shoulder. A wonderful horse, the twin of the one behind us, except that where one was as black as coal, this was as white as the stars.

'It's us they were after, sir,' said Josie, 'not you.'

'No, I mean, outside of Heston. You can't tell anyone, ever.

Will you promise?' He was knitting his fingers together then undoing them and knitting them again, over and over.

We promised readily and he looked relieved. 'Good. I shouldn't have wanted to see the groundsmen either tonight. They don't know about the tunnel.'

'We *thought* as much,' said Josie. 'We fell through and they didn't seem to know where we'd gone.'

His eyes darted from me to Josie and back again. He looked like a twitching mouse, wondering if it dared take crumbs. 'Are you poachers?' He didn't sound accusatory, just curious.

'Nay, sir. It's a long story but we were on our way to Silvermoor. We heard Paulson and his dogs in the lanes and he's not best known for his patience with the likes of us. We ducked through the hedge to escape him, so there we were on your land, sir . . . that is, on Heston land. We beg your pardon. *Is* it your land, sir?'

I was starting to wonder if he even *was* a Barridge now. Perhaps he was just a house guest or a distant family member staying a couple of nights. He was behaving more like a prisoner than a master.

He ran his hands over his face as if trying to rub all the fear and confusion out of it. Three frightened mice we were, that night, all frozen to the spot, trying to take each other's measure. 'I'll never have it,' he said and I wasn't sure how that answered my question. Then he added, 'You know this is a bad place, don't you?'

I thought of the man traps and the tripwire. I thought of Paulson crushing Josie's bluebells. I thought of the fortune made off that long-ago accident, the deaths of all those men. I nodded.

'I'm sorry you got caught up here,' he said. 'Might I help you?'

We looked at each other in amazement. This was the most extraordinary turn the night had yet taken.

'That is . . . very kind, sir,' I said carefully. 'We want to be off Heston land as soon as possible. I don't want to put you to any further trouble but my friend here has fair turned her ankle and we've lost our bearings in the chase . . .'

'They're expecting you, at Silvermoor?'

'No. It's only that . . . well, sir, I need to get Josie to safety and it was the only place I could think of.'

'Safety? Are you in danger, young lady?'

Josie looked down and shifted her weight off her painful ankle. 'Yes, sir, one way or another I think I am.'

It was quite bizarre. It was as if he were our friend now, taking on our problems to solve without even knowing what they were! Who *was* this strange soul haunting the stables in the middle of the night?

Suddenly realisation struck and I gasped. The long pale hair, the very white skin, the white horse. He was my ghost! This was the man I had seen on his dancing horse in the moonlight nearly three years ago. Of course, I did not *really* think he was a ghost –

he was flesh and blood before me. He *must* be a Barridge, but . . . his behaviour made that theory equally improbable. There was so much I wanted to say to him but he still looked tremulous and I didn't want to frighten him off. Even so . . .

'Sir, I beg your pardon,' I burst, unable to contain myself, 'but who *are* you?'

His eyes filled with tears, as if the fact of his identity was the greatest of burdens. He looked at the horses as if wishing they would explain. 'I realise it's the height of bad manners not to introduce myself,' he whispered, 'and yet . . .'

'You don't have to tell us anything,' said Josie. I felt frustrated, but women are always better at reading the needs of others. 'Please, sir, you don't know us, you've offered to help us. It's enough.'

'I can show you to the edge of the property,' he said. 'There's a way out. You will find yourselves far from Silvermoor. But to try to take you nearer would mean passing Paulson's cottage. I shouldn't like to attempt it.'

'No more should we,' I muttered. All the same, I was already dreading the following morning in the mines. There would be no sleep tonight and a day in the pit without rest wasn't merely torturous, it was dangerous. 'We'd be grateful to be safely off the property, sir. The rest isn't your difficulty.'

He consulted a silver pocket watch. 'Only eleven,' he said. 'The men still patrol regularly at this time. We'll stand a better chance if we wait an hour or so. Would that be acceptable?'

My heart plummeted at the prospect of another delay. 'Whatever you think best, sir.'

'Would you be willing for me to take a look at your ankle?' he asked Josie. 'I'd take no liberty and I have some skill in the medical line. If you must use it later tonight, perhaps binding it would give you a better chance.'

'Aye, sir, thank you,' she said.

Perhaps he was a doctor then, summoned to care for one of the staff who looked after the place. Perhaps he'd taken the liberty of exploring the stables and feared being caught in the act. He took a roll of horse bandage from a shelf. 'How rude of me,' he said. 'Might I offer you a drink? Port?' As though we were in a parlour at sherry time.

I just looked at him. It was like some bizarre child's tea party.

'Thank you, sir,' Josie said. She seemed far better able than I to take events as they came. Perhaps, after being locked up by her own parents, she had every reason to hope for improvement.

Our unusual host reached into the horses' feed bin, of all things, and brought out a crystal bottle containing a dark ruby liquid and a crystal glass. Probably not a visiting doctor then. 'I only have one glass,' he apologised. 'I never entertain, you see. Perhaps you would be so good as to share it and I shall use . . . this!'

Looking around, he found the wooden cup normally employed to measure out the horses' rations. He gave it a good wipe with his voluminous sleeve and poured a generous measure into the mismatched vessels.

'This is Ebony,' he said, handing Josie the glass and stroking the velvety nose of the black horse. Ebony whickered fondly. 'And this is Equinox.' He crossed to the white horse's stall. 'Let us rest and inspect the injury in here.' We all crowded into the white horse's stall. 'She will tell us if anyone's coming,' he added. 'Please.'

He gestured for us to sit on the ground, so we did. Josie stuck her legs out in front of her and he respectfully felt for damage through her skirts. They both took a hefty slug of port then he started bandaging, with fingers that weren't shaking or knitting any more but were deft and gentle. She bit her lip but stayed quiet until he was done.

Then we settled to watch the hands of the stable clock creep towards midnight. The port was good for us, I think. There had not been just one shock that night, but a whole succession of them. As precarious as this moment of peace was, we needed it. The giant hooves of Equinox – at least, they looked giant to me after the nifty little pit ponies I was used to – scraped gently on the cobbled floor as she moved between the stable door and her hay net. A grey moonbeam fell through a small window and an owl could be heard in the woods.

'I have no right to ask you anything, when I am being so very evasive,' said the gentleman, 'but we have time, and if you're willing to tell me your story, I should be very happy to hear it.'

Josie told him everything. The lease of Drammel Depth, her family's growing hardship, their decision to send her to the mine. She told him of the great row with her parents and about Miss Honeycroft and Miss Embry. She told him about being shut in the coal shed and rescued by me – at which point he reached across and shook my hand.

I think it was the first chance Josie had had to think through all that had happened to her. I think there was healing for her in telling the story, though it seemed to leave her exhausted. She slumped against the wall and her eyes closed. Soon she was asleep and didn't even stir when Equinox bent her beautiful white head to nuzzle her.

While Josie slept, the pale stranger and I talked of cabbages and kings: of the ills of the coal mining industry and the courage of horses, of the places we should like to visit one day and the splendours of a good book – of which he had read countless and I had read nine.

Midnight came and went. I was tired myself and in no hurry to leave this dreamy haven and I could tell that our host was enjoying the company, but at last he stirred himself.

'We should go,' he said regretfully. 'I have greatly enjoyed our conversation but you're not safe here. It would be selfish of me to linger.'

While I roused Josie, he bridled the black horse and led him to a mounting block. 'Ebony will take us,' he explained as we said our sleepy goodbyes to Equinox. 'He will disappear in the shadows. Without a saddle the three of us will comfortably fit.' It was true, Ebony was enormous. Eighteen hands at least, I hazarded.

He mounted up and between us we got Josie up in front of him. Then I scrambled up behind and we rode from the stables. He reigned in and looked all about. All was silent and still. He turned Ebony's head to the north and we trotted briskly through the night. At last something was uneventful. We reached the edge of the property in no time. A narrow iron gate laced about with chains and padlocks barred our way but he leaned forward and slipped the chains and the gate swung open.

'Paulson doesn't know,' he said. 'He thinks it's locked a dozen times over.'

I was about to dismount when he stopped me. 'I'll take you,' he said very hastily, as if he might change his mind in a second. 'I'm not allowed to leave . . . and if they found me . . . but she can't walk. You'll pass Paulson in the lanes on his dawn patrol and be back where you started. Ebony is fast. I'll take you to Silvermoor.'

I had walked these lanes so many times, in every mood and season, at every time of day and night, but I had never travelled them so swiftly. Our friend urged Ebony into a smooth canter – none of the rocking and bobbing of a pony; it was more like flowing down a river. The horse's long legs ate up the miles.

At the bottom of Silvermoor's drive, our rescuer looked up between the lines of oaks and his shoulders curled. 'I'm so sorry, I can't,' he whispered and I saw that his hands, which had been so at home on the reins, were twitching again.

'It's no matter,' said Josie, swinging a leg determinedly over Ebony's neck. 'You've done so much. Thank you from the bottom of my heart.' Then she saw the great distance to the ground.

'Wait!' I slid off and helped her down. It was an ungainly descent but she got there without further jarring to her ankle. Then I reached up and shook our saviour's hand. 'It's as she said, sir, you've done so much for us. You have my gratitude. If ever I can do anything for thee, I'll do it. I know there's likely nowt but I am in your debt.'

'Only tell me that you are my friend,' he replied gravely. 'An academic arrangement to be sure, since we're unlikely to meet again, but I should like to know that somewhere out there I have a friend. Two friends.'

'You have our friendship and our gratitude, sir. I'm Tommy Green of Grindley.'

'I'm Josie,' said Josie, reaching up to shake his hand in her turn. 'Josie Westgate of Arden.'

He hesitated a long time and started Ebony back slowly towards Heston. Then he looked back over his shoulder. 'Manus,' he said. 'But remember, not a word to anyone.'

# Chapter 25

*~~~*

# Tommy

That night we slept in the shelter of the oaks on Silvermoor's front lawn. Always a godly place, this felt. No demon hounds or spectres or deathly traps here. It was terribly cold, though. I wrapped my coat around Josie and we slept in each other's arms and passed the rest of the night in no great comfort but relative safety. The sun came up, a white disk behind the veil of grey that ever covered our sky, and I thought that the industry was mighty indeed that could dim the sun. The earl came out with his two dogs and I stumbled from the trees to greet him.

He was understandably astonished to find a stranger there at such an hour but I hastened to invoke Miss Honeycroft's name as soon as possible and press home her promise to Josie. I apologised fifteen times in three minutes. He was nonplussed, not least by the fact that his dogs greeted me like an old friend. Roused by our voices, Josie limped to join us. A shocking figure she looked, with her shorn hair and filthy countenance. He did not look impressed or happy but he was not an unkind man after all and she did look pitiful.

'You'd better come in and explain the matter,' he sighed. 'No, not to me, to my housekeeper. She will see to the girl.'

I sighed with relief. 'Thank you. But I'd best leave Josie here if tha can promise she's safe. I've a shift at eight.'

'One of mine, are you? What's your name?'

Da wouldn't like this. 'Tommy Green, my lord.'

I was surprised to see that the name meant something to him. But he didn't look best pleased to hear it. 'Tommy Green, Tommy Green,' he muttered, looking at me narrowly.

I wished I hadn't been out all night, that my eyes weren't puffed and squinting, that I didn't have a head full of leaves. I looked down and saw a small caterpillar wriggling up my left sleeve. I detached it gently and set it on the grass, as if the adjustment would make me respectable.

'I seem to hear your name more than that of any other villager,' observed the earl. 'What's all the fuss about Tommy Green, I'd like to know? Well then, I'd better see for myself. Come along.'

'My lord! I mean, I should be honoured, but Mr Bulford will have me guts for garters if I miss a shift, and so will Da if I lose the wage . . . I beg pardon, sir, to speak so plain.'

'I shall send word to Bulford and secure your wage just this once, since your absence is caused by my demand. Come.' He led the way to the house and we followed, holding hands like two tired children, even though we were both sixteen now and in the usual way of things would not have been spending a night curled together. Under the circumstances such considerations were far from my mind. I was too weary even to know if the decisions I'd made were sound, whether I had made things better or worse by coming here like this. All I knew was that I'd got Josie away from her foolish parents, and that I couldn't relax yet because if I'd misjudged things, then she might be sent back and the fight wouldn't be over.

The earl ushered us into the library where Walter had allowed me to write my note the night before. I knew that Josie had been here before too. If he recognised her, he gave no sign of it. Then again, Josie without her distinctive swinging plaits looked like a very different creature. She kept putting her hands to her head as if smoothing down an invisible cap and when she did I saw her eyes fill. She'd never been vain but she had her pride.

'Now,' said the earl, when we were seated. No drinks were offered. 'Explain yourselves.'

We exchanged a glance and I began. I told the story all over again, just as Josie had told it to Manus in the stable. When we got to the part about Miss Honeycroft, he stared at Josie.

'I've met you before!' he exclaimed. 'You were the one who rescued my niece that day?'

'Aye, m'lord.'

'Well, good heavens. I had no idea. I'm sorry, child, your hair . . .'

'They cut it, sir,' she said defiantly. 'Tommy told you. To disguise me as a boy.'

'Yes, of course. Carry on, Tommy Green.'

I completely missed out the part about straying onto Barridge land. We had promised Manus, after all. As far as his lordship knew, we escaped from Arden and ran straight to Silvermoor, where we spent the night on the lawn. I insisted that Miss Honeycroft would wish to save Josie from Drammel Depth, even though I was the only one of the three of us who'd never met her. I was immeasurably relieved when the earl agreed.

'My niece is due to return next month,' he said. 'No doubt it will be sooner now that Walter has sent your note. I know just how she would deal with Josie so I must do likewise if I am to escape her ire. Child, are you willing to stay in the servants' quarters for now? It will give your ankle a chance to recover and you can help Mrs Roundsby with some light duties. I won't pay you but you'll have shelter and board and be out of harm's way. Then when my niece returns you can agree a longer-term solution with her. How does that sound?'

'Like the kindest thing I ever heard,' she said softly, her eyes glimmering again. 'Thank you, my lord. I'm not a Grindley lass, you've no duty of care to me . . .'

'Except for your service to my niece,' he reminded her.

'Aye, there's that. Anyroad, I can't tell you how much I didn't want to go underground. It were like a big black pit of dread swallowing me whole before I even got there.'

'Well, think of it no more. Coralie wouldn't hear of that happening. If I allowed it, she'd . . . have my guts for garters, I believe is the expression? I shall ring for Mrs Roundsby.'

The housekeeper was a more sympathetic personage than the butler, but not by much. Even so, when the earl explained the matter, her face softened. Miss Coralie was a great favourite in the household and everyone at Silvermoor knew the story of the brave Arden lass who'd saved her. A bath and a square meal were first in order, she said, then there was some silver that needed polishing.

Josie stood to go with her. 'Thank you, ma'am,' she said. 'I'm that grateful.' Mrs Roundsby looked further mollified. Then Josie turned to the earl. 'I've said thank you once, m'lord, but it doesn't seem enough. Thank you a hundred times. Thank you for the rest of my life.' Then she came and knelt in front of me, took my hands and kissed them. 'And thanks to you most of all, our Tommy,' she said in a thick voice. 'If it wasn't for you, I know where I'd be this very minute. I'm safe thanks to you, Tommy.'

I rested my head on top of her tufty red one. I kissed her hair and realised I didn't know when I'd see her again. The earl had granted us many indulgences but I hardly expected that he would say to me, *Tommy, my boy, treat my home as your own while your friend is staying here and visit whenever you wish.*

'Come on, child, I haven't got all day,' said Mrs Roundsby and Josie got to her feet. The shock of recent events still lurked in her eyes and I knew that she wouldn't be so cavalier as to pass up a chance at improvement again, not even for my sake. I was glad of it. She needed to fortify her position, make sure the mines, and Arden, could never claim her again. My chance hadn't come yet. But it would, I told myself, as I watched her limp away. At least, I hoped it would.

When we were alone, the earl walked me out of the house and kept me talking on the drive. He established that I was the same Tommy Green who had spoken to his son Walter at the new-century party, and to whom Walter had sent books. I agreed that I was. He said I looked familiar and asked if we'd met before. I told him about the school prize-givings, all three.

'Indeed?' he said, looking very puzzled. I wondered why it should be quite so surprising. He knew that village boys won prizes, after all.

Then he asked me what Bulford would say about me if the earl were to go to him and ask for an account of my character and work.

I scarcely dared hope that he were thinking of offering me some other job. 'I don't mean to brag, sir, but he'd speak highly of me. He'd say, like as not, that I'm a good worker, I keep a civil tongue in my head and I do what has to be done. I'm strong, and the others know they can depend on me, sir.'

'*Indeed*,' he said again, clearly confounded. He seemed decent enough, for the gentry, but perhaps he found it hard to accommodate too good an opinion of a working boy. 'Well, well.

An interesting development. You realise, of course, that I can simply ask Bulford about you and verify your claim?'

I scowled. 'I've said nothing I don't stand by, m'lord.'

'I see. Now, boy, you look as if you can hardly stand. I will ask Matthias to drive you back. Make sure you sleep the rest of the day. You'll need to be back to full strength for your next shift or you could affect the safety of others.'

I felt resentful; I knew the dangers of the mines far better than he. And he wasn't offering me a job, merely indulging his curiosity. Even so, I thanked him, and as we parted I couldn't resist asking about something that had been bothering me all night. A suspicion that was growing inside me, even though it made no sense at all. Manus.

'Sir, might I ask you something? The eldest Barridge son, the one who died. What were his name, sir? Did you know it?'

He looked at me suspiciously. 'Why? Not thinking of causing any trouble, are you, Tommy Green? Not poking around in things that don't concern you?' He sounded like my father.

'No, sir. Only Josie and I were talking about the sad story last night to while away the hours and we couldn't remember his name.'

He nodded. 'A sad business indeed. I'll tell you, then off home with you. His name was James.'

'Oh.' I'd been wrong. I was oddly disappointed.

'James Manus Barridge,' added the earl. 'Poor fellow.'

# Chapter 26

# Josie

*April 1902*

Three weeks later, my new life in York began. At first I could hardly believe it was real. Every morning I expected to wake in my family's cottage, Martha and Tansy in bed with me, their hair smothering me, and Ma downstairs screaming about some grievance or other. Yet every morning I woke to the sound of the Minster bells drifting over the gates and snickleways of the city to reach us on the Mount.

Every day in York, when I got out of bed, I stood at my window for a moment before dressing. It was only ever brief; I was a servant now and it wasn't a lazy life. But it was a better life in so many ways. Perhaps it wouldn't have been in a different household but the Honeycrofts were good to work for and Mrs Crane, the housekeeper, was a decent woman. I'd been so lucky to come here.

Of course, Miss Coralie had long ago replaced Sheila with a new lady's maid, a fish-eyed creature called Sarah. But she let her go and replaced her with me. This was not as callous as it sounds for it was not in Miss Coralie to be anything of the sort. It had not been a comfortable arrangement from the start, I learned. Miss Coralie had never been able to take to the girl, who was reticent and cheerless, though efficient. She was also efficient at removing silver spoons from the pantry, Mrs Crane confided in me, and the Honeycrofts would have sent her packing but that Sarah cried and cried.

She had a sister with a crook leg who lived in Ripon, she explained. There was a doctor who could help her, but he was expensive and that's why she stole. When Miss Coralie found me at Silvermoor, with my sprained ankle and my hair like copper feathers, she applied herself at once to finding a new position for Sarah. Within the fortnight the girl had gone to a place in Ripon – a larger household, which meant a higher wage, and she could visit her sister on Sundays. Miss Coralie had extraordinary energy when it came to making things happen.

And so I found my place at Gravenagh House, on the Mount, in York. It was spring, which seemed the perfect time for such a momentous new start. That brief pause at the window at the start of the day became important to me. I looked out over a square garden with dark-leaved fruit trees that would, I learned months later, bear plums. It boasted a neat lawn and whimsical topiary. Stone walls surrounded it and I could see fragments of gardens and roofs beyond. In those first weeks, purple and gold crocus blazed in every corner. It was all ordinary enough in its way, yet unlike anything I had ever seen. I marvelled at the simple beauty of a townhouse view and felt grateful. Grateful and guilty.

We humans are confounding creatures. Here I was in a life better than anything I'd ever dreamed of and every day I wrestled with guilt. Guilt because I felt more at home here than in Arden, because I felt safer and happier with Miss Coralie than I did with my own mother, and most especially because I had found a way out and Tommy hadn't. I tried to quell the feeling by writing to Tommy every single evening when my work was done, and by sending my entire salary home to Arden every month. Miss Coralie was not happy when she found out about *that* arrangement.

'No, Josie,' she would scold. 'This is the beginning of your new life. A life for *you*. You're not a guest here, you're an employee. You're paid a certain amount because it's commensurate with the work you perform. I know you're young now but one day you'll retire. How will you live if you've given all your money away?'

I thought my head might explode. Independence and a future of my own choosing? Earning money, with no demands or duty? It was too soon for me to realise that these were real possibilities. Miss Coralie and I were from two different worlds.

I tried to explain that where I came from, I belonged to my parents, therefore any money I earned was theirs too. At home I would hand my pay directly to them, my contribution to the household. But she just shook her pretty head.

'But you're not in Arden now. You're not living in their home and they don't provide you with food and board. I do. Do you think you should hand your pay straight back to me? You're not part of the mining community any more. You're in service, and domestic staff manage their affairs very differently.'

Shivers ran all through me when she said that. Shivers of delight and fear. *Not part of the mining community any more?* Had I really escaped? Was I really *allowed*?

I learned the tasks of my new job: dressing hair, mending clothes finer than I had ever imagined, pressing undergarments so white they might have been made of roses. I learned the folk around me, their temperaments and tendencies – Miss Honeycroft and her brother, their father and aunt, and the other servants: kind, clever Mrs Crane, mousy May the housemaid and Norman the footman, a likeable fellow who doubled as aide to the two gentlemen.

Next I learned the city. At first I was actually afraid to venture out. Arden had been as familiar as the back of my hand. I didn't understand how to read a map, ask the way, or draw on my own resources. Before, my life had all been so very *known*. But I had to run errands for Miss Coralie. I needed to know where the post office was, the bookshop, the haber-dasher, the sweetshop. (The sweetshop was important to Miss Coralie.) And before long I stopped feeling afraid of the paved and cobbled ways, the carriages that dashed past, the bustling crowds. As I pieced together the route from Gravenagh House to the doctor's surgery, or from the bakery to the jeweller's, I learned where other things were located too: the Minster, the racecourse, the concert hall. And they were all more beautiful than I had words to tell Tommy in my letters.

All the while, as I puzzled out my new environment and my new role, half my mind dwelled on home. I missed Tommy, every minute, and worried about him. There was no doubt in my mind that I loved him and that worried me too for I had no hopes that he might feel the same. I never knew, any more, when I might see him. And it still felt so *wrong* that life had pulled me out from the coalfield before Tommy.

Another preoccupation was the sequence of events that had brought me to York. My parents. My *mother*!

They were set to send me down Drammel Depth. Even though I had other solutions to offer, that was what they wanted. That was good enough for me. It all tumbled through my mind as I walked through the streets of York, and when I was writing to Tommy, in that last hour of the evening before sleep took me. Then I would find myself holding my pen in mid-air, staring into the shadows and frowning.

I'd never thought I came from a *bad* home. Though I'd never got on with Ma, I hadn't thought that especially unusual or tragic. But now I had seen the way Lord Sedgewick spoke to Coralie and Cedric, the way their father and aunt behaved with them here at Gravenagh House. Although Tommy had a difficult relationship with his father, his mother sounded like an altogether softer, warmer person than mine. Well, no two people were the same. Still . . .

It was the *way* they had told me that I had to work underground. They didn't even *wish* they could save me from it. Our folk were not sentimental, I wouldn't have expected them to weep and cover me with kisses. But there was another extreme and my parents were beyond it. I remembered my mother's face when she told me what they had arranged. It hadn't been grim determination to break painful news that I had seen in her eyes that night, it had been satisfaction. Almost . . . – a word from a Christmas carol came to me, strange and out of place – *exultation*. I let out a shuddery breath as I remembered and my pen dripped three huge blots onto Tommy's letter. She would have been *glad* to see me underground. But why?

# Chapter 27

━━━━ ◁◈▷ ━━━━

# Tommy

*Summer 1902*

That May, we heard that the Boer War had come to an end. The Transvaal was now part of the British Empire. I still dreamed of Africa, the herds of black and white zebra streaking over the plains, the dark-skinned people who knew . . . well, who knew what they knew, but I was certain that it was utterly different from anything we knew here and that I would love to learn it. The Zambezi, I remembered from school, was the fourth longest river in Africa. The Nile was the longest and I still dreamed of Egypt too: of Moses in the rushes, of soft-footed, rubber-lipped camels and green palms, blue water, gold desert . . .

The Zambezi flowed into the Indian Ocean and I longed to see India more than anywhere, purely because I could barely imagine it at all. Sometimes I felt that if I listened very hard,

I might hear the song of India, whatever its music may be, or that if I breathed very deeply, I might catch its scent. But very firmly in Grindley I remained . . .

Josie lived in York now, and although our friendship continued by letter, this left me with time on my hands on Sundays. How I missed that girl. I still walked out when I could, needing air and daylight like salvation. I would climb the rise and remember our talks and our laughter. Without her it was an unloving landscape.

My eyes rested comfortless on the pale streaked skies and the wheeling black shapes of birds, on those abrupt crags of rock that burst out of the grass and reigned over the moors. I suffered the glistening winds, sweeping and swooping like great powers come to lay us low. I thought that if God was as the preacher maintained, exacting and axe-like in His judgement, then we were probably closer to God here than the inhabitants of any other place. But if the Divine were how *I* liked to imagine it, a guiding force of growth and light, this might be the most godforsaken place on earth.

Most Sundays I went to church, thinking to seek comfort in God. But I didn't find Him, no God that I recognised in my secret heart anyway. Preacher Tawney's sermons were all of duty and devotion. 'A working man's religion,' they called Methodism. What did that mean? No one but me seemed to question why a working man should have a different religion from any other man.

I listened hard and thought about all that Tawney said. This system of belief helped dozens of us to reconcile ourselves to our life in the yoke, to various descriptions of tragedy. All my life I'd been told that God had created a wonderful order where everyone played his or her part, that He had made the likes of us to do exactly what we did.

It struck me that this was a very useful and comfortable thing to believe if you were an earl or a coal owner. It was also useful if you were a preacher, and your living was in the hands of the earls. But if you were a miner, it wasn't so convenient. In fact, it was downright unfortunate.

I decided to go and see Miss Embry. She was an educated lady. She had helped Josie to improve her reading and writing. I was sure she would help me too. My dreams had too long been neglected.

I hadn't been back to Arden since Josie left. That night of high adventure had only been a month or so ago, but it felt like another lifetime. Two days later, Sam Westgate had come hammering on our door, looking for his daughter. We could tell him quite truthfully that she wasn't there. It didn't take long to show him around our small property and prove the absence of Josie. As for the rest, we lied through our teeth.

Sam had somehow learned that I'd missed a shift the day after Josie's flight and drew the obvious (and correct) conclusion. But my father, of all people, lent his weight to my story that I had been struck down with a fever.

'No son of mine would go traipsing about t'countryside over some bint of a girl,' he stated. 'Your daughter's always been trouble for our Tommy and I'm not sorry she's gone. Not surprised, either, if you were sending her underground. It's no place for a lass. But that's your affair. And this house is mine.'

Such was the weight of my da's character, the authority he carried as the type of man who formed the backbone of communities like ours, that Sam Westgate left, defeated.

At first, Da had been fit to flay me when he heard I'd missed a shift. Men had lost their livelihoods over less. But the earl was true to his word and squared it with Bulford, who squared it with my father. I think Da was fairly stupefied that the earl himself had taken an interest in my affairs. The fact that Josie was gone reconciled him greatly; he'd always considered her a distraction to me. He hadn't been lying when he said he was glad to see the back of her. And so the incident receded into memory, in Grindley at least. Not so in Arden.

A little while after my seventeenth birthday I returned my church attendance to its earlier occasional pattern and instead began visiting Miss Embry on certain Sundays. She had readily agreed to give me some schooling, to take in hand my speech and expand my knowledge of the world. It was only a couple of hours on a Sunday, but it was a respite in my week, a mental treasure trove to take into the mines with me.

But after my fifth visit to Miss Embry I was attacked in the lanes by Sam Westgate and three of his friends.

'I'll teach you to steal my daughter!' he puffed as he applied his boot to my ribs. 'I'll teach you to rob me of a wage! I can't feed my family now, thanks to you!'

I happened to know this wasn't true. Josie still sent a portion of her wage home each month and it was more money than she would have brought home from the mines. Martha was working at the surface at Hepzibah now – older girls and women often worked there and there wasn't much wrong with that – so that brought in a little extra too. And of course, he had one less mouth to feed. But an imagined grievance can take hold of a man just as strongly as a real one, and Sam was not a man of any great character. He liked to hold the world responsible for his woes and had started spending the extra money, so I'd heard, in the White Rose in Steepley. What a thing for Josie's hard-earned money to go on.

The attack took me by surprise, both the fact of it and its viciousness. I knew that I was taking the brunt of many more frustrations than Sam's. Reduced wages, inhuman working conditions, a sense of powerlessness, all of these rained down on my body under the guise of righteous punishment.

'And what did you do to her when you took her?' Sam howled, nearly losing his balance with the force of his kicks. 'I always knew she was a dirty slut like her mother. I always knew she'd come to bad. I'll teach you what happens in Arden when a man makes a lass go to bad.'

As if he were avenging her! As if he gave two bits for her

honour or her dignity *or* her wellbeing. I put up a wild struggle, but four against one is not fair odds. As I said, they took me by surprise and they were angry men.

'And don't show tha face in Arden again!' they spat as they ran off and left me. 'Else we'll finish the job.'

A light rain began to fall. I lay on the ground, pulpy and bleeding. It was a sign of my circumstances that as I lay there, my prevailing thought wasn't whether I would live or die, but how I would manage to work in that condition, and whatever would Da say now?

# Chapter 28

~~~~~~~

# Tommy

I was off work for a week and received no pay for it, of course. My father wanted to beat me himself, I could tell, but it would have rendered me unfit even longer and thus would have defeated his purpose.

As I lay abed I pondered Sam Westgate's attack. I could easily understand his reasons: by taking his daughter I had taken his property, and when a man had as little as we did, this was a significant violation. I had cast aspersions on his fitness as a father, a family man, an elder. What I had done was a public declaration that I knew better than he, so of course I must be brought down for it. Even so, I had the feeling that I was missing a piece of the puzzle. It was not his actions that confused me but his words. *I always knew she'd come to bad.*

Why on earth would Josie come to bad? She was the most straightforward, bright-hearted person I knew. She'd never courted, she never flirted, there was no duplicity of any sort about her. Then I remembered:

*I always knew she was a dirty slut like her mother.*

What a thing to say to an enemy, in the presence of other men from the village! I'd certainly never seen or heard anything of Maggie Westgate to warrant such a claim. But even if she'd had an affair, or come to the marriage bed not a virgin, there was a way such things were handled in communities like ours. Even if we all knew, the wronged husband or wife never gave one sign of it in public. Sam had been wild that night. Now, several of his fellow workers had heard him call his wife a dirty slut. Never mind *her* humiliation, *Sam* would never live it down! What extremity had driven him to say it?

I'd always thought of Maggie as a hard woman, insufficiently loving to my precious Josie, unimaginative and unsympathetic. But lustful? Flighty? Passionate? No. Apart from anything, all Josie's tales cast her mother at the fire, at the mangle, wielding a needle, with three daughters close around. She'd have a devil's job finding the time to be wicked.

*I always knew she was a dirty slut like her mother.* Speculation poured over me like iced water. Was it possible that . . . ? Had she . . . ? Was Josie not Sam's child? Maggie's antipathy towards her had always seemed to me extreme. A second idea came to me, causing the breath to catch in my throat. Josie's red hair. Exactly the same shade as Miss Honeycroft's. The Earl of Silvermoor and his many conquests. We had spent many an hour weaving tales about me being related to him but what if it was Josie all along?

Of course, it didn't have to be either of us. There may be no substance behind Sam's words; Maggie may never have done such a thing. And if she had, it could have been with anyone. It didn't have to be gentry; they weren't the only folk who took their pleasures. Only, that hair . . . Other people besides Josie and Miss Honeycroft had red hair, I told myself. They weren't *all* related.

I couldn't tell her my suspicions, I realised. They had not a shred of grounding, for one thing. And how could I tell her what her father had said? They had hurt her enough between them. She was in a better life now, happy at last. I would forget the whole thing. We weren't children any more to play at secret identities and mysteries of birth.

A handful of Grindley men went to Arden one night and threatened Sam if he ever laid a finger on me again. No violence was done — most miners were too respectful of each other's struggles to render a man unfit for work — but the message was clearly understood.

I was, needless to say, utterly forbidden from returning to Miss Embry's. I had no business messing around with shop-keeping ladies who were high above the likes of me, Da said. Why must I always go where I didn't belong and cause trouble? he demanded, before he stopped speaking to me altogether. The freeze lasted nearly a month.

I lay like a sack of potatoes, but on the inside I was a raging bull. Why was it that every single thing I wanted for myself was denied me? I enjoyed quite a plastering of self-pity as I slept and fumed and slowly healed.

During that time we received the worse kind of news. Arnold Moore, a fellow from our village, was killed in a black-damp explosion. Little Benny Larkin went back to drag him free, but Arnold was already dead and Benny was killed too. Two young men gone from among us. Two families sporting gashes of loss. And in church Preacher Tawney told us that they had died in a noble cause. But was it? *Was* it?

Certainly Benny had been heroic, and I wondered what they all had to say about him now, those men who had made his days a living hell. When I thought of what Ben's life had been, my heart was broken by it. I thought of the men pulling his trousers down and laughing. I thought of his pinched face lighting up in the sunlight reflected off the river as he showed me his bucket.

*Look at the bullstang, Tommy, eee, that colour!*

I knew Benny had dreamed of another life. I strongly suspected Arnold had. But they had not been given that option. Dying whilst doing what someone else said you must – *was* that noble? What enormous irony that Benny had been teased as a weakling and made little of and tormented, when he was so brave.

My twin comforts through that time were my sister Connie

and my letters from Josie. We understood each other, Con and I. She looked for joy and beauty in a world where there was very little. Finally there had been another concert, several years after that first one, and we had all been pleasantly surprised when Da put up no resistance to Connie taking part a second time. Connie was given a solo. Mrs Tawney had commended her warmly on her singing and told her she had a remarkable voice for one so young. Connie had told us proudly and Da had snapped that it was all foolishness and that she was becoming vain. She wasn't, of course. Even when she received yet more praise, after the performance, it didn't turn her head, but she did make the mistake of saying at home that she wished she could be a singer. When a third concert was discussed, Da forbade her from taking part.

'Airs and notions. I knew it!' he growled.

During that week I rested. I wrote to Miss Embry, explaining why I could visit no more, and received a kind reply which Da snatched before I'd finished reading it and threw on the fire. Then he did likewise with the rest of my letter paper which I'd saved hard for and bought from our local shop. So for a while I couldn't write to Josie; I knew she would worry.

It was painful to be cut off from any way to communicate with the larger world. Da didn't mean to be cruel. It was just that he was at a loss as to what to do with me. My unpredictable actions and inexplicable inclinations just kept sprouting up, like shoots on a giant beanstalk, and he kept swiping at them with a metaphorical axe, trying to stop them invading his life, unearthing chaos. The branches were one thing; he could lop them off, one by one as they presented themselves. He could even hew down the trunk. But the roots were something else entirely and they went deep.

Any being faced with extinction fights back; it's nature. So although I put up with it on the surface, my rage grew. The schoolmaster wouldn't teach me, the preacher wouldn't entertain debate, Walter wasn't allowed to see me and now I couldn't even visit Miss Embry. Anyone who knew more than I did, who could have improved my mind, was out of my reach. I had no channel by which I might receive a little grace. I was entirely out of options. Until it occurred to me that perhaps I wasn't.

On the last day of my convalescence I went out walking. I was still sore but I needed to get my body back in the habit of motion. I was stiff and clumsy and that wouldn't help me in the pit. I said so to my parents as I pulled on my boots.

'Don't go looking for trouble!' my father shouted after me. It was the only thing he said to me that summer. 'Don't go to places you shouldn't go or talk to people you've no business with, understand?'

'I won't, Da,' I said, then walked to Heston Manor.

I made one stop on the way, at the Grindley schoolhouse, which was empty at this time of day. I opened the cupboard door to the 'library' and took out a book at random. I tore out the flyleaf and replaced the book. I scribbled a note on the page, folded it and addressed it on the outside simply to 'Manus'.

Then I walked to Heston's iron gate with its mass of chains and padlocks, the gate through which Manus had ridden us to safety. I reached up, unwrapped the chains and went in. What possessed me? It might have looked like resignation, as though I no longer cared for my life, but it wasn't that at all. It was an ice-cold fire that burned a challenge to Paulson, to Barridge, to Da, to Sam Westgate and all of them. *Come on then. If you want my soul, come and fight me for it.* I repositioned the chains and set off through the woods in broad daylight.

Funnily enough, it was the most uneventful walk I'd ever had in those grounds. There was no need for Barridge's men to watch for poachers during the day and the estate was large. There was a chance I might cross paths with someone, but there was also a good chance I might not. I found my way to the stables without incident. Ebony and Equinox were both there, their curious heads looming over their stable doors like giant chess pieces. I rubbed their noses and fetched a small handful of oats to treat them.

I looked for the entrance to the tunnel through which Josie and I had arrived. It was hard to find and I wondered if I'd dreamed the whole thing, until I discovered a trapdoor, hidden under thick hay in an empty stall. I waited, and hoped Manus would come, but he didn't.

After a while I gave up. I attached the note to Ebony's hay

net then walked back through the woods and out of the gate, as blithely as though I were a regular caller. Then I went home.

'Where didst tha go?' asked Ma fearfully when I got there. 'Tha's been an awful long time.'

'Down past Crowhill Farm to the river,' I said and kissed her. 'Nowt to worry thissen about.' Then I ate my supper and went to bed.

# Chapter 29

~~~~~

# Josie

*July 1902*

I had been at Gravenagh House for three months. My hair was still short but I no longer looked like a plucked chicken. It was growing back fast, with a slight curl that hadn't been there before, and arranged itself around my face respectably enough. Even so, I ached to have it long again. I was starting to fill out. I worked long days and was never idle but the food here was good and plentiful and the little money I did save for myself I was pleased to dispose of in the chocolate shops of York. I'd never had access to such things before, nor the means for them. The first time I tried Mrs Hendrix's chocolate lemon parfait I was almost blind with joy. If Miss Coralie was right and I should be saving for the future, I was contentedly eating my way through my retirement fund.

Whenever I passed a mirror I didn't recognise myself. Curves and curls, a slight flush to my cheeks where before I had been white as white, and the smart, clean dress of the respectable lady's maid. The skinny, aproned miner's lass with her plaits and clogs was quite gone. On the outside at least.

Every day I didn't get a letter from Tommy there was an ache inside me, a fear that something dreadful had happened to him. Every time I got a letter I lit up with delight, then I'd be clutched by the dreadful thought that although he'd been alive two days ago when he wrote it, he wasn't necessarily now. I never used to worry on a daily basis like that in Arden.

Then came a time when I didn't hear from him at all for weeks. I was beside myself; it was like a bleeding wound in my side. I tried not to think the worst. Money was scarce and paper and stamps were luxuries he could ill afford, I told myself. Still, that hadn't stopped him before. I even wondered if he'd met a girl and the thought gave me an odd stabbing feeling just under my ribs. But I didn't think it was that. Our friendship was too special for him to abandon me if that were the case. If he'd met a girl, he would tell me. So that left only disaster – or something else.

I toiled through the tasks I had hitherto taken such delight in. Compared with the drudgery of housework in my home, my work in York seemed so different, so elegant. Yes, I had to do needlework. But it wasn't just taking buttons off so they didn't get crushed in the mangle then sewing them all on again afterwards; it was embroidery, or sewing ornaments on hats or silk roses on gloves. It all had a purpose, which was to make the world more beautiful, or at least, to make Miss Coralie more beautiful, which had the same effect. And yes, I had cleaning to do, but only to keep her room lovely. My eyes quickly grew used to marble mantels and porcelain candlesticks and delicate watercolours. *This is how the world is meant to be*, I thought, and then I would think wistfully of Tommy, who had always longed for a finer life.

A day came when I couldn't bear not knowing any more. I rose as usual and stood at my window, gazing at the garden, today drenched in dew and draped in spiders' webs like tiny pearl necklaces. We were due back to Silvermoor in three weeks to stay for a fortnight; Coralie, myself, her brother and cheery Norman, the footman, who was becoming my friend. Normally the prospect would have filled me with wild joy. Now my pleasure was superimposed with painful *doubt*. I must ask the Honeycrofts to investigate.

Coralie was unsurprised by my request. She could always tell when I was downcast in the absence of a letter from Tommy. Apparently, my face lengthened and my shoulders drooped. She sent word and a Silvermoor servant was despatched to Grindley to enquire. Then word came back and she sent for me one evening, when she sat in the parlour with Mr Cedric.

'He's alive and well, my dear,' she said as I hurried in, fearing the worst. 'You have nothing to worry about.'

'Oh miss, *thank* you!' I forgot myself sufficiently to sink onto the nearest seat, which was a pale blue brocade chaise longue. I leaped up again at once, as if I'd sat on hot coals, and they laughed.

'Sit down, Josie. It's only us,' said Cedric in his languid manner that was very lovely and very deceptive. He might appear like an affluent young gent with little on his mind besides parties and young ladies but Cedric was sharp. He was planning to stand for parliament. His visits to the mining villages were not due to idle curiosity but to a sincere wish to make things better. He said there was so much wrong with the coal industry that he hardly knew where a man might start.

'Thank you.' I collapsed again. 'I'm so relieved I can't feel my legs. Thank you so much for finding out. Why hasn't he written?'

'From what we can gather there was some sort of . . . incident and he couldn't work for a week. His father was . . . very angry. I believe he confiscated his writing materials, so you see, he simply has no means to put pen to paper. I've written to Walter, asking him to send some down, but perhaps his father will intercept them again so you're not to worry if you still don't hear anything.'

'What sort of an incident?'

They exchanged looks. 'He came in for a dose of rather rough punishment from some village men, apparently,' said Cedric. 'A disagreement. But all put right now, nothing to worry about.'

'Grindley men?' I puzzled.

'Arden men. He'd been visiting the shopkeeper, I understand, and they . . . objected.'

I understood at once. 'Because of me. They think he stole one of theirs, don't they? Oh,' I added, seeing Miss Coralie's face. 'It was my father, wasn't it? Him and his stinking pals. They attacked Tommy for helping me, didn't they?'

'I'm afraid so,' said Cedric, 'but it won't happen again. Tommy's staying away from Arden and away from trouble. They've made their point. It's done with.'

I hoped so. But I knew that village memories were long. 'Oh, I wish he could come here,' I sighed.

'I know, Josie. But we've no capacity in our household, you do understand that?'

'Oh, I do. I didn't mean . . . You've all done so much for me. I just wish he could have a chance too. If you hear of any positions among your friends . . . would you tell me, please, so I could let him know?'

'From what you've told us of him I wish I could employ him myself,' said Cedric. 'When I get into politics I shall need a clerk and perhaps Tommy might be the chap. But I've a way to go yet, Josie – I'm frustratingly young, you see. I need more experience. And more money! But yes, I'll keep my ear to the ground. And perhaps when we're next at Silvermoor, I might talk with him myself, so that if I recommend him, I can do so from personal experience.'

I could feel my eyes glitter. A clerk. Oh, how Tommy would love that. 'Thank you, sir, you're very kind. Tommy would be so pleased to meet you.' His chances were coming. I knew it. Now he only had to stay alive in the meantime.

# Chapter 30

Tommy

*July 1902*

Work was harder after the beating. Though I was greatly recovered, every bit of me was still sore. Swinging the axe, lifting the tools, bending and walking for miles on cramped legs were all painful in new ways. I did everything gingerly and the mines were not a place to accommodate a soft approach.

'He doesn't like hard work,' more than one man teased, and they weren't teasing *entirely*. That was the worst insult you could offer around there. It meant you were less than a man, not part of the tribe any more. They knew I'd been injured but that didn't matter; down here we all had to pull our weight, no matter what. I knew that, and I tried. But sometimes my shoulders would twitch involuntarily, or my ankle would give way for no reason. It was out of my control. Just for now I wasn't as strong as I used to be and it was my strength that had always made up for my differences and stood me on comfortable ground with these men. Even so, I only had to remember Josie's face on the night I'd rescued her to know that I'd do it all over again if I had to.

One day Bulford came and watched me work in the flickering light of his lamp, while I swung the axe and ducked the showers of debris from the roof. I expected a reprimand but he left in silence and the next day I was sent to the stables. Bulford, thinking to do me a favour, had put me back on the ponies for a while. Tay Chandler had just started hewing so his pony, Flinty, needed a driver. A good little lad, Flinty, one I'd trained myself. I was pleased to be back, but I'd forgotten that there *was* no easy option in a mine.

The tunnels, with their steep inclines and sharp descents, could be fatal to an inexperienced or inattentive driver. I was experienced, but my mind was elsewhere; at Silvermoor, in York, at Heston. I kept thinking about James Manus Barridge.

It was madness, and yet it made perfect sense. I marshalled everything I had ever heard about the dead Barridge. He was said to be an expert horseman, yet he died in a riding accident. I remembered Manus floating on Equinox over the lawn, the horse performing impossible feats. He was said to be a marvellous scholar, with a particular talent for medicine. I remembered his nervous hands becoming suddenly capable as he inspected Josie for damage and bound her ankle and I knew the truth. The dead Barridge heir was not dead at all, but living in secret at Heston.

But why? It was inconceivable that the Barridges had faked the death of their eldest son. Wasn't it?

More than once Flinty nudged me with his nose when I wasn't moving fast enough, or refused to budge when I absent-mindedly steered him wrong. He showed me more forbearance than the men. It was dangerous, so dangerous to be distracted down here.

The ponies often pulled as many as five loaded corves, which together might weigh thirty hundredweight. If that weight ran out of control, that would be it: pony crushed, back broken, driver sliced into cuts by the sharp steel wheels. Yet I couldn't force my reluctant limbs to their old deftness. I bumbled and bungled and hated Sam Westgate for making me so vulnerable, when he knew what vulnerability meant down here.

Grandpa passed away. He had improved these last months and we'd begun to breathe easier, but then he left us after all. I cried again; it was becoming a habit. Da clipped me, but his own face was filled with such sadness I felt almost close to him. Grandpa was in his sixties, a good age for around here, and the night before he died we'd had such a talk, about his life and all the things he felt grateful for.

'I'm that grateful for all my grandchildren,' he'd said, 'and you most of all, Tommy, for all that you're odd. Like a blackbird's song you are for me. I'm grateful for your Grandma, of course, and I'm grateful to have such a good son. Yes, I know you two butt against each other like hammer and coal. But he's a good son, a good man. All these bairns but he and your ma still found room for us in this house. They wouldn't see us cast out when I had to stop work. I've had a long life, Tommy, honest work and love aplenty. I wish the same for you, though I'm a simpler man than you, so you'll need more besides.'

I rested my head against his. His face was, indeed, that of a contented man, so there was comfort to be had. I knew Grandma wouldn't last long after him. Thin as mist she looked without him. One of those two without the other was unthinkable.

He was buried in the village churchyard and we were all there. After the funeral I walked, my steps marking the beginning of a new phase of my life, without one of the people I loved. I followed the river past the spot where Benny had shown me his dragonfly that day, all the way to the bridge where I'd watched Walter and his friends playing. Today there were no young lordlings splashing about, and there was no Benny crouched in the shallows. He was gone, Grandpa was gone. I meandered home, feeling heavy with the loss of good people. Next day, despite our grief, we were back underground.

# Chapter 31

———— ❧ ————

# Tommy

Like stones tumbling down a slope and gathering momentum, my beating by Sam and his cronies had repercussions. No one besides Flinty was with me down there to see my beginnerish performance, but the hewers and rippers waiting for my corves knew that something was amiss. They were paid by the ton. Their wages therefore depended on the speed with which I could get the corves to and from the coalface. The journey in this particular stretch of the mine was just under a mile and the temperature was ninety degrees Fahrenheit. I wasn't fast.

It wasn't unusual for the men to beat a boy if he didn't bring the coal quickly enough. I could tell that Al Crace and Ed Stoneley were itching to, but I wasn't a boy any more. I might not be at my best now, but I would be again and I was bigger and stronger than either of them. Plus I was Da's son and everyone was afraid of him. So I got through the days but I could feel the tension building.

Then I received an astonishing note, addressed simply to *'Tommy Green, Grindley Village'*.

*Dear Tommy (if I may),*
*Thank you for your kind correspondence. I wonder if you would*
*do me the honour of visiting me at midnight any night next week*
*that might be convenient. Perhaps I might offer you a little light*
*refreshment at the stable block. Ebony and I will wait a half hour*
*at the gate nightly, to escort you safely.*
*    Yours with gratitude,*
*    Manus*

I smiled. The dead heir of the wealthiest family in the county inviting me to a forbidden manor, to drink port in a stable. The oddest situation imaginable wrapped up in the most conventional language. An invitation like any other, but for the specifics. I burned the note. Me consorting with a Barridge! Da would love that, wouldn't he?

The days were long until Monday. I struggled and pretended to be stronger than I was but Al and Ed grew increasingly frustrated.

On Sunday I stayed home and rested, to my parents' relief. On Monday I slid from bed at eleven, promising myself I'd be home no later than two.

At a quarter past midnight I arrived at the tall, narrow gate. I gripped the bars and peered in, unsure whether I should unwrap the chains or wait here. A moment later a large shape condensed from the trees: Ebony. Manus let me in and pulled me up behind him without a word. We rode quickly back to the stables. He fastened the main door behind us, checked everywhere to make sure we were alone – all very cloak and dagger – then showed me to Equinox's stall again, as elegantly as the Earl of Silvermoor showed people into his library. Two upturned buckets were waiting for us and he shook my hand and thanked me for the call. When I was comfortably seated, he went to fetch not only port but a little cold ham and two slices of cake. There were china plates and silver cutlery. I remembered a story Miss Embry had once read to Josie and me, about boys in a boarding school having a midnight feast.

I did my best to match his mannered courtesy despite being eaten alive with curiosity. When we had eaten and drunk a little he told me how pleased he had been to receive my note but begged me not to risk the stables another time. 'If you wish to communicate with me, tuck your message into the chains at the gate,' he suggested. 'I shall check it regularly. And you must check too for I shall reply to you the same way. On this occasion I took the chance of slipping your letter into a pile of servants' post that was waiting to be sent. I didn't know if it would reach you. I really can't emphasise enough how unforgiving Paulson would be if he were to find you here.'

'I know it,' I nodded. 'I shouldn't have done it but . . . it were a strange day that. I'd had some trouble and I weren't thinking straight.'

He nodded. 'You have some nasty bruises, Tommy. An accident?'

'No, sir, no accident.'

'A beating then. I've received a few myself. If I had known, I would have brought some arnica. Do you think you might visit me again soon, Tommy? If so, I'll bring some for you. It's a folk remedy, German in origin. I find it very effective. I use it to treat bruising, knocks, skin lesions . . .'

'You're a doctor, sir?'

'Not by profession, but I started training, yes, and retain a keen interest in the subject. I've had some modest success healing birds and animals . . . I've had no opportunity to prac-tise on human patients.'

The dead Barridge heir, brilliant at many things, including horsemanship and medicine . . .

'You said you're not allowed to leave, sir. So, you *live* here?'

He took a very deep breath and sat up straight upon his bucket. 'I do, Tommy. I have decided that you are someone I can trust and that we can be friends. Am I right?'

'Aye, sir, you are. I'll break no confidence you give me. Though I don't know why you'd want a friend like me.' I thought of Walter's note: *My father says you are not a suitable friend for me.*

'Ah, but I don't want a friend *like* you, I want *you* for my friend. You strike me as a thoroughly decent and somewhat unusual fellow, both qualities I value. I suppose you refer to the differences in our stations, education, things of that nature?' I agreed that I did.

'Well, in the first place my station is so odd – unique, in fact – that it renders all other factors null and void. In the second place, I never understood or agreed with those distinctions. I am one of those subversive, dangerous types who value people for their own self, their character and qualities, rather than external factors like birth, sex, wealth, skin colour . . .' He trailed off and sighed. 'Do I shock you or do I strike you as a kindred spirit?'

'The latter, sir, definitely. Please tell me your story.'

So he did. He was, as I had already worked out, the eldest son of Sir Winthrop Barridge, hidden away in an allegedly deserted estate. It was the strangest circumstance.

'My father never loved me,' he said. 'For a long time in my childhood he believed me to be another man's child. My mother had been unfaithful to him and he thought I was the result. By the time I was six, it was apparent that I was not. Though we are nothing alike in any other way, the similarity in our appearance was undeniable. Our colouring is opposite – he has dark hair and eyes – but we have the same sharp cleft in the cheeks that makes us look as though a pirate has taken a blade to us. The same flared nostrils and tilt to the chin. Though on my father these features look arrogant and cruel, I believe they do not produce the same effect on me.'

Indeed they didn't. I couldn't think of a less apt word to describe Manus's face than cruel. The best word for him was *fey*, a word I had learned from Miss Embry. All I could think then was that he looked gentle and strange and as though the world were just a bit too real and solid for him.

'But by the time the doubt was erased from his mind, the habit of hating me had grown strong. He couldn't shift it, and when my brothers were born, twins you know, he was able to enjoy the uncomplicated joy and pride of fatherhood he had never experienced with me. Two sons, as like him in temperament as I am in looks. A brace of heirs! I was very much surplus to requirements.

'They liked to hunt and shoot and play sport from a very young age. I preferred to read and paint and ride, though not to hounds. I liked to disappear into the woods, and be at one with nature. I liked to draw the trees and mosses and the creatures I saw. My father and brothers just wanted to shoot them. Heston is full of their trophies. Not dozens of them, Tommy, but hundreds. I try not to look at them. When I come here, I hurry straight from my quarters to the tunnel, escape to the stable and back again. The rest of the house sits around me like a far-too-big shell, filled with unpleasant things. I have one bedroom, one bathing chamber and a small study attached. And sometimes I go to the kitchen and talk to the servants but that doesn't always go very well; I believe they think me very odd.'

He was quiet for a minute and looked so sad. I reflected in

awe on his curious life and still had a million questions. But this was no sensational tale, this was a man's hours and days. I couldn't resist just one question, though. 'The tunnel, sir, what is it? It doesn't have the look of an old mining tunnel.'

'No indeed. I found it quite by accident many years ago. I looked through many tomes of family history and learned that it was commissioned by an ancestor, rather eccentric by all accounts, who preferred animals to humans and wanted a direct route from his kennels to his stables. I can relate very well to old Ansell Barridge,' he mused ruefully. 'There are no kennels now, but the entrance is close to the house, hidden in a thicket of briar, and I can make my way there unnoticed. I often can't sleep and I take comfort in the horses' company at night.'

'And the hole we fell through, is it some kind of skylight?'

'I assume so, though I never noticed it before. After you appeared that night I checked the whole length and it appears to be the only one. I hope the groundsmen never fall through or my secret will be discovered.'

He fell silent for a moment then continued his story: 'In Willard and Joss, my father had sons he could understand and take pride in. I was not such a one.'

I waited and wondered. Surely a father did not disown and pretend the death of a son simply for an interest in botanical drawing?

'As I grew older, it all got worse. I am the heir – or rather, I *was* the heir. The fact was a daily irritation to my father. It was all wrong, he used to say, the wrong way round. I didn't understand anything, I couldn't do anything right. There were expectations of the Barridge heir which time and again I fudged. When it came to athletics I embarrassed him. It isn't that I'm not strong, Tommy, I am. But I'm not co-ordinated at team games. I've never enjoyed seeing large men barrelling towards me intent on grabbing a ball. I do not wish to experience or inflict unnecessary pain. Oh, there are a thousand stories I could tell you to make you understand the great rift that evolved between us but we don't have time tonight. Suffice to say that there are several important matters on which an heir and his father need to agree for happiness to ensue. I agreed with Winthrop Barridge on precisely none of them.'

I nodded in full understanding. Differences between father and son – didn't I know something about *that*.

'We disagreed about my choice of bride – at least, she whom I *wanted* to be my bride. I shall tell you about her another time, Tommy. We disagreed about my preferences in friends, about our treatment of animals and servants and, most fatal of all, about the mines and the people who work there for us. Oh Tommy, be glad you live in Grindley. Be glad the Sedgewicks have your keeping, if anyone must, for Hepzibah and Drammel Depth are . . .' He shuddered and put his head in his hands.

I ate a little more ham. It was delicious, seasoned in a way I had never tasted before. The simple act of eating nourishing food helped to keep me anchored in something resembling the reality I knew, for in every other respect I felt I was spinning away into a storybook.

'Did you go down there?' I asked. 'Did you see it?'

'Yes, and the villages around: Arden, Steepley, Craddon. I don't believe it's right, Tommy. Yet my father is defined by the mines, by the extraction and selling of coal, always building his coal empire. To threaten his way of life, his way of making money, is to threaten *him*. Of course, I never *meant* to threaten him, yet I became a threat, because of the opinions I expressed in the wrong company. He imagined how I'd run things after his time – and it wasn't the fate he wanted for his empire. I was a problem. And he solved it in the most creative of ways. I am as you find me.'

'But can you not change it? How can he strip you of everything that's yours? How can he keep you prisoner here? It's insane! You're *entitled* to that fortune, that position; it's the law!'

'He's never cared too much for the law.'

I thought of the man traps in the woods and Josie with her hair shorn and I knew it was so.

'I don't mind the fortune, all of that. It's just that . . . I don't want *this* life either. It has its compensations – the horses, the peace and quiet, a level of comfort that I'm sure *you* would appreciate, my friend – but I'm not free. What sort of a life is it if you're not free? Surely that's a question that you've asked yourself often?'

'Aye, many times a day! I just can't . . . wrap my brain around your life, sir. My sort of limitation is shared with many, many men. That doesn't make it any better – sometimes it makes it worse for I feel more alone when not one of them feels as I do – but at least it makes it –' I laughed, 'normal. A normal sort of prison. One we all recognise and say, "Oh aye, that happens." But *yours*! Can you not leave, if heritage don't matter to you? Can't you go far away and start a new life on any terms you choose? For though you have no fortune, you have your upbringing, the manners of a gentleman. You have your education and abilities . . . you could shape a life from that.'

'You say it so longingly, Tommy, that I can see you speak of your own heart's desire. But I am a prisoner of more than just my father's peculiar drive to bend all things to his will. I hate to admit it to one who risks his life on a daily basis but . . . I am a coward.'

'No you're not.' I said it instinctively.

He looked surprised. 'Oh, I assure you I am. While I stay in this life, I'm safe. I'm untried here; I don't have to stand against other men and perhaps be found wanting. I don't have to make the commitment in my own mind and heart to break with my old life entirely, by starting to be someone else. My old life was hard and imperfect but it was familiar. My old life, you might say, broke with *me*. It pushed me out and declared me dead. But *I* have not broken with *it*. I acquiesce with my father's wishes by staying here and keeping his secret. For all that the world thinks me dead and gone, for all that I am Yorkshire's best kept secret, I am still, very much so, James Manus Barridge of Heston Manor.'

# Chapter 32

———⟨⟩———

# Tommy

The next day I paid for my midnight visit. My head was buzzing and weighty and I was irresistibly preoccupied with all I had learned from Manus. His confidences had knocked me off my feet. It wasn't just the amazing revelation of his story, it was the way his experience mapped onto mine, as if one outline had been traced on top of another, two identical shapes, though with details and colours entirely different.

There had not been time to ask all the questions I wanted to ask and it would have been too much for him anyway, I could tell. He had trembled throughout most of his narrative and his nervous hands had knitted, knitted ceaselessly. He would have made a deft basket weaver. I wanted to know about the woman he had hoped to marry and what became of her. I wanted to know what he had seen in the Barridge mines. I wanted to know what his mother thought about the removal of one inconvenient son; was she was even party to the deception? Did she believe him to be dead too or had she been complicit?

I wanted to ask about the vision I had seen that night. Surely it had been Manus riding Equinox in the moonlight, but how had they been floating and dancing? And I could still hardly believe that his father had done this. So Manus had values inconvenient to his father, their temperaments were incompatible. There must be many, many families across Great Britain suffering a similar predicament. They didn't all go around pretending their sons were dead.

As I drove Flinty up and down the tunnels, my thoughts returned repeatedly to what he'd said about the things that kept him trapped. How effortlessly I understood them. They were exactly the things that kept me going underground again and again for a shilling a day, for all that I protested it was no life. I claimed that the reasons were my family, necessity, the masters, the lack of opportunity and there was truth in all that. But what Manus had said did not need adjusting in any particular to give an exact account of *me*.

*I'm untried here; I don't have to stand against other men and perhaps be found wanting. I don't have to make the commitment in my own mind and heart to break with my old life entirely, by starting to be someone else. My old life is hard and imperfect . . . But I have not broken with it. I acquiesce with my father's wishes by staying here. I am still Tommy Green of Grindley.*

Out of nowhere I remembered with startling clarity that

long-ago day when I finished school. I saw myself standing there in the classroom, twisting my cap, watching Mr Latimer go about his tasks. I remembered words that had long escaped my memory, though the sense of them had remained within me like fetters.

*The world out there is more complex and difficult than you could ever imagine. Its realms and reaches are not for the likes of you. Here, you may be the star pupil. Out there, you would be nothing. You would be crushed in an instant . . .* Dear God. All this time I had seethed and seethed, sworn blind I wanted a chance to leave, but all along I had been afraid of failing. Petrified.

Life was not going to come down here and find me. *Nothing* would find me, not light, not hope, not opportunity. There were no paths here except for those that had been hewn from the rock so that we could take out the coal.

I'd been waiting for someone else to hold out a hand to me and perhaps there was nothing so unusual in that. We all want that. But there was no place for me in the Honeycroft household. Walter was just another boy who could not defy his father. Miss Embry was a solitary woman in a world where it was hard to be a solitary woman. Preacher Tawney was confined by his beliefs perhaps more than any of us; after all, he made his living out of them. And Latimer . . . well, I didn't know what *his* problem was.

I had seen all this as a sign that I was not meant to leave yet, that I must stay here and wait. But I did not see it that way any more. I was now the very age that my brother Dan had been when he was killed underground; what *exactly* was I waiting for? I would finish this shift and then I would leave. I would hew my chance out of the rock. I would *make* it.

I must have been about halfway through my shift when it happened. We were on a steep descent, heading away from the shaft. Flinty baulked. My heart sank; the ponies always knew before we did when something was wrong. Almost immediately the tubs started sliding. Flinty's high-pitched whinny sliced through the darkness. I jumped from the corve rails and hauled at his head to make him step off too.

'Step over! Step over!' I screamed.

In the flash of a second I saw every kind of bloody disaster in my mind's eye. The tubs crushing Flinty, breaking his back. Myself beneath the sharp steel wheels, sliced in horrible ways. All I could think of was to get my pony from the path of those running tubs.

Flinty stepped over. The tubs kept running but at least they were empty. The first of them was pulled sideways when Flinty left the tracks and the rest crashed into the first. I heard a horrible splintering and winced at the thought of the damage to mine property. Poor Flinty was yanked back by the weight of the tubs. He stumbled and fell.

'Oh, be all right, there, Flinty lad,' I cried, the fear in my voice outweighing the reassurance in my words. 'You'll be right, Flinty, stay down, lad, I'll get thee free.' I set down my lamp at a careful distance, grateful beyond expression that it had withstood the jolt, and hurried to Flinty's side. He was writhing in an attempt to right himself but the space was cramped and the harness was holding him back.

When I reached his side he stilled. He knew I was trying to help. I could hardly see but I daren't bring the lamp closer. A sudden lunge from Flinty might knock it over and I couldn't risk that. All the same it was a hellish job. Flinty was dark brown, the harness was dark brown, its buckles dulled with use, and we were in near darkness. I worked mostly by feel and undid one buckle, then another until he was freed. Then the challenge was to help him to stand up in that narrow space, with a low roof above us, a huge pile of crashed corves to our left and a treachery of rails underfoot. We thrashed about and first he bumped his head, then I did, then I spotted the flash of a wheel sticking out from the heap of crashed tubs and I kept him from slicing himself on that. But he trusted me, and we made it in the end. We stood, breathing heavily. Thank God those tubs had been empty. Full, they would have been the death of us.

I frowned. Accidents like this happened when a driver missed his lockers, the bits of metal or wood that we put into each wheel to make it slide like a brake. I knew I hadn't been working to standard lately. I knew I'd been distracted. But one thing I knew with every kind of certainty that exists: I had not missed my lockers. I could remember fastening them as soon as we turned to make our descent. It was second nature and I had done it.

But before we set off, Ed Stoneley had called me aside. He asked if I couldn't make it a bit faster this time. A horrible sneer he wore while he said it and I had breathed slowly to keep my temper. I said I would, that my injuries were all cleared up now and that I'd be back to full strength before he knew it. I made sure to put a threat into those words. I held his eyes and I could see that he wouldn't dare lay a finger on me. I'd gone back to Flinty, only to find Ed's crony Al Crace stroking his mane. It was an odd scene, since Al wasn't an animal lover.

'Good lad,' said Al, stepping out of my way, with an ingratiating smile that was very out of character. I realised now that Ed had distracted me to give Al time to pull out my lockers. Not all of them, I reckoned, from the length of time the wheels had held. Probably just two, but that was enough. Cruel, destructive, stupid-minded tomfools. I wasn't sure what made me angrier: the thought that they were too cowardly to attack me directly, or the fact that they were content to carve up Flinty to settle their imagined score with me. I wasn't sure yet what I would do to them when I got out.

'Right, lad,' I said evenly. 'Let's get us going. Let's get out of this place and I for one am never coming back.'

We set off and my mind was all on my new plan. I would get back to the shaft, I would punch first Al, then Ed, plain in the face – oh, my strength had come back to me fully now and no mistake! Then I would take Flinty back to his stable, feed him treats and say goodbye. I would walk to the cage and ride up to daylight for the last time. I would go home, wash and change, eat my dinner, then talk to Da. I would tell him man to man that I was leaving. I would tell him that as soon as I could make my way, I would send them money that would show my miner's wage up for the pathetic pittance it actually was. He would jeer and tell me not to make promises I had absolutely no way of keeping.

My mind zigzagged like a dragonfly, darting here and there, landing then taking off again in a new direction. I might go to Silvermoor and ask the earl for a loan. I might go to York, where Josie was. Leeds, where Miss Embry had family and could perhaps give me a contact. Barnsley, the town of industry – surely there would be jobs aplenty there. From feeling I had no possibilities at all, it suddenly seemed I had countless, and all because my mind had broken through that barrier of perceived impossibility. So what if my father didn't speak to me for twenty years? So what if every other person in my village said it couldn't be done? There was no price too high for liberty, no price too high to . . .

Flinty baulked again. What now? He started whinnying, high-pitched and urgent, and my stomach pinched in on itself.

'What is it, lad?' I asked, fearfully.

It happened all at once: a great crack like a bolt of thunder and then, like torrential rain dropping out of the sky in a sudden downpour, so did the ceiling drop in front of my horrified eyes. Flinty spun round in his own length and bolted. I was too horrified to move. I just stood and stared at the blockage in front of me, the whole tunnel filled, floor to roof. I watched the progression of collapse that kept coming towards me, slower and less dramatic now, but still, it was the mine falling in on my head, just as I had always known it would. I was seventeen. I was the age my brother Dan was when it happened to him. Green family history was repeating itself.

# Chapter 33

## Josie

I could feel myself sparkling like Christmas. The house on the Mount was in disarray; Miss Coralie was packing. We were returning to Silvermoor!

I ran on light feet up and down the stairs a hundred times, fetching her boots from the boot room, pressing her dresses, packing the dainties from the kitchen that she needed to sustain her on the journey. It wasn't half a day by carriage but Miss Coralie liked her sweets every bit as much as I.

It was early. The summer mists were lifting and shifting over the gardens and the sun was already burning through. Magpies chattered, thrushes sang and the air was full of joy. I was bursting with impatience; it seemed the tasks would never be done, that we would never be ready, that the cases must be opened for 'just one last thing' forever until the end of time. But at last the carriage was loaded and we were seated inside and Mrs Crane was waving us off.

We passed the long row of Georgian houses of which ours was one, with their smooth columns and paved front paths that invited you in. We passed the Knavesmire, pale apple-green in the sunlight and smooth as water. And then we were out of York, driving down through the country, towards Silvermoor, towards Tommy.

We enjoyed some pleasant conversation on the way. Conversation was always pleasant when Miss Coralie and Mr Cedric were together and they didn't stand on ceremony because Norman and I were with them. Many families would have sent us separately, but not the Honeycrofts.

Norman and I got along splendidly. He was quietly knowledgeable and we had twice attended concerts together. I loved concerts with a passion. Norman had a sweetheart in Acomb and they planned to marry next year. When he told me of their plans it made me wish that Tommy and I had plans like that. But we had a long way to go before that would happen – if it ever did. Tommy wasn't even out of the mines yet.

When we neared our destination, I grew quiet. Now we were passing Arden, Heston Manor, the lanes where Tommy and I had walked and talked and fashioned our beautiful friendship. I craned my neck for a glimpse of him. There was none, of course, for there was no reason that Tommy would be out walking at such a time on such a day. It was just that the memories were so strong and dear it seemed impossible that a curly-headed, froggy-eyed boy and a ginger-plaited young girl would not forever be swinging their way along.

When we turned into Silvermoor's grand avenue, more memories assailed me. Walking hand in hand with Tommy on the eve of the new century. Limping beside him on that fateful night when he'd somehow got me out of Arden, away from Heston's gamekeepers, and safe to Silvermoor. I even remembered how it had looked to five-year-old Tommy on the occasion of Lord Walter's christening, though I hadn't been there. He had described it to me so fully and vividly that the memory had become my own. Was it like this for Tommy? Did he see me at every turn? Was the memory of our treasured hours together the brightest thing in his world? Was the distinction between him and me fading so that his memories were my memories and my happiness was his?

# Chapter 34

———

# Tommy

The silence was absolute, broken only by the occasional mysterious groan or crack the earth made deep underground. And yet I fancied I could hear the march of hundreds upon hundreds of miners' boots, tramping through the decades, bringing me to this inevitable today.

Rocks had knocked me to the floor and pinned me in place. I did not know what was broken or crushed, I only knew that there was pain and I was trapped. Behind me I could just feel another warm body with the fingertips of my right hand. Flinty wouldn't abandon me. He had come back to die alongside me.

For a while the lamp, miraculously, continued to burn. I could see it somehow standing tidily upright on the tunnel floor. There were three inevitabilities, three more events that must be played out in that caved-in spot deep in Crooked Ash: the lamp must go out; Flinty must die; I must die. I wondered in which order they would happen. The lamp went first, as was my guess, and there I lay in that absolute dark that had haunted me since I first experienced it and has always haunted me since.

I could feel pain in my chest, both physical, from some injury I could not guess at and spiritual, for having wasted my life. This morning's insights had come to me too late. If only the mist had dropped from my eyes one day sooner. If only I had realised that I didn't have to wait for someone else to give me a chance. If only I had understood that failure was nothing to fear. Oh, the things I thought about, trapped down there in the blackness.

I thought of Dan, of course, and wondered if this was how it had been for him, a long slow waiting for the end. I thought of my living brothers and said a million prayers for their protection.

I thought of Josie, candle-bright. I wondered how and when she would hear that I was gone. I thought of the world outside the mine, the world above that deep, rude shaft into the earth. That beautiful landscape in its gauze of black. Our heritage of people in harness . . .

And I thought of Da. I thought of the rows we'd had over the years and how we'd always been at odds. He just could not understand why I was made the way I was, why I couldn't settle to the yoke like the rest of them. I didn't understand it myself. All the things that fascinated me had always been things from beyond our world. When I told myself that *this* was my place, that it must be enough, the effort was as unnatural as twisting a leg in its socket so the foot faced the other way. And yet, if there had been one person holding me here, it was Da. It was a complicated love, but I did love him, I realised now. Despite all of it, I admired the man he was, his wholeheartedness in his life, the fact that he was the first man among us, respected and feared, utterly straight in his integrity and absolute in his courage. My father was an impressive man and I wished I could tell him. He did not understand my ambition. But I understood his pride.

# Chapter 35

### Josie

Within the hour we were settled. The Honeycrofts were taking tea with their aunt and cousins. The earl was out and about on earl business. I was permitted some time at leisure, which I began by going to the kitchen for my lunch. Some of the Silvermoor servants, like Dorcas and Mrs Roundsby, were pleased to welcome me. Others, like Portis, were not; clearly they couldn't shake off their first impression of me as a scrappy miner's lass with no finesse, undeserving of a position with the Honeycrofts. I cared little. I was more than aware that many people thought that I had a place where I must stay. But the Honeycrofts had shown me that there was another way to think and that was the way that I chose. So I beamed at Portis and tucked in.

I was so excited that soon Mr Cedric would meet Tommy. I would engineer it somehow! No matter what he said about being unable to promise anything, I knew that when he met

Tommy he would love him and do anything he could to get him from the mines. I just *knew* it. Oh, I could hardly breathe!

I was just wondering whether to go outside and beg some fresh flowers for Miss Coralie's bedside when a small maid called Sylvia came looking for me. Miss Coralie wanted me in the drawing room.

Tommy! It must be Tommy! I ran, smoothing down my hair, straightening my dress, wondering what he would think of me now.

He wasn't there but Cedric was. She wanted to talk to me about when I might see Tommy, the times when she couldn't spare me, and so forth. And so the three of us laid lively plans together until we were interrupted by the sudden arrival of the earl.

'Uncle!' cried Coralie, embracing him in a flounce of green silk.

'Here we are, under your feet again, drinking all the good brandy,' observed Cedric from the sofa, doing just that.

But the earl didn't greet them with the deep affection I'd seen before and he seemed not to notice me at all. His face looked grey and his hair unusually rumpled. Was he ill? He gave Coralie an absent-minded kiss and strode to the drinks table. Perhaps he was afraid Cedric would drink all the good brandy after all.

'Coralie, dear, Cedric. Welcome. I'm sorry not to be more

effusive but there's been a collapse at the mine. Years without, and one forgets how bloody awful it is. There's a fellow trapped, apparently.'

'Tommy!' I shrieked, leaping up from my seat and causing the earl to spill his brandy all over his snowy cuff.

'What the . . . ? Oh! It's you, Josie, is it?'

'Sir, it's Tommy, isn't it? I know it is, I just know it.'

Coralie wrapped an arm around my shoulders. 'Now, Josie, wait, I'm sure it's not. Is it, Uncle? Is it Tommy?'

'I'm afraid I don't know. I didn't hear a name. I went to see Bulford but he missed the meeting. I found the place in disarray. Horrible business. I offered to help but they wouldn't hear of it. They like to manage things in their own way. They're putting together a small rescue party, but of course, no one knows the damage till they get there. They think it's just the one chap trapped, and a pony.'

I could feel the room spinning and everything grew far distant. I fought to hang on to consciousness; fainting wouldn't help Tommy. 'Oh miss,' I whispered. 'Tommy's on the ponies this week. He said in his last letter.' My legs gave way but her firm arm around my shoulders kept me upright.

'Sit, Josie,' she commanded, manhandling me back to a chair. 'Cedric, give her some brandy. Uncle, we must know for sure. How do we find out?'

'I'll go straight back there myself and I won't come home until we know. I'll take Beauty and be as fast as I can.'

'I must go,' I said, gulping the brandy and recovering myself enough to sit up straight. '*Please*, miss, say I can go! I *have* to go.'

'No,' said Coralie with a determined expression. '*We* shall go. Maverick can carry us both.'

'And I shall go,' declared Cedric. 'Dig him out myself if necessary.'

# Chapter 36

## Tommy

Every time the earth made one of its curious groans, I braced myself for another fall, the one that would crush me in an instant. I didn't know whether to dread or hope for it. When I'd first started mining those sounds had unnerved me so. It was impossible to hear them and not think it was the start of the whole world breaking. But I grew accustomed to them in the end, as we can grow accustomed to almost anything with time and relentless exposure. As I lay there waiting to die I wondered if they were the comings and goings of some underworldly demon, through a great portal of stone. Perhaps he was coming to claim me now.

For a long time I had drawn a little comfort from the faint puffs of Flinty's breath reaching the back of my neck but they had stopped a while back and I believed he was gone. It made me cry deep, painful sobs, the thought of that brave little pony spending his days pulling tubs of coal up and down, up and

239

down, and now killed in the line of duty. We were all so very dispensable.

I wondered whether the vibration of the tubs crashing had caused the roof fall or whether it would have happened anyway. In other words, were Crace and Stoneley to blame for this? I couldn't lift my head, I seemed to be devoid of all strength. I couldn't move my legs either but whether because they were trapped or due to injury I couldn't tell. I could reach my arms to left and right, although it hurt to do so. If I stretched my right arm back, my fingers touched Flinty's rough coat. And to the left I found my snap tin, empty. My sandwich was under this rubble somewhere.

I had an idea. I felt about for a piece of hard shale. I held it in one hand, the tin lid in the other, and tried scratching letters in the tin. Between my recumbent posture, the awkward angle of my arms and the fact that I couldn't see a thing, I had no idea whether the marks I made bore any resemblance at all to what I intended. But it gave me something to do to pass the time.

Long hours they were. It was so hot I grew delirious, or perhaps it was hunger or thirst or nearness to death that caused that. I could hear the ghost miners tramping and the demons shrieking and the earth weeping.

Behind me, Flinty started whinnying. I tried to say his name but I couldn't sound the word. I'd been so sure he was dead. He started thrashing and kicking and made that same high-pitched sound over and over, piercing in the darkness. Then I heard his head thump to the ground and I knew that this time he was really gone. I felt tears trickle tracks through the dirt on my face. And then I heard a new sound, the strangest yet. *Tap, tap, tap.*

I couldn't make sense of it. It seemed to me that a demon would make a much more sinister noise – a dragging or a rasping. Were dwarves coming, as in the fairy tales? I was too weak to puzzle overmuch, so I simply continued scratching away at my tin. Perhaps I would fall asleep at the task and not have to suffer my final moments.

*Tap, tap, tap.* It was a most persistent noise. It continued, never varying in volume or rhythm. It sounded tentative, like a very timid child knocking at a door. It was faintly irritating. Must I have an unsolved mystery to itch at my soul in my last moments? And then I heard voices. Human voices.

I knew right away that I wasn't dead and hearing angel voices because they were familiar and very much of the earth.

'Steady, Stan. Keep yer 'ead down. Not too hard now.'

'Aye, Jim, I know. Canst tha see owt?'

'Not yet. But I heard a pony, I'm telling you.'

I was suddenly very much awake. I hardly wanted to hope at such a late, desperate stage, but it was obvious that it was a rescue party. My father and Stan Baldwin. Moments later I heard Bulford: 'Shut tha mouth, Adam Slater. I don't care if you do think it's a fool's errand. We're staying till we find him, alive or dead.'

Adam Slater evidently expressed the opinion that the latter was more likely for I heard my father's voice again: 'You can leave if you think like that, Slater. Go on, we don't need you here. Go and polish china with tha missus.'

'Da?' I hadn't been able to form Flinty's name but I could call my father. 'Da? I'm here.' My voice was feeble.

A pause. Then a voice I didn't recognise, one that didn't belong down here: 'What are you waiting for, Mr Green? Every moment is critical, we must carry on.'

'Aye, I know that, sir, only I thought I heard . . . never mind.' *Tap, tap, tap.*

My throat was raw and I thought maybe I only had a few more words left in me. I would save them till they were more useful. The tapping continued, and occasional remarks drifted through the rock. I kept listening out, hoping to notice some variation in sound that would suggest they were getting closer but it remained steady. It was frustrating, and yet reassuring for it was this soft, tentative approach that convinced me that it was real and not a product of my desperate imagination. Of course they must be ginger – there was nothing more dangerous than a mine in the wake of a fall. A single breath in the wrong direction could bring the whole lot down, crushing them all. That had happened in Horizon Drift a year or more back. Three men lost in a fall, twelve lost in the rescue.

'I *know* I heard a pony!' Da again. He was seething; I knew that tone so well.

'Perhaps here?' suggested the voice that was different from the others, the man my father called sir. 'I do believe the rubble is less dense.'

I had an idea, started tapping my piece of shale against the tin. At once the tapping on the other side stopped. 'Sir! Did you hear?'

'Yes, I did.'

'Stan?'

'Aye, I did. Tommy? Is that you lad?'

'Tommy?' My father's voice was so close it was as if he'd spoken into my ear. Suddenly there was hope again. That I might see my father, and hold my mother again. That maybe I could see my brothers and sisters and Josie and Manus . . . my life had never seemed so full of precious things.

'Da! I'm here!' I cried, the words cracked and squeaky like a boy only just coming into manhood. But he heard me.

'Hang on, lad, hang on. We're coming. Steady now, Stan, he's just through there. We'll have to go easy. Shine the lamp, aye, that's it.'

The tower of rock and shale started to trickle and shift. I cowered, heart hammering. If that came down on me now . . . But it didn't. A rock was removed and passed along a line out of the way, then another, until the gap was enough for me to see lamplight. I saw hands, carefully feeling their way around stones and finding a way through. More rocks were lifted away and eventually I saw my father's face, grim as ever, ducking through the gap. He clambered into the space where I lay.

'Tommy!'

'Careful, Jim,' said Stan, unnecessarily. My father was born careful. He made no joyous dart towards me, no sudden movements at all. He reached an arm through the gap and brought a lamp in. He looked all around. I saw his gimlet eyes taking in the dead pony and every contour of the rocks around me. Then he looked down at me.

'Tommy,' he said in a low voice, as if words could break me. 'What's harmed?'

'I don't know, Da.'

He nodded and crouched by my feet. He started picking things up and moving them, as stealthily as he used to move through the woods on poaching nights. I knew then that I would get out alive. This was the man who could take deer by surprise, who could slip through old Paulson's traps like a ghost. He was an invisible man, when he wanted to be, someone who made no impression on the material world. Suddenly there was no weight on my legs. Da came to my side. He laid his rough hand on the side of my face. 'Tommy,' he said again. 'My boy.'

'Aye, Da,' I said. 'I am.'

'Canst tha sit up? Easy now.'

I tried but I was too weak. He supported my head and lifted my back and then yes, I was sitting. Standing was a task too far, though.

'Stan, get through here,' he ordered. Stan's left leg appeared over the low wall of rock, then the rest of him. 'We must lift him out,' said my father. 'Is Bulford ready?'

'We're ready, Jim,' said the deputy's voice from the other side. Da took my shoulders and Stan took my legs and they fed me head-first through the gap where Bulford and another man received me and they began a slow, cautious trudge through the tunnel. There were two men in front and they took turns to carry me in pairs, while I slipped in and out of consciousness all that long while.

Finally, we reached the bottom of the shaft. I could hardly believe the wondrous sight of the cage and all the men waiting around it with lanterns, all that light. A shout went up: 'They've got him. He's alive!'

They laid me carefully in the bottom of the cage. Da got in with me then pulled the grille to, leaving behind all the others who had rescued me. I was surprised at that, until we started our way upwards, alone, and then he bent his head to mine and wept fiercely. 'My boy,' he croaked. 'My special, precious, wonderful boy!'

I was so amazed I couldn't answer. By the time we reached the surface he was dry-eyed and stony-faced again.

# Chapter 37

# Josie

I think I'd been holding my breath the entire time that we waited there – three hours or more. Whatever frost had existed between me and Tommy's family had long since melted by the time the shout came up from the depths of the earth that he was alive. I found I was clutching the hand of his sister Mary, always the least pleased to see me, or, indeed, anyone. Relief poured through me as hot and thick as the treacle the cook at Gravenagh House used to make peanut brittle for Coralie. Then it set and cracked. Alive but in what state? I tried not to imagine Tommy injured, perhaps for life. I just held my breath instead. It was only when the cage reached the surface and we saw his father bent over his limp body that I broke into tears.

Everyone crowded round. Tommy looked up at us swimmily, his green eyes roving over the faces that loomed above him. The earl took charge, ordering people back, demanding the facts, and a sigh of relief seemed to pass through the gath-

246

ering, so I guessed the news wasn't too bad, as far as anyone could tell at that point. I collapsed into Coralie's arms and she told me I had been very brave, though I didn't feel it.

When the cage rattled up a second time, discharging the rest of the rescue party, Coralie handed me over to Mercy and ran to Cedric. Bulford came over to the Greens and gave them the possessions of Tommy's that had survived – nothing but his cap, with the newspaper stuffing gone, and the lid of his snap. His mother rubbed her fingers over both of them and I knew what she was thinking. What good was newspaper against the might of the earth? And what sort of life was it in which she must send her son to such a place with nothing but bread and jam? The questions hung in the air.

She frowned and turned the tin over and peered at it in the watery sunshine. Wordlessly, she handed it to me. I looked down in surprise. There were letters scratched on it, as though he had etched them with a stone. I'd heard of it being done before, dying men leaving messages for their wives or children. There was a whole mass of scratches all over the lid, curves and lines overlaying one another – he obviously hadn't been able to see what he was doing. But somehow two words were legible against the mass of marks. Very rough, very shaky were the letters, but it was clear what they said: *Josie I . . .*

In what he believed were his last moments, his thoughts were of me.

# Chapter 38

# Tommy

There was sunlight on my face and fresh air stirring my hair and a crowd seemingly composed of every person I had ever met in my life. Ma was there, of course, crying with joy, and nearly all my brothers and sisters; only little Alfred was missing. Ma would have made him stay at home with Grandma in case the news was bad. Josie was there and Miss Coralie. When the cage rattled up with the rest of the men, she ran with a shriek into the arms of a blackened and sweating young man. Then I realised that the 'sir' whom my father had addressed during the rescue was Mr Cedric Honeycroft himself.

Even the earl was there. He would not hear of me going to the hospital in Rotherham but said I must be taken to Silvermoor and attended by his own physician. My mother said nothing but, 'Thank you, my lord, thank you, my lord,' over and over again. My father said nothing at all but he seized my hand before I was loaded into the carriage, so tightly I feared that if I came away with no other injury, I would have a broken hand.

I wanted to tell him there and then of my decision never to go back down the mines again but I couldn't. I did not wish to trade on the brief, bright crack in his emotional armour to gain permission or blessing; I didn't want to take advantage of his being momentarily thrown out of character. Or perhaps it was just that I did not want to spoil the simple truth of that moment. My father loved me. He had saved me. Just for then I wanted nothing more.

I lay alone in the carriage for a few moments while plans were laid, decisions made. In the end two people accompanied me on the journey to Silvermoor: Josie and my mother. My father took my siblings home to bear the news to Alfie and Grandma. And the other men arranged themselves into a suitable configuration to complete the shift and address the damage.

My mother looked like an angel to me. Her face, prematurely lined and set into a frown – a worried frown as opposed to my father's grim one – had been smoothed out by relief. She looked beautiful. And if I didn't dream it, she was holding Josie's hand. Josie looked brighter, more shining than ever. I was in a great deal of pain, so thirsty I could hardly breathe and no doubt in a state of shock. Yet none of this stopped me seeing that her hair fell below her chin in ruddy waves held back by a white ribbon. Her figure was taller and fuller than when she had left. Her cheeks glowed and her eyes sparkled and she even had a dimple in her left cheek. She was a woman now, and pretty as a picture in her grey and white striped gown, even though her face was the mottled red and white she detested from crying.

The earl and his niece and nephew must have galloped all the way for they had arrived at Silvermoor before us. While Cedric dispatched his manservant to draw him a bath, Coralie joined Josie and Ma in arranging my own bath and getting me to a bed before the doctor arrived. It was a strange time; a sequence of people and events in quick succession with me passive at the centre of it all. I was at once grateful for every moment because I had not lost my life after all, and exceedingly desirous of rest.

# Chapter 39

## Josie

I had always sensed that Tommy's mother was a good woman, not least because of the glowing way he spoke about her. But on the one or two occasions we had met, her special qualities had been withheld from me behind a barricade of suspicion and unconditional reserve. I never took it personally; I was an outsider and that was the way of things around here. But during the days that I stayed with the Honeycrofts at Silvermoor while Tommy recovered in one of the guest rooms, and Sarah Green visited him every day, that barricade evaporated.

At first he slept and slept, while we sat together beside his bed. Initially I would excuse myself when I walked in and found her there. I wanted to give her time alone with him and I didn't want her to think me disrespectful or presumptuous; it was as easy to offend one of our lot as it was to catch a cold in February. But each time she gestured me in and soon it felt as natural to be at her side as if I were one of her daughters.

Perhaps it was because of what he'd written on that snap tin lid. Or perhaps because she'd seen the depth of my caring. Or maybe because Tommy fast asleep was not the best conversation.

We spoke in low voices of gentle things: our villages and families; how I liked my job in York; small memories of Tommy. And we gazed at him, with his cuts and bruises, his pale skin and the long eyelashes that rested on his cheekbones as he slept. I longed for him to open his pond-green eyes so I could see the glimmers in them once again.

I had known for some time that I loved him as more than a friend. This was my first opportunity since then to be able to look and look and look at him and I was startled by the responses in my body. If I looked at his arm lying above the covers, I could not help but admire the mass of his muscles and wish that arm were wrapped around me. When I looked at his tawny curls I wanted to touch them. I wanted to run my fingernails over the stubble growing on his jaw. When I looked at his face I was flooded with memories of a hundred conversations and escapades. They made me feel so close to him that I wanted to be close to him physically too. Two feet away on a chair might have been a hundred miles.

When I looked at his lips it was impossible not to remember the time that he'd kissed me. Well, he had kissed me twice, but I didn't count the one for the new century. Everybody was kissing everybody then. But the kiss he'd given me when I told him about turning down Coralie's offer . . . that memory turned my legs hot and as weak as water as I sat demurely and chatted to his ma. His mouth was perfect, I noticed; Michelangelo couldn't have drawn more exquisite curves. I wanted to press my own lips against it . . . these were new and visceral feelings which alarmed me; I didn't know if they were normal. I wished it was easier to see Dulcie now; she was the only person I could conceivably ask about this. I loved Coralie, but such a conversation with my employer was unthinkable!

Surely it was the shock, I told myself as the days went on. I had nearly lost him. Relief was taking funny forms; it would pass off along with the nightmares and the anxiety I felt first thing on waking every morning before remembering and going through my day with a welcome refrain in my mind: *Tommy's safe, Tommy's safe.*

# Chapter 40

~~~

# Tommy

I had never experienced a sleep so sweet and profound. No siblings' limbs thrown over mine, no feet beneath my nose. A large bed all to myself, dressed in linen fragrant with lavender and soft as clouds. Silence and darkness uninterrupted, not the crushing darkness of the mines but the tender darkness of safety. I emerged from it blinking and marvelling. I tried to sit up, discovering bandaged ribs and wrist, and in so doing roused Josie and Ma who were sitting in chairs at either side of my bed. They fluttered to attention at once.

In the end I stayed in the house at Silvermoor for two months. I had two cracked ribs and a broken wrist, though neither was as profound a harm as the shock of the affair. It took a long time for my appetite to come back, to feel like myself again, and most of all for the nightmares to stop. My legs, miraculously, were unharmed. The only reason I couldn't move them in the tunnel was that a timber had trapped them, but its injuries were no more than flesh wounds, which healed quickest of all.

The earl insisted that his physician continued to attend me, so the pain in my chest was expertly managed and never allowed to lead to any complication. He also insisted that I receive half-pay throughout my convalescence, which I immediately sent to Da. Even so, it was a far cry from my grand plans to find work and send them more money than they'd ever dreamed of. I felt uncomfortable being in such a dependent position.

In the only lengthy conversation I had with the earl during that time I told him honestly of my plans. 'I'm not entitled to any pay, my lord,' I was at pains to tell him; I wouldn't have felt right otherwise. 'I'll never go back. I'm not your responsibility any more.'

He looked thoughtful. 'Very well, Tommy, I accept your resignation on behalf of Mr Bulford,' he said at last, 'but we shall let the arrangement stand. You have given me three years' excellent work at Crooked Ash, and another two at the surface before that. Your injuries were incurred during your employment. Because of the accident you can't secure new work for some time. We shall let it stand.'

'Why, sir? I mean, I thank you, sincerely, but you don't do this for everyone.'

'No. I run an imperfect system, as my nephew keeps pointing out. But I do my best, and your father has been one of our finest workers for many a long year. I owe it to your family as much as to you. Furthermore, I have been unfair in my estimation of you over the years. I listened to hearsay instead of using my own discernment, so you might consider this an apology of some sort – reparation. Then of course your bosom friend is my niece's maid, my nephew takes an interest in your future and my son holds you in affection . . . in truth, Tommy, I could not turn my back on you if I wanted to. There is wisdom in accepting the inevitable.'

I laughed a little and thanked him again. 'What do you mean, sir, that you listened to hearsay? Has someone spoken against me?'

He sighed. 'You may remember years ago, my son Walter wished to initiate a friendship with you?'

Of course I remembered. How much it had meant to me.

'Well, I wasn't altogether against him having a friendship with a village lad. He's a lively chap, Walter, and it's hard on him having only sisters close to his age. I happened to see Latimer in the village that day so I asked him about your character. I'm afraid he said you were very difficult, arrogant and not to be trusted. I didn't like the sound of that for my son. I have learned otherwise since, but at the time I had no reason to doubt his word. Of course a man is entitled to his own opinion. But still I think it strange.' As did I.

And so I succeeded, temporarily, in securing my boyhood dream. For a little while I lived at Silvermoor, though not through any sequence of events I would have chosen. My meals were brought to me, I received the best of care and my surroundings were luxurious. I watched the weather change through a tall window framed by blue curtains and I had leisure, for the first time in my life, to think for hours. I thought about what mattered to me, about what I believed or no longer believed. I revised many of the judgements I had forged in the fire of angry, disappointed youth. Now they were tempered by a brush with death, the experience of my father's love and a growing perspective. My dreams and plans remained unchanged. That I had a second chance to try them was a miracle. I was grateful for it every day.

Ma visited me every week. At first she was as bewildered to be treading the corridors of Silvermoor as she would have been to find herself on the moon. But she slowly grew used to it and struck up something of a friendship with Mrs Roundsby. She could hardly bring the crowd of my eight siblings a-visiting with her, but twice she brought my precious little Connie, who sang me a pretty song, once Alfie and Ernest, and once she came with Mercy. Da came not at all.

Mr Cedric and Miss Coralie both came to make my acquaintance. I felt as if I knew them already from Josie's letters and I thanked them for their kindness to her. Coralie stayed only a short while, squeezing my hand when she left and telling me she hoped they would see a lot more of me. Cedric lingered and we talked about mining, about my dreams and aspirations, and about his.

'You didn't have to crack your ribs on my account,' he observed. 'I had hoped to meet you at Silvermoor one day but, my good man, you are too obliging.' He was funny and several times had me laughing until he realised that was very painful for me. Then I saw that underneath his lively charm, he was shrewd and conscientious. I didn't see that he could help me, when he was very young himself, but he was the sort of person it could only ever be a good thing to know. I thanked him most earnestly for going underground to save my life.

Best of all was seeing Josie. Sometimes she was busy with her duties and could only manage an hour or so at my bedside. Other days were quiet family days for the Honeycrofts so she could sit with me for hours.

Josie had changed in so many little ways, and yet in all the ways that mattered she was still the dear friend of my youth. She was less tossed around by her fits of anger or enthusiasm, more steady and graceful. She spoke of new things: classical music concerts and lemon parfaits, which were a delicacy I could not imagine, and of saving for the future. But her vivacity and cheek, her curiosity and humour were all as they had been. As was her affection for me. I had wondered in the briefest of moments whether the change in her circumstances might cause her devotion to fade, but no such thing had happened and really, I should have known it.

More than once I wanted to kiss her during that strange time of my convalescence but I didn't for two reasons. Firstly, doing so would have made me gasp, and gasping was too painful with my broken ribs. Secondly, I valued our friendship too much ever to risk it. I had kissed her once, long ago, and she had never spoken of it again. I guessed that she preferred to think of it as a momentary impulse.

Talking was so much better than letters. I could imagine her standing at her window first thing in the morning and taking a deep breath before starting her day. I could imagine her strolling through the chocolate-scented streets of York while the bells rolled through the air like ribbons. I could see for myself how happy she was. It gladdened my heart as nothing else could have done. My Josie was lovely, and her life was lovely, and this was the way things ought to be.

In return I told her everything I had not been able to tell her while my letter paper was confiscated – well, almost. I said little of her father beating me and nothing of what he'd said while he did it. I still did not see how it could help her. But I told her everything else. It was luxury to have such long hours of conversation day after day.

I told her about Grandpa passing and Grandma fading. I told her about my night-time visit to Manus and who he was. Her shock was delightful. I told her his extraordinary story and she had all the same questions as I, questions to which I still had no answers. And I told her how his words had made me see everything differently, resulting in my sudden and unshakeable resolution that I must leave and seek my fate. 'I still must,

Josie,' I confided. 'There'll be no more waiting. No matter how hard it is.'

She took my hand and I tried to ignore the strange thrill that ran through my whole body at her touch. 'I'm glad,' she said. 'There'll be risks, of course, and hardship, but what are they to a man like you who has lived a life like yours? Now you can use all your strength and grit to do something you *want* to do.' She bent her head and rested it on my hand. I reached over with some difficulty to lay my other on her shining copper head. 'Oh Tommy, you don't know how it was for me when you were trapped. Promise you'll never change your mind! Promise you'll never go back, not even for your father.'

It was an easy pledge to make.

# Chapter 41

~~~~~~~~~~

# Tommy

*October 1902*

The following week Josie brought me an old scrapbook that
Coralie had found in the library. It was a big, unwieldy tome
and, as Josie leafed through the pages, dried flowers and concert tickets from fifty years ago fell out, like ghosts of more
gracious times. She showed me an old newspaper article from
1891, pasted in neatly. It was an account of Manus's funeral. The
accompanying picture showed a glass hearse draped in sable,
drawn by four black horses wearing black ostrich feathers in
their headbands. Eerie figures in tall hats and crepe veils flanked
the hearse and a large crowd was gathered.

I shuddered. A funeral! Had I thought about it, I'd have
realised that of course there must have been one. But to see the
evidence that Winthrop Barridge had gone through the entire
gruelling rigmarole of a public event – one of some pomp

and grandeur – all the while knowing that his son wasn't dead at all, truly made me wonder if the man was quite human. Ghastly to reflect that the entire world thought my friend's lifeless corpse had been inside that glass coach. I could see that Josie was similarly affected.

The Honeycrofts had stayed longer than planned but eventually returned to York, taking Josie with them. The last month of my convalescence would have been boring indeed if not for Walter. I felt much restored in my spirits and mind but my body lagged behind. The doctor urged the importance of rest, of straining nothing and waiting, waiting, until I was completely healed. I could not afford to be impatient but I was used to an active life. Indolence was delightful for a while but soon paled. I had plans and wanted to forge them. I had a second chance and wanted to seize it! I had heartily had enough of lying abed.

But Walter had taken to visiting me every evening and showing me his lessons. Now aged twelve, he was as charming a young fellow as he had ever been. In the years since our New Year's Eve conversation, Walter had developed no greater love of study; it was for my sake that he brought his books to my bedside. At first he explained things to me. I think he liked the novelty of playing tutor and presumably it helped him digest his lessons too. Presently I found that I could help him with the things he found difficult, based on my new understanding of what he had shown me; in short, I quickly overtook him.

Then he suggested that I join him for his lessons with his tutor. His parents were ready to agree to anything that encouraged him to work. I'm not sure the tutor was especially happy with the arrangement, since the lessons must take place in my room, with me languishing like a maiden on snowy pillows. However, I did my usual trick of asking every question that occurred to me and Mr Farthing soon lost his resistance when he found himself engaged in debate, which also drew Walter in and furthered his learning.

Walter was a lively, good-natured classmate. The tutor was exacting, and I thrived on that. I read more in that month than in my whole life before: philosophy, history, economics, religion. The earl came to see me a second time and told me he had heard excellent reports of my intelligence from Mr Farthing. He asked me what I thought of a scholarship. I told him I did not know what that was.

When he explained to me that a scholarship was a means by which people of outstanding abilities but negligible means might attain an education for free, and seemed to suggest that I might be just such a person, I wanted to cry. This was exactly what I had hoped Mr Latimer might suggest when I stood before him aged twelve, searching for words to ask about concepts of which I had no knowledge. He must have known of such things, he *must* have, but he didn't tell me anything. Instead, years of my life had disappeared in the darkness. But the past was gone. All I could concern myself with now was what lay ahead.

Once the seed was planted, I was compelled to speak to Mr Farthing about it. He hummed and haaed and sighed about what an unfeasibly large amount of work I would have to do to stand any chance of reaching the standard at all. Maybe another year, he suggested. But it was October. The exams weren't until the following May. I would work hard, I promised, if only I could try right away. I had wasted too much time. Eventually he relented, and even began to display a little grudging excitement.

Of course, I could not stay in the guest room at Silvermoor all that time. I had prevailed enough upon his lordship. So on a misty day when orange leaves spun through the grey air, with my ribs healed at last, I dressed and left. But I did not go far. I only went to the spare room of one Mrs Murphy, a widow who had a tiny cottage on the estate. I worked for my room and board on the land and in the stables all that autumn and winter and half of the following year besides.

The work left me tired, especially after two months of inactivity, but it was nothing to the exhaustion of working in the mines. The work was physical and the hours were even longer, but here I was out in the daylight all day long. I could breathe clean air, tend animals, hear birdsong and watch the seasons turn. These things soothed me, made me not mind the demands of the work. Perhaps the key was how well the work suited you, how far against your own true nature you had to push to perform it. *We are who we are and we have the temperament we were born with. That,* I told myself as I forked hay and shovelled manure, *is why choice is important.*

I visited my family and told them they wouldn't see me for a while as I would be studying in every spare moment.

'A scholarship?' asked Ma, looking blank.

'What's that?' asked Ernest.

'For Pete's sake,' growled my father, looking as if my perfidy would never end.

Every evening, every Saturday afternoon and every Sunday, my brain was challenged as never before. I spent long hours reading and puzzling out problems. I had lessons with Mr Farthing while Walter was out riding Merrylegs. I promised I would recompense him when I could. He only sniffed. I took practice tests that Farthing devised for me and failed, miserably. Then failed modestly. Then I failed by only a whisker until one day I did not fail at all.

'Well, I suppose you might just about stand a chance,' said Farthing. 'I wouldn't have guessed you could come so far in such a short time.'

But I shook my head. 'Not good enough,' I said.

I munched apples by the dozen to fuel my efforts and the smell of apples hung about me as once the smell of damp and coal had done. When the sun shone I worked in the corner of a field where the horses grazed. When the rain came or the wind blew my pages, I worked in the stables and when night fell, I worked in my room in Mrs Murphy's cottage, in the small pool of light cast by my lamp. My heart still caught with fear sometimes, lest the light should go out.

# Chapter 42

———— ❧ ————

# Tommy

*March 1903*

Months passed. A new year dawned. The scholarship exams were looming and my body was fully recovered. My thoughts turned to Manus more and more often and I knew I must go and see him. I was sent on an errand to Steepley one day and took the opportunity to tuck a note into the chains on the gate. Doing so gave me a slight chill. The sinister subterfuge of it, returning to those lanes, to Heston, felt like returning to my old life, my old concerns and stolen comforts. It was no such thing, I reassured myself. Those days were over.

Even so, I was glad to be away from there and uncomfortably aware of the risk I took, even leaving a note, let alone venturing into the grounds. But I needed to see him again. My curiosity was burning holes in me and I wanted to tell him how profoundly our last conversation had affected me.

So although I was no longer the Tommy who had swung up and down those lanes on a regular basis and run the gauntlet of Paulson's traps with defiance, I told him I would call there at midnight five nights hence.

They were an uncomfortable five days full of doubts all new to me. I learned an interesting lesson about life: when you had nothing, you could afford to be careless. The more I had to lose, the more I wanted to protect it. Nevertheless, for all that we had only met twice, I thought of him as my friend and he was in a rare predicament.

My trip was not in vain. Manus was waiting for me in the shadows and, after a brief, hearty handshake, he swung me onto Ebony's back and we trotted to the stables. Once again he had brought food: some buttered bread and cheese and a slice of fruit cake. I was well fed at Mrs Murphy's but the habit of perpetual hunger hadn't died in me yet, and cake could never be a bad thing.

'I was so glad to get your note,' said Manus. 'It's been months and I was worried about you. I thought perhaps Paulson found you after you left here last time, or that there was some sort of accident in the mine.'

'There was.' I swallowed down my last square of cheese and wiped my mouth with the back of my hand. Then I told him the story of the collapse, my rescue and subsequent convalescence. 'I meant to write sooner and explain but it's been hard to get out at night . . .'

It was true. I struggled to wake at night now. Perhaps it was having a bed to myself, or the long hours of fresh air, or perhaps I was simply exhausted from the last five years and would take quite some time to recover. Besides, poaching with Da had been one thing. It was a different affair stealing out from the respectable home of a lady tenant.

'Such a narrow escape!' said Manus. 'I'm only glad you're well. Thank you, Tommy, for remembering me.'

'*Remembering* you? Oh sir, if you only knew.' I tried to express how moved I was by his kindness to me despite the risks to himself. And how grateful I felt to him for making me think so differently about my life. 'What you said to me last time we met, sir, about the reasons you stay here, they helped me see my way forward in life. They were the push that I needed to leave the mines . . . I say again to you, if ever I can help you, you've only to call on me.'

'My dear Tommy. I'm happy that admitting what a feeble fellow I am proved to be so valuable to you!' he said with a self-deprecating smile.

'Sir, how could your father shut you away like this? You are so very different, yes, but to pretend your death? He must be a very extreme man.'

'Oh, he is, Tommy. The most extreme. There was another thing that made my family despair besides my interests and politics. I would have told you before except that it is very painful. And telling my story is tiring for me. I am unused

269

to having someone to trust; for years now I have been secret and silent.'

'I understand. Some confidences cannot be rushed.'

'Just so. Well, I fell in love, Tommy, with a girl from Arden, from the mining community. Helen. She was an ordinary girl, from an ordinary family, like your Josie. She was the most beautiful thing I ever saw. I don't just mean that she was pretty, though she was. I mean that she lit up the world like starlight. She was kind and gentle and she loved me . . . Anyway, suffice to say that my mother found out, and she told my father. They were so appalled by the wrongness of my choice, as they saw it, that they took it as solid and incontrovertible proof of mental deficiency in me. Helen and I were kept apart and I became extremely melancholic . . .'

The look that flooded his face was so anguished that I reached over and grasped his arm. 'Sir, you're here now, it's done with. You're with a friend.'

He shook himself and reached up to stroke Equinox. I suspected it was his ritual to ward off pain. 'You're right. Thank you, Tommy.' He took a deep breath. 'When I heard that Helen had married and moved to Suffolk it got worse. I know my father had arranged it. The physician pronounced me very deficient in mental resources indeed. Such symptoms were common in women, he said, quite usual among such delicately balanced creatures. But in a man, they were a sign of a weak disposition and an unstable mind.

'Suddenly my father had a new complaint about me as an heir. I was mentally ill, I might pass the condition on to our descendants. I was a fault in the mighty Barridge line, with the potential to topple the whole clan.'

'Oh sir.'

'Please, Tommy, call me Manus. Sir is just . . . well, it's just not *me*. Anyway, I know that I am not what they said. My interest in medicine included the health of the mind. My melancholia was not only understandable, it was the only healthy reaction to separation from the woman I loved and the cruelty of my family. However, it gave my father the excuse he needed to take drastic measures; the straw that broke the camel's back, as we say. I am as you find me.'

I drew a long breath, pondering his astonishing tale. Hearing yet new dimensions of his father's cruelty, I thought perhaps I should hurry from that dangerous place as soon as I could, but now that I was here I had the opportunity to ask months' worth of questions.

'Sir, I came poaching here once, years ago. And I saw you in front of the house riding Equinox. Dancing you were, in the moonlight. I couldn't make sense of what I saw; I thought you were a ghost. How? What . . . ?'

'Ah! Fancy that, you saw me before we ever met! You were there, yet I had no inkling that a friend was nearby. Have you heard of dressage, Tommy? No? It's a form of horsemanship – the highest form, many would say, since it requires absolute harmony of horse and rider. My father, of course, rates it not at all. *He* uses horses and ponies to haul his coal, pull his carriage or chase foxes. He's an impressive rider in his way but brute strength and determination are what he relies on. Dressage is a subtle art, Tommy, I think *you* would appreciate it. It is a poem of movement created by a level of training that can only be reached through trust, patience and intuition.'

'Do you really float?' I asked. 'When you do dressage?'

He smiled. 'I'm happy you thought we did. It only appears that way when the unison of horse and rider is at its peak. You must have seen what some people call "airs above the ground". Jumps, in other words, but that doesn't sound so romantic, does it?'

'It sounds magical. How did you discover it, if your father has no time for it?'

'My aunt Pheenie, my father's sister, was an excellent equestrienne; she taught me the basics of dressage when I was just a young boy. She lived in Scotland but used to visit during the summers. My father was furious with her for encouraging me. "Don't make him more unmanly than he already is," he told her. She was very scathing; I think she was the only person who wasn't afraid of him. She died when I was eighteen and left me her books, written by experts like Antoine de Pluvinel and de La Guérinière. So I continued studying and practising. I still practise at night, when there is no one to watch or jeer.'

It struck me how unbearably solitary he was. I knew all too

well how it was to feel different among your own kind. But at least I had lived in a bustling noisy family. Alongside the tension and expediency in our home, there was affection and comradeship. My lessons had been short-lived but they had taken place in a schoolroom filled with other children. Even in the mines I was part of a community, though I found fault aplenty with it. Manus studied medicine alone. After losing his aunt he studied dressage alone. He was no longer part of his own family. He lived alone. He rode by night. He must be so terribly lonely.

'Sir, Manus, if I'm not speaking out of turn, I'm worried about you. How long do you plan to keep living like this? It's a half-life. You're so alone!'

He looked uncomfortable. 'It's familiar to me,' he said. 'And perhaps I'm better off alone. My own family found me impossible to tolerate. And remember, I was not hidden away until I was two-and-twenty years old – I know enough of the world to know that people in general take a very dim view of oddities and outcasts. I have my horses, and the woods and the stars. They are my friends and my comfort. I think perhaps it's enough for me.'

He was convincing, almost. I frowned. 'It's not. Trust me, I understand you better than you might ever imagine. My father never was happy with me either, because I'm different, because he can't understand the things that lift me up. I know how it is to feel apart from *every single person* in your own community.

For years I believed I'd always be alone in my true heart. But then I met Josie. Then I met Miss Embry. Then I met Walter. And then I met you. It would be like that for you too. The horses and the trees and the stars are all very well — they're beautiful — but they're not *people*. And people need people.'

To my dismay he hunched forwards, elbows on knees, and buried his pale, gaunt face in his pale, thin hands. Equinox nuzzled him and stamped. I could have kicked myself. I had shone a bright light on this sensitive, fragile, hidden person and it was too much for him to bear. I was such a *boor*, such a mining lad. Josie would have handled it so much better!

'I'm sorry, I'm sorry,' I said and, for want of anything better to do, topped up his glass.

He shook his head. 'You've done nothing wrong, Tommy. It's only that your words have hit home. You see my secret heart. I told you before, I'm a coward. But how would I do it even if I *had* courage? Even aside from the small matter that I'm supposed to be dead, how could I want to be back in that world where love can be thwarted, where people hunt other species for sport and even turn on their own for scant reasons? Tommy, only a fool could want to be part of such a brutal parade.'

'There's cruelty aplenty in the world, aye. But there's beauty and kindness too . . . And there's nothing wrong with being afraid. I was afraid in the mines. I was afraid coming here tonight. It doesn't mean we shouldn't do things.'

He looked at me pitifully. 'I do know it. Only . . . I am thirty-four years old. How can I start anew in my middle years? What would I call myself? Where would I go? What sort of life could feel right when I'm not even supposed to be alive at all?'

'I've answers to none of those questions. But I think you must promise yourself that you'll work them out. As long as you're working towards it . . . well, that's something. We won't solve it all tonight,' I added gently. 'You need some means behind you and a plan. You need friends, and I assure you that you have Josie and me, for all the use we are. And Miss Embry, I'm sure she would help you too.'

He grasped my hands. 'Tommy, stop now, it's overwhelming. But thank you for stirring me from the stupor I have come to live in since I was consigned to this desolate existence. Thank you for showing me that it is untenable.'

'I'll stop. And I beg your pardon if I've spoken out of place. Now I've escaped the mines I've a zeal to see everyone happy! We'll change the subject. I've some news for you, Manus. I'm studying for scholarship exams for a school in Derbyshire called Westonbury Academy.'

'Westonbury? I know it! My cousin Aloysius went there. Oh Tommy, a scholarship! What a fine thing that would be for you.'

'If I don't get it, it won't be for lack of effort. Even if I don't, I can't keep labouring at Silvermoor forever. If Westonbury doesn't happen, I must go to York or Leeds and find a way to make something of myself. I won't always be nearby. How shall I write to you then? I can't just send letters here addressed to Manus Barridge.'

'Indeed no, we must think of something before you go.'

Uncertainty about the future made it hard to say goodbye. We were pensive as we rode Ebony back to the gate.

'You won't start at Westonbury till September,' said Manus, 'so we have time yet, during which notes at the gate will still serve us.'

'*If* I go to Westonbury,' I reminded him, slipping into the lanes. I looked back at him through the gate and for all the world it was like looking at a prisoner behind bars.

'Oh, you will,' he said with certainty. 'That's one thing I do know.'

# Chapter 43

## Tommy

*June 1903*

Manus was right. I passed my exams with flying colours. On the afternoon of my eighteenth birthday, the letter with the Westonbury crest found me at Mrs Murphy's. I was filled with joy that felt like champagne. No, it was headier than joy; it was pride. Real pride. The first thing I did was write to Josie and tell her. She was due at Silvermoor in a week but this news couldn't wait. I walked up to the house to beg one of the servants to post it with the family's mail and then I asked to be shown to the schoolroom, where I told Mr Farthing and Walter.

Walter was a small explosion of excitement; I think he felt responsible for it all since I had been, briefly, his protégé. Mr Farthing took Westonbury's letter from me with a blank face and read it minutely.

'An impressive result,' he said at last. 'A very impressive

result. I must say, Tommy, I didn't think you could pull it off, but pull it off you have. Well done.'

Later that evening the earl sent for me. I was unused to paying a call of an evening. But the long, unvaried nights of studying were over for now. The exams were behind me. Freedom was a new and unimagined state. He received me in the library with Walter and the dogs. He congratulated me heartily and insisted we toast my success in brandy, which I thought very gracious of him.

'Write to us, Tommy, let us know how you fare,' he said. 'You're a friend of the family now.'

My jaw dropped a little at that; I had come a long way without knowing it then. I nodded and shook his hand but Walter was not so reserved.

'I guess you think he's a suitable friend for me now, Papa,' he chided. 'You didn't once, you know.' I felt my cheeks flush red.

'I remember,' said the earl. 'But I have learned that Tommy is no ordinary lad. And one of the marks of a man, Walter, is that he is able to admit when he is wrong and adjust his course. I hope you will remember that.'

'Yes, Papa, only *I* knew it from the first, didn't I?'

'Magnanimity in victory is another fine quality . . .' said the earl. I smiled.

They were special weeks, those last few before I went to school. And they were speedy – I'd never known time go so fast. The week before I was due to leave, I walked to Grindley to see my family. Mrs Roundsby surprised me by giving me a basket for the family. She remembered my mother kindly, from all the times when she visited my bedside.

'There's plum jam and chocolate cake and a Victoria sponge,' she told me. 'There's a roast chicken, a bag of potatoes, a cabbage from the kitchen garden, carrots and a wedge of the good cheese. I'll pop a bottle of currant wine in too if you can carry it all.'

'I can carry it,' I beamed and kissed her cheek. When had my family had such things?

I set off early in the morning and walked to Grindley with a light heart. In all my years of walking these lanes, I had never thought I would one day be doing so as a scholarship boy, bearing riches for Ma and the rest to enjoy for weeks.

I arrived during a flurry of familiar tasks. Da had already left for work. Jimmy and John were just heading out with their snaps and packed caps. It hurt, seeing them go, but they were sunny enough. 'We'll be back later,' they said, thumping my arms and taking a quick greedy peek into the basket. 'You can tell us all your fancy news then.'

I sat by the fire and shelled peas for Ma and counted pegs and rolled yarn. The sight of idle hands hurt Ma. While I did these tasks we talked of past and future and she asked me a million questions about school that I could not answer.

Grandma was pale and slight as a wraith. It was as if she had drawn in on herself as deeply and totally as she possibly could, as if she was searching for Grandpa deep in the fathomless space of her soul. I knew I would not see her again. Just for a minute, it made me not want to go. But as if she could read my mind, she leaned over and took my hand. Her hand had no strength in it but her eyes did.

'Tommy boy,' she whispered. 'You've given me a good memory to take with me. A good thing to tell your Grandpa.'

Useless to hush her, and disrespectful too. I could see she was going and that it was what she wanted. 'You tell him I love him when you see him,' I told her. 'And I love you, Grandma.'

She smiled and patted my hand with hers, like a little vole's paw it was. 'You're a good boy, Tommy lad.'

Duly, Connie insisted I take her to the stream for old time's sake. She was a dab at fishing now and deftly trapped a hearty tea for us all. She sang as she sat on the riverbank and I swear she sang the fish to her. She was eleven now and chattered without guile about her friends and her dreams and hopes. I wished all the good things in the world for her, but they didn't seem likely to come her way unless I got them for her so that was another reason to do well in school and live up to all my grand ambitions.

We walked back and I played jacks with Ernest and Alfred, sitting on the rug. Da, Jimmy and John came home from work and took turns to splash in the bath before coming in to join us. Georgie came too, with Agnes. Da shovelled his dinner as if food were going out of style, barely even glancing at the basket which Ma had left packed up so that everyone could see it in its glory before it got dismantled and stored away sensibly. All my brothers and sisters were over the moon. Not Da. Straight after the meal he said, 'I've to see Bulford,' and disappeared.

I watched in dismay. 'Is he coming back?' I asked.

Ma looked annoyed. 'I don't know,' she said. She must have been dreaming about a family evening round the fire just as much as I. But the small facts of having saved his son's life, of my going away on an adventure the likes of which had never befallen anyone in my family, would not stop Da being Da.

The rest of us sat in the lounge until the summer evening shadows came strolling in and I knew it was time to start thinking about walking back. It had been one of the best evenings I could remember, Mercy playing harmonium, Connie singing, Mary scowling. The little ones stayed up past their bedtime and Grandma fell asleep. I gazed all around our little house, long and lovingly. It might be foolishly small for that many folk. It might belong to us only as long as our menfolk worked the mines. But there was love in it for all that.

I was furious at my father for being absent at such a time. Wasn't he proud of me? Wasn't there *anything* he wanted to say to me before I left for Derbyshire? But as my gaze ranged towards the kitchen and Mrs Roundsby's basket sitting on the wooden table under the window, I saw a drift of smoke rising on the other side of the pane and I understood.

I excused myself and went out to our little yard. Da was

there, sitting on the wall, puffing on his pipe, all alone. I shook my head. It wouldn't have been in me to spend my son's last evening in such a way but my father was different from me in most respects.

'Da,' I said. He looked up, his face softened by the puffs of smoke from his pipe. 'Da, what are you doing out here, you stubborn fool?'

'Can't a man take a minute to relax and smoke a pipe after a day at work?'

'Aye, and how long have you been smoking it? An hour? Two? I have to go soon, you know.' I sat on the wall next to him, swung my legs over so that we were facing opposite ways, as we always did.

'Well then,' he said eloquently.

'Aye,' I responded in kind. And there we sat.

After an age, when I truly thought we would have no conversation that night, he spoke. 'When do you go?'

'Day after tomorrow.' I was fairly sure he knew that already.

'Yer mother says you'll be back to see us at Christmas. I've told her not to count her chickens. I've told her you'll likely not come back now.'

'Ma's right,' I said mildly. *And you don't know me at all*, I thought silently. *But that's nothing new.*

'Down the mine that day . . . I didn't want you to leave me,' he said in a voice so soft I could hardly hear him. 'And now you're leaving me anyway.'

282

So that was it. I knew his was not a selfish love – he had risked his life to save me after all. It was only that his view of the world was so narrow, so rigid, that this seemed almost another death to him.

'That's different,' I said, still calm. I doubted I'd ever rage at Da again. Things had happened that were too big for that. 'I'll only be gone from the house, the village. I won't be gone from your life. I'll visit. I'll write to Connie and she can read the letters to you all. And in time I'll make things better for all of us, you'll see. Before you ask, no, I don't know how. No, I don't have all the answers. No, I'm not too big for my boots. And yes, I do think I'm special.'

'No point me opening me mouth, is there?'

'Well, it's not like you were saying much before, Da.'

I saw a glint of mirth in his eyes then. It was the first time I had ever seen it. 'I wish you weren't going. Leastways, I wish you could be content here like the rest of us. But yer not and you won't be because yer so bloody *different* and in that case I suppose . . .' He sighed weightily.

'Aye, it's for the best,' I finished for him. 'You know, Da, I used to pretend you weren't really my father. I used to pretend the earl was . . .'

Da did chuckle then. 'Yer mother would have summat to say about that arrangement.'

I smiled. 'Aye, she would at that. But now I'm glad with all my heart that you are my father and I wouldn't want any other.

When I was trapped in the mine that day, I was thinking of you. I'll always be glad that I was saved so I had the chance to tell you this. But you never came to see me at Silvermoor and you've been hiding from me since. We'll always be a mystery to each other, Da. But you've shaped me. Butting heads with you has made me who I am. And you're the best man I know. You're brave and strong and you have more conviction in your little finger than most men do in their entire selves. If I can be half the man that you are, I'll be proud, for all that I must do it in a different way.'

There it was. All that had been in my heart since that last day underground, out in the open at last. I had finally made peace with our relationship, the good and the bad of it.

Da puffed on his pipe a couple of times and looked up and down our dreary, deserted little street as if it were the most fascinating place. 'Go on then, best get back to tha mother,' he said.

# Chapter 44

# Tommy

In the final months before my departure for Westonbury, Manus and I had continued our friendship by note, courtesy of the thickness of chains wrapped around the gate. It was just too risky for me to keep wandering onto Barridge property and with the chance of a lifetime in front of me it would have needed a thicker head than mine to keep doing so.

Once a week or so we exchanged notes – I encouraged him to plan a future of his own and he congratulated me for getting into Westonbury. We shared unexciting stories of our days, and we each grew accustomed to having the support of the other. By such small increments our friendship became more established, though in intensity it had been formed from the first: Josie and I fleeing, Manus hiding, all of us terrified, then his unselfish rescue . . . these made for an unusual friendship and the bonds had been forged quickly.

As I counted down the days to my departure I came to

understand better his reluctance to leave Heston. All my life I had dreamed of going to a school like Westonbury and now that it was upon me I learned what a terrifying thing achieving your heart's desire could be. I had no idea what awaited me, how I would fare . . . There would not be one particular in which my days would be like the days I had known so far and although this was precisely what I had striven for, I was astonished to find that I was very nearly as frightened as I had been on my first day in the mine. And so my surroundings felt dear – the villages, the voices around me, even the pitheads – just because they were known.

The night before I left Yorkshire, I met Manus again, though only at the gate. That way we could see each other without my setting foot on Heston land and without Manus leaving it. We knew we were only observing the letter of the law, wilfully turning a blind eye to the spirit of it. We kept a watchful eye out so that Manus could melt into the trees and I could shoot down the lane if there was any sign of trouble. When an owl swooped low overhead, lamp eyes intent on some scuttling creature, we were all startled, Ebony most of all. I think the owl brushed the tips of his ears.

I watched Manus calming him with some awe. Ebony was such a wild beast in that moment, all flying hooves and rolling white eyes, yet Manus was the very picture of calm competence. Faced with a powerful, volatile animal, he showed not a jot of fear. Yet when it came to taking control of his own life, he shrank to a shadow.

'I'll miss you, my friend,' he whispered through the gate when all was quiet again.

'I'll be back at Christmas. And we'll write.'

'Yes. We'll write.'

For we had devised a system. Manus had agreed that I might let Miss Embry into our secret and I would send my letters for Manus to her. When she was able to go out walking, Miss Embry would tuck my letter into the thick collar of chains on the gate at Heston, taking good care to make sure that no white corner stuck out, to get drenched by rain or alert a passing groundsman. She would collect any letter that Manus left for me in the same fashion and send them on. It would be a sporadic correspondence but better than nothing.

It could only be Miss Embry for there were few enough people I trusted. Josie wasn't at Silvermoor often enough to be our messenger and besides, I didn't want her anywhere near Paulson. Walter was far too young to be mixed up in something like this. Miss Embry knew a little about life and the world and she would do anything for Josie and me. It was a lunatic solution, probably, but it gave us some comfort.

'I brought you this,' Manus murmured, drawing a leather-bound book from a pocket. 'I know you've had your fill of scholarship over these last months and I didn't want to deflect you from your course of study, but I wanted you to have something from me. This was my favourite when I was a child and in truth remains special to me today. Take it with you to Westonbury for company, even if you don't have time to read it.'

I said a heartfelt thank you and we shook hands through the bars then I jogged back to Silvermoor. When I had gained my room in Mrs Murphy's cottage I lit the lamp and examined my gift. Kipling's *The Jungle Book*. A little thrill went through me. India! Jungles and panthers and rivers and wolves . . . Miss Embry had a copy that I'd always hoped to borrow but I'd never had the chance. Now I had my own copy, the leather soft and the pages satiny from use. I opened it and saw an inscription written in fountain pen:

*For Tommy Green,*
*May your adventures be many and magical. With gratitude from*
*your sincere friend,*
    *JMB*

# Part Three

# Chapter 45

———⚬⚬⚬———

# Josie

*September 1903*

I had been in York nearly eighteen months when tragedy struck in Arden. Against all the odds, that tragedy was not mining-related. The mines churned away, the miners limped along, the families continued to struggle. When death came, it slipped in subtle and unsuspected and took my sister Tansy.

I received a note from Martha that Tansy was mortally ill and Coralie sent me back at once. I say *back*, rather than *home*, because it didn't feel like home to me any longer. I hadn't been there once in all this time. I'd met up with Martha several times when the Honeycrofts were at Silvermoor; either we fetched her to the house, or we met on Silvermoor Rise. Once or twice she'd brought Tansy too, a dancing, sunlight-haired little fairy. But I'd never gone back to the village.

As the Honeycrofts' carriage rolled into Arden, several folk whom I'd known all my life stopped to gawp as if I were a Persian princess. I was appalled at how mean and cramped and dirty it was. How had I ever thought this was normal? There was the schoolhouse. There was the lane Bert and my father took when they set off to Drammel Depth each morning. There was the end of my street. I rested my eyes on each landmark in turn, willing myself to feel some nostalgia, but I felt only a strange hammer of fear knocking away in my chest, driving in nails. For anything but this I would have turned and run.

I would *not* get stuck here, I told myself firmly. If I had no other reassurance, there was the fact that my employers expected me back after a week. There was no need to be superstitious. Even so, there was nothing comforting about having finite business ahead of me when that business was the death of my sister. According to Martha's letter, Tansy was not expected to last more than three days.

The carriage dropped me at the end of the street. The last time I had been here I was fleeing with Tommy, in the dead of night. My hair had been shorn, my heart broken and soon afterwards my ankle had been sprained falling through the skylight at Heston. So much had changed since, but walking this road made me young Josie from Arden again, feeling all wrong and afraid of going home. I hadn't realised then how much I had always feared it. To me that sinking, constricting feeling had been normal.

I knocked at the door, an odd thing to do. My mother opened it and stared at me a long moment with a face like curdled milk. I wondered if she was going to let me in. Then she stood aside and I saw my father and Bert at the fire, smoking. My father looked up and nodded. "'Ow do, our Jose?' he said in a flat voice.

Bert came and hugged me. 'It's that good to see thee,' he whispered into my hair. He was twenty-one now and quite the young man. I could see worry lines already, around his eyes and carving his forehead. I laid my hands on either side of his face.

'Oh Bert,' I murmured, and realised I missed him.

Then I heard clattering footsteps. Martha came haring down the stairs and threw herself into my arms. 'Oh, you're here, you're here,' she gasped and I could hear how she'd been longing for it. 'Oh Josie!' She burst into tears.

I held her tight. 'I'm here, Martha. Oh, you poor pet, oh, what a terrible time. Where is she then?'

'In the bedroom. She can't be moved. We're all sleeping down here to give her peace and Ma and I take it in turns to sit with her through the night.'

'Can I see her?'

'Of course, come up.'

I dropped my bag and slung my coat over the back of a chair. Neither Ma or Pa made a move to take them or to welcome me. I followed Martha, and Bert came too.

Tansy had typhoid. No one knew how she'd contracted it;

she appeared an isolated case. But the doctor had explained that it was possible to carry the bacterium symptom-free. Tansy never went anywhere but school, therefore it was reasonable to suppose that there was an asymptomatic carrier among the other children in the village. One little ticking clock, who could spread illness and death at any moment.

My younger sister's beautiful face was flushed and when Martha pushed back the bedclothes I saw that her white chest was covered with pink blotches, like a curtain patterned with roses. She was asleep, breathing hoarsely and moving restlessly, but when she heard my voice she opened her eyes.

'Josie?' she whispered. 'I'm that glad you've come back. Oh, I've missed you.'

'I've missed you too, my love,' I told her and took her in my arms, heedless for a minute of health risks and precautions. 'I've missed you, my little fairy sister.'

She giggled, as she always did when I called her that, and asked me to tell her about York, so I described the glinting shop windows and the apple-green racecourse and the chocolate factories that scented the whole city with sugar until she fell asleep again. The three of us sat there for hours, until night fell.

'I'm glad I've seen thee, Josie,' said Bert into the darkness. 'I've a day shift tomorrow. I won't see you unless you're still here in the evening.'

'I'll be here,' I promised. At last, when owls started calling over the village and moonlight touched the little room, Martha dozed off on my shoulder. Bert woke her and beckoned us to the stairs.

'She's that tired,' he told me in a low voice as she stumbled behind us. 'She's still workin' at surface and she'd been up wi' our Tansy all night most nights.'

'I'll stay up with Tansy tonight,' I said as we stepped into the lamplight and fire-glow of the downstairs room. 'Give Ma and Martha the chance to have a decent rest.'

'You'll not stay here,' said Ma in a voice that was low but determined from her chair in the corner.

'Ma!' said Bert in astonishment.

'Nay, I mean it. She's left this house and she's left once and for all. She'll not come back at her whim now.'

'But Ma! She's here because of our Tansy! She's come all the way from York. She has to stay, it's her home!'

'No it isn't. And she didn't spare a thought for Tansy or for any of us when she ran off into the night with her Grindley lad, did she? And we haven't seen hide nor hair of her since. No, I'll not have her type under my roof.'

'Ma,' I said wearily. 'I'm no type, I'm just me. And even if you don't like it, even if you don't like *me*, let me stay so I can help you. We're going to lose Tansy. Let me help you.'

'We've managed just fine without you all along,' she retorted. 'I won't stop you seeing your sister in her last days, but you'll not stay here and that's flat. Go on, get out!'

'Ma!' protested Martha. 'Where's she to go? I want her here! She's my sister too. And I need to sleep.'

But my mother's face had closed down, shutters drawn. I hastened to make peace. 'It's all right, Martha, I'll stay with Miss Embry. I'm sure Ma will stay up tonight and let you sleep and I'll be back in the morning.'

'But I'll have to go to work! I won't see you!'

'I'll come early. I'll see you before you go and I'll come and see you at work, too, if I get five minutes. Don't worry, get some rest. I'll be back first thing.'

I picked up my things, hugged Bert and Martha and walked back down the coal-black street. Truth to tell, I wasn't sorry not to spend another night under that roof. When it had just been me, Bert and Martha, gathered around Tansy's bedside, it had felt comforting, like family. But the minute I was back in that room where my father had shorn my hair and I'd baked hundreds of joyless loaves under my mother's critical eye, I felt unsafe and small.

I rapped on the door of the emporium and waited a long while until I saw a candle flicker inside. Miss Embry's voice came cautiously through the door: 'Who is it?'

'It's me, Josie,' I called.

A sharp exclamation and a rattle of bolts. 'Why Josie!' she exclaimed. 'Come in!' She held out her arms but I shook my head.

'I've held Tansy, Dulcie. I must bathe and wash my clothes

before anything. I'm so sorry to come unannounced but . . . may I stay the night? The next nights, in fact. My mother won't have me there.'

'Oh gracious,' she said, closing the door behind me. 'Even at a time like this? How can anyone be so bitter? Of course you can stay, Josie. Follow me. I'll fetch you towels and salts and I'll heat some water for you. Do you have a nightgown? A change of clothes for tomorrow? Then we shall manage perfectly.'

An hour later I was boiled and scrubbed and hygienic enough in my own estimation to submit to the embraces of my old, dear friend. 'How much you have done for me, dear Dulcie,' I murmured when she released me. 'And still you're helping me out of the predicaments caused by my family.'

She smiled sadly. 'Oh Josie, we should be so merry, you staying here with me, if it were not for the circumstances. Your heart must be breaking. Dear little Tansy, such a beautiful child. I cried when I heard the news.'

I sighed. 'I know. I can hardly believe it. I don't *want* to believe it, of course. Oh Dulcie, why did it have to happen? I wanted to send for her and Martha one day and have the two of them with me in York. I wanted better things for them both. Now Tansy will die never having known any place but Arden and I'm so afraid Martha will never leave now. You know how good and loyal she is. I'll bet she'll feel sorry for Ma and think she can't leave her and be tethered to this place forever.'

'I thought she was tethered anyway. What happened to that fellow she was seeing? I thought they were engaged?'

I sighed again. I had done little *but* sigh since returning, I reflected. 'Aye, she's engaged all right. But you know . . . I kept hoping anyway . . .' My opinion of Luke Stevens, the beau in question, was not high. He was handsome enough in his way but possessed all the sensitivity of a troll. Martha was a bright-eyed blackbird. I could all too easily imagine her crushed underfoot. Was she really going to marry that great lump of a man? Now seemed hardly the time to ask.

Dulcie squeezed my hand and ushered me into the parlour. 'Sit, Josie, I shall fetch food. At least we don't have to keep an eye on the clock tonight, you don't have to rush off home like the old days. Small comfort perhaps but we shall relax and I shall tend you very well.'

It *was* a comfort. If I had to be back in Arden at all, this was the only place of peace within it. If Tansy had to die, then only true affection could be balm for the injury. I looked around the dimly lit room, the spines of dear book-friends on the shelves, the fuzzy balls of lamplight hovering in the corners. Hours I had sat here in my younger days, feasting on stories and good conversation, dreading the moment I would have to leave. I marvelled anew that I'd managed to be contented for my first twelve years. Ignorance was a gift God sent us, I decided, until it wasn't any more.

Dulcie returned with a tray of sandwiches and cake and

lemonade, with a small glass each of sherry. 'Something warming,' she said, setting the glass on the table at my side. 'Now let us talk till we fall asleep of everything our hearts need to share.'

And we did, until late into the night. Even so, I kept my promise to Martha and was back at the old place bright and early the next morning – the knocker for the miners had woken me banging on the window next door. I spent half an hour with Martha while she ate her breakfast. Da and Bert were gone already and Ma stayed upstairs with Tansy. It would be a long day just the two of us watching her, I thought gloomily.

I walked Martha to work, then dragged my feet back again. Somehow Ma and I managed the day by alternating our time with Tansy, an hour apiece. By keeping the arrangement simple and inviolable we didn't need to speak. While I sat with Tansy I heard Ma knocking out the chores downstairs: pounding loaves, attacking the mangle, clattering dishes . . . When it was Ma's turn I couldn't bear to be in the house. I walked briskly up to the pit to see Martha, though she wasn't at liberty to chat. I went to Dulcie's for my lunch. I called on one or two neighbours I thought might be pleased to see me and didn't bother with the rest. At last Martha came home, then the men, and it grew a little easier to be in that house until night fell. Then we repeated the whole performance the following day.

# Chapter 46

## Josie

The days were so tense and so sad that I sat up late every night with Dulcie. It might not have seemed like common sense since I grew increasingly tired, but I needed that fortification against Ma's animosity and my utter desolation at my little sister's fate.

Each day felt interminable, yet Tansy's death, as expected, came very rapidly. On my fourth day in Arden, she slipped away, only a few hours later than the doctor had predicted. Martha was at work and Ma had run out for a few things, and so it was just me and Tansy in the house when she passed. I was holding her hand and she opened her eyes and smiled at me – such a brave smile for such a little girl.

'Oh Tansy,' I said, struck with the sudden knowledge that the moment had come. 'Not yet my darling girl.'

But Tansy, who hadn't said a word for more than a day now, opened her parched lips. 'I must, our Josie. But don't worry, it's better in fairyland,' she whispered, using our old joke to tell me that she wasn't afraid.

I kissed her brow and told her I adored her forever and more. She nodded and closed her eyes again and a moment later she was gone. I couldn't move. I held my own breath when she stopped breathing, unwilling to accept it, just waiting for her narrow chest to start rising and falling again and for it all to have been a false alarm. But she breathed no more and I finally gave a shuddering gasp and sank my head onto her soft tummy.

Yet I was glad Ma wasn't there so that I could have a little time with my sister alone. I cried scorchingly. My poor little sister. She had never had a chance to bloom and now she never would. She would never see a city, or a sea, or a sequined gown. And my world was a dimmer place without her. Although I had hardly seen her in this last while, we carry home with us wherever we go, however glorious or disappointing it may be. It is a shape which sits within us and dictates how we arrange our lives around it. For me, Tansy and Martha were the best part of that shape.

I couldn't imagine returning to York without the hope that one day she would join me and I might show her everything there that I loved, see the delight all over her face. But perhaps she was somewhere even better. In her very last moment she had spoken of fairyland. It was the language of sisters; I had always told her it was where she belonged. Was she just saying it to reassure me or had she glimpsed some shimmering, blissful iridescence? I hoped the fairies would come in rainbow legions to take care of her.

After a while I heard Ma returning and I wondered what words I should use. I dreaded her reaction. Would she be somehow angry with me? Would she keen and wail? I wasn't sure I could deal with seeing Ma in distress, it would be so out of character. I kissed Tansy one last time then took a deep breath, squared my shoulders and went downstairs.

I didn't need words. Ma took one look at my treacherous, blotchy, pink and white face and she knew. 'She's gone then?'

I nodded. 'Oh Ma.'

A stricken look flashed through her eyes as though life had betrayed her one too many times. Just for a moment, for less than a moment, I thought she would hold me. But she only turned her back and started setting out the small purchases she had brought home on the kitchen table.

'Aye, well, you've done your bit here then,' she said. 'You can go now. Now don't you start, we'll send word about the funeral, don't fret about that.'

I wondered how long it would take her to go upstairs and see that small, still figure. But that was her business.

'Send for me if I can do anything for you at all,' I said.

She continued occupying herself and I walked away.

I went to Hepzibah and told Martha. The foreman agreed she might go home and keep her job, though she would lose the day's wage. Then I went to Drammel Depth, found the office manager and asked him to get a message to my father and Bert. Martha followed me numbly, then we walked back into the village together.

Outside the gate, Martha cried in my arms. It was brimming up in my heart to ask her about Luke Stevens, to beg her to come back to York with me, but I knew she wouldn't want to think about all that now.

'Come and see me at Miss Embry's whenever you like. She said she's always happy to have you,' was all I said. My heart yearned after her as I watched her drag herself into that sad cottage. At least Ma wouldn't be alone. I wasn't sure comfort could be had, but if she would appreciate anyone's presence, it would be Martha's.

The funeral was three days later. As I walked to the church with Dulcie, it seemed impossible that I would leave again the next day; this tragedy had swallowed me whole. Yet what was there to stay for?

We sang hymns around a tiny grave. Ma and Da stood side by side and didn't look at me. Then again, they didn't look at anyone. Alice was there with her Fred. Her hair was as glorious gold as ever but she was getting plump, no way around that. Luke Stevens stood with his meaty arm around Martha, bending his head to hers at regular intervals and staring around as though daring anyone to come near what was his. Or perhaps I did him a discredit. If I had Tommy with me now, I would want to be held by him, I would want to take refuge from the world in him. Perhaps that's how Martha felt. And he was here; had he rearranged shifts, foregone a wage? Perhaps he was more caring than he looked.

Dark earth fell and the crowd dispersed. We returned without Tansy. Our little angel gone. Only ten years old.

# Chapter 47

## Josie

I had always wondered at the fact that Ma, who had not a jot of poetry in her blood, and valued beauty far below Bovril, or Reckitt's Blue, had given us girls rather lovely names. Alice and Martha were usual enough but both very pretty, I thought. Josephine wasn't a village name at all, so I have no idea what prompted mine. And Tansy, as pretty and golden a name as my little sister had deserved, not only evoked a beautiful image but meant immortal. I remember being astonished when I learned that Ma knew what it meant, and chose it deliberately. It was a glorious name to bestow, though sadly ironic in the event.

I had always taken it to mean that Ma had a soul after all, some softness and fancy folded up very small, in some out-of-reach corner on the shelves of her being. The day of the funeral persuaded me otherwise once and for all.

I left the churchyard with Dulcie, gulping with undignified tears but unable to help myself. It was just too great a loss, an insufferable wrench. Luke had relinquished Martha and walked with Alice's husband Fred, while Martha, Alice, Bert and my parents walked together in a sad little group. I hurried after them and Dulcie went on her way. Martha and Bert hugged me. Alice kissed my cheek and squeezed my hand. Even Da clasped me in his arms for a short minute.

'Oh Josie, lass,' he said in an unsteady voice. 'Did you ever think we'd see the day?'

Then they all carried on and, to my surprise, Ma hung back to walk with me. I slowed my steps, grateful for any small moment we could share and willing, in the shock of the day, to move beyond any past hurts.

'Oh Ma,' I said. 'It breaks my heart. She was so beautiful, so good. I have to go back tomorrow, Ma, but if I can ever do anything to help you, I hope you'll think of me. I'm still your daughter, even though I've moved away.'

She stopped dead and the crowd of mourners flowed around us as they passed. 'Aye,' she said, in a voice like cold ashes. 'You're my daughter. I'll always remember that.'

I looked at her uncertainly. She didn't make it sound like a good thing. 'Well then . . . Ma . . . can't we be friends? Or . . . be kind to each other at least? The bad things are a long while past now.'

'No, the bad thing is standing right in front of me. The bad thing is a living memory before my eyes every minute I see you. That's why I've let them go on ahead. I have one thing to ask of you, Josie, as your mother. Go away and never come back. I don't want to see you again.'

I felt like a frightened child. 'Ma? You can't mean it. Why do you hate me so? I don't hate you, for all it's been difficult. You're my mother!'

'Aye,' she said again. 'I am. But Sam Westgate is not your father. You're a shame and a disgrace. You're a *bastard*! You torture me, with your red hair and your fancy ways. And it gets no better as the years pass, it gets worse. So leave tomorrow and never come back, do you hear me?'

Galaxies spinning away, nations falling, stars igniting in the heavens . . . all sorts of vast, unfathomable things flooded through my mind, dizzying me. Nothing was more enormous than this.

'Ma?' My voice came from a long way away. I reached for her to steady myself but she stepped away. I nearly fell, but a passer-by caught me.

'Dizzy with grief, poor lass,' he said and moved on respectfully when he deemed me steady on my feet.

'Ma, for the love of God, don't say such things!' I implored her in a low voice. 'What a time to tell me, if it's true!'

'Oh, it's true all right,' she said indifferently.

'But . . . but . . . it *can't* be true! Da has to be . . . my da. He has to be. If he's not, then who . . . ?'

'Never you mind. He wouldn't want to know you, believe me that. Sam's done his best, he's brought you up and given you a roof — though you threw it all back in his face! But he couldn't bring himself to love you. How could he, knowing? How could *anyone*, knowing what you are? You never belonged here, Josie. You wanted to get out and you got out. So do us all a favour and stay away. Let me pretend you never happened. That's the only daydream I've ever had!'

So saying, she strode off and I watched the remnants of my small family disappear into the distance without me. Tansy gone. Da not my da. Ma disowning me. Only two sisters and a brother remained. I was standing, I realised, by the bushes where Ma had hidden my apron on that long-ago day when I'd been late for Alice's wedding. She'd slapped me and combed my hair with violence and yanked me to the church. But afterwards, thanks to Tommy, there had been bluebells. But Tommy was far away at school now. And all that felt like the childhood adventures of another girl. I wasn't Josie Westgate of Arden any more.

# Chapter 48

## Josie

I don't know how I made it back to the Emporium. My legs were weak. I don't know who spoke to me as I walked, but I suppose if I was odd, they would have put it down to the sad day. Dulcie was looking out for me and I stumbled through the open door with a gasp.

'Oh Dulcie!' I cried. 'It's worse. It's worse than anything!'

She gave me sherry and threw a blanket over me although the day was warm. 'Tansy, dear?' she asked but I shook my head. I couldn't say more for nearly an hour.

Dulcie came and went, giving me time alone, but always checking on me. She bustled discreetly around the little parlour so I didn't feel alone, but she asked me not a question. I stared into space for a good stretch of time and eventually, somehow, came back to myself.

'Dulcie?' I said, and she was at my side. 'Dulcie, I'm a . . . bastard.'

'I beg your pardon, dear?'

'It's true. Ma just told me. I'm a bastard. I'm not my father's child.' I gazed at her in terror. Would she hate me too?

'Oh . . .' she said slowly. 'Well, that explains a lot, doesn't it?'

And really, it did. After the initial shock wore off, we discussed it all and started to make sense of it together. Quickly I realised that in practice nothing had changed. There had never been love lost between me and my parents. Alice I could take or leave. Martha and Bert would never think less of me. Tommy wouldn't. Dulcie didn't. And bastard or not, Westgate or some other name unknown, I had, as Ma pointed out, got out. Of course it rocked me to the core to have my whole foundation called into question, to learn that I wasn't who I'd always thought I was. But my father had never done much for me; I'd never felt he was the defining element in my life.

I couldn't begin to understand how I'd come into being. If I was the eldest, it would be easy enough to imagine an early love gone wrong, then Da coming along and agreeing to marry Ma and pass me off as his own. But I was the *fourth* child! The last before Tansy! I could *not* imagine Ma sneaking around and risking everything in the name of love. I couldn't imagine her seized by a grand passion. I couldn't imagine her being so impractical as to think an affair could end well. I didn't *want* to think that I was the product of violence, though that would certainly explain her attitude to me. But surely if that were the case, the early years, just after the terrible happening, would have been the worst? Ma's antipathy towards me had become worse as I'd grown older.

Perhaps as I'd grown up I'd started to look more like my father. I hoped not! I didn't want anyone else noticing a resemblance while I was still in ignorance. Dulcie and I wracked our brains that night but I didn't look like anyone! No one in the village and no one I'd ever seen. The only thing that might possibly link me to anyone I knew was my hair. I had exactly the same hair as Coralie. The earl, her uncle, was a famous lothario with a weakness for village girls. Was it conceivable that he was my father? Or another member of that family, carrying a red-headed inheritance?

'Good God!' I cried, throwing myself on the sofa after pacing doggedly for some time. Dulcie passed me another sherry. 'Tommy and I spent our childhoods spinning make-believe that he was one of the earl's by-blows. Don't tell me that all that time it was *me*?'

She spread her hands, as baffled as I. 'The hair isn't conclusive, Josie. In other ways you don't look a thing like her.'

'It's true, I don't,' I mused, 'more's the pity. God, what if Ma tells someone else? What if Coralie and I are related? She might regret taking me in then. Oh Dulcie, I couldn't bear for her to hate me, I love her. But if she was going to discover a long-lost sister, or cousin, she wouldn't want it to be a girl from this place, would she?'

'Josie, I think you're forgetting all you know of her! If it *were*

the case, I can hardly imagine Miss Honeycroft being preju-
diced against you. After all she's done for you? No. And I doubt
your mother will breathe another word. She'd cause herself a
lot more trouble than she'd cause you. But this way, by telling
you and only you, well . . .' She trailed off and looked angry.

She was right. Ma had achieved nothing but to vex and
torture me, and that was enough for her.

'I *hate* this village, Josie,' said Dulcie unexpectedly. 'I've
tried and tried to be happy here for my uncle, to keep his shop
going, to keep his memory alive. But nothing *grows* here. The
business improved when New Arden was built but now it's
levelled off again. It isn't thriving, but it isn't failing either. If
I want to keep Embry's Emporium just as it is, I can probably
do so till the end of my days. But I'll never make any real
money and I'll never be able to develop it. I'll never marry
and I'll never have any real friends now that you've gone . . .'
She ran out of breath and stopped. Then she added, 'I'll be
surrounded by resigned, sad people like your neighbours and
bitter, angry people like your mother. And I'll sell them flour
until the end of time.'

I'd had no idea Dulcie ever questioned her place in the village. She always seemed so composed and constant. But of
course, it was hardly surprising. She wasn't old. She was clever
and lively and cultured. And she was beautiful, whatever those
nasty Barridge twins had said. This was not a place in which
she could thrive.

'So what are you going to do?' I asked her. It was a relief to think and talk about someone else's woes and set my own aside for the rest of the night. Dulcie's might have some happy resolution; mine were with me to stay. Ma had done a spiteful thing in sending me away with such partial information. It would poison everything, and leave me always wondering. Worrying. Even so, I left the following morning in higher spirits than I would have believed possible the day before. I was, after all, leaving Arden. By itself that was cheering. But there were other reasons. Martha came first thing in the morning to say the sweetest goodbye. I hadn't decided whether I wanted to trouble her with Ma's revelation, and she had to hurry to work, so I said nothing about it. I did, however, comment on how caring Luke had seemed at the funeral. I thought that a very tactful way of broaching the subject. I was able to ask if everything was going well without sounding like a nosy or disapproving sister. She said she'd write to me. I went away hoping there was a little doubt in her heart, or surely a simple yes would have sufficed?

I was also excited because Dulcie had charged me with a mission. 'Keep your eyes open for opportunities for me in York,' she said as we waited outside the shop for Norman to come in the carriage and take me home.

'In York?' I queried in delight. 'I thought if you left here, you'd go back to Leeds.'

'No, dearest, I prefer not to go back, only ever onwards. I

313

love York, as you know, and having you here this last week has made me remember all over again how lovely it is to have a friend nearby. Another addition to York's long list of inducements . . .'

'I'll scour every shop and business the minute I'm back,' I promised. 'Why, if you were there too, what fun we should have! You're the only thing missing to make it perfect. And Tommy. And Martha . . .'

'We shall have to work on getting them both to move there in due course,' she twinkled. 'We'll swell the population with our acquaintance alone.'

'How long do you think it would take you to sell up here and be able to move out?' I wondered.

'Not long, I hope. When I arrived, there were two other parties interested in buying the business. You can be sure that when word got out that a woman was taking over the emporium, male buyers came out of the woodwork.'

'But if it's different this time, how long would you wait? Are you dependent on a buyer?' Now that she'd put the idea in my head, I was impatient for it to happen.

'I suppose I am really. But let's not run to meet trouble, Josie. I'm sure it will happen when it's meant to.'

I rattled out of Arden atop the carriage, sitting next to Norman. It was a grey, squally day with sun and rain coming in unpredictable outbursts but I didn't feel like being alone with my thoughts in case they returned to Tansy and Ma. I was happy to take my chances with the weather and bump along in the bracing wind. I feasted my eyes on the sight of Arden disappearing into my past, one landmark at a time.

When we passed Hepzibah, the great pithead that reared above us like a gorgon about to strike, I squinted at the crowds of surface workers for a glimpse of Martha, though I didn't catch one. It hurt to leave my sister behind washing coal. But as we left the village behind altogether a double rainbow surged into existence. Intense colour blazed across the grey.

'Look! A good omen!' I pointed and Norman looked up.

'You could do with one,' he said. 'I'm sorry about your sister, Josie.'

'Thank you, Norman.'

# Chapter 49

———— ∽≈∽ ————

# Tommy

*Autumn 1903*

My first weeks at Westonbury were hard. More than once I remembered Mr Latimer's words to me on that long-ago day: *Here, you may be the star pupil. Out there, you would be nothing . . .* More than once I was to wonder if Latimer was right after all.

I had arrived on a cool September day, driven, thanks to the earl, by Matthias. I gazed in awe and fear at a large building of Jacobean grey, lit by autumnal sun and laced by deep, cool shadows. On that first day a rainbow hovered over its chimneys and brown leaves skittered about its walls.

'Rather you than me,' remarked Matthias when he drove off, leaving me alone at the boys' entrance. It hardly seemed the right place for me; I wasn't a boy, I was eighteen years old, tall and strong for my age and I'd been working for more than six years. I wished Josie were with me. Westonbury was not unlovely but I had not a friend there. Yet soon I came to know it well enough.

Inside, the place was a maze of long, straight corridors, featureless except for a succession of oil paintings in ugly frames along their walls – old boys who had gone on to success and glory. At first I wished I had Rogue or Flinty to help me out, but in time I came to know my way around by those portraits. My maths classroom was the second door after portly and pink with a blue cravat. The refectory was to the left of angular old boy with the cane and the spaniel. Whenever I passed curly moustache with mean little eyes I knew I was in for trouble, for that hung just next to the headmaster's office.

My little corner of this strange new world was a bed in a dormitory that housed eight boys in all, the others all three years younger than I. It was a light room, with tall windows overlooking the sweeping front lawn.

The lessons themselves were not hard to follow, yet when it came to raising hands and answering questions, the other boys answered with a sophistication that seemed forever beyond my grasp. I sometimes got the answer right, but they could add comments and references to other learning that I had never had, weaving the day's information into a larger tapestry of knowledge that seemed to hang together, secure in every stitch. I knew only ragged strands here and there. To the others the world was knowable, and known. To me it was only glimpsed in moments.

I had long been made acquainted with all the reasons why *my* people, mining people, thought that I shouldn't aspire and didn't belong in any other life. But now, it seemed, I had come to school only to be educated in all the reasons why *these* people thought exactly the same thing.

'I say, old chap, you've done awfully well to get here, but wouldn't it have been kinder to yourself to stay in a more . . . *familiar* environment?'

'Tommy Green spent half his life wielding a coal shovel, don't you know? *Lord* knows what made him think he could make any sort of impression here.'

'You don't belong here, Green, and no scholarship will convince me that you do.'

I was provoked to two fights, both of which I won in about four seconds. The fights landed me in no end of trouble with the staff, but put an end to trouble from the boys once and for all. Even so, I missed friendship, as anyone would.

*I'm here for my future*, I told myself over and over again, silently and fiercely. *I'm here to learn. I'm here to find a way to become a man of means, to ease things for my family and to help a little in the world. I'm not here for friends or pleasure.*

Christmas sparkled like a star in the distance, marking the end of my first term. I'd hoped to return home in triumph, telling tales of tests passed with flying colours, awards won, perhaps even the promise of a job when I finished at Westonbury issued by some wealthy visitor unable to overlook my extraordinary potential. So far, however, there was nothing whatsoever about which I could brag and I was beginning earnestly to wonder if I were growing more stupid as the weeks progressed.

It was all very disappointing of course. I felt uneasy when I imagined explaining to my father how I was just barely hanging on by the skin of my teeth. I was sure it would take nothing short of banners of glory to reconcile him to my choice. But when I felt disenchanted I thought of all the people who'd helped me get here. Miss Embry, Manus, Walter, Mr Farthing, the earl . . . even my father, who had taught me to stay alive down there long enough to make it here.

The letters I received from home were my biggest pleasure at Westonbury. Not all the news was happy, though. Back in Grindley, Grandma had slipped away to join Grandpa. Connie's letter had big tear splashes on it and I wanted to be with them all, attend the funeral. But the school had rules about things like that and besides, I had no means to get there. It was the first, but not the last, time that I wished I'd earned a wage on the Silvermoor estate, not just board and lodging.

I also learned that Josie's sister Tansy had died, though she only wrote to me after it was all over and she was safely back in York. She hadn't wanted to upset me during my first weeks at school. I hated that I had not been there for her and was only consoled that she had had Miss Embry to shelter her through that terrible time. My hair stood on end when I read that she hadn't been allowed to spend the night in her old house.

*And there's something worse*, she wrote. *Something I can only tell you when I see you. You're not to worry, I'm not ill or anything like that, I promise. But I've learned something shocking and I can't write it down.*

It was hard not to fill my next letter with a barrage of questions, but what would be the point of that?

Manus was still struggling to make a decision. He was cursed with that unhelpful temperament that dreamed and longed to roam the wider world, yet which feared to leave all that was familiar. His conflicting urges held him at an impasse.

I longed to go home and see them all but first I had end-of-year examinations to prepare for. If I could acquit myself well, it would restore my faith in my ambitions and give me some good news to carry home. I so badly wanted to succeed. I applied myself, working harder than ever before. I wrote fewer letters to my friends and concentrated all my efforts on this one goal. A week before the end of term, the results were announced. I was third from bottom.

# Chapter 50

<hr/>

# Tommy

*Winter 1903*

Christmas was a mixed blessing. On the one hand, it was one of the happiest times of my life. On the other hand, I knew I would miss everyone twice as badly when I left.

I spent two uninterrupted days at home with my family, then I received a note from Josie inviting me to tea in the library at Silvermoor. I ran all the way from the cottage to the grand house, laughing aloud with the improbability of it. Five years ago, when Josie and I were windswept wanderers in the lanes between our two humble villages, if anyone had told us that she would one day receive me in such a place and pour tea from a silver pot, we would have laughed ourselves delirious.

After our first excited reunion and the novelty of feasting on Christmas treats in someone else's sumptuous home, Josie quickly noticed that something was on my mind. I didn't want to start things off with a complaint but within ten minutes she had dug it out of me, that with the best part of two weeks still ahead of me, I was already dreading going back. I admitted it most sheepishly.

'This first bit was always going to be difficult, we knew that,' shrugged Josie through a mouthful of mince pie. 'Grindley's all wrong for you, but you know who you are there. School's a step in the right direction but it's so new! You lack years of learning that the others have had and once again, you're different.'

I nodded, spooning a little more brandy sauce over my slab of pudding. 'It's painful to have the same old feelings in such a different life,' I agreed.

'Natural,' she declared in a tone of finality. 'But you'll finish there – only five more terms to go – then you'll strike out and live life on your own terms. You'll be glad of your time there then. Westonbury's no more your place than Grindley is,' she said. 'It's not your dream to be at Westonbury, it's your dream to gain an education. Westonbury is just the place where you must do it.'

She was right. She cheered me sufficiently to abandon the topic for the rest of my stay. It was what it was; I would make no other choice. On Josie's side, however, there was much to discuss. She told me everything she had noticed about Martha and Luke and I comforted her best as I could, which wasn't particularly well, when all was said and done. There were many men like Luke in our sort of community and no doubt people would say Martha could do worse. I reminded Josie that her sister was smarter than many girls and would surely keep herself out of any situation that would spell her unhappiness. She nodded and sniffled and talked about Tansy's last days and at last I asked her the big question. What was the dreadful thing she could only tell me in person?

So she told me. My old suspicions, confirmed from the horse's mouth. At last I recounted what her father had said that night when he beat me. 'I never told you because I didn't want you to have that worry,' I explained. 'But now you have it anyway. I think it must be true, Josie – leastways, your father believes it.'

'Oh, it's true,' she said bitterly. 'It's the only way to understand why Ma has always been so hard on me, why they would've sent me down Drammel Depth, even though I had other choices. Who do you think it is, Tommy? Do you think I'm one of the earl's little accidents? Or do you think I'm just anybody's, some man my mother took a fancy to when things got hard, or dull, with Da – with Sam?'

'I don't know,' I said truthfully. 'I don't know how much of a clue your hair is. It's likely just a coincidence. I don't see as how we'll ever truly know. I mean, who would we ask?'

'Exactly. No one. I daren't spoil my relationship with Coralie *or* the earl, come to that. Silvermoor is a big part of my job, of Coralie's life. I'm pretty sure it's never occurred to either one of them. And I'd bet a million pounds Ma will never tell me. I'll wonder about this all my life.'

'Maybe one day you won't wonder because it won't matter,' I said. '*I* don't care who your parents are. You never really were a Westgate, not even half a one. You're *Josie*, my Josie, my best friend. Whoever you've come from, you're more *you* than anyone else I know . . . and that's that, really.'

She smiled. 'Thanks, our Tommy,' she said softly.

I wanted to say more. She looked so pretty sitting there in the firelight, putting away mince pies as if she didn't get three square meals a day. And I was so happy to see her. But she was, as I'd said, my best friend, and we'd been a long time apart so maybe that was making me sentimental . . . She was my *friend*. I daren't confuse that with anything else. She was too important to me to mess things up.

Loving being with her, loving the way she looked, loving listening to her, loving how she understood me, loving storing things up to discuss with her . . . did that add up to . . . *loving* her? Or was that just friendship? One thing I did know, I was going to treasure every minute of the two weeks we had together.

I stayed with my family, which was at once strange and heartening. It was strange to be back, of course, and because Grindley held so many difficult memories it wasn't entirely nice to be there. Yet inside our little house, as had always been the case, there was love and teasing and I was glad to be amongst them again. Because Grandma and Grandpa were no longer with us I was given their old bed that folded away under the stairs. Jimmy and Alfie had been using it and I was loath to oust them but they said they didn't mind going back upstairs for the holidays.

'Our John's married now anyhow, and he was always the fartiest and the kickiest of us,' said Alfie. 'It's not so bad.'

Da and I were more cordial than we had ever been; I could hardly believe it. 'Earning money yet?' he asked.

'Nay.'

'Top of the class?'

'Nay.'

'Making your mark on the school? Winning prizes and that?'

'Not yet, Da.'

'Aye, well,' he said. 'Constance, pass us the gravy.'

Ma had been hoarding to have extra treats for my homecoming and Mrs Roundsby had sent a small Christmas basket. Alfie said he'd celebrate my return for that reason if no other. Connie's delight was infectious; she was transparent and bright as a mountain stream. My married brothers dropped in and out and clapped me on the back and asked how my studies were going. Mercy was married too, and happy. She gave me a scarf she'd knitted for me, which I told her I would cherish. Ernest's health, against all expectation, seemed to be improving and though he was now working in Crooked Ash he seemed no worse than when I left.

I spent part of almost every day at Silvermoor. The Honeycrofts were there for the whole of Christmas, their father and aunt joining them from York for the middle four days, and of course, this meant that Josie was there too. As was Norman, Cedric Honeycroft's manservant.

It wasn't that I disliked him for himself. I knew that he and Josie were friends and it seemed plain that he was everything she had said: a decent, straightforward, hardworking fellow with no pretensions about him but a taste for good music and beautiful architecture. No dullard then, and ready to share his interests with Josie. Very ready. No, the reason I disliked Norman had everything to do with the way he looked at her. I could tell that he worshipped Josie.

When I said so, Josie laughed out loud. 'Norman's engaged!' she gasped through her guffaws. 'I told you! He's to his marry Sally next summer and I'm to be at the wedding. I met her in October and we got on well. You don't suppose she'd be extending the hand of friendship if she thought her fiancé had designs on me, do you?'

'And do you wish it were different?' I couldn't help asking. 'Do you wish he were free?'

She looked at me as if I'd gone stark staring mad. 'They don't teach you much at that school, do they?' she observed. 'I could never think of Norman like that. How could you think it?'

'Well, you're of an age and you're lovely looking, Josie. It's not such a stupid question really, is it?'

She opened and shut her mouth a couple of times and looked at me with an expression that told me I really needed to cut my losses and change the subject. I wasn't sure why she was annoyed, but I did just that. Even so, Josie could tell me till she was blue in the face that Norman only liked her as a friend and that he was going to marry his Sally, but I knew differently.

# Chapter 51

## Tommy

Between Josie and Walter and the Honeycrofts and my family, I was home for a week before I saw Manus. We arranged it in the customary way and on the twenty-eighth of December I slipped out late at night while the others slept. It was a perfect December night, the earth sleeping soundly as an enchanted princess. The moon was a wire-thin curve. My footsteps were crisp and clear despite my wish for stealth; the lanes rang with the darkness and coldness of that powerful time of year when humans should know better than to be abroad. Most of us did. As always, Tommy Green of Grindley was the exception.

Manus was waiting. We exchanged a quick handshake then he hoicked me up onto Ebony and off we trotted. I hadn't seen him for months; a rapid conversation through the gate would not do. His long hair was a little longer but his pale face hadn't changed a jot and his billowing sleeves and cravat were as snowy white as ever. Once we were safely inside, he embraced me like a brother. As ever, he had provided a small feast for us as well as a cloth bag containing a Christmas pudding, a bottle of brandy, a loaf and a round of duck pâtépate. 'For your family at Christmas,' he said.

'My dear friend, this is so kind of you!' I said, peering into the bag and getting a rich whiff of the pâté. 'But how shall I explain it?'

'Tell them you went poaching,' he grinned.

We were more or less up to date on each other's news, thanks to Miss Embry's postal service, so instead we were able to go about the business of spinning plans. Mine were vague at the moment, separated from me as they were by the vast barrier of eighteen more months at Westonbury. Manus's were also vague, much to my frustration. The tale he told me of his Christmas alone at Heston, the day exactly the same as every other day except that he had to fetch his own meals because the house servants had the day off, made me want to cry.

'But I don't mind fetching my own meals,' he told me. 'In fact, I prefer it.'

'Hardly the point!' I told him. 'What about your family? Don't they *ever* visit you? Do they even know you're alive?'

He sighed. His hair was silvery as Equinox's mane in the starlight. 'They all know. Mama, Jocelyn, Willard, the girls . . .'

'And they've never visited you once, not even at Christmas?'

'No. The girls would want to. But they'd be afraid to say so and they would never be allowed.'

'Your mother?'

'She is as hard and unrelenting as my father. They make a marvellous match.'

I couldn't imagine such a family. 'I cannot believe they leave you here to be so utterly alone.'

'Sometimes I wonder if my isolation is harder on you than it is on me, Tommy,' said Manus gently.

Perhaps he was right. Perhaps I had so long been fighting to get myself out that now I couldn't live without the fight and had simply transferred it to someone else. Oh, but to see his fingers knitting and knitting when we talked about his family, but still and relaxed when we laughed and talked of wider matters. To know that day after day, night after night, he rattled around that huge house, this vast estate, with never a soul to talk to . . . I was lonely enough at Westonbury but for Manus the scale and context were entirely different. How could I not wish it were better for him?

'It's so good of you to come, Tommy. I'm more grateful than you can ever know. But I feel I should stop you now that you have so much to lose. A place at Westonbury, a promising future. You shouldn't risk it all to give me a few hours of company.'

It was true that I felt unhappy about breaking into Heston. When its forbidden acres were all I could aspire to see of a world beyond my own, I would see them come what may. But now everything was different.

'If I'm honest, I feel the same. If I were caught by Paulson now that I'm not poaching any more, it would be the most horrible irony. He'd have me for trespassing in the blink of an eye. And I *must* do well, Manus. Not just for me but to help my family — I promised them I would — and to help *you*. As for Josie, we're just friends, of course, but . . .'

He smiled. 'I understand, I understand perfectly.'

He said it so knowingly that it made me colour and change direction. 'Of course, if you would just *leave*,' I continued, 'then I wouldn't *have* to take the risk. Anything must surely be better than this.'

But his face closed over with the obstinacy of the timid man. 'I'm sorry, Tommy,' he said flatly. 'I'm doing well enough for now. I still want to leave one day but . . . in the meantime perhaps you'd better not come again. We can write, and even a correspondence is a great deal more than I ever thought I'd have.'

I sighed. 'I fear I'll be stuck in Derbyshire till I finish school anyway. The earl was very kind in sending the carriage for me this time but he's made no mention of Easter and I can't expect he'll keep treating me every holiday I have. So the decision might be made for me.'

'Then we must make the most of our time together tonight,' said Manus. He topped up my port glass and asked after Walter. He was always very interested in his counterpart, my friend from the other mining family, one so different from his own.

Walter's news was twofold. At last he had a new mount, Windfall, a tall grey, for Walter's legs were sprouting like onions. Finally he had a mount who could jump the way Walter had always dreamed. The other news was that Mr Farthing would be leaving, to be replaced with a new tutor. Actually, this was bigger news for me than for him. For Walter, a tutor was no more than a necessary evil. I, on the other hand, already felt sad at the thought of Silvermoor without the gruff tutor who had done so much for me.

'He's moving to Liverpool to be close to his ailing mother,' I told Manus. 'So, come the spring, there'll be a new fellow to teach Walter. I hope they find someone sympathetic because he has the loveliest nature imaginable but he's no natural scholar. He has to be carefully coaxed into learning anything that doesn't pertain to horses.'

'I think I'd like him very well,' said Manus.

'It's a shame *you* couldn't be his tutor. You'd be able to bribe him to learn with promises of sharing your horsey secrets.'

He laughed, and we talked of my family and friends until a shift in the sky told us that I'd stayed far too long.

'I must go,' I gasped, scrambling to my feet. 'Da will be up for work at this rate. Lord knows what he'll think if he finds me gone.'

Manus took me back to the gate in a trice. 'This might be goodbye for a long time then,' he said sadly. 'Thank you again, Tommy, for all you've done for me.'

'But promise me you haven't given up,' I pleaded. 'Promise you'll keep looking for a way out. You deserve better than this, Manus, greater happiness. And it's not goodbye forever. I might be away for a few months, but surely you'll be away from here by next summer and we can meet . . . *somewhere*?'

'I'm certain of it,' he said, in that bland, sideways way that people talk when they tell you what you want to hear but have no confidence in the truth of it.

As I hurried home, I had an awful sinking feeling that he might *never* strike out for a better life. He believed himself safe at Heston, and perhaps he was. But if ever there was an illustration that safety was not enough for a life well lived, Manus Barridge was it. But what help could I offer? I had done the impossible; I was firmly on the path to my own dreams. But in terms of my power and influence in the world, nothing had changed at all.

The time flew by. All too soon I was saying the rest of my goodbyes: to Dulcie, who had spent Christmas with family in Leeds, but visited me and Josie in Grindley when she returned; to my family, to Walter and the earl and the Honeycrofts. It was a strange collection of acquaintances that I had in South Yorkshire. But they were dear to me, every one.

Josie saw me to the Sedgewicks's carriage and, when I was seated inside, she wrung my hands through the window. We gazed at each other intently, knowing these last looks would likely have to sustain us a long time. I had the feeling that although we had just spent two weeks talking without pause, there was more she wanted to say to me.

Although the earl was ever courteous, he still hadn't made any mention of another visit and I certainly couldn't ask. I was sure he had more pressing things to consider than what I might be doing in three months' time; there were rumours of a strike brewing, something which hadn't happened in a Sedgewick mine for more than fifty years. Since, with every low blow the Barridges dealt their men, the Sedgewicks looked better and better as masters by comparison, I was sure it wouldn't happen.

The carriage jolted into motion. Josie's hands slipped from mine and I was on my way. Through the windows I watched the winding lanes and gentle hills and brutal pitheads of South Yorkshire dissolve in a shroud of rain.

# Chapter 52

*Josie*

*Spring 1904*

Spring was very slow in coming round that year. Life in York was good, on the whole. Yet something weighed on me. It wasn't even the question of my paternity, though my thoughts did still twist anxiously about the matter. Gravenagh House offered me a life as happy as ever and Coralie continued to be the best employer a girl could dream of. The rhythm of back and forth between York and Silvermoor still satisfied. What then was the reason for my creeping dissatisfaction, I wondered, as February slugged by, bringing with it my eighteenth birthday?

Long reflections in the drear-blue evenings revealed that I was frustrated not by my own lot, but by everyone else's. Oddly, it was a little lonely being the only one happy. I wanted the people I loved to be happy too. But everyone else was stuck.

Tommy, of course, was still at school and would be for more than a year. There was nothing unexpected in this and yet, as my birthday came and went, I grew gloomier by the day. He was far away, still preoccupied with circumstances which meant he was unable to think of love. And why *should* he think of love? He still had so much to do in his life. And when he *was* ready for all that, would he even think of me? I had been under his nose for so long now. I knew he cared for me deeply but our total of kisses still amounted to just two and surely, if he felt anything *close* to the way I did, he wouldn't be able to help himself.

I knew I'd improved a lot in terms of looks, but I didn't flatter myself that I was the most beautiful girl in Yorkshire or anything of that colour. And Tommy was handsome, no doubt about that. I wasn't being partial. He'd always been lovely, if slightly funny looking, but he'd grown into himself now. He would be nineteen this year. He was no longer a dreamer, he was moving forward in reality. This gave him an air of purpose and progress, imbued him with a light and a determination that made him really very . . . well, *I* thought he was very appealing and I could see that the maids at Silvermoor thought so too. Tommy, of course, was oblivious. I wasn't sure whether to be glad of it or to scream. He was always so wrapped up in his own world, his own goals. Of course, I wouldn't want him to be like the earl, accidentally captivated by every pretty girl who passed. But oh, if he could allow himself to enjoy just a *little* bit of love and desire, and if he could aim it at me . . .

My only comfort was that he had seemed a little jealous of Norman. Which was ridiculous – who could fancy Norman? Besides Sally, of course, and a good thing too; everyone has their someone. But Tommy was *my* someone and he'd have to be stupid not to know it. And we all knew he *wasn't* stupid, so where did that leave me? When Tommy finished school and went to work, would I even figure in his new life, except as erstwhile correspondent?

Dulcie hadn't found a buyer for the emporium and so she languished in Arden through the grey season; the only point of excitement in her life seemed to be in running messages for Manus and Tommy. And Manus was just as bad. Still declaring his torment and loneliness, according to Tommy, yet going nowhere. Perhaps most painful of all, Martha was still in Arden too. Still engaged to Luke. They'd a date set for this Easter.

*I hope you'll come*, she'd written. *I know it will be difficult for you to come home. I know that something happened between you and Ma. But I can't get married without you and you would see Dulcie, so perhaps it would not be so very bad for you . . .*

I'd folded the letter grimly and didn't know how to reply. Seeing Ma would be the least of my worries compared with watching Martha bind herself to such a life. She hadn't written to me of cruelty from Luke or doubts in her heart. In fact, she

337

hadn't written of her heart at all. Although life in Arden was not sentimental, Martha was tender and loving, and I *worried* . . . Eventually I put pen to paper promising I would be there, for what else could I do?

March eventually drove February out. Daffodils started blooming in the gardens and along the city walls. Rain and sunshine spat at each other like squalling cats and I never knew what hat to wear when I went out. My new straw hat was a spring dream, with little yellow and white flowers piled along the brim, but it wasn't resilient to the weather so I more often, reluctantly, wore my sensible winter one still.

Then at last something did happen. Something so unexpected that I didn't know how to write of it to Tommy. I was walking home one gusty afternoon when I saw Norman hurrying along the Mount towards me.

'Josie! Hello!' he cried, looking all feverish and excited.

'Hello, Norman. Is everything all right? Has something happened to Cedric?' It was the only explanation I could think of for his uncharacteristic demeanour.

'Cedric? Oh no, he's fine, everything's fine. Only . . . I must speak with you. Will you take a turn about the racecourse with me? I've brought an umbrella in case of rain as you've only your pretty straw hat . . . Here, I'll carry your bags . . .'

Sure enough, he grabbed the bag of books and the bag of fine lilac lawn I'd purchased on behalf of Coralie and thrust a battered umbrella into my hands in their stead.

'I'm happy to have a walk with you, Norman, but perhaps I should take these in first. Coralie's expecting me.'

'Not for half an hour,' he said and I checked my watch. He was right. When had he come to know my daily timetable so well? When had he started taking note of my choice of headwear?

We fell into step and made for the Knavesmire. It was a pretty day and Norman was my friend. It was a lovely place to walk. Yet I knew something was wrong and I soon learned what it was.

'Josie, I'm sorry if this is sudden, but perhaps you've guessed after all. It's long overdue for me . . . Will you marry me?' asked Norman, as soon as we were away from other walkers. 'Oh!' he added, falling to one knee beneath a sprightly, budding chestnut tree.

I thought he was joking. I stood there and stared at him and suddenly I understood. He wasn't joking. Tommy had been right. He loved me, I could see that. Norman wasn't the sort of man to fling proposals about for fun. He wasn't the sort to break an engagement for a fresher fancy. He was in torment, and I felt awful for it. Poor Norman. And now his knee was covered in mud.

'What about Sally?' I asked faintly, while my head readjusted itself. Then I kicked myself. That wasn't the salient point here, in terms of my response, anyway.

'Oh, I know,' he said eagerly. 'I feel awful about her, awful.

A part of me will always love her. Not in the way I love *you*, Josie, you must never think that, but as a part of my youth, like a sister . . . But you, you're my future, Josie, or at least, I wish you to be. I hope you are. Please say you are . . .'

'But, but . . . what would she say?' I whispered. 'Think how upset she'd be.' Again, I was annoyed with myself. I didn't want him to think that Sally were my only objection but I couldn't quite marshal myself to dash his heart there in the mud without a moment's warning.

'She was heartbroken,' he admitted, hanging his head. 'It was very hard indeed. She cried and I felt that bad . . . but she's a reasonable lass. She could see there was nowt to be done.'

'You've *told* her already? *What* have you told her exactly?'

'Well, only how I feel about you, of course, and that I was going to ask you. I assumed nothing, Josie, how could I? Only I have *hoped* . . .' His left knee had also sunk into the mud now, as if the weight of all this hope was too much for one knee to bear.

'Oh Norman, get up!' I came back to myself and tugged at his elbow. There would come a time later on when it would all sink in and I would realise that I had hurt a dear friend. Perhaps I would even regret my answer; Norman would make a wonderful husband and it wasn't as if anyone else was asking me. But for now I had to push all that aside because my instinctive response was clear and true. 'You're getting filthy. Stand up.' I started walking and he followed. 'Dear Norman, I'm so very sorry but I can't marry you.' There, it was out. 'I'm flattered – astonished! I hold you in such high regard. But I can't . . . I don't feel that way about you. I think you're a very good man, but you're not *my* very good man.'

Oh, the look on his face. I stopped talking. Piling on words wasn't going to remove the sting. It was awful to take away someone's dreams like that.

'I'm sorry if I've done wrong by being your friend,' I added, my face burning. 'I never meant to give you false hope. I was happy with the way things were and I never stopped to think . . . I should have.'

'No.' His voice was hoarse and he took my hand. 'You've done nowt wrong. I knew when I asked you I had no guarantee. I knew it but I had to ask anyway. You're a woman that would light up my days if you stood at my side. But you don't feel the same and that's enough. I'll not push you. Will you forgive me for asking a painful question?'

'Of course,' I whispered.

He took my hand and tucked it into his arm and we walked around the Knavesmire, one long, slow funereal loop in silence. I dared not ask him what he was thinking or what would become of us now. Soon we would return to the house, where he would see to his duties and be the Norman he was before, but with everything changed. He had broken his engagement with Sally because of his feelings for me. I groaned silently on the inside. I wondered if that would ever mend. But how could she take him back now? And he was probably too decent to ask.

'Thank you, Josie,' he said when we returned to Gravenagh House. He took back his umbrella and handed me my shopping and went down to the boot room. I stood in the hall a long moment and felt sick. Then I went into the drawing room where Coralie was standing at the window.

'Here's the lawn for your Easter dress, Miss Coralie,' I said in a small voice, 'and the books you wanted from Coulson's.'

She turned. 'I suppose Norman has asked you to marry him?' I nodded, face flooded with fire. Had everyone seen this coming but me?

'And you refused him.' I nodded again, eyes tingling. She looked at me sympathetically. 'Poor Josie. Hard, is it not? Poor Norman too, of course. Well, it was inevitable.'

'Was it, miss? *Was* it? Only I never saw it coming! I had no idea he had those . . . thoughts. Oh, I wish I'd realised in time to stop him . . . I wish he'd never . . .'

'But he did, dear, and we must deal with what's before us, not what we wish. You've done nothing wrong, only it may take you a while to realise it.'

That night I sat down to answer Tommy's latest letter but I didn't have the heart to tell him what had happened, nor to write a letter of evasion and half-stories. He would have to wait until I knew how to tell it properly. In bed, I tossed and turned and had one of the worst nights' sleep I could remember.

I dreamed I was on board a great sailing ship, an old-fashioned galleon, and Tommy was tied to the mast. We were going down, the ship listed in the giant navy waves, and water gushed onto the deck from countless holes. Norman was there, scooping away with a tin mug, determination written all over his face.

'Don't worry, Josie,' he kept saying. 'I'll keep us safe.'

I turned my back on him and tried to reach Tommy but the boat was tilted at such an angle that I couldn't climb the incline. Even when I stretched my arms out I couldn't reach him, even when the galleon started breaking up with a great crack, crack, cracking . . .

And then I was awake. I sat up, gasping, clutching at my sheets and piecing reality together one fact at a time. The ship had been a dream, of course. But the noise went on. *Bang, bang, bang.* That was real. There was someone at the door!

I leaped from bed and lit my lamp with trembling hands. The small clock on my mantel showed four in the morning. What an hour! The household would stir at six but for now it was still night. I pulled on a robe and went onto the landing. I saw Coralie and Cedric burst from their rooms, and their father, on the floor below, wrapped in a plum and red paisley dressing gown. He looked up and saw our anxious faces lined above.

'I'll see to it,' he said.

Norman appeared from some lower part of the house. Had

he spent all night in the boot room? 'I'll see to it,' said Mr Honeycroft again. 'It's all right, Norman.' Norman glanced up, saw me and vanished.

Mr Honeycroft unbolted the door and gave a cry of surprise. 'Gracious heavens! Who are you?'

The younger Honeycrofts and I leaned over the bannister like a theatre audience in the gods. We saw a young woman with dark, bedraggled hair, drenched in the rains of a wild March night.

'Please, sir,' she sobbed. 'I'm so very sorry to disturb. And it's such an hour, I know. But please might I see my sister, Josie?'

# Chapter 53

## Josie

I ran down those stairs as though I were a creature of air, born on the wind to my sister's side. Mr Honeycroft had drawn her in, closed the door. She stood shivering in a puddle of her own making. Before I even hugged her I inspected her, holding her away from me and looking her up and down for damage, but I saw none.

'Are you well, Martha? Is anything hurt?' I asked to be sure.

'Nay, leastways, no cuts or bruises, you needn't be afraid to hug me. Though I am very wet . . .'

'Never mind wet!' I exclaimed and threw my arms around her. 'Oh, I'm so glad to see you, Martha. Whatever's the matter, you did right to come to me.'

I felt gentle hands detaching me from my sister. 'Josie dear, let Martha be dried and changed,' Coralie murmured. 'She mustn't catch cold.'

'Of course!' I watched Martha turn several shades paler as

she saw Coralie, unmistakeable with her riotous red hair in a curly, escaping braid and a fine satin robe. Martha had never seen a lady before. She curtseyed, looking as if her legs were giving way beneath her. My unassuming, humble sister would never have burst into a stranger's home in such a way if she had a choice. She looked mortified.

'Don't worry, Martha,' I said. 'This is Miss Coralie, who I've told you so much about. She's as kind as can be, so don't feel embarrassed.' But Martha seemed to have lost her tongue.

'Take Martha to your room and dry her off, Josie,' said Coralie. 'You know where the towels are. Then bring her down to the sitting room to get warm. I'll have Norman set a fire and Mrs Crane can bring you something to eat and drink. Take as long as you want to talk, don't worry about your duties this morning. And of course, you're welcome to stay here as long as you need to, my dear,' she added to Martha. 'Don't worry about a thing on our account.'

'Come on.' I led my drooping river nymph of a sister to the foot of the stairs, where she paused and looked up in wonder. Compared with Silvermoor it wasn't a big house, only three storeys rising above us. But compared with our little pit worker's cottage in Arden it was a palace.

I took Martha's hand and pulled her after me up to my little attic room. It was cold now that the adventure had subsided, and I was damp from hugging her. I unbuttoned her familiar brown coat and flung towels and some spare garments of mine at her; I wanted to get her warming by the fire as fast as I could. While she dried herself and rubbed at her hair, I dressed in my usual grey and white work dress. I wanted to be ready to start work as soon as I'd got to the bottom of things with Martha.

Moments later we were seated before the fire in the sitting room, with great tankards of hot, spiced apple juice and bowls of porridge with honey. Martha was dry, apart from her hair, and that was on its way. She was dressed in a warm navy dress of mine and I'd wrapped a shawl around her shoulders for good measure.

When she'd eaten and drunk she looked at me with such relief on her face. 'I made it,' she marvelled, 'I'm here! Oh Josie, I felt that terrible, barging in on the family, looking such a fright. I could die from having them think I've such manners. If it had been any better a night, I would've waited outside till a more respectable hour, but I was so cold I was frightened to stay out any longer.'

'And wouldn't I have scolded you if you had. You did right, Martha, and now that your wits are returning, you'll see what sort of people the Honeycrofts are. They won't think ill of you.'

'No, I can see that,' she said thoughtfully. 'Aren't they good to give us this time alone together? Even so, I can't stay here forever and I can't go home . . . Oh Josie, whatever shall I do?'

I snorted. 'Why don't you tell me what's happened before

you worry about what next?' I suggested. 'Quick, for I'm imagining all sorts of horrors.'

'Well, I had to leave,' she said. 'I told Luke I wouldn't marry him. He was that furious, Josie. Said I'd made him a laughing stock. Said I was a hussy who didn't know my own mind and he'd make my life a misery in any way he could . . .'

'In other words, he showed himself for the gent he truly is,' I carped. 'Well, I'm not surprised, Martha, but *why* did you change your mind? Your last letter was all wedding plans – much to my dismay. I thought it was what you wanted.'

'I did at first! Oh, I did. I thought he was handsome and dashing and the most interesting fellow I was likely to get. He was sweet at first too – brought me flowers when we started walking out, said I was pretty, that sort of thing. I thought it would be all right. And I never thought I'd leave Arden, never imagined I could. But we'd only been together a year when he started acting like I was such a nuisance. Told his friends I was a nag and I kept following him around. Rolled his eyes over every little thing I said. He made me feel so stupid, Josie, and boring and . . . like I was nothing. I didn't want to feel like that. I thought he didn't want to marry me any more, but he said he did! But why would he, when it was plain he found me so irritating?'

'Because you're a good girl, Martha, and he wasn't going to get what he wanted if he didn't marry you. And you *are* pretty, very pretty, so you were a catch. He wasn't thinking about happiness, yours *or* his, just gratification and proving himself in the village.'

Martha frowned and pulled the blanket close about her. 'I suppose there's nowt so queer as folk. Anyway, all hell broke loose when the word got out that I'd let him down. That's how everyone saw it anyway. You know what they're like. Luke's mother came and stood on our doorstep and gave me a right dressing-down at the top of her voice. Said I wasn't good enough for her son and what gave me the right to turn down the best offer I'd ever get? She said I was getting as jumped up as my sister and maybe you'd given me airs . . .' She paused, looking concerned, as if I'd care in the slightest what Millie Stevens thought of me.

'Oh, it were awful, Josie. The neighbours hanging out the windows and lining up in the street to listen. All I could say was I was sorry but I didn't love him and I wouldn't make him happy. But you know how it is in Arden – love and happiness don't seem to matter very much. I just kept saying it over and over again . . .'

'And where were our dear parents through all this?' I asked wryly.

'Da just sat by the fire, saying nothing. You know what he's like. And Ma stood off to the side of me, out of sight, with her arms folded across her chest. In the end she came over to the door and stood next to me. 'That's enough now, Mrs Stevens,' she said. 'You've had your say. I don't say as you're wrong but

that's enough. I'll make her see sense.' Mrs Stevens said Luke
wouldn't have me back now, not even if I came crawling back
on me hands and knees, and Ma shut the door in her face.

'Then Ma turned on me, Josie. Oh, she were that angry.
It was the first time she'd ever hit me. She said she were that
disappointed in me . . .'

'So when was all this then?' I asked.

It had been the day before yesterday. Martha had told Luke
when he came off his shift, his mother had sailed into attack
that evening and Ma continued the good work through most
of the night. The next morning Martha had gone to work as
usual and no one would talk to her.

Every village liked to have an opinion over something like
this, Arden more than most. Luke was from an old Arden
family, good-looking, if you liked that sort of thing, and
didn't have an idea in his entire brain that didn't come from
his forefathers – in other words he had good, steady values. By
turning down the chance to join herself to him for life, Martha
had hinted that she wanted something more for herself, and
thrown everyone's choices back in their faces. Several of the
young women who worked with her at the surface fancied
Luke themselves and had envied her the engagement. Now
here she was saying she was too good for him.

The whole village came out on Luke's side; he was the jilted
party, he was the good, staunch lad, Martha the callous heart-
breaker who'd been infected by her subversive sister. Who else

would have her now that she'd shown herself to be fickle and unreliable? She'd stay at home with Ma forever. And Ma was of the same mind as everyone else, which she made perfectly clear from the minute Martha got home that day. 'I'm ashamed of you; you're a disgrace; you think you're special, you do . . .' all the old favourites. Exhausted from her day, Martha had been able to do nothing but sit at the table and cry.

An hour or two later there came another knock at the door, another Stevens. Only this time it was Luke, not his mother, and it turned out she'd been wrong: he *would* take Martha back.

'I'll only say it once,' he said, 'but I expect you've had time to think upon it and I expect you've realised tha's made a mistake. I'll take you back, Martha, for I said I'd have you for my wife, and so I will. But I'll soon knock the nonsense out of thee when we're wed.'

Despite this heart-rending declaration of romance, Martha said no all over again and Ma shrieked with fury. 'Get out! Get out of my house, you ungrateful beast!' she yelled. 'Go on, I've not raised thee for this. Oh, I've been cursed with my daughters. Tansy dead, Josie wrong from the minute she was born and now you! Get out!'

Martha said Ma was hysterical at this point; she had no choice but to grab her coat and go. Luke stormed off into the night. Of course, she went straight to the Emporium, thinking to stay the night with Dulcie, then borrow some money to come to me in York the next day. But Dulcie wasn't there and though Martha waited two hours she didn't come home.

'Where was she?' I asked, curious.

Martha shrugged. 'I've no idea. Anyway, I waited and waited and the wind was howling and the rain was spitting and I thought I'd catch me death of cold so then I went to the church. I thought of our Bert but I knew Frannie wouldn't like it. All she cares about is keeping in with the village, and now she's expecting again she's that moody.

'What about our Alice?' I teased and Martha snorted. Alice had only grown more vain and unsympathetic with the years.

'Preacher took me in, of course, but only to lecture me about how women should be guided by their parents and menfolk and not look outside the appointed order of things . . .

'Then he started on about how disappointed in me he was and how he'd always thought I was such a modest, humble, sensible girl . . . And I found that the way *he* said it, modest and humble and sensible weren't things I wanted to be. I mean, they *are* . . . but not if they mean doing what others tell me to do for the rest of my life!'

I grinned and clapped my hands quietly. At last.

Preacher left the room to give Martha time to reflect. The clock struck nine and she realised that if she ran, she might catch the last carriage heading north. There were some coins on the desk and she scribbled a hasty promissory note, snatched them and ran. The carriage took her as far as Askham where one of the horses threw a shoe and then she walked, all the way to York, through that awful howling night.

I felt a great weight lift from my shoulders to have her there with me, her long dark hair growing fluffy in the fire's warmth, the colour returning to her face. I wasn't worried that she'd change her mind and go back. She was quiet and certain in herself, and besides, she couldn't. She'd burned her bridges in Arden more surely than I ever had. I'd merely run away from a future in the mines. Whereas good, sweet, sensible Martha had not only broken Luke's heart but stolen from the minister. I'd never felt prouder.

# Chapter 54

## Tommy

*Spring 1904*

As winter grudgingly yielded to spring it looked increasingly unlikely that I would get home over Easter. There was no suggestion of it from anyone with the means to make it happen and I wouldn't ask for a favour. To go home would be a treat, not a necessity, and I didn't feel entitled to treats. It was still hard for me to believe that I was here at all.

Yet in March I received a letter from Josie that made me feel that going home was entirely necessary after all. That damned Norman had proposed! To Josie! The blood boiled inside me as surely as if I'd been placed in a pot above a kitchen range. That sneaking, oily manservant! *My* Josie! Of course, she *wasn't* mine, in any official way. I had no claim on her for I had made no proposal. But how could I, penniless and suspended in schooling as I was? I hadn't even made my feelings clear, and that was because I was afraid.

As I clutched the offending page, a million thoughts bubbled through me and I understood as never before how the thought and the hope of Josie shaped my days. Her friendship was unspeakably dear to me, as much a part of my own self as my arms and legs, or my love of learning. Yet I couldn't deny it had grown into something more, young as we were and as unfinished as I was. Life without her friendship was unimaginable, yet it was equally impossible to be near her without these newer feelings rising out of me and swirling all around us. If they should be distasteful to her, if she didn't return them, my life would be a drab thing, robbed of colour and light. It would be as if a film of coal dust had settled over everything once again.

Josie had been established in a good position for some time now. She was earning a respectable wage where I was still a schoolboy. She was younger than me yet she was surging ahead in this game of life. It was entirely reasonable that Norman should have asked her to marry him (his poor fiancée aside, of course). It was entirely likely that others would do the same. And what if she said yes to one of them before I was out of here and able to take my place at her side? A horrific thought: *what if she already has?* I hadn't got past the astonishing news to reach the end of her letter; I'd assumed her response rather than actually read of it. Hastily I shook out the paper and resumed.

*Of course, I refused*, she had written. *I have no feelings of that sort for Norman, nor ever could. Poor Norman left Gravenagh House within the week. He said he couldn't bear to be near me knowing I would never feel the same, and he is too kind a man to hope I would give up my place. So he is gone and I feel sad for the change in our happy little household. I did not wish to hurt him but how could I have helped it? I miss his friendship, but friendship alone cannot stand for love. Friendship is an important part of love but love is ever so much bigger. You see, Tommy, I am a woman now and spend some time pondering these matters.*

I breathed a huge sigh of relief. *Of course I refused.* Of course. And Norman was gone. He had bowed out, left her to her life. Perhaps *his* life was drab and dusty now. *Poor Norman.* I couldn't truthfully claim that my sympathy outweighed my relief. I'd had a narrow escape.

Yet over the days that followed I found myself poring over the rest of the paragraph. *Friendship alone cannot stand for love . . . Love is ever so much bigger . . . You see, Tommy, I am a woman now and spend some time pondering these matters.*

Was she trying to tell me something? If so, what? My worst fear was that she was warning me, telling me not to hope, that we were friends, yes, but that friendship wasn't enough. Or . . . faint hope . . . was it because of me that her thoughts made such comparisons? Norman had been just a friend. Dare I hope that *I* could be that something bigger?

I knew I must ask her but the prospect was more terrifying

than a week in the mines without a light. I must conquer this unmanly desire to hide in faint hope and unexpressed longing. I must know one way or the other. If she did harbour hopes too, she deserved to know that I felt the same. If she didn't, then surely it was better that I know now, before these feelings took hold more than they already had? So I told myself, though I knew they were so deeply rooted that their ends curled firmly around the glowing bedrock of the earth's core. There was no going back from this, for me.

I thought about writing a letter. This course had much to recommend it. I could do it at once. I could pour out everything I wanted to say, and perfect it, guard against any bumbling or blundering. I could strip my entire soul bare without having to watch her face fall, and learn, as Norman had done, that we were no more than friends. And it would be a gentlemanly approach; she would have time to compose her reply, without having to deal with my pitiful hopes laid before her.

Yet I could not write. It would not serve. It was a pale, distant solution and my love had nothing of pallor or distance to it. I must be beside her. I must be able to watch her face, confront the moment when I would have all to lose or to gain. And – faint hope – if her answer was *yes*, then *how* I wanted to hear it in person. How I wanted to take her in my arms, see her face light up, watch as I gave her the happiness that she would give me if our feelings were matched. I must wait. I must be patient. And I must pray that she would not give her heart to

357

someone else in the meantime, which was such a horror of a thought that I nearly wrote the letter after all.

My hopes of getting home at Easter were embers. Even if I found a way to go in the summer, that was yet three months away. If I were stuck at Westonbury for every holiday until I completed my scholarship, I would not see Josie for fifteen months or more. Unendurable. It seemed impossible that someone so lovely, so rare, could fail to be snapped up during the span of so long a period. Though, of course, it was Josie's heart that would ultimately dictate the matter. If she did love me, she would turn down a hundred suitors. I knew it because if the goddess Diana herself threw herself before me and laid the moon at my feet, I would still choose Josie.

# Chapter 55

───◦⌒◦───

# Tommy

I was quite right: I didn't get home that Easter. They were two long, solitary weeks indeed, alone at Westonbury with no classes and no company. I was privileged to be at school, to have access to a magnificent library, to have time and solitude to work on my lifelong goals. But I was only human and I longed to see an interested face before me, to share a sudden laugh, to trade dreams and ideas. Cicero, Descartes and Herodotus, though stimulating, were quiet company, confined as they were to the page. What really comforted me were the letters that came from Yorkshire. They were my connection with my heart's desires, living reminders of all the reasons why I was here.

Josie's news continued interesting. No more proposals, thank goodness, but her sister Martha had arrived in York one dark and stormy night. It was good to hear how happy Josie was to have her there. I was pleased myself; I liked to think of Josie having someone she loved nearby and I had always thought Martha too good and lovely for Arden. She stayed with the Honeycrofts for two weeks, during which Miss Coralie asked around and made a solution appear from thin air as was her wont. Now Martha had a position as undercook in the home of a grand old lady.

*She lives not ten minutes from Gravenagh House*, Josie wrote exultingly. *She says compared with living in Ma's house, the work is a bed of roses. While she was here Mrs Crane showed her how to make a few more refined treats than we were used to in Arden but other than that she was amply qualified! So that's something to thank Ma for!*

And at long last, there seemed to be a shift for Manus too. Like a nervous horse gathering itself to jump a fence, he was finally preparing to leave Heston. He and Miss Embry had begun a little correspondence of their own. She too encouraged him to break out of his odd, ghostly prison and to build a new life for himself on whatever terms seemed fit to him. Whether a woman's entreaties could do what I could not or whether it was simply that the timing was right and Manus was ready, he began enclosing money with his letters to her. His escape fund, he called it.

*Miss Embry will store it for me*, he explained in one letter. *I don't have much, but think how terrible it would be if I needed to leave of a sudden and did not have it with me — for I have no way of knowing when or how the opportunity will present itself.*

His next letter told of another, more startling scheme. *All the money that I have is now in the possession of good Miss Embry,* he wrote. *It is not very much to start a new life, as she has pointed out to me. I will not steal, though I know some might say I am owed all that Heston can yield to me and more. However, I remembered what you told me of the villagers' custom of sinking their money in possessions . . .*

It was true: at Christmas I had told him, for what reason I can't remember, about a way in which mining folk purchased themselves a little security in a dangerous world. Poor though we were, if a family had several sons, several wages coming in, they might manage to put a little aside and eventually buy something for the home: a mantel clock, a musical instrument, some brass candlesticks. We didn't trust the banks. Banks were run by gentlemen and frequented by gentlemen. We preferred to keep what we'd earned where we could see and touch it. Then, if a man reached retirement, and was asked to leave his cottage, he could take these possessions and sell them. It was our version of a pension. And it seemed we had inspired Manus.

*There are several of these, at least, to which I can legitimately and morally lay claim: a pocket watch, a valuable antique snuff box, some onyx cufflinks . . . It has pleased me to collect them up, two or three at a time, and stow them in the bushes directly across the lane from the gate. Thence Miss Embry can extract them and keep them, too, for me to sell when I am finally free of this place. My fund is building . . .*

361

This news filled me with horror. I regretted most acutely ever having asked Miss Embry to become involved in our intrigue, if it meant her rooting around in the undergrowth, carrying aristocratic goods about the countryside in her skirt pocket. Imagine if Paulson should come across her pocketing a gold watch! He would have her before the magistrate in seconds and how would she ever defend herself? By explaining they'd been willingly entrusted to her by a dead man? It was ludicrous.

I wrote to them both at once to point out the dangers and tell them it must stop. Miss Embry replied courteously that she was a grown woman, well able to calculate the risks. It seemed she had taken up Manus's plight as her own personal cause. Manus, thankfully, saw sense:

*I would never put Miss Embry at risk, not for all the horses in the Spanish school. I see now that we both became carried away with our scheming and lost sight of the dangers. Not so much as a gold tiepin shall I leave in future, rest assured, Tommy.*

Relieved, I went back to Cicero, and a mug of cocoa. With such startling missives as these, the days passed more bearably than I had anticipated at first.

The lonely holiday had its benefits. I'd made good use of the time to read around all my subjects and start building a wider network of knowledge. Because of this, I was finally able to do as the other boys did, referencing and cross-referencing my comments and questions. I earned praise from the masters and even a little admiration from some of the boys. Most importantly, I started to see each piece of knowledge as part of a larger whole and learning took on a new glow of excitement.

When it was time for the end-of-year exams, I came top of my class, jointly with another boy. We were each awarded a leather-bound volume of Shakespeare's plays, inscribed by the headmaster. I set it next to my Kipling, beside my bed. At last I was getting somewhere. At last, something to tell my father.

Even so, when term ended and summer stretched ahead, *two and a half months of it*, I couldn't help sighing. I had hoped I might work in the school gardens for a few hours here and there throughout the summer term, and earn a little money to pay for a carriage to Silvermoor in June. But this idea was quickly dashed. The housemaster, Mr Talbot, told me that scholarship boys weren't allowed to work during their time at Westonbury. The standards were rigorous and no distraction could be allowed.

And so I found myself as penniless as ever and faced with another lonely vigil at the altar of learning. I never stopped feeling grateful that I had all these channels for learning at my fingertips; I just wished for a little company. And, of course, there was Josie . . . Sometimes I would begin a letter telling her how I felt but no words I could summon were adequate to make such a declaration on paper. My love was too visceral, too real.

I began working my way through the school library, following a self-determined course of study, and for my leisure I read still more, this time for interest, of European capitals and Middle Eastern temples, of the ancient sites of Greece and the cherry blossoms and Buddhist deities of Japan. I devoured *The Jungle Book* for the second time and once again India coiled its way into my mind like a vine, like a cobra, like the Brahmaputra River. I took three walks around the grounds every day to keep body and mind healthy. I chatted to the servants when they would tolerate me and took tea with Mr Talbot once a week in his study for some variation. A month passed. I realised I was counting days.

Then one day, returning from a walk, I saw a familiar carriage in the drive and I wondered if my isolation was giving rise to strange visions. It was the small, navy-blue second carriage of the Sedgewicks, with Matthias raising a hand to me from the seat. Was something wrong? I broke into a run but was reassured the instant Matthias opened the door and Lord Walter came barrelling out. The huge grin on his face told me this was not a sorry errand.

'What on earth?' I marvelled. 'Am I seeing things? This is an awful long way for you to come for a visit!'

'Indeed it would be, Tommy old chum,' he cried, holding out his hand in an attempt at a manly greeting, then giving it up and throwing his arms around me. I responded with a bear hug that set us staggering and laughing like brothers. 'But we're not visiting! We're taking you home!'

I released him. 'Really? How?' I turned to Matthias and shook hands.

'It's quite right,' Matthias assured me. 'His lordship sent me for you and his young lordship insisted on coming along. We're to take you home this very day. I hope that suits,' he added.

'It suits!' I laughed. 'I have no prior engagements. I can be ready in ten minutes. But perhaps you'd like rest and refreshment before we set off again?'

'I would,' Matthias agreed, while Walter jumped up and down.

'Can I see your room while Matthias rests?' he asked. '*I* don't need to rest. I'm too excited.'

'Aye, so am I!' I towed them to the kitchen where the cook was persuaded to let Matthias sit a while and drink tea and eat boiled eggs and fruit cake. The cake persuaded Walter to sit with him while I went to find the housemaster and clear my absence with him.

Talbot readily agreed. 'I approve,' he said. 'Paid employment, no. A holiday, yes. Make the most of it, Green, you've been working hard.'

Walter chattered incessantly while I packed. 'You sleep with *seven* other boys?' he asked in horror. 'All the beds in one room? However do you put up with it? I'm *so* glad I'm being schooled at home. I never thought I'd say it but Papa does have good ideas about some things . . .'

'At home, my lord, I used to sleep in one *bed* with all my

brothers. It didn't make for the most comfortable night's sleep but it was all the space we had. This is an improvement in that respect.'

He shuddered.

'Where am I to stay while I'm home? Do you know?' I asked. I didn't expect hospitality at Silvermoor, yet I hoped my visit might be a long one and didn't entirely relish sleeping with my brothers *or* in the fold-up bed for several weeks.

'Mrs Murphy's tenant has moved on,' Walter explained delightedly, 'and my father has paid her to let you use the room for the next six weeks. You'll be back in your old place on the estate. Shall you like it, Tommy?'

'I'll like it right well and that's a fact.' It was true. It felt right — more comfortable than Grindley, more appropriate than staying in the grand house, but near enough that I could see Josie and Walter whenever they were around, and visit my family every day if I wished. 'And is everyone well, your lordship?'

'Oh golly, call me Walter. We've been through all this. I'm your friend, not your . . . your *master*! Yes, everyone's quite well. My sister Flora is practically engaged to a gentleman called Devon Ashcroft. He's no fun at all. My sister Elizabeth has *never* been fun, and that hasn't changed. But little Humphrey is growing up right. We've made up this wizard game with the molehills on the lawn . . . But I'm glad *you're* coming, Tommy. Won't we have a fine old time?'

It struck me that I would see Josie any day now – perhaps even tonight. I would have the chance to tell her everything I longed to, in person, at last. And suddenly I did not feel nearly man enough for the task. I sank onto the edge of my bed. Well, I needn't tell her right away. Six weeks, Walter had said. Perhaps we could have just a few days of enjoying our old ways before I did something that might rock the very foundations of all I knew.

'And how are you here, you and Matthias? Have I missed a letter or something?'

'Oh no, it was Josie's idea to keep it a surprise. She said you'd like it and we needn't worry that you wouldn't want to come back with us. It was the funniest thing, Tommy. One day Papa just said out of the blue, "Where the devil is Tommy Green these days? Westonbury must have broken up for summer by now. Why hasn't he been to see us?" Honestly, Tommy, Papa can be *so* naive.'

Walter's air of world-weary superiority almost made me gasp with laughter. He shook a finger and adopted an admonishing tone. 'I explained to him! I said, "Papa, what you must understand is that Tommy hasn't the *means* to come back. He's stuck in Derbyshire. He was stuck there all Easter too. Not everyone can come and go as they please, you know!"'

'Gracious, and what did your Papa say to that?'

'Well, he said it was remiss of him not to have thought of it and he would send Matthias as soon as a carriage could be spared. I asked if I might go along and he said yes. And *then* he said . . . Oh! I'd forgotten. I'm to give you this, Tommy.' He dug into a pocket and gave me five shillings in a small cloth pouch. 'It'll feel nicer to have a little something of your own, Tommy, won't it?'

'It most certainly will. I must thank you father kindly. He has done more for me than I deserve.'

Well, with money in my pocket and six weeks ahead of me in Yorkshire and a sudden end to my monastic existence, I felt as if a cloudburst of riches had emptied over my head. I was packed in minutes, as promised.

'Come on then, Walter,' I said, casting a last unsentimental glance around the room. Let's go home.'

# Chapter 56

## Josie

*Summer 1904*

I ran to the window at least twice a minute but the drive remained empty. I knew they wouldn't be here before tea time yet I couldn't stop myself checking. I couldn't bear to miss that first moment. I couldn't bear to miss a single second. Tommy was coming!

My life had transformed when Martha came to York. Though the old lady over in Fossgate kept her busy, we met most Sunday afternoons. It was pleasant, too, to know that there was the possibility of seeing her by chance when I was out and about. Best of all to know she was happy; she had taken to life in the city like a duck to water. In Martha I could confide the changing nature of my feelings for Tommy and this was an immense relief. Still, I missed him in a way that nothing could alleviate. He was part of me and he was just too far away. Often I found myself crying – not feeble, self-pitying tears but great, wrenching tears that seemed to come from a fathomless place. They were brought on not only by the absence of him but also from the mere fact of him, and how I felt about him.

When the Honeycrofts packed up for a month at Silvermoor, my customary glee at staying in the big house was dampened by Tommy being confined to school. I didn't think I'd see him all summer. I was starting to wonder if I'd see him all *year*. But now he was coming after all and there was no containing me.

Miss Coralie was reading a novel that had her captivated, so she sat quietly and turned the pages while I buzzed around her, knocking her pearl-handled letter opener off her bureau, tripping over a pair of shoes. From time to time she lifted her eyes from the page, watched me with raised eyebrows and said nothing.

All day I had been in a dither of excitement. Quite foolish I became, scorching Miss Coralie's blue striped poplin, dropping one of her crystal earrings and crawling under the bed to fetch it from where it bounced, that sort of nonsense. But then, it had been six months since I'd seen him.

'Hadn't you better go and have your supper?' Coralie asked when the bell rang for the servants' tea. I looked at her in mute despair. I'd never hear the carriage if I was away under the stairs. Her eyes danced. 'Or perhaps you'd like to take a sandwich or two with me in the drawing room.'

'Oh, *thank* you, miss,' I gasped. I could have sworn she winked.

# Chapter 57

## Tommy

Oh, how good it was to watch those miles towards home vanishing beneath the carriage wheels. And by home, of course, I meant Josie.

'So she's at Silvermoor now? She'll actually be there when we arrive?' I kept asking poor Walter, who answered me the same way each time.

'Yes, Tommy. Josie is at Silvermoor. Today and for the coming weeks. You'll see her this evening,' Walter repeated patiently. It was as though he were nineteen and I were the younger boy.

For most of the journey Walter chatted on about his lordly concerns. His new pony had started napping at fences. It had never happened before, he couldn't understand it. His father had received sixteen applications for the post of Walter's tutor but had refused to so much as interview any of them. Not that Walter minded being without a tutor but he was concerned

371

that his father was overlooking some jolly fellows in his quest for perfection. He didn't want to be sent to school because there was no tutor who could meet his father's standards. And *why* had he been in such trouble for putting a frog in Elizabeth's bed? She didn't have to be such a ninny as to run all over the house screaming. In the story the frog had turned into a prince!

I told him sisters were difficult creatures. With the exception of one, my youngest sister Connie, who had more sense than the rest of the family put together.

When we passed Grindley, I stared out of the window. It was a sort of grim fascination I felt. I had no sentiment for the place, yet it was where I had spent my formative years, and I felt it demanded some sort of respect for that. It had formed me. Like coal I had been pressed into Tommy — dreamer, scholar, oddball. A one-man revolution, as I'd told Josie once.

As we rattled past the pithead, I saw the cage open and a dozen weary men step out. I shuddered. We continued along the lane and passed the turning that afforded a glimpse of the long rows of dismal cottages; there I saw a familiar figure walking out of the village. My brother Jimmy. He looked up as we passed and I waved madly. Jimmy didn't wave back; for a minute I wondered if he'd seen me. Then he spun round and bolted back to the village as fast as could be.

I grinned. Straight back to the house to tell them all brother Tommy was heading for Silvermoor in a fancy carriage. Oh, there'd be a right kerfuffle. They'd all be wondering if I was too grand for them now, if I'd decided to come to Silvermoor and not let them know. I'd have to go down there this very night and set them straight.

But now we had reached the Silvermoor estate. We swung off the lane onto the wide driveway, where the avenue of oaks cast a dappled shade over the carriage. Soon we pulled up outside the front door. Walter scrambled over me to jump out first because the door on his side was sticking. The dogs came hurtling from the house, down the steps and across the gravel. And then Josie came running, just seconds behind them, almost as if she'd been looking out for us. Her black buttoned boots flashed as she held up her grey and white striped dress and flew into my arms.

'Oh Tommy!' she shrieked. 'There you are at last. I was starting to think I'd dreamed thee!'

I laughed like a fool, transported by the warmth of her reception. 'I'm real, Josie,' I said into her hair. 'Oh, it's that good to see you.' I let my arms wind their way right around her back. She was so narrow I could encompass her easily. But she wasn't skinny; I could feel the swell and softness of her chest against mine, and the edges of my hands sensed the curve of her hips just below them. I ached to move my hands downwards but I didn't. I did, however, have trouble letting her go. The embrace deepened and softened, from frantic and exultant to peaceful and eternal. I felt as if all my life, all the trials and adventures, had been to bring me to this point.

'Tommy!' yelled Walter. 'Let her go! Come on, I want to show you Windfall! And look, here's Father to see you. Oh, Cedric, hullo there! Coralie, I've had the most splendid time. I saw Tommy's dormitory. He has to share with *seven* other boys . . . !'

Walter insisted on dragging me out to the stables before I was allowed to talk to the others or take tea or anything, but I didn't mind; it was good to stretch my legs after the journey.

At last I was permitted to take tea in the drawing room and submit to the general enquiries of the family. As ever, Lady Amelia was nowhere to be seen but Lady Flora had decided to take an interest in her young brother's unusual friend and joined us. She was a beautiful young lady and cordial, but I didn't know her as well as I knew the others and I found her presence a little inhibiting. The younger children crept in but soon grew bored and crept out again. Cedric was with us only briefly. He was on his way out to a meeting in Grindley.

'It's good to have you back with us, Tommy,' Cedric said, shaking my hand as he left. 'Do you have particular plans for your weeks at Silvermoor?'

'No, sir. It's just such a grand surprise to be here at all. Just seeing everyone is all I care about.'

'I've no doubt you'll fill your time most enjoyably. However, I have a proposition for you. May we speak in private when you're settled in?'

I glanced at Josie but could see from her face that she had no idea what this was about. Curiosity was burning in her dark eyes; it was still her defining characteristic.

'I'd be delighted, sir. Whenever it suits you.'

The earl was in and out, wanting to sit and talk, then remembering another urgent message he had to send or another note to himself he must make. He seemed genuinely interested to talk to me and horribly distracted in equal measure. At last he sat and stayed a while. Only Coralie and Josie were left at that point. Josie sat quietly at Coralie's side, mending a bonnet, for form's sake, but really we all knew that she was the person I had really come to see and everything else was just a way of facilitating it.

'Now, Tommy,' said the earl, looking tired and a little pale, 'tell me about school and your plans. How has your first year been?'

So I recounted the initial struggle, the highs and lows of hope, the solitary Easter at Westonbury and my final triumph in the end-of-year exams. How glad I was to be able to report that the year had reached a happy conclusion.

'I'd like to thank you greatly, my lord,' I concluded. '*None* of it would have been possible without you. If you hadn't had me to stay here when I was injured, I would never have met Mr Farthing, nor had him to coach me, nor heard about the scholarship. You wrote me a recommendation, you provided my transport . . . You've opened up a whole world of opportunity for me, sir, and I'll never forget it. Thank you too for bringing me home this summer. And for the five shillings that Walt . . . his lordship passed on to me. You're more than kind to me.'

'You're entirely welcome. I haven't done much, really. Forgot all about you at Easter, truth to tell. Shocking of me. You've helped my boy as much as we've helped you and it's always inspiring to see a young man pit himself against circumstances and thirst to learn. Ah, Farthing,' he sighed. 'He was a good tutor. A crying shame he's had to leave us. I haven't found a replacement, you know.'

'His lordship did mention, sir. I'm sure you'll find someone. It's such a fine position.'

'I hope you're right. As if I hadn't enough on my mind.'

'You do seem preoccupied, sir, I hope nothing's too badly amiss.'

'It's the mines, Tommy,' said Coralie. 'There's trouble brewing, talk of strikes and goodness knows what. Uncle has his work cut out trying to salvage matters. I shouldn't be surprised if it has something to do with why Cedric wants to talk to you.'

'What's happened, sir? I've heard nothing.'

'Tysen's are destroying the new pits,' he said bitterly. 'Already! They treat their men like slaves. Barridge, of course, needs no encouragement to axe costs, cut corners, boost profit, by any means necessary. It's creating a culture that can only lead to revolution and riot, in my view, but they're taking the hard line. Short-sighted fools.'

'I can't say I'm surprised, sir, and it's good of you to care but, begging pardon, sir, how does it affect you? Nothing's changed at Grindley, has it? I know the men have always felt most thankful to work for you.'

'Oh, you see the state of my mind? I've left out the most important part. The men in Arden and New Arden, and those at Steepley too, have joined together to fight for wages that are even higher than those I pay. I can't blame them. If you're going to risk your relationship with your employer and all your security, it may as well be worth your while. They've leaned on Grindley to join them and Grindley finally have. It was a long while coming.

'Half your lot, Tommy, held out against it, your father included, saying that I'm a good master, that my wages and conditions are fair, and not to rock the boat. Sorry as they might feel for what's happening in Arden, they said it's Arden's fight, not Grindley's. The other half were all for anything that might lead to a rise in wages. They won, eventually.

'Now we have three communities, four if you count Arden and New Arden separately, all banded together, demanding higher pay. That's Sedgewicks, Barridges, the Spackles who own Steepley's mines and the Tysen's lot all put to the test. We're all responding differently but the miners are standing together. We have to reach a unanimous answer or there'll be a strike in Grindley for the first time in fifty-six years. Production would come crashing to a halt and we have contracts to fulfil. If it was just Grindley, I could handle it. And Spackles is reasonable enough. But how I'm ever to reach a consensus with the likes of Winthrop Barridge I simply cannot envisage . . .'

'I see,' I breathed. It was a huge piece of news. While I'd been suspended in my ivory tower, my old world had kept turning and in a few short months was on the brink of unimaginable change. Knowing as I did the capacity of mining men to accept the intolerable and preserve a modicum of security at all costs, I could only imagine how Tysen's and the Barridges must have pushed and pushed them for it to come to this.

'Anyway, Tommy, you did not come home to talk strike and politics,' said the earl, slapping his hands on his thighs. 'You came to relax after your hard work and your admirable progress. I shall leave you to it for now but I hope I shall see a lot more of you before you go back.'

'I hope so too, sir.'

He went out again, and Coralie watched him go thoughtfully. 'It really is too bad,' she said. 'He's always done his best for the men. Oh, I know they still get the rough end of the deal, Tommy, believe me. But he really has tried, and now he's being brought down with all the rest. The villages feel that with the influence of a more open-minded patron, their cause might do better, and that's why they leaned so hard on Grindley to join them. But really, Uncle has just about as much influence over Winthrop Barridge as anyone else.' She sighed. 'But there, you have better things to think about now, do you

378

not, Tommy? Josie, why don't you take him for a walk about the grounds for an hour or so? You two must have so much to catch up on.'

'Thank you, miss,' said Josie demurely, laying aside the bonnet. 'I'll finish this later, it won't take me long now.'

And soon we were walking through the dusky woods, listening to the pigeons call and breathing in lungfuls of wild garlic that made my stomach rumble. It was good to be alone with her, in the peaceful outdoors. My head was fairly spinning from all the news and from seeing so many familiar faces after so long away.

For weeks I had promised myself I would tell her I loved her the moment we were alone . . . But something stayed me. We only had an hour. Not that it would take an hour for her to slay my heart, if that was how it was to be. But if her answer were good . . . I would like to have longer ahead of us to kiss and cry and make plans. And Josie was rattling on about the strike, telling me the Arden point of view, as related to her by Miss Embry. It was big news, affecting our whole families. Although Josie never saw hers any more, it would have been impossible not to take an interest. Perhaps we should get all this out of the way first, I wondered, and turn to romance at a better moment. Or perhaps it was just cowardice on my part.

It was a blissful hour. Just to see Josie again, to hear her laugh, watch the light darting across her lively face, to share thoughts there and then, instead of unfolding a letter and reading them two days later, was a luxury. And we had days and weeks ahead. When Josie took her leave of me at the servants' entrance, I wanted to kiss her, but settled instead for a quick squeeze of her hand.

'Goodnight then, our Tommy,' she said, her eyes sparkling. 'I'll see you tomorrow.'

'See you tomorrow, Josie. Oh, but it's good to be able to say that.'

There was a moment when she hesitated, and I hesitated, but we went our separate ways, like the chaste friends we were.

# Chapter 58

─────❧─────

# Tommy

That evening, after settling in at Mrs Murphy's and eating a hearty meal there, I walked over to Grindley. Not wanting to go empty-handed, I begged leftovers from Mrs Roundsby. She found a couple of loaves of still-warm bread, baked that day, and a jar of honey from Silvermoor bees.

When I walked in, Ma shrieked, and threw her arms around me. 'Oh Tommy! You look such a gent! Oh, it's good to see yer face.'

My sisters crowded round me fondly with kisses and smiles and my brothers nodded and clapped me on the back.

'Remembered your family then, have yer?' remarked Da. 'Not too grand to mix wi' likes of us then?'

I rolled my eyes. 'No, Da.' They were mostly gathered there, so I explained my astonishment when the carriage had arrived for me, unannounced, at Westonbury. 'So they whisked me off and here I am to see you, *my first evening back*,' I concluded with some emphasis.

'It's lovely,' said Ma. 'Just lovely.'

My brother George walked in with Agnes. They obviously hadn't heard that I was in the vicinity and had a great surprise.

'Eh,' said Agnes when they'd recovered and George had shaken my hand several times. 'Not too grand to mix wi' likes of us now you've gone all posh, then?' And so the evening progressed.

I only stayed a couple of hours, well remembering how they would need a good night's sleep with a day in the mines ahead. We'd caught up briefly on all the news and I asked Da about the strike. 'It's a bad idea,' he said. 'It's a disgrace what's been happening in Arden and they need to take action, yes. But it's not our fight. Sedgewicks have never used us ill. Nowt but bad can come of this.'

Da and my brothers were all yawning and Ma was drooping too by the time I left, though the girls were disappointed I wouldn't stay longer. I promised I'd come back the next day. I wasn't tired, though. Despite all that had happened that day, I felt exhilarated and happy. I wanted to walk, and let all my thoughts and impressions settle. Without much thought I set off in the direction of Arden. How often had I done that in the past? By day, hoping to see Josie and during the dark wash of night, poaching with Da or visiting Manus. How life had changed. How grateful I was for it.

It was ten o'clock. There was still a dream of light in the sky, pinkish and soft over the grey. A flock of jackdaws circled overhead, neat, swift shapes clacking in the evening hush. When I looked back over my shoulder I could see the fireside lamps of Grindley glimmering through the almost-dark, going out one by one. Ahead the lanes were full of fairy dust and just for a minute they felt magical, promising, before I remembered that they led nowhere I wanted to go. I walked and walked, thinking about Josie, home, and the weeks of leisure ahead of me. I would give two or three of my five shillings to Da, I decided. I wouldn't give it all, for I would need it at Christmas, to come home, but how good it would be to contribute something at last after all my fine talk.

I wondered idly if I might run into Miss Embry, collecting letters for Manus. I wished I might. Perhaps I could sound her out about Josie. Women talked, I knew from my sisters. Perhaps she could give me hope, or prepare me for disappointment. But I didn't really imagine I'd see her by chance and I wouldn't go to Arden. I wished I'd thought to scribble a note for Manus. But I hadn't expected my steps would bring me so far.

As I neared the gate to Heston, my footsteps slowed. All those years of speculating with Josie about the family, that great, empty house. The long years of Manus being shut up inside. There was no sign or sound of Paulson or his dogs, but my heart started beating faster just from habit. I found myself creeping, rather than striding. 'The poachers' walk,' we called it, as if every step was to land on velvet.

To my astonishment, I saw a figure inside the gate, equally silent, fumbling with the padlocks and chains. He was dressed in dark clothes, but his hair was as white as ever, and a large, dark shape loomed behind him, making small, cautious noises.

'Manus!' I whispered in delight.

He wheeled around in terror, and dived into the bushes on his side of the gate, all in one swift, startled movement.

'Manus it's me, Tommy,' I hissed, afraid he'd take off and we'd miss this opportunity to talk. 'I never thought I'd see you tonight! Let me in, won't you?'

'Tommy?' A strangled voice came from the ferns.

'Yes, it's me! It's all right, Manus, only me.'

I'd forgotten what a nervous, highly strung creature his life had made him. His emergence from the undergrowth was preceded by a lengthy rustling and he came only slowly to the gate, as though expecting trickery at every turn. I stepped forward so that he could see me.

'Oh Tommy,' he said with great relief. 'It really is you. Well, how marvellous! What a wonderful surprise. Will you come in and take a glass?' As he reached for the chains his hands were shaking.

I nearly said yes, for old time's sake, but thoughts of Josie stopped me. I had too much to lose, that which I already had – and that which I had not yet claimed.

'I mustn't, Manus,' I said. 'I daren't get caught in Heston now. You see . . . well, it's Josie . . .'

He smiled, and looked angelic in the light of the rising moon. 'Of course it is,' he said. 'I always knew you would come to it, Tommy. Are you engaged?'

'No! That's just it. I've never said a word to her about it, Manus. She doesn't know how I feel. I don't know if she feels the same or if this is going to break my heart. But I must tell her. I haven't seen her for six long months and I can't wait another day. This is *not* the night for me to get arrested.'

'Quite right,' murmured my friend, unfastening the gate at last and drawing me in. 'Then let us simply sit here and talk in whispers. It's a warm night and we can be comfortable.'

I did as he suggested. We embraced, then settled ourselves on two springy tussocks. Ebony came to greet me and chew on my hair. It must have been nearing eleven but there was not so much as a chill in the air.

'The earl sent for me today, without warning, and suddenly here I am, for six weeks,' I explained.

Manus's eyes sparkled. 'Oh Tommy, I do hope I might see you again, even if it's just here, like this. I have missed our conversations. The loneliness can become . . . well, it gets crushing, actually. Sometimes I can't think for it.'

'I've only had the smallest experience of it at Westonbury and that was bad enough. Manus, six weeks is a long time for me to be around. There's no reason we shouldn't meet somewhere else altogether if you would only leave.'

I was dismayed to see that same defensive hunching in his

shoulders, a stiffness coming into his face. 'It's not that easy,' he murmured, as he had so many times before.

I couldn't hide my disappointment. 'But Manus, I thought everything was moving along. You have your escape fund, and Miss Embry. I thought surely the time must be drawing near now. You've had so long to think of a plan. You've been here *three* years since I met you.' But then he looked so sad I wished I hadn't spoken so strongly.

'I know I'm very disappointing, Tommy,' he said. 'Altogether a rather pathetic creature. I can only try to explain . . . The loneliness, as I said, stops me from thinking clearly. And the fear goes so deep! Ten years is a long time, and I've been made helpless in many ways. I've forgotten so many of the skills I once had, like charm, logic, small talk – though in truth, I was never very good at that. I try to imagine myself stepping out into the real world, approaching a landlady for lodgings, applying for a position in a bank, and it just seems impossible. Manus Barridge does not do those things. Manus Barridge lives in secret at Heston Manor, confined to his rooms. He lives life between the pages of his small private library by day, rides his horses on the lawn by night.'

'Yes,' I admitted. 'He does. I do understand. You couldn't possibly feel otherwise. However, it comes to this, my dear friend: you will *never* feel otherwise, not for as long as you're here. The change must come first, I feel it strongly. Make the move, no matter how scared you are, and then you will see it all so differently and be so very glad you did. I'm sure of it.'

'Miss Embry said something very similar to me. You're both so clever and wise, I'm sure you must be right. But Tommy, what if I don't have it in me? I know *you* stepped out of your life, started anew. But if it was easy, everyone would do it, wouldn't they?'

'No, not everyone is moved to do so. Not everyone has been locked away from the world by their own father, their death declared. You have it in you, Manus, trust me. Within the week then, won't you promise? Do it while I'm still around for a while and can help you, perhaps.'

He laughed softly. 'Within the week? I was wondering if I'd manage it this year.'

'Manus, *no*, you can't stay *months*. The longer it goes on, the harder it will get. Take the plunge.'

'By the end of your stay then,' he bartered. 'How about if I say I shall come up with a plan and leave here before you return to Westonbury?'

'Well, it's better than the end of the year,' I conceded.

We moved on to other matters: the brewing strike; my schooling and Josie; Miss Embry and Ebony and Equinox. We must have talked an hour away and I was just thinking I should go when Ebony whickered, a low, nervous sound of warning. We looked at one another, frozen.

Through all those months of sporadic meetings in the stables we had never heard so much as a whisper of a groundsman, only that very first time, when Josie and I hid in the straw just before we met Manus. I hadn't forgotten the dangers of coming to Heston, that's why we were sitting here in the bushes! But on another level all our conversations seemed to have taken place within an enchanted bubble and I had come to believe that our friendship was protected. But although we could hear nothing – no voices, no dogs, no footsteps – Ebony continued to stamp softly, uneasily. The horses always knew.

I got to my feet and slid soundlessly through the gate. Manus rose too and stood looking at me. It struck me that he had more to lose than I did now. I wasn't trespassing, even if Paulson grabbed me, he would find no motive for poaching – I was a scholar, a friend of the Sedgewicks, I had no need of Heston pheasants. It would be unpleasant, I was sure, but I would get through it. Manus, however, stood to lose every chance of escape. The gate would be sealed, measures to guard him redoubled, perhaps he might even be moved, if they ever found out he had a friend. As we stood like men of stone, I wondered why we had never thought to hatch a plan for this very eventuality.

Then we heard it: a bark in the near distance. Ebony's nostrils flared, Manus's pupils dilated. I stepped forward and pulled the gate to, so that it wasn't obvious it was open. The chains lay slack, however, unhooked and useless. I flapped my hands at Manus to tell him to turn around and start his way back. He had every right to be wandering around his own property. I backed away into the lane planning to walk back to Silvermoor quickly, but without any appearance of guilt, if such a thing were possible.

But before I could set off there was an almighty eruption in the bushes. Two dogs suddenly exploded from the brambles and knocked Manus to the ground. I wondered where the third was. Ebony reared, whinnying; I caught a glimpse of his black hooves scrabbling at thin air. Strong hands grabbed me from behind, taking me unawares, pinning my arms behind my back. And I heard the third dog growl.

# Chapter 59

—◦◦◦—

# Josie

I went to bed that night with stars wheeling in my mind. Tommy was home. Oh, the way he'd held me when he stepped off that coach. How wonderful it had been to walk in the woods with him, to talk directly instead of through the distance and delay of letters, to hear his voice, see his face! There had been moments when I thought he was going to say something . . . When I thought *I* was going to say something. But we didn't have much time and there were six weeks ahead and there was so much to catch up on in the old way. I found myself pouring out to him all my thoughts about a variety of situations – because I could.

Still, now that it was night time and I was alone again, knowing that he was so close, I could hardly sleep. I tried to talk sense into myself as it struck midnight, as one o'clock came, when it turned two . . . How vexing. Now my eyes would be puffy and I would be bleary-headed tomorrow, when

I wanted to be at my captivating best for Tommy. I huffed and turned and punched my pillows and gave up at a quarter to three. I rose and dressed quickly. I ran silently through the house and out into the night. Teacup insisted on coming with me, a tiny warrior to keep me safe in the shadows. It took me twenty minutes or so to walk to Mrs Murphy's cottage through a moonlit night blooming with summer scents. The quavering call of an owl thrilled me.

Fortunately the two bedrooms of the little house faced opposite ways so I was able to throw small stones at Tommy's window without fear of waking the wrong person. I waited, heart beating joyfully, for the moment when a dark shape would fumble with the window latch and a tousled curly head would lean out. What was I going to say? I had no idea. Perhaps I would tell him I loved him – why wait to learn my fate? Perhaps I would make up some implausible excuse. Perhaps I would simply say I couldn't wait for the morning to see him, which was true.

Either way, I knew it was right that I was here now, in the privacy and immediacy of this beautiful night. I waited.

I threw more little stones, then slightly bigger ones, then a largeish stone that made a crack I didn't like the sound of. Impatience had got the better of me. I waited. And there was no Tommy.

I sat on the grass and Teacup hopped into my lap. 'He's not coming, is he, little one?' I murmured. That last stone hadn't been subtle. Tommy could not be so heavy a sleeper that he would sleep through that. He wasn't there. I sighed. Perhaps he'd just decided to stay the night with his family in Grindley. Perhaps he was even now tucked up on that funny bed of theirs under the stairs. Safe. I hoped so. But I very much feared he'd found another adventure.

# Chapter 60

## Tommy

'What right have you to hold me? I've done nothing wrong!' I cried. 'Let me go at once! I'm a friend of Rufus Sedgewick, on my way back to Silvermoor.'

A growl at my left ear. 'A friend of Rufus Sedgewick, is it? *I'm* sure. Do his lordship's guests always stroll about Heston lanes at midnight? A proper funny arrangement, that.'

'The lanes are public,' I spat. 'People may use them as they please. I'm not trespassing. Let me go.'

'Oh aye, and who's going to make me?'

'Paulson, let him go!' Manus had scrambled to his feet. The dogs sat back on their haunches, growling, wary. 'Whatever you're imagining, you're wrong. This fellow was simply out for a stroll on a summer night. I was exploring the estate on Ebony and didn't realise we'd strayed so close to the boundary. We exchanged a few pleasantries and were about to go our respective ways. You can hardly think he was poaching, surely?

Look at his clothes. Listen to how he speaks. He's no impoverished mining lad.'

'He's no guest of the Earl of Silvermoor neither,' declared Paulson, turning me to take a good look at me. His eyes were rolling a little, however, and a strong stench of whisky rose from him. His suspicions were dogged but I doubted how sharp his senses were. 'I don't know who he is and I don't much care. Mr Barridge wouldn't like this at all. There's something funny afoot and I intend to find out what it is.'

I took a good look at him too: his broad, florid face, his tweed hat with its crest of feathers, his ginger cravat. His blue eyes were cold and a little wild. He was more than fifty, heavyset and puffing. I could take him, I knew it. But what about Manus? And there was the dog . . .

'Your vigilance does you credit,' I said, playing the gentleman. 'I'm sure Mr Barridge would be impressed. However, you're barking up the wrong tree on this occasion. Let me go and we'll say no more about it.'

He laughed. '*Pup!*' he sneered. 'And as for you . . .' he turned to Manus. 'You needn't think I'll keep this to meself. There'll be measures put in place, strict measures.'

'But why?' Manus sounded innocent, but I could see how frightened he was. His hands were twisting again, in silent, pointless loops. A second groundsman had caught up with the dogs and was holding them, looking to Paulson for instructions. 'This fellow knows nothing . . . of a private nature. He

394

was very courteous but not curious in any way. I'm sure he realises a great many people reside on the property, caring for the horses and the grounds and so forth.'

'Indeed,' I said. 'I've very little interest in the arrangements here. I'm a scholar at Westonbury and my studies are more than enough to occupy my mind.'

'And I suppose you've never set eyes on each other before tonight,' said Paulson with great sarcasm.

'Never,' said Manus emphatically. Too emphatically. 'Well, I've had enough of this, Paulson. I shall go to bed. Goodnight, young fellow, I can only apologise.' He took hold of the reins and started leading Ebony back towards the house. The groundsman and his dogs watched him but made no move to follow.

I held my breath. Was he really going? Would he be well? What would happen to me? Paulson I could handle, but three dogs as big as calves? As I stood there weighing my options. I wished with all my heart that I had told Josie I loved her today. Even out of the mines life was precarious, people were harsh, time was short and unpredictable. Six weeks had seemed a luxury of time; now who knew what would happen? I should have told her.

'Aye, get back inside,' Paulson snarled after Manus. I was shocked by the lack of basic respect he showed to the man they were all guarding. 'I'll be speaking to Mr Barridge tomorrow. As for *you*,' he added, shoving me hard, 'you'd best come with me.'

'I certainly won't!'

'Oh, I think you will. Here, Breaker.' The dog growled louder and stood at his master's side, bulky and powerful. I thought of Josie. If I ran, the dogs would savage me. If I went along with them, perhaps I could talk my way out of this yet. But oh, my blood was up. Much as I knew I should play this wisely, I wanted to fight. My hands twitched with it.

'What's yer name?' he demanded. 'Tell us and I might go easier on yer.'

Suddenly I thought of poor Flinty and gave a little smile. 'Al Crace,' I said clearly. 'Al Crace of Grindley.' Any trouble this might cause him would be small payback for that brave little pony's death.

I glanced after Manus; he had mounted up. I could see Ebony still walking away from us and Manus's white hair, disappearing among the trees.

'Al Crace, is it?' repeated Paulson dubiously.

'Yes. Now I've given you my name and I've told you where I'm staying. I think that demonstrates a great deal of good will on my part. I strongly recommend you let me leave. You're welcome to call at Silvermoor tomorrow and verify my story.'

'Oh aye, *verify*, is it?' He was one of *those* people; suspicious of a new word. 'No, I think I'll take you with me, Mr Crace. A night in the cellar will give you time to think, no doubt. Mr Barridge can deal with you, seeing as you're so friendly with the gentry.'

'Oh I say, young fellow!' Manus's voice came from among the trees. 'Regarding our earlier conversation, I believe, after all, that you're right . . .' *What was he talking about?* 'It's time to *leave!*' He wheeled Ebony round and cantered hard at the gate.

'I *know* I'm right!' I shouted. I yielded to the twitching in my hands and threw an almighty punch. I caught Paulson smack in his bloated, red-veined face. It gave a satisfying crunch and he staggered backwards. I leaped for the gate and wrenched it wide open.

'Breaker!' cried Paulson, writhing on the ground. The dog sprang. It was like being knocked down by a flying bull; the thing was massive. His huge jaws closed around my arm and I howled. I punched and kicked it but he was hefty and muscled and savage. Paulson had struggled to his feet and was cocking his rifle . . . but the counterpoint to all this was the steady beat of Ebony's hooves coming closer. The enormous horse was in the lane, squealing. The dog dropped me as this far bigger opponent careered towards it and I staggered to Ebony's nearside, bleeding profusely.

'Paulson, put that thing away unless you intend to shoot *me*,' commanded Manus.

Paulson looked at him insolently and raised the rifle, pointed it directly towards us. He might do it; I wouldn't put it past him.

Manus reached out a hand to me, but my arm was altogether too shredded for him to grab it helpfully. I stuck my foot in the stirrup and tried to leap up but Breaker made a lunge for me, closing his teeth on my right ankle as surely as if I'd stepped in a steel trap. My father's voice flashed through my head: *That's our limit. Go no further, never ever, if you value yer life*. I had never been good with limits.

Ebony wheeled away from the dog and, with my foot hooked in the stirrup, I was dragged after him and out of Breaker's jaws. I nearly fell but Manus grabbed my armpit and hauled me up. I roared with pain and the effort of flinging myself onto the huge horse from such an unlikely angle but somehow I made it. It wasn't easy to arrange myself on his broad, slippery back with Breaker leaping and snapping and Ebony spinning and prancing. But eventually I righted myself and Manus nodded when he felt my weight come to centre.

'Come on, Tommy,' he whispered, 'it's time to run.'

Ebony flew down the lane, faster and straighter than an arrow. Paulson fired two shots after us but missed; whether he intended to or not I never knew. Ebony didn't even flinch. He was such a mightiness of horse he seemed to defy hounds and bullets alike.

I had never travelled so fast. The motion was so fluid that even with only one foot in a stirrup, and no saddle beneath me, it was easy to keep my seat. The dogs chased us but we soon left them behind. We pounded through the lanes and fled up onto Silvermoor Rise. I glimpsed the dark huddle that was Arden away to our left. I saw the Heston boundary where Josie used to break in and pick her bluebells to our right. Ebony galloped, never once missing his footing. We flew down the other side and out into open country, out onto the moors, farther than I had ever been, apart from Westonbury, of course. At last we stopped.

The night was silent. No hounds, no gunshots, no shouting. We had outrun them all.

'So,' said Manus, sliding from Ebony's back. 'I've done it. I'm out.'

I made to dismount then remembered my chewed ankle and stayed where I was. 'This wasn't quite what I had in mind.'

We looked at each other in the darkness and started to laugh. It was such an improbable, ridiculous situation.

'Well, Miss Embry has your money,' I mused.

'And you must get back to Silvermoor,' said Manus. 'It's a pity you told Paulson you were staying there. He'll go looking, asking questions.'

'He didn't believe me. I also told him I was called Al Crace. The Sedgewicks can truthfully deny they know anyone of that name.'

'Well played.' He leaned against Ebony's tall shoulder. 'What a to-do, what a to-do. Oh Tommy! How am I going to get Equinox?'

'I don't know. For that matter, what are we going to do with Ebony? A man might hide easily enough but you're huge, aren't you, old fellow?' I murmured, rubbing the horse's neck. He arched it in pleasure.

'First things first,' said Manus. 'Get me off the moors and you back to Silvermoor . . . I think I know what our first steps should be. The rest will have to follow.'

He was rising to the occasion. It was just as I'd said: he was more afraid locked away from the challenges of the world than when he was actually confronted with them. Or perhaps it was exhilaration and the shock would set in later.

# Chapter 61

## Tommy

I rode into Silvermoor early the next morning. The sun was rising and summer mists were lifting; the estate was silent and still. But I had only been in the stables a moment when Josie came running in.

'Tommy Green!' she cried furiously. 'Where've you been all night? I've been that worried! Every time you're out of my sight I'm worried that you'll get buried alive, or forget me, or get mauled by those great big bloody dogs . . . Wait, you're bleeding! You *did* get mauled by the dogs . . . Wait, is that *Ebony*?'

'It's a long story,' I said, stumbling towards her and wrapping her in my arms. I was bone-weary after another narrow escape at Heston and a night of roaming the countryside. I sagged against her, let my head drop onto hers, and though she was small and slim, she held me up. This time it just felt like coming home. I had learned my lesson. I would not wait another minute.

'I love you, Josie,' I said, my eyes closed, her face tucked into my neck. It wasn't the declaration I had planned, gazing intently into her face to read its every reaction, communicating the force of my love with the intensity of my gaze. It just had to be said, before anything else happened. Just in that moment, with the relief of seeing her again, it almost didn't matter what she said, only that she knew. Perhaps it was a good thing that the words just came out like that, true and matter of fact.

'Tommy,' she said sternly, 'I love you too but you're bleeding and no doubt in some sort of trouble. What do you need?'

There was her woman's pragmatism again. And she was right. Soon, people would be about and I couldn't be seen like this. My limp I could explain with a story about turning my ankle in the dark but it was obvious my arm had been bitten by a dog and, since there was no way to explain it, I limped back to the cottage before Mrs Murphy rose. I left the door on the latch for Josie, who soon brought bandages and carbolic acid from the house. Fortunately the wounds were easy to clean and I soaked the bandages in the carbolic before wrapping my poor chewed appendages tightly. I gritted my teeth against the pain.

'Well,' said Josie when she was finally done and I'd sunk onto my narrow bed in exhaustion. 'I want to hear what's happened, of course, but first I must ask you one thing. Just then, when you said you love me, was that just a heat of the moment thing, like when I told you I'd turned down Miss Coralie and you kissed me, or was it . . . well, *what* was it, Tommy?'

Her face was whiter than I had ever seen it and I realised she was afraid. I understood suddenly why that kiss had never been repeated. I'd always assumed she hadn't wanted it to be, but now I realised that she hadn't really believed I meant it. I reached out the hand of my non-bandaged arm and she took it. I pulled her until she was sitting on the bed beside me. My moment had come at last.

'First of all,' I told her, 'that kiss was not a heat of the moment thing. That kiss was pure feeling. I was horrified that you'd missed your chance, but moved that you'd done it for me. Our existence was downright impossible back then, and you were the most precious thing in it to me. You always were, you still are and you always will be. I've been wanting to do it again ever since, but I was afraid you wouldn't want me to and I didn't want to risk our friendship.'

'Oh,' said Josie, very softly.

'Secondly, my friendship for you has caught fire, Josie. I've been wanting to tell you for the longest time but I didn't want to write it, I wanted to tell you face to face. You once said that friendship is an important part of love, but love is bigger. My friendship for you is still there, if that's all you want – you'll never be without that. But there is more, so much more, that I feel for you if you . . . unless you . . .' At last my eloquence ran out and I gazed at her beautiful face imploringly.

'Oh,' she whispered again. 'Oh, I'm so relieved.' She looked unusually shy and uncertain.

'Then . . . it's what you want?' I checked.

'It's what I want more than anything. I've been waiting and wondering . . . thinking I could wait forever if I only *knew*. Oh Tommy, yes, it's what I want.' She lifted a hand to trace the line of my cheekbone, to stroke the side of my face, to touch my lips. She did it wonderingly, as if I were a miracle sitting before her. I took a moment to absorb the fact that all my hopes had not been dashed, that everything I had ever wanted had just come true in that moment. Then I kissed her hand and went on.

'I want us to marry one day, Josie. Will you? Months I've been at that school waiting to tell you in person and feeling very afraid of what you'd say. Then last night I thought maybe I'd never see you again so I couldn't wait another minute to tell you everything. I love you. Thank you for being the bright light that got me through those years underground, that gets me through the days at Westonbury now. I want to share every bit of my life with you, even though I don't have a damned thing to offer you yet. Well, two shillings . . .'

'Shh,' said Josie. 'Of course I want to marry you. How could it be otherwise? I was afraid too, Tommy . . . but it's all right now. Oh . . .' She drew me close and we sat for a long moment wrapped in each other, then I took her face in my hands and I kissed her. For the first time it wasn't hasty, or unexpected, it wasn't the expression of a fleeting emotion or a special occasion. We both knew it was coming and we both meant it with all our hearts. Her lips were soft and sweet and I might have been a miner's lad but her kiss made me a prince. I pulled away to gaze into her dark eyes and smiled a smile that spread through my whole body and warmed it. Plans with Josie. A life with Josie. That special, bright spark always at my side, illuminating everything we saw and did. Never had anyone been so happy not to have been savaged by dogs.

# Chapter 62

---

# Josie

I fled across dewy grass back to the big house, to conduct my morning chores for Miss Coralie. I was surprised to find my shoes and hem wet, so certain was I that I had wings. Tommy loved me. After all this time I knew . . . We were to marry, one day, when his schooling was done. I longed to tell Miss Coralie but it was too new. This new us was only moments into existence; I wanted to cherish it in the privacy of my heart a while longer first.

Later that morning I had some free time. Since Tommy couldn't walk far, we borrowed Walter's pony to ride to Arden. Ebony would have been far too conspicuous a mount.

We rode with my arms around his waist, the warmth of his back pressing against me, and he told me more about the night before. He and Manus had ridden to Arden last night and taken the great risk of tying up Ebony on the outskirts. I could see that there was no other way. If anyone had chanced to see two men riding an enormous black horse through the village, the news would have been everywhere in an instant.

Fortunately Miss Embry was a light sleeper and they roused her easily enough from the little backyard where Tommy had hidden all those years ago. They explained the situation through the window in whispers and she had Manus climb in through the window rather than opening the door onto the street at such an unlikely hour. Then Tommy returned to Ebony and rode back to Silvermoor the long way round; there was no way he was returning to the lanes that night. No wonder he hadn't made it back to Silvermoor till dawn.

When we got to Arden we didn't bother trying to hide. No one would beat Tommy in broad daylight and we decided we had both broken with the place conclusively enough that we could go and visit our friend Miss Embry if we wanted. We found her behind her counter, business as usual.

When she saw us, Miss Embry's eyes lit up. Oh, the dear, lovely woman. I had never been gladder to see my friend.

'I *thought* you two would come calling,' she said, hurrying over to hug us. 'Oh Josie, how lovely to see you, my dear, and how well you look. Tommy, what a gentleman you are now! Welcome home, if ever such it was. I'd better not shut up shop until lunchtime, for I don't want to arouse any suspicions with my, er . . . guest staying. You can go back and see him, though; I believe he's awake.'

We were quite torn between wanting to see Manus

immediately, and lingering with Miss Embry, whom we hadn't seen in some time. After all, we had important news.

'Dulcie, we've something to tell you!' I burst out, unable to contain it any more.

'You don't need to, my dear, for I can plainly see. It's the two of you, isn't it?'

I nodded, grinning, feeling my face flame and not even caring. Dulcie embraced me again. She kissed Tommy's cheek. 'I'm so happy for you, darlings. It couldn't have been any other way. Are you engaged?'

'Yes!' I said rapturously at the same time that Tommy said, 'No'.

I looked at him in stupefaction. We had agreed it not three hours ago. Were men even more confusing than I had been led to believe? I wouldn't have believed it of my Tommy.

'We *are* going to marry, yes,' he explained. 'But I want to ask her properly, with a ring and a plan. I haven't done that yet.'

I was relieved. So like Tommy to want to do things properly, to make a distinction between an official engagement and what we knew to be true. *I'm engaged, I'm engaged!* I thought in the privacy of my own head.

Just then the bell jingled and my old over-the-road neighbour, Mary Mallen, came in. When she saw me she gave a great start. 'My, haven't *you* become grand, Josie Westgate?' she said, her lips pursing as if grandness was the very devil's work.

'Good morning, Mrs Mallen,' I said. 'I hope you're well.' I was proud of myself.

'Go through, my dears,' said Dulcie. 'Make yourselves comfortable and I'll join you when I can.'

We found Manus in Dulcie's drawing room, eating cream cakes and scribbling feverishly on the leather-bound jotter on her desk.

'Tommy!' he cried and leaped up. 'And . . . why, *Josie*! How *wonderful* to see you again after all this time. How very different you look from the last time we met.' He shook hands with Tommy heartily and kissed my hand with his old-fashioned manners. I could hardly believe I was seeing him again after all this time of only hearing about him in Tommy's letters.

'Tommy, wasn't that some night?' he asked, his eyes shining. 'We did it! I'm finally free! I can't thank you enough. But how are you? How are your wounds? Has there been any trouble? Is Ebony all right? How am I going to get Equinox? Oh!' he caught himself when he realised how many questions he was firing off. 'Sorry. Let's sit. Cake?'

Tommy shook his head while I helped myself.

Tommy answered those questions that he could, then recounted his furious gallop back to Silvermoor, his dawn arrival and our happy news.

'Oh, I'm overjoyed for you both,' said Manus. 'No wonder you look so well, Tommy, despite your hair-raising night. And Josie, you're positively sparkling. In fact . . . my God!' He stopped talking and stared at me in what can only be described as shock.

'What?' I asked, pausing mid-bite. 'Have I cream on my nose?'

'None whatsoever. Only, won't you do me the favour of putting the cake down for a moment, so I can look at you properly?'

'What is it with you Barridges?' I groused. 'When I met your brothers years ago, they looked at me as though I had two heads, and now *you're* doing it. I know I'm not the fairest maid in Yorkshire but for heaven's sake!'

'It's not that,' said Manus. 'You're sufficiently fair, believe me. Really very comely indeed. It's just that . . . well, *gracious*! You're the very likeness of my dear Aunt Pheeney.'

# Chapter 63

───◦∾∾◦───

# Josie

All I could hear was the ticking of Dulcie's mahogany mantel clock. I suddenly felt very calm. I suspected it wouldn't last.

I tore my gaze from Tommy's at last – I knew that he was thinking the same as me – and looked at Manus. 'Your Aunt Pheeney?' I asked in a small voice.

'Yes, my father's sister. I've told Tommy about her; she was a magnificent horsewoman, the one relative I could count on through my childhood to take an interest in me.'

'Your *father's* sister?' I echoed and looked at Tommy again. He moved closer to me and took my hand.

'Yes,' said Manus, looking a little sorry that he'd mentioned it. 'I'm sorry if I've upset you in any way, my dear. She was a lovely woman – the only really decent Barridge, in fact – and very handsome.'

I smiled. 'It's not vanity that's troubling me,' I said. 'Heavens, I should be glad to take after someone so fine. It's just that . . .

can I tell you something, sir? It might shock you, though, and I don't want to upset you more – you have enough to deal with at the moment.'

'What's one more shock? And for goodness' sake, call me Manus, Josie. I can't be sir to you!'

'Very well. Then it's this: a few months ago I learned that Sam Westgate is not my father. My mother told me, but she wouldn't tell me who my real father is. She's left me wondering and worrying, as was no doubt her intention. But she made some remarks that led me to believe he might be gentry, or someone from outside Arden anyway. All this time I've been wondering if it might be the earl. He has a reputation with the ladies and his niece, my employer, has bright red hair like mine. But there's no other resemblance, and it seems more than unlikely, the earl and my mother. Now I'm wondering . . . What colour hair had your aunt, Manus?'

'Red,' he said at once. 'A little darker than yours, but red. But it's not the hair that made me notice it, Josie, it's your eyes, your bone structure. I mean really, it's uncanny.'

I sighed, recasting many events in my past – indeed, my whole self – in light of this new information. I felt like the pieces in a kaleidoscope, shifting and reshaping with every turn of the wheel. Would I ever reach a fixed position?

'I always thought,' I said slowly, 'that your brothers were laughing at me. It was long ago that I saw them, here in the shop. They'd come to see Dulcie because she was new, and they'd heard she was pretty. They were very rude. They both stared at me and said to one another, "Do you see it?" I thought they meant the state of me, but perhaps they saw a likeness even then.'

'It's entirely possible. I didn't notice it the night I met you but then your hair was in tufts, your face was all swollen from crying and it was dark. We were all in a state of quite some agitation and all any of us could think about was how to get you to safety. But today, well, it's as clear as day.'

'It makes sense, Josie,' said Tommy. He'd been quiet all the while. 'You said yourself that your mother wasn't the sort to have a love affair. And I've never heard of the earl dallying with an Arden woman. Why would he even be here?'

'And my mother's never gone anywhere else,' I finished. 'He'd have forced her, wouldn't he? I can't see Ma conceiving a passion for Winthrop Barridge, I really, really can't. No wonder she hates me. Oh, poor Ma. I never thought I'd say that but . . .'

'Winthrop Barridge,' sighed Tommy. 'Oh Josie.'

I dared a glance at Manus. I knew he had no fondness for his father but still, this was a harsh assumption to make. To my surprise, his eyes were gleaming. He looked radiant.

'Oh Josie,' he said in a small voice. 'I'm deeply sorry for what your mother must have undergone. Only I can't help thinking . . . that this is *wonderful*!'

'How?'

'Because he's my father too, of course. That means you're my sister!'

My jaw dropped several feet, I felt sure. Why had that not occurred to me sooner? And not only Manus, but those Barridge twins, the boys and the girls . . . I was half-sister to all of them.

'My God,' I said in a low voice, squeezing Tommy's hand fit to crush it. 'My God, Manus. You're my half-brother.'

'I am!' he cried, leaping up. 'Oh Josie, I'm so happy!' He pulled me to my feet and threw his arms around me. 'I know this must be a shock for you, but can you imagine what it's like for me? All those years cast out of my family, all that time fearing what would become of me in the world . . . And on my first day of liberty I discover a *sister*.'

The kaleidoscope locked, with a decisive click. I knew it was true. *Everything* fell into place, everything. All those snide remarks from Ma about how I thought I was special, different, too good for the likes of them, when nothing could have been further from the truth. I always thought it was odd she would say that, of all things, to me, rather than to Alice, who'd always had notions. Ma's persecution of me, getting worse over the years, as, presumably, the Barridge resemblance grew. Not only had I been a painful reminder, I had been a living, walking possibility that someone would realise the secret. I hated to think I was a part of old Winthrop so I concentrated instead on my aunt, the wonderful Pheeney.

It also explained Da's indifference to me. Oh, and that comment he'd made once about the bad taste of villagers christening their by-blows with aristocratic names. He'd been having a dig at Ma. But how like her to do the one small thing within her power that she knew Winthrop Barridge would hate. I felt almost proud of her. Quickly I told Tommy and Manus.

'Yes, it's frowned upon, I know,' said Tommy. 'Everyone knows it happens but they all like to brush the evidence under the carpet.'

'Well then. Is Josephine a Barridge name, Manus? Is that what Pheeney was short for?'

He looked stunned and nodded. 'Yes. She never used it because she said it was like a mouthful of feathers. So Pheeney it always was, and it suited her. I'd almost forgotten she *was* a Josephine.'

'And I'm not sure I ever knew *you* were,' said Tommy, staring at me. 'All these years and I've never even thought about it. I just thought you were Josie.'

'I always loved Josephine. I wished they might call me that, but it didn't really suit Arden. My God, I don't just take after your aunt, I'm *named* after her.'

'*Our* aunt,' corrected Manus.

At that moment the door opened and Dulcie joined us. I glanced at the clock and saw to my astonishment that it was somehow midday. We'd have to start back for Silvermoor shortly.

'I've closed the shop,' said Dulcie. 'It's a little early but I did so want some time with you all. Are you all right, Manus? It can't be nice skulking out of sight. I hope you're quite comfortable.' She looked around at our stupefied faces. 'What? What's happened?'

# Chapter 64

## Tommy

I don't know when anything had ever astonished me more. And this from someone who had been rescued from certain death and won a scholarship on very little schooling. But I had become reconciled to the unexpected on my own account; this was Josie. I hoped with all my heart that this would be a good thing for her — an answer at last, a wonderful connection with Manus — for certainly no one would wish Winthrop Barridge for a father.

Once Miss Embry had been duly appraised, the conversation moved on to the other great matter at hand: what was to become of Manus? But really, he was like a different man today. The experience of just one night under Miss Embry's roof appeared to have galvanised him.

'Congenial company, home comforts, a reminder of the real world . . . these are only the start of what I've been missing,' he vowed, gathering up the papers he had been writing when we arrived.

On them, he had estimated his net worth, between the small sum Miss Embry had kept for him and the possessions that he could sell. He had written a list of possible courses he might pursue with that capital, some of them a little wild, to be sure, but in his position perhaps no idea was a bad one. He had also drawn up the pros and cons of each and a theme recurred: he had spent quite enough time alone, without love. If it were in any way possible, he would prefer not to move too far from the area where Miss Embry and Josie lived and to which I returned periodically. Of course, the biggest drawback of starting a new life anywhere near here was the proximity to his family. But really, it was that or seek refuge alone in some anonymous city or country; none of us were in a position to go with him.

'It's a pity you can't be a groom at Silvermoor,' sighed Josie, thinking of his gift with horses. 'You'd be quite hidden away from your family there, yet not in the horrible way you were hidden at Heston. I'm there every few weeks . . . Dulcie could come and visit us both . . . But the stables are full – with staff, I mean, not horses. And there's nothing at Gravenagh House.'

'No, he can't be a groom at Silvermoor,' I agreed, 'but there is something else.'

'Oh!' said Josie, immediately realising what I meant. 'Oh yes!'

Quickly I explained to Dulcie. 'Young Lord Walter – *you* remember him – needs a tutor. His has left, his lordship's not been able to find a replacement to suit and he needs someone by the summer's end or it's off to school with Walter and he doesn't want that.'

'But how perfect!' Dulcie clapped her hands.

'I couldn't,' said Manus immediately, of course.

'You *could*,' I persisted. 'Think about it. You're highly educated, a gentleman. You'd be more than able to tutor Walter. Silvermoor is a wonderful place. The earl is kind and fair. Walter is just lovable, *and* he lives for horses. He's not the keenest scholar, but he's able enough when he tries. Oh Manus! You could live in a beautiful place, you'd have a wage, and freedom. Even if you only stayed a year, you'd have such a different perspective from which to decide your next steps. And by then I'll be finished with school, perhaps we could go into business together . . . why, *anything* could be possible. And you'd be perfectly safe from your father – I don't think a Barridge has been to Silvermoor in twenty years.'

'Hide in plain sight, you mean,' mused Manus. 'It's a daring scheme, I grant you. I'm not sure I'd have quite the stamina for it . . . after being so long alone, to be around people *all* the time, to work with someone of Walter's age. I haven't any experience of youngsters.'

'Wouldn't someone recognise him?' asked Dulcie.

I stared at Manus, my spirits diving. I had thought it such a perfect plan.

'I don't know that they would,' he said thoughtfully. 'I haven't seen the Earl of Silvermoor since I was a very young boy.

He didn't take much notice of me then. My father kept me away from people as much as possible even before he killed me off. My appearance is distinctive, but it's not very well known.'

'But didn't you say you resemble your father?' I asked. 'One of the first times we talked you said it.'

'Yes, but our colouring is totally opposite. He has dark hair, and eyes like Josie's. I am as you see me.'

We all stared at his pale, pale hair, blue eyes and skin that was whiter than white. 'It's your colouring that catches the attention, not your bone structure,' Dulcie admitted.

'What about the Honeycrofts, or the servants?' asked Josie. 'Might they recognise you?'

'The Honeycrofts no, I've never seen them. The servants? Well, theoretically I suppose there might be someone working at Silvermoor who saw me thirteen years ago. There *might* . . .'

We looked at each other. We all wanted this to work; we wanted it for Manus. Purpose, respite, company, after the insanity of his last thirteen years. It wasn't a safe option, nor foolproof. Pure sense would dictate he go elsewhere. Yet I wasn't sure which of us could be accused of possessing pure sense. And any of the obvious places, Newcastle or London, would have connections with a large family like the Barridges also. Nowhere could be considered truly safe. Here, he would be, as he said, hiding in plain sight. If there was a phrase for it, one could only suppose it stood a chance of working.

'How would we achieve it?' asked Dulcie. 'We could say

that you're a cousin of mine from Leeds, Manus, and that's how you heard of the post. But we can't waste time going back and forth to Leeds to post letters . . . No, better you go in person, say you were visiting me and the vacancy came up in conversation . . .'

'Wait, wait, dear Miss Embry. You are quite tearing ahead of me. How could I possibly just walk up the drive at Silvermoor and ask for a job? Besides, I'm sure I come across much better by letter than I do in person.'

'You'll come across beautifully,' Dulcie corrected him. 'The earl won't be able to say no to you and that is the result we desire.'

# Chapter 65

—◦◦◦—

# Tommy

Accordingly, two days later, I sat with Josie and Miss Coralie in a small lounge at Silvermoor and had the oddly displacing experience of seeing Dulcie driving up to the house in the borrowed mine cart, with Manus beside her. He looked notably nervous and notably groomed. The intervening day had been put to good use: they left Arden before first light and went to Leeds on the train, where Manus visited a barber and bought a new suit – one that wasn't terribly out of date. Dulcie had persuaded him that though his eccentricity was endearing, it had no place in an interview with the earl. They returned during daylight hours, realising that with further comings and goings ahead it would be too difficult to hide the fact that she had a house guest.

'A cousin you must be then, or scandal will abound!' Dulcie chuckled.

It was agony for Josie and me to pretend we knew nothing

about it when Coralie heard the wheels and went to the window. 'It's the shopkeeper from the next village over with a very pale companion,' she announced. 'Is she here to see you, do you think, Josie?'

'Miss Embry?' queried Josie innocently. 'No, I've no plans to see her today. Do you, Tommy?'

'Not me.'

'Well,' said Coralie, 'I'm sure Portis will show them in if they're calling for one of us.'

It was all we could do not to jump up and go and see how they were received. How would the earl take to a surprise visitor? As the minutes passed without the cart rattling off again, we could only assume that Portis had admitted them. Were they still waiting or was Manus talking to his lordship even now? Our suspense crackled.

Josie was busy with some embroidery. I wished I had something to do with my hands too. When Cedric wandered in and offered me a sherry, I accepted even though I did not much like it, just for something to hold.

'You said you wanted to talk to me, sir,' I reminded him. 'Would you like to do that now, or would you prefer another time?'

'Now's as good a time as any,' he beamed. 'Would you prefer to go to the library or shall we talk here? It's nothing I object to the ladies knowing. In fact, I've discussed it with my sister already.'

I glanced at Josie's face and laughed. If I made her wait any longer to learn the mystery, she'd kill me. 'Here's grand, sir.'

Cedric had never forgotten his idea of employing me as his clerk when he went into politics. 'Well, I'm starting out at last,' he told me. 'I know you're tied up at school as yet but I heard you'll be here for over a month and I wondered, would you consider working for me in a part-time capacity these coming weeks? I'm helping Uncle campaign for better mining conditions to become legal requirements and now, with this strike brewing, I've turned my hand to a bit of journalism too, articles and letters in various papers, don't you know? What I need is a fuller understanding of the mining life. Oh, I traipse into Grindley all the time, and they tolerate me, but I know they'll never fully confide in me. The us and them mentality is too deeply ingrained.'

'Aye, we're close people, for the most part,' I agreed.

'But you, Tommy, you're not . . . close. And you lived that life for years. Won't you fill in the gaps in my understanding?'

'Yes, sir, gladly, but you don't need to employ me for that. I'll just talk to you, whenever you want.'

'Bless you, Tommy, that's good of you, but I'd rather a formal arrangement. Then I won't feel guilty about drawing on you heavily. I'd also like you to read through some of the articles and papers I've written before I send them off, correct them if necessary. I want to be sure the picture I'm painting is fully accurate. And I'd like you to come with me to meetings with the other coal owners and with the miners too. I hope they'll listen to me more readily if I'm accompanied by one of their own.'

'I'll readily come, sir, but I don't know how much use I'll be. My folk already think I'm odd and some think I'm a traitor for leaving the life. I might be more hindrance than help.'

'Well, that we shall see, but if you're willing, Tommy, I'd very much like to try. So you see, what I'm proposing is a proper job. This work is very important to me and whilst I don't wish to commandeer your whole holiday – a few hours a week should do it – I would like to make the most of having you here, you're a tremendous resource.'

I smiled. I had thought of my underground years as wasted time, but it took only one truly interested person of influence to render my experiences in the Stygian darkness suddenly valuable. If they led to helping others that came after me . . . well, perhaps there had been riches down there besides coal after all. And Mr Talbot would never need to know.

'Am I? Well then, who am I to say no? Thank you, sir, I'd be very grateful for the experience of working with you.' And of course, any wage he saw fit to pay me would be welcome too. I saw no reason to press him for a sum since I would, as I'd said, have done it all for free. But I knew he would not allow that and I saw myself leaving in September with money in my pocket, which meant that I could afford to come home at Christmas *and* Easter. No more six-month dearth of Josie.

'I think it's splendid,' said Coralie. 'I do admire you, Cedric. One minute you were just an indolent young man with an eye for the ladies and the next you've grown up and you're making a difference in the world.'

Cedric smiled. 'I'm not sure how much difference I'm making. But I'm trying.'

'Thank you, sir, for everything you're trying to do,' said Josie. 'Thank you on behalf of my brother Bert, who's in the mines. Even now, with the distance between me and my family, I still dread the news that something's happened to him.'

We toasted my new appointment in sherry and a little later the mine cart carrying Dulcie and Manus drove off. 'They must have come to see Uncle,' mused Coralie. 'I wonder why.'

'I wonder,' said Josie, gazing after them.

# Chapter 66

# Tommy

A curious sort of time followed, and by curious, I suppose I mean that it was happy. For me there was no danger, no trouble and I had everyone I loved nearby. I saw Josie every day, my family every few days, Dulcie once a week or so and, strangest of all, Manus was living at Silvermoor.

He had presented himself to the earl as Dulcie's cousin, Mr James. He kept his story simple: he'd been a tutor in Leeds, the situation had ended when his charges grew up, he'd come to visit his cousin and she told him of the post at Silvermoor.

The question of references never even arose. By meeting Manus in person, the earl could gauge his obvious intelligence and gentlemanly qualities. The two men talked of literature, mathematics, history and horses. They also talked of politics and the earl was apparently surprised by how well Manus understood the mining industry.

'It's hard not to have some awareness, living in Yorkshire,' Manus had commented and, of course, that was true.

The earl sent for Walter and introduced him to 'Mr James'. My two friends hit it off famously and the earl could see that here was someone with the passion for horses to win his son over, as well as the scholarly talent to educate him. When he showed Manus out, Miss Embry was waiting. She spoke so glowingly of her cousin's qualities that a character reference was immediately established. I think that between the pressures of warding off a strike and desperation about finding someone even remotely suitable to tutor Walter, the earl was quite determined not to let Manus slip through his fingers.

'When can you start?' he'd asked.

'Next week?' suggested Manus.

And so it was.

They were easy days for Mr James of Leeds. He spent long hours with his young charge but during these summer weeks there were no lessons, so they simply established a friendship. They spent a great deal of time riding on the estate or in the field nearest the house where Manus schooled Walter and Windfall. Walter was delighted by how Windfall's performance and his own horsemanship improved.

It was natural, of course, that Mr James would want to see his 'cousin' and Josie and I were a little surprised by how determined Dulcie seemed to play her part in this story. She visited Silvermoor more often than she ever had when Josie was there alone. She had had no luck selling the Emporium. After several months of advertising and writing letters to anyone she could think of who may have suitable contacts and cleaning the shop twice as much as usual so that it looked as appealing as any business in Arden could, she was despondent.

'It's starting to feel like a millstone around my neck,' she told us, 'whereas here at Silvermoor my three dearest friends can all be found and I feel my back is firmly turned on that place. Oh, my dear uncle. I loved him, but I heartily wish I hadn't taken on his legacy. But I wanted to prove I could . . .' she admitted ruefully. 'Well, I can and I have, but it's not making me happy.'

Manus had wasted no time in 'meeting' me and Josie, and we formed what to everyone else appeared an instant friendship. Josie and I often watched Manus and Walter at their riding lessons, and sometimes the earl came too.

'Unusual fellow,' he remarked, 'but a decent sort, no doubt about that. Stroke of luck that he's a horseman; he's got Walter eating out of the palm of his hand. I hope he'll fare the same in the classroom come the autumn.'

'I'm sure he will, sir,' I told him. And I was. Manus's gentle nature, which had caused him to suffer at the hands of his father, made him perfect to work with horses – and Walter. He would not force the boy to do anything, but would encourage and enthuse him, and these were the things that would best enable Walter to learn.

Ebony, whose presence had gone unexplained for a few days,

was simply Mr James's horse. If anyone had noticed that Mr James's horse had arrived days before the man himself even secured the appointment, it was not remarked upon. Similarly, if anyone thought it odd that he had only one suit and no books, these oddities seemed slight in the midst of what was clearly a very satisfactory arrangement for everyone.

No one from Heston ever came searching at Silvermoor. I don't know how the conversation between Paulson and Barridge might have gone but really, how *could* Barridge come calling on his aristocratic neighbour, accusing him of harbouring his dead son? And how could they come after me? I'd been in the lane, that was all. They couldn't accuse me of theft since Manus had ridden off on his own horse and taken me with him. We could only presume that they had decided to hope that Manus had ridden off to forge a new life far away. I did, however, hear that Paulson paid a visit to a very confused Al Crace. It had been dark the night that Paulson detained me, and he had been drinking; I believe that a fair bit of unpleasantness took place before Paulson was persuaded that Al was not his man.

It seemed that the plan had unfolded better than any of us could have hoped. It was perfect in every detail but one. Manus fretted on a daily basis about Equinox. He hated being parted from the horse who had been one of his only two friends for years of his life. And he worried what would become of her.

'What if my father mistreats her, to get back at me? Or takes her to Alderway Chase and rides her hard and breaks her spirit? Oh, I can't bear to think of it, Tommy.'

I couldn't bear it either. Yet exactly which of us could venture into Heston and rescue her? After Manus's escape security would have tripled and more. And we could hardly visit the Barridges and say, 'By the way do you happen to have a white horse going spare that I might buy?' We wracked our brains but came up with no answers.

The only other cloud on the horizon was the unrest in the villages. I heard all about it when I visited home. The strike would commence in the autumn if the masters didn't increase pay across all the villages. Stories of acts of insolence against the deputies became more common, as if things had already changed – the sullen yoke was lifting and the oxen were snorting.

Preacher Tawney redoubled his efforts to inspire the people to obedience but church attendance dropped off in favour of 'secret' meetings that everyone knew about, in the old shed where Grindley had once kept its racing pigeons. Da would have nothing to do with those and though no one dared challenge him to his face I heard from my brothers that people were starting to pass comment behind his back, saying that because I was such a friend of the earl, Da was going soft.

Da didn't care. 'Just let them say one thing to my face,' he said briefly, if the subject arose.

'I still don't like it,' he said one afternoon. 'They want

Grindley involved because they want the earl involved, I see that. He's the only one of the masters who cares what happens to us and the only one with the authority – *perhaps* – to make a change. I'd go so far as to say that everything now is riding on your earl, Tommy. It all rests with him.'

'And he feels it,' I said. 'It's a weight on him. He'll do what he can, Da, I know that, but don't forget who he's up against.'

'Aye, Barridge,' Da agreed, glum. 'I've not a lot of hope, lad. God only knows what all this'll come to, where we'll end up. All the same, though,' he added, brightening for just a moment, 'imagine if it did pay off! Imagine if we all had higher wages . . .'

I smiled. The strike was like a storm blowing in, an ominous rumble over the horizon. But it was an ill wind that blew no good, and a strong one, if it had the power to make my father dream a little.

# Chapter 67

## Josie

Winthrop Barridge had not decided to let his son's escape go unchallenged after all. We realised it one morning when Manus burst in on us in the copse, interrupting a rare and precious moment of privacy for Tommy and me – and making not a word of apology about it. I didn't mind too much. Our kisses were wild and sweet as briar roses and I could have indulged in them all day long, but we both knew where that could lead and it was getting harder and harder to pull away. Tommy must finish school and I must not disgrace myself and altogether it was probably a good thing that Manus arrived just then. Besides, he was my brother. Every day now I woke to the joyful remembrance that I had a brother and a fiancé. I was no longer a Westgate but somehow, magically, I had family. I had never known such happiness.

Manus was panting and brandishing a newspaper. 'Look!' he demanded. 'Look!'

We sat up hastily, brushing moss from our clothes and leaves from our hair.

He had folded the page not to some dramatic news, as I would have expected, but to the livestock page. I frowned. Did he want to buy a cow? Then Tommy pointed at an advertisement in the equestrian column. Equinox was for sale!

'He's doing it to flush me out!' Manus exclaimed. 'He knows I won't let her go to any old home. He knows that if I'm in the area, I'll see this and he hopes it will drive me to rash action.'

'Well, don't let yourself be driven, for goodness' sake,' I said, studying the advertisement. 'You've too much to lose. At least we know where she is now and we can think of a plan.'

'Another one,' Tommy remarked.

'Aye, another one,' I smiled. 'We seem to be forming one after the other, don't we, each more unlikely than the last. But surely we can think of *something*?'

The answer was simple and obvious: someone would have to go and buy Equinox. The tricky part was who. Tommy couldn't go, lest Paulson was there to recognise him. Obviously Manus couldn't go. And I, with my marked resemblance to Aunt Pheeney, could hardly beard Barridge in his den either. That left only Dulcie, but where would the Arden shopkeeper get the money to buy a fine horse and why would she even want one? It was a difficulty. And there was no time to lose; if someone else bought Equinox before us, she would be lost forever.

In the end there was only one way to manage it. We had to let Coralie into the secret. I spoke to her that very afternoon. Her astonishment was evident but as was her habit, she wasted no time in arranging things. She went to the earl and told him that she wanted to buy a horse she had seen advertised in the paper for Walter.

'It's the perfect mount for him,' she enthused as only Coralie could enthuse. 'Look, Uncle, eighteen hands and an inch. Even Walter can't outgrow that. A dressage horse – perfect to match his skills now that Mr James is bringing him on so beautifully. *And* a reasonable price.'

The earl was understandably puzzled as to why she should suddenly take such an interest in her cousin's riding, and why she should want to buy him an extravagant gift two months after his birthday. 'Walter doesn't *need* a new mount yet,' he argued disapprovingly. 'He and Windfall are a good match for each other still. And why buy a horse that's been advertised in a paper?'

'It's not just any old horse,' argued my determined employer. 'The Barridges are selling it.'

'All the more reason to avoid it, surely? Old Winthrop's probably ridden it to within an inch of its life. And I'm not sure I want any more dealings with him at present, I've more than enough with this strike business.'

'It could help. It might smooth things over to have an inter-action with him about something else. Oh, do say you'll come with me, Uncle, I can't go to Alderway Chase on my own. I'm afraid they'll eat me alive. Cedric's in London till Tuesday as you know or I wouldn't trouble you. We must strike at once!'

'I really don't have time for this, Coralie. Can't someone else go with you? Take Mr James, he knows horses, he'll be able to advise you.'

'Oh no! Not him,' Coralie gasped, then added clumsily, 'I mean, he's terribly busy.'

'*I'm* terribly busy,' the earl complained, looking at her with narrow eyes. Coralie told us afterwards that she knew she'd bungled it, but to her relief her uncle didn't press the matter. 'I'm sorry,' he said briefly. 'I really don't have the time.'

'Oh, Uncle dear,' said Coralie. '*Please?*'

Three days later Equinox, unharmed, came to Silvermoor.

# Chapter 68

# Tommy

Between my family, Josie, Manus, Dulcie and Cedric, my weeks at Silvermoor spun away. I had never known time go so fast.

My 'few hours a week' for Cedric soon became much more. A full-blown clerk I quickly became, drafting all his correspondence, which was considerable, running errands, taking notes at meetings. The situation rumbled on. Despite threats from the Barridges and pleas from the Sedgewicks, the miners remained mutinous and strike reared its unthinkable head.

'A dinner,' said the earl one afternoon. 'I shall host a dinner. Winthrop Barridge grows more obdurate with every passing day. He cuts off his nose to spite his face. Little would I care if he weren't cutting the rest of our noses off too. I don't know that it's possible to talk any sense into the man but let us try once and for all. If we're to go down, let's go down knowing we've done everything we can. We'll invite the Spackles, the people from Tysen's, the Barridges – I suppose he'll bring his dreadful sons along – and we'll force them to stay and drink brandy until we have a workable plan of action if it takes all night.'

'An excellent idea, Uncle,' said Cedric. 'I shall invite one or two politicians I know to give a broader perspective and why don't I pen a letter to a fellow in Wales I've heard about who resolved something like this a year or so ago? He might lend weight to the argument. And Tommy must come . . . We'll show them such a well-rounded picture they'd have to be blind not to see our point of view.'

'Agreed, agreed,' muttered the earl, getting up and wandering out. 'Shall we say two weeks from today? That should give us time to make arrangements and send out the invitations, but I don't wish this thing to drag on any longer than that. Let's have an end to it.'

Josie and I looked at each other in alarm. I knew we were both thinking the same thing. A dinner for everyone, including Winthrop Barridge. The one thing we had been sure of, when we encouraged Manus to come to Silvermoor, was that his father never would.

But as the days passed we calmed down. The dinner was only one evening; Manus would just have to stay out of the way. There was no earthly reason why the tutor should make an appearance. And if the earl did insist on inviting him, he could simply become ill on the day. It could all be very easily managed.

Manus, however, was understandably spooked. Even the thought of being under the same roof as his father was enough to undermine the new mesh of happiness he wore around him. The memories were too painful, the associations too bad. We arranged an emergency picnic in the woods one sunny evening, Manus, Josie, myself and Dulcie.

We settled ourselves on a tan picnic blanket Josie had procured from somewhere and feasted on cold chicken, boiled potatoes and ginger ale. Josie looked as beautiful as could be in a new pink dress that Coralie, with her great love of colour, had encouraged her to buy. Manus was looking more upset than I'd seen him in a while and that was sad to see. Dulcie was looking unusually fine, I noticed, with a white flower tucked into her dark hair and a string of pearls glistening around her neck. I hadn't seen Dulcie in pearls before. There wasn't much call for them around Arden.

As usual, she was decisive with her council. 'I shouldn't worry about it,' she advised him. 'You probably won't lay eyes on him. But even if you do, what then? Usually first sons who disappoint, discredit or in any other way disgrace their fathers are scared of being disinherited. In your case, the worst has already happened. What can he do to you now that you're dead?'

It was a good point but Manus was little reassured. 'He can ruin everything I've built so far. He can tell the earl that I'm degenerate, fatally flawed, possessed of a diabolical streak, all the things he used to tell me. The earl may believe him. At best he'll know I've been lying to him and let me go. I would hate to leave here under a cloud. I love Walter. I love Silvermoor.'

'But you forget,' said Josie, 'he can't expose you without exposing himself. It's he who declared you dead and hid you away. He has far, far more to lose than you, Manus. If I were you, I'd walk right on into that dinner just so that he *can* see you, just for you to see his face. He'd sweat like a pig.'

And then it dawned on the rest of us that of course Winthrop Barridge was also *her* father. The fact was so improbable and our knowledge of it so new that it was easy to forget. *Josie's* father, who presumably didn't even know of her existence, and on whom she had never even laid eyes, was coming to dinner.

'*I'm* going to get a look at him,' she went on. 'I'll have a word with Ally the maid and get her to pretend to be ill. I'll serve in her stead. I want to be at that dinner. I want to see that Barridge.'

'Is that wise?' asked Manus. 'The resemblance . . . he might notice.'

She shrugged. 'See if I care. Why shouldn't his mistakes come back to haunt him?'

'*Can* you serve?' wondered Dulcie. 'There are quite specific customs at an event like that. You've never done work of that sort, have you?'

Josie snorted. 'I can stick potatoes on a plate as well as the rest of them. Coralie will be there, Cedric will be there, my father will be there and Tommy will be there. Do you think *I'm* going to miss it? Oh no. I'll be there, don't doubt it.'

We didn't.

# Chapter 69

## Josie

I woke on the morning of the dinner with my stomach churning. For all my bravado, I was going to set eyes on Winthrop Barridge – my father – for the first time in my life. That alone was daunting; add to it the fact that he was known to be the cruellest man in five counties and I hardly knew how I could keep my composure through it all.

I wanted Tommy to hold me and tell me all would be well, but we were unlikely to see each other today. Coralie needed me; Cedric and the earl needed Tommy. We had done very well for time together this summer. The Honeycrofts and the earl had indulged us and we knew it. This was just one day and it wouldn't have mattered at all . . . if it hadn't been the most momentous day of my life.

I was subdued as I went about my morning tasks. My stomach was griping and I was worried. I'd bribed Ally (with money and the promise of trimming her old bonnet before Sunday, when she was meeting a new sweetheart) to pretend she had stomach flu this evening. At this rate I would be the one laid up in bed.

Although I didn't lay eyes on Tommy in the household whirl, I did see Manus – my *brother*! That thought still filled me up and made me smile. So did knowing that I wasn't related to Coralie; our lovely arrangement need never be spoiled.

In the time Manus had been at Silvermoor he'd started to look healthier. His skin had lost its moonlight pallor and acquired something of a summer glow. It made his hair look whiter than ever by contrast but it suited him. His nervous mannerisms hadn't made a showing for some time; around the horses he was always relaxed and confident. His old-fashioned clothes had aged him; now, in his new clothes, he looked his age, which was thirty-five. Now he wore a ready smile which made more difference to his appearance than anything. Altogether he had emerged as an attractive man. I knew that Dulcie had noticed, which made me think mischievous thoughts.

Today, however, Manus was so white he was almost sickly. In fact, he looked very much the way I felt.

'Josie,' he murmured when we passed each other on the stairs, 'you're so pale.'

I laughed. 'That makes two of us,' I told him. 'You look like the ghost you're supposed to be. And *you're* not even going to see him! Oh Manus, I've bitten off more than I can handle. I can't be in that room with him all night, knowing who he is to me, knowing what he's done to you, to my mother. For two pins I'd tell Ally the plan's off, but that if he came here and I never even saw him . . . I'd regret it, I know I would.'

'You can do it, Josie,' he said firmly. 'You're the bravest person I know. I'll never forget the night I met you. If someone had told me then that you were my sister, it would have been such a balm to me. I may even have left much sooner. Anyway, I'm proud of you.'

My eyes filled with tears. My old family had never shown such faith in me, except for Martha. My brother Bert was a good sort, but he was a *different* sort. He didn't think beneath the surface of things, didn't say much. That Manus saw something admirable in me made me feel warm and worthwhile. I remembered my mother accusing me of thinking I was special and me desperately denying it. Well, perhaps I *was* special. Perhaps I wanted to be.

Somehow I made it through the day. It was a long while since I'd known time to go so slowly. At five o'clock Ally and I slid into the library to go over the plan. She would take to her bed, I would carry the news that she was ill to Mrs Roundsby, along with the solution: that I would take her place. I'd cover her duties the next day too to make it convincing, and I'd volunteer to run up and down to check on her, so the others wouldn't see her looking healthy. The day after that she'd resume her duties bravely, though she must remember to yawn a lot and have a couple of dizzy spells. I would then trim her hat with satin buttercups, something for which she had a great yearning.

When I'd coached her through the next two days for the

tenth time, she lost patience. 'All right, Josie, all right!' she exclaimed. 'Never mind a poorly stomach, you're giving me a headache. I'm going to bed now. You can go and tell Mrs Roundsby whenever you see fit. I know the plan.'

The library door was ajar and just then we heard voices along the corridor. The earl and Portis.

'Really, Portis, it's most inconvenient,' said the earl. 'Today of all days! Can't you tell him to come back tomorrow?'

'I would, m'lord. In fact, I did. But he insists it cannot wait. I've had quite the tussle with him or I'd not have bothered you. In short, my lord, I cannot get rid of him.'

'Oh, very well, Portis, show him into the library. I'll give him ten minutes, no more.'

'Very good, sir.'

'The library!' squeaked Ally and darted out like a shot squirrel. She vanished while the earl's footsteps could still be heard approaching.

I should have followed her lead but my lamentable curiosity got the better of me. I hesitated just that moment too long. I had no reason to be in the library. I didn't want to make a fumbling explanation and arouse suspicion before the dinner. At least, that was the excuse I made to myself for the shocking thing I did next. I jumped behind the long curtains and sat on the windowsill, as still as could be. The moment I was there I felt awful. Deliberately eavesdropping on the earl, who had always been so good to me, was a terrible thing to do. But it was too late now; he was in the library, pouring himself a glass of something and swearing softly under his breath. I grimaced. Not in the best humour then. I had to stay put.

A moment later Portis showed the unwelcome visitor into the library and the earl greeted him tersely. 'How do you do? You catch me at a very inopportune time but Portis said it was a matter of urgency. Make it quick, if you please.'

'I'm sorry to come at a bad time, my lord,' said a voice I didn't recognise. 'It's something that's been bothering me for some time now and, well, it just can't wait any longer.'

The earl sighed and did not offer him a drink.

'It's been a thorn in my side for years now. It has to be said, only I didn't know how, or when, or *what* to say . . . it's not easy, my lord.'

'Yet inspiration came to you today of all days,' said the earl wryly. I winced on behalf of the visitor but his next words made all my sympathies vanish.

'It's not to be borne any longer, the way you favour Tommy Green. You've singled him out, you've sent him to school . . . it's all over the village that you think he's your son. And now he stays all summer at Silvermoor, working side by side with your nephew as if he's a gentleman. And he's *not*! He's just a common miner's son, no blood in him beyond that which is black with coal.'

My jaw dropped. *Who* was this who spoke of my Tommy with such venom? Who cared enough how Tommy spent his summer to broach it with the earl in his home? I ached to tweak

445

the curtain, to see who this person was. He didn't sound like a miner. But I daren't. Any indulgence the earl allowed me and Tommy came from trusting us and despite our unusual freedoms, the appropriate barriers were always maintained. It was different with Cedric and Coralie, who were of a younger generation. But the earl was always the earl, and this was nothing he'd want me hearing.

'Let me understand you,' said the earl in a low voice. 'You have taken it upon yourself to call on me in my home, uninvited, on what is for me the busiest, most important day of this whole year, in order to tell me that you disapprove of the way I treat a young protégé of mine? You feel that it is somehow appropriate to hold opinions about the way I conduct my household, and *share* them with me? You come here with a load of cock and bull nonsense — common *gossip* — that I think he's my *son*? What are you thinking, man? Have you no care for your living?'

No care for his living? He was dependent on the earl then, for all he sounded educated. Was it the *preacher*?

'My lord, I haven't told you all of it.'

'Nor do I wish to hear it! I presume you've come here to throw more aspersions on Tommy's character. You've always spoken against him — quite falsely it turns out. These are not the actions of a gentleman. For God's sake, man, have you lost your mind? Why should you care what I do or don't do for Tommy Green? What has he to do with you?'

'Nothing, sir, nothing.' The man was mumbling; I could

446

hear his mortification through the curtains. 'Only he doesn't deserve your favour . . .'

'Latimer!' The earl shouted the name and I nearly jumped out of my skin. Latimer. The schoolmaster. Oh, I saw it all now. I knew what was coming before it was spoken. 'Get this through your skull – I have no interest in your views on Tommy Green. I most certainly do not have to explain myself to *you* but whilst we're having this bizarre conversation, let me assure you that I do *not* think he's my son, I never *have* thought it. I support Tommy because he's an extraordinary young man, clever, ambitious, determined, yet never ruthless. He does not pursue his dreams at the expense of others nor seek to bring others down . . .'

'*That's not it!*' My eyes widened as Latimer raised his own voice to be heard. 'He doesn't deserve your favour and I *do*. He's not your son, but I am.'

There. I knew it. Oh, this made my being Winthrop Barridge's daughter very small news indeed. I wanted to giggle, nervous and tense as I was.

'I beg your pardon,' said the earl, sounding as menacing as I had ever heard him.

'It's true. I've wanted to tell you ever since I knew but I could not. And yes, today is the day I've found the nerve. I want you to do something for me, as you do for Tommy. I am your son. I deserve it.'

'You're lying. You're a jealous, petty, troublemaker. Get out, Latimer. Go home, pack your bags and don't expect a reference.' I was shocked. The man was insufferable but to cast him off without a living?

'It's not lies, sir. My mother was Kitty Makepeace. She was the daughter of Makepeace the baker. You met her by chance in Harrogate one day. She was beautiful. You recognised her from the village and struck up a conversation and one thing led to another, sir. I beg pardon to speak of such delicate things, but she was finished when she realised she was with child. Her father wanted nothing to do with her. The bakery closed down and he moved away. She never troubled you, sir, never asked for anything.

'She brought me up in Leeds and never told me a thing about my father until she was dying. When I heard there was a post at the village school in Grindley, I took it to be near you. I thought that something in you would recognise me as your son. But you never did. I thought if I was patient, respectful of your family, the time would come. I thought if I worked hard and well, I would earn your regard. But you never noticed a thing. Whereas Tommy Green won prizes, caught your notice, earned your indulgence. Well, I won't have it any longer. I demand you recognise me. Father.'

My eyes must have been saucer-like by then. Of all the things! Imagine me making a speech like that to old Barridge. Fat chance. A long silence followed. I held my breath. You could have heard a pin drop in that library.

At long last the earl spoke again. 'Well then. You have said what you came to say and you are unburdened. You must go now, for I have urgent matters to attend to tonight.'

'And must I still pack my bags, sir?'

'Not today.'

'And should I come back tomorrow, sir? Or Friday?'

'You are never to set foot in this house again. I will come and seek you out when I'm good and ready. Say nothing of this to anyone.'

It was harsh. But there was nothing the gentry liked less than having their imperfections cast up to them. It wasn't as if Latimer was the only one; he couldn't be, not with the reputation the earl had. But he was the only one standing there telling the earl about it.

'Good day then,' Latimer said, with impressive dignity, I thought. I heard the door open and close and then a silence.

*Oh go away*, I begged the earl silently, hoping against hope that he wasn't going to stay in the library for an hour or two of introspection. Quite apart from my fear that Mrs Roundsby would go looking for Ally and my plan would fall apart, I was getting cramp. I heard the creak of leather as the earl sank into a chair.

'Well, confound it!' he swore. 'Jesus God confound it all!' I bit my lip. He gave a loud, angry groan. 'Dammit,' he muttered. 'Latimer. Latimer of *all* people. Shame it *couldn't* be Tommy!'

I sat through another few groans and some extraordinary swear words that I'd never heard before. The chair creaked again and I heard the clink of a decanter. Then came the wistful sigh that often follows a drink being thrown back, then at last, footsteps and the door. He was gone.

# Chapter 70

## Tommy

An hour before the big dinner, I found myself in the dining room with Cedric and the earl, going over last-minute tactics with Cedric while the earl made adjustments to the seating plan and drove Mrs Roundsby mad. He was unusually short with everyone. I supposed the importance of the night must be taking its toll.

Josie was there too, taking a crash course in formal dinner-time service. She had swapped her grey and white striped gown for the black uniform and white apron of the domestic maid and her fiery hair was tucked beneath a white cap. Already a wisp was escaping.

At last the table was arranged to perfection. Josie had been hustled out to the kitchen. Lady Amelia drifted in. In all the time I had spent at Silvermoor I had never seen her before except at public events. I remembered my first sight of her when I was five years old. She was just as beautiful tonight.

Years older, of course, but that made no difference. Her pale hair was done up in coils and braids, with a burgundy flower tucked in one side. It matched a burgundy gown of some sheeny, glowing fabric which gave colour to her face.

'Come, Rufus,' she said in a deep, gentle voice that made me think of elven forests and river nymphs. 'Your guests will arrive and you won't even be dressed.'

'*Our* guests, my dear,' he amended. 'Yes, you're right. I should go. Cedric, you're done with me?'

'Yes, Uncle. Hello, Aunt Amelia, you look wonderful. Aunt, do you remember Tommy Green? He's been my right-hand man these last weeks.'

She looked at me and I was fairly dazzled. I was sure there were stars in her eyes, actual stars. *How* could the earl be unfaithful to her? But as she looked at me those stars hardened to flint.

'Ah yes, the miner's boy,' she said lightly. 'Good evening.'

And for me the spell was broken. She thought I was his son, I realised. As did many, no doubt. It was incredible that I was here – so much so that the wrong explanation seemed the only possible one. I sighed.

'Remarkable woman,' said Cedric, looking after her as she glided out, 'but she can be a little . . . chilly. Poor Uncle. It wasn't a love match. Anyway, she's right. We must dress, Tommy. Off with us!'

I ran back to the cottage and stepped into the black suit with evening jacket and bow tie that Cedric had loaned me. I slicked down my hair with water and a little pomade, also courtesy of Cedric. My curls seethed under the restraint but for once I looked respectable. In fact, I looked like a gentleman. I took a few deep breaths. There was really no need to be nervous. It was the earl and Cedric who had to influence people. I was only going because Cedric was so generous and wanted to include me after the work I had done for him. I would make small talk, I would stay in the background; I wouldn't be significantly affected by the outcome either way. My family would, the earl would, but I would go back to Westonbury next month and after that I would leave and seek a position wherever I chose and I knew one thing: it would have nothing to do with coal.

Yet I *was* nervous because I had never been present at a function of this sort before. How would they view me, these rich folk who might also think that I was the earl's son? It might not be a comfortable evening. Well, I had promised to be there and I would. I must be there for Josie, too; we would see Winthrop Barridge for the first time tonight. I took a deep breath and set off across the lawn to the house.

The guests were already assembling for pre-dinner drinks in the drawing room. I hesitated on the threshold, intimidated by the large number of dinner jackets. They looked like a flock of jackdaws, while the women stood like a bouquet of blooms, quite separate. Cedric detached himself from the flock to usher me in and introduce me. There were three men from

Tysen's alone: Mr Tysen himself, the founder of the company, Mr Wickleton, the partner who'd had the dubious honour of having the new pit named after him and Mr Hallow, another partner. Three very senior people at one dinner. They were taking this seriously and intended to be heard.

There was Mr Spackles from Steepley and Mr Howells, the Welshman Cedric had invited to inspire us with his stories of managing a similar situation in the South Wales valleys. Except for Mr Howells they had all brought wives. The earl was there, of course, and Lady Amelia, Lady Flora and Coralie. There was no sign of Josie or the Barridges.

I couldn't shake a sense of menace in the air and found myself altogether wishing the night could be over. The earl glanced frequently at his watch and I could tell he was annoyed that the Barridges were so late. In fact, he still seemed remarkably tense, as if the slightest thing might set him off. I was put in mind of firedamp lurking in a mine.

Winthrop Barridge and his two sons arrived just as we were going in to dinner. To be so late was wildly discourteous; I thought the earl might make a cutting remark. But breeding, it seemed, was stronger than inclination. He greeted them graciously, quickly introduced them all around and showed them to their places. You could not fault his manners; no one would guess at his discomposure unless they knew him.

I stared in fascination at the newcomers. They made me think of a tribe of warlocks. They brought no womenfolk; no

Mrs Barridge, no Barridge sisters. Like Manus, they were all tall and rangy. They all wore heavy dark coats over their evening dress despite the clement evening. They all had beaky noses and straight dark hair combed back from a proud brow. The twins were identical. I knew I would never be able to tell them apart and hoped that Jocelyn stayed to the right of Willard at all times. Not that *I* would be engaging in conversation with them, I could tell that at once by the way their eyes swept over me, incurious, disdainful.

The father – Josie's father – was a hatchet, I could tell at once. His cheekbones were sharp, his nose was a hook. His presence was undeniable, though he was neither handsome nor charming. Beside him, the earl – good-looking, mannerly, charismatic – faded, as if the darkness of one sapped all the colour from the other.

Most notable were Barridge's eyes. They were dark, like obsidian, like a night without stars, like *Josie's*, I realised with a sudden shock. Just like Josie's. Except that *her* dark eyes danced with questions and merriment and warmth. His were as cold and flat as the bottom of a well. I understood Manus all the better. Any son might find it hard to stand up to an autocratic father – *I* knew that well enough. This man was something different. He was a force, like gravity, who could bend and influence by his very presence. I looked at him and thought, *We will lose the argument tonight*.

I was grateful to be seated next to Lady Flora at dinner. At least there was someone I knew a little beside me. To my right was Mrs Wickleton, who was tall and statuesque and seemed uninterested in the proceedings. Coralie was opposite and she winked at me when we were all seated.

The earl made a toast, welcoming everyone, talking of changing times and the need for harmony, for creative solutions and new approaches. I felt inspired and dared a glance at Winthrop Barridge. Inspiration was doused. His two sons had the same dark eyes, although whereas their father's were blank and shadowy, theirs glittered like coal. They looked like wild creatures waiting for a kill. Where had this diabolical family come from? Were they sprung from the depths of the earth, from the very coal seams? Were they the demons I had imagined during my days in the tunnels?

The first course was announced, a soup of celery and mint, summery and elegant. Josie was suddenly at my side, serving as though she'd been doing it all her life. 'Thank you,' I murmured.

'You're welcome, sir,' she murmured back. She moved along the table and I watched as she reached her half-brothers and her father. They ignored her, of course, and when the bowls were all filled, she took her place at the side of the room with Portis and another maid. She looked demure and professional. I knew she was taking in every detail and every word.

The dinner party made polite, general conversation for all of about ten minutes before one of the Barridge sons – Jocelyn on that side, wasn't it? – brought up the matter at hand. 'So

Sedgewick, what's to do about this strike?' he asked, as though the earl were a deputy or a manager. 'You're not still proposing we give in and up their wages, are you?'

There was a tangible ripple of shock around the table at his insolent tone. His father made no move to check or reprove him. I was put in mind of Paulson, always flanked by his savage dogs. This seemed a similar arrangement.

I saw a muscle twitch beneath the earl's eye, but his tone was light and even. 'As a matter of fact, I am, young Jocelyn,' he said. I smiled. Insolent met by patronising. One all. 'I've thought long and hard about it. The fact is, they do have a point.' He began to list all the arguments that we'd been rehearsing all week. There had been no pay rise in the local mines for fifteen years. As a result, some of the South Yorkshire pits, including Hepzibah, Drammel Depth and Wickleton's, were the lowest paid in Britain.

'If we accede,' he said, 'we wouldn't be setting a harmful precedent, nor engaging in some lunatic strategy the likes of which has never been seen before. We would merely be raising our rates of pay to a level commensurate with the rest of the country. I think no one here can deny that our workforce are the legs we stand on. We have a long history of attracting the best workers, the strongest, the least contentious.'

'Pah!' snorted Barridge Senior. 'They want to strike. I call that contentious, Sedgewick. Perhaps we have different definitions of the word.'

'*In general*, the least contentious,' the earl continued, unperturbed. 'We've enjoyed an unusual period of calm for our industry. This is the first uprising we have had to deal with in a very long time. I believe that is cause to consider it most carefully. Our men are not firebrands, willing to start up over any imagined grievance. They're doing essential work for money below the industry standard. Let us right the wrong. I say it's simple.'

'Impossible,' said Wickleton. 'Just think what it would do to our profits.'

'It would decrease them,' shrugged the earl. 'But think what a *strike* will do if we cannot raise our own coal, cannot fulfil our orders, if we lose contracts . . .'

'We must brazen it out,' said Winthrop Barridge lazily. 'We are men. We cannot be held over a barrel by a mob of unwashed ruffians. You sound like a woman, Sedgewick.'

This time there was an audible gasp. He had insulted the earl *and* all the women present in one fell swoop. And we were only on the first course. I couldn't tear my eyes from the earl and I think that everyone was wondering the same thing. How could one respond to such a statement?

The earl was charming. Charming could have been his middle name. 'If sounding like a woman means responding with prudence and foresight, if it means having the intelligence to learn from decades of experience, if it means having the wisdom not to cut off our nose to spite our face, then I thank you for the compliment,' he said with a smile. 'Like the invaluable women who dine with us tonight, I hope my boorish male pig-headedness has been tempered by finer qualities. The men here tonight are not callow youths – well, most of us are not,' he added, with a disdainful smile at the Barridge twins. 'We are looking to the future, we are part of a bigger picture than our own selfish concerns. Let us all take a bold stroke together and avert disaster.'

'Hear, hear,' said Mr Spackles. 'I agree, Sedgewick. Let us stand together and fall together. Let us secure the continuation of our mines, and do something for the greater good while we're at it. What's to dislike in that plan, Barridge? Jesus, God, they're only asking for a shilling!'

'What's to dislike? *What's to dislike?* I'll tell you! We don't mine coal for the good of our health. We mine it to make money. We have a massive workforce. *Only a shilling*, multiplied by all the miners in our employ, makes a good many shillings, Spackles. It's prohibitive, it's impossible. They're lucky to have jobs, all of them. Time was, they knew it. Now they're getting ideas, no doubt because of what they've heard about the indulgences at the Sedgewick mines. Oh yes, Sedgewick, safety measures and money for widows and parties on special days . . . *you've* given them ideas and now they've spread. And we've mutiny on our hands. Well, *they* might say mutiny but I say war!'

A hubbub broke out around the table as everyone turned to

their neighbour to mutter urgent opinions they were too timid to lay before Barridge or the earl. I lifted my eyes to meet Josie's for the first time. Hers were wide and incredulous. I knew what she must be thinking: *This man is my father?*

'War?' cried the earl. 'Barridge, hear yourself, man. Let's try for a little perspective. We are employers deciding a course of action to best suit ourselves and our employees, that is all. We are not leaders of nations invading far-off lands—'

'No,' interrupted Barridge. 'You may be trying to suit us and them but I am not. I am trying to suit myself. Because we *are* the leaders of the nation. Where would Great Britain be without us? Our economy, our railroads, our export industry. We are the gods in this society!'

'*Gods?*' cried Cedric, anger sparking in his eyes. 'Could you be any more grandiose? How can you rest in these placid Victorian certainties when the world is changing all around us? The industry is fragile. The fabric of power threatens to tear! I have sad news for you, Barridge, and this is the fact: we are not gods. We are men, with men's faults and failings. We have come together tonight so that we might watch out for each other, prevent each other from falling prey to our own blind spots. So that together we might come to a course of action combining our greatest wisdom. Yet you are deaf and blind to all but yourself.'

'Hear, hear,' said Coralie clearly. 'Well said, Cedric.'

I looked at Josie again. Her face was flushed.

'Ah, here is the callow youth of whom you spoke, Sedgewick,' said Barridge. 'I hear idealism, I hear naivety, I hear dangerous liberalism that will beggar all our companies. But I hear no sense.'

'Beggar our companies? Barridge, we are wealthy men, all of us. We are beyond wealthy. If we cannot weather a temporary drop in profits, then we have managed our fortunes very ill.'

'Sedgewick, we are better than these men. It *is* appropriate that we maintain our standards and our lifestyles. To compromise in the way you propose goes against the very order of nature. I won't do it, I tell you. You can pay your workers more if you wish and that is your business. But I will not, and that is mine.'

He stood up and threw his napkin into his dish. I glanced at Josie once more. Was he *leaving*? 'And I think you'll find that Tysen's are of a mind with me,' he added.

But the three Tysen's men looked unsure. I could see that they had come here of one mind but that they had changed their views in the face of the earl's persuasive logic, and the support of Cedric and Spackles. They said nothing.

'But as you well know, Barridge,' replied the earl in a low voice, 'there is no point in me paying my men more if you will not do the same. They will strike anyway. They stand together now, your men and mine, Tysen's and Spackles', for the first time in memory. Persist in this and you will bring us all down.'

'So be it.'

'Mr Barridge, won't you sit down and enjoy the roast lamb that is to come?' asked Lady Amelia in her soothing tones. 'Perhaps we should postpone further talk of this matter for a while and enjoy the dinner. Josie, please fetch Mr Barridge a clean napkin.'

Josie darted to a table where clean linen, glassware and cutlery were laid out and took a snowy napkin to her father. 'Sir,' she said in a small voice, holding it out to him. He snatched it without giving her a look. He remained standing, as if debating whether to stay or go, while the twin watchdogs observed him attentively with their glittering eyes. Josie watched him too; I could see her taking in every detail of his face from close quarters. Seen side by side like that, there was a noticeable resemblance between them. I looked cautiously around the table to see if anyone else had noticed it but, of course, there were greater dramas unfolding.

'Josie,' snapped Lady Amelia and Josie was startled back to herself. She resumed her place at the edge of the room. The lamb was brought out and the servants stirred themselves to continue the dinner party, while Winthrop Barridge remained standing and glowering and it wasn't until a plate of fragrant lamb was laid before him that he consented to sit down again. He chewed with a dogged air and another course passed with only a little small talk, as did the lemon ice to cleanse the palate.

But when the Baked Alaska was brought out, Barridge began again. Mrs Henrietta Tysen was recounting her elder daughter's triumph singing in a regional concert when he cut right across her, mid-sentence, as if the last forty minutes of peace had never been.

'Then tell me, Sedgewick,' he said. 'How *exactly* do you propose to pay this surplus salary? You must have managed your fortune very wisely indeed if you can fund an annual increase of that amount without feeling the sting of it.'

And that was the end of the earl's patience.

'Dammit!' he bellowed, slamming a hand on the table, making the guests jump and the cutlery jingle. 'Will you mind your manners, Barridge? A lady was talking. Please excuse our excitable companion, Mrs Tysen,' he added in an aside then returned his attention to Barridge. 'The point of the exercise is not for us to avoid sting. A sting will not kill us, I daresay!'

'How then?' pressed Barridge, inexorable.

'If necessary, I shall sell my daughters' diamonds!' roared the earl, pushed beyond endurance.

Everyone looked startled, none more so than Lady Flora, who raised an involuntary hand to her throat where a magnificent choker sparkled in the lamplight.

'For God's sake, man!' the earl continued. 'My wife and daughters alone are wearing more money's worth tonight than these men, who risk their lives and their sons' lives every day, see in a year! We could give them *all* away and still be wealthy. We could give them all away and know that within a year our fortunes will be on the rise again – and we can buy more diamonds.'

'You grow a little wild, sir,' said Barridge in amusement. 'My wife and daughters do not wear diamonds.' No one would disbelieve him. His wife and daughters wore dark weeds and ashes no doubt. *They* had no reason to sparkle or shine.

Then Lady Flora did something that made me understand why I had always loved the Sedgewicks and aspired to be like them. 'Here, Father,' she said, unfastening her gleaming collar. 'What you say makes perfect sense.' She reached across the table and dropped the diamonds beside her father's plate.

'A pretty gesture,' sneered Barridge. 'I suppose you will give away your fine gowns to the women of the villages next. I suppose you will give them your next fine dinner of roasted lamb and sup yourself on bread and cheese.'

Lady Flora shrugged. 'Perhaps once in a while,' she agreed.

At last, Tysen spoke up. 'I'm with Sedgewick, Barridge,' he said. 'I didn't think I would be but I agree; we have worse times ahead if we persist in our obstinacy. I would view a pay increase as an investment in the business, just as we would the cost of building a new office, or sinking a new mine. That's the way of business. Let us give them the raise and be done with it.'

Barridge merely shook his head, lips pursed.

'Oh, he will not!' exclaimed Spackles. 'He's a hard, cruel man. Yes you are, Barridge, we all know it. It's known throughout the county. We all know you don't care tuppence for your men.

You'd see all your workers and all of us besides in hell before you'd climb down off the mighty pedestal where you've put yourself. You don't care a spit!'

'Gentlemen,' said the earl decisively, rising to his feet. 'The evening gets out of hand. There is no reason for the ladies to be subjected to high temper. Let us retire to the drawing room and bring our debate to a civilised conclusion over brandy and cigars. Ladies, please excuse us and enjoy your sweet.'

# Chapter 71

## Josie

The men rose, the women looked somewhat relieved. I could not have moved for all the chocolate in York. As I watched the men go I didn't take my eyes off my father, for probably this would be the last I ever saw of him.

Then, as Willard Barridge passed me, he stopped dead and reached out to detain his twin. 'I say, Joss, look at that!' he cried. I was thirteen years old all over again, standing in Dulcie's shop and clutching a bag of flour. Jocelyn Barridge stopped and looked and so did everyone else.

'She looks familiar,' he said. 'Who is she, Will?'

'I've been wondering all night. I've been casting my mind back over dinner parties and servants but that's not it. Look again.'

Jocelyn stepped closer. I knew I was bright red but I lifted my chin as high as it would go. Even so, I was shrinking inside myself. Anyone would, with that crow of a man advancing on them. Suddenly, without a word, Tommy was at my side.

'I see it!' Jocelyn said. 'God save us if she isn't the absolute image of Aunt Pheeney.'

'That's enough!' exclaimed Cedric. 'You've no business scrutinising our staff like that. I won't stand for it. Come away now. Josie, if you wish, you may be excused.'

But now Winthrop Barridge had stopped. 'Josie?' he asked. 'You have the same name as my sister? Whose are you, girl? Who is your mother?' I wanted to answer him – oh, how I wanted to. But I could not. The man had turned my tongue to stone.

'Barridge!' cried the earl. 'Leave the girl alone. Come into the drawing room to resolve the issue at hand or get out of my house.'

Barridge took another hard look at me then turned on his heel. 'It doesn't matter,' he said. 'Come on, Will, Joss. It's time we left. There'll be no agreement tonight.'

They started from the room, Willard looking back over his shoulder, an unpleasant mixture of curiosity and dislike on his face. Tommy was still beside me, letting them know I wasn't alone in the world. Coralie was looking on, wide-eyed.

At last they were gone. Cedric looked back at us and nodded, understanding that Tommy would stay with me. But then the strength returned to my legs and I found my tongue. This *was* the last I would see of my father, and I could not let him leave on these terms. I could not have him ignore me, inspect me and then walk away, with me only standing like a terrified mouse. I was not Manus. He had not cowed *me* since birth. I walked out of the room and into the hall, where the Barridges were calling for their coats and Spackles and the Tysen men were being shown into the drawing room. I walked right up to Winthrop Barridge and addressed him, knowing all the while that Tommy was at my shoulder.

'Yes, sir, I am named after your sister. My mother is Maggie Westgate and I have only recently learned, to my very great disappointment, that you are my father. But in one thing you are right. It doesn't matter.' I was pleased to hear that my voice came out strong and scathing.

A hush fell over the hall. The other men hurried discreetly into the drawing room but stopped short of closing the door. The scandal was too delicious. One of Barridge's by-blows serving him soup under his very nose! The earl raised his eyebrows.

'Well, what of it?' Barridge demanded. 'I see you've somehow made something of yourself. You have influential employers and no doubt wish to call in a birthright now, extort some money out of me. Well, you shan't get any.'

'How perceptive you are, sir, how well you understand human nature,' I said with great sarcasm. 'No, I wish nothing from you. You disgust me. I merely wish you to know that I know, and that I am not one bit afraid of you. I am glad with all my heart that I've never had anything to do with you. I intend to keep it that way.'

I turned on my heel and began to walk away, with great dignity, towards the staircase. Behind me, the earl spoke up.

'I think you should know, Barridge, that Josie is an important part of this household. I need your promise that you and your sons will make no trouble for her. She has my absolute protection.' I smiled and began climbing the stairs.

'Strong words,' drawled Barridge. 'I make you no promise, Sedgewick. You have tried my patience tonight. What do I care if one of my mistakes is living under your roof? What do I care if my men strike and yours along with them? My fortune is vast, I can wait out whatever lies ahead without bending or conceding. This country has a hierarchy for a reason. You seem to have forgotten the way things are meant to be. I am Winthrop Barridge. No one can touch me.'

'Really?' said the earl and I noticed a change in his tone. As if, all of a sudden, he had discovered that he held the winning card in a game. As if he knew that everything was within his power and the next roll of the dice would bring about his opponent's downfall. I paused halfway up the stairs and turned. I noticed the drawing room door had opened a little wider. The other men were listening. 'No one can touch you?'

'No one,' said Barridge. 'I bid you goodnight.'

'Not even a scandal that would close every door in the country to you? Not the revelation of a secret that would reveal you in the worst possible light and be the ruination of your entire family? You know, Barridge, no one would ever do business with you again if they knew that your child was living incognito under my roof.'

Barridge looked at him scornfully. 'I don't *care!*' he said slowly, as if speaking to an idiot. 'I don't care if she works here, I don't care if it's known I've fathered a bastard or two. I'm not the first and I won't be the last. That child is no threat to me.'

'No indeed,' said the earl, 'but I'm not talking about Josie. I'm talking about your son.'

Now the dining room door had crept open too and I saw the faces of Lady Flora and Coralie peeping out. Barridge scowled. 'What the devil are you talking about?' he demanded, casting a glance at Tommy as if fearful that he might be his too.

'I'm talking about your legitimate son, your rightful heir, whose death you feigned and whose existence you've kept a secret all these many years,' said the earl. I was shocked. The earl knew about *Manus*?

My half-brothers hovered, composure chipped for once. 'I'm talking about your eldest son, James Barridge, whom you've kept hidden away God knows where for ten years and who is currently living in my house, masquerading as my son's tutor.'

Oh, it was glorious! You could have heard a pin drop. I heard a gasp from the dining room and the ladies drifted out silently. Mr Spackles stepped into the hall as well. Barridge looked around, at all the people listening, all the people who wanted him to capitulate. He looked as if he might, just might, be considering how this could ruin him. Then he laughed.

'The pressure of managing your mines has affected your mind, Sedgewick,' he said. 'I'm sorry for it, but we're not all cut out for hard times. You're utterly deluded. My son is dead.'

'On the contrary,' said the earl. 'He is teaching my son and he goes by the name of Mr James. Now, a father who would pretend the death of his own son and heir, and lock him away for above a decade is a rare thing. If it were known, the scandal would be incomparable. There are already quite a few people here tonight who have heard the truth and usually I would say that's too many for you to stand a chance of keeping the secret. However, I'm sure everyone here would be willing to maintain silence . . . *if* you let go of your determination to drive us all to a strike.'

'I always knew there was something fishy about that boy's death,' said Spackles, stepping forward. 'How the devil did you manage it, Barridge? Where did you keep the poor lad all these years? How on God's earth did he end up here?'

'They kept him at Heston Manor,' I said, smiling sweetly and starting my way back down the stairs. A dignified exit was one thing but this was too good to miss. 'No one was ever allowed to the estate and he was kept to the house by daylight. No one laid eyes on him for a very long time. But he escaped a few weeks ago and came here to live his own life.'

'*You* had something to do with this?' growled Barridge, glaring.

'Of course. He's my brother.'

Barridge turned to his sons. 'Go home,' he told them.

'But . . . Father . . .' stammered Jocelyn.

'If what they say is true . . .' interjected Willard. He was thinking of his inheritance, you could see it plainly.

'Go *home*!' repeated Barridge, in a tone of ice and thunder. They went. Then Barridge turned to the earl. 'We'll talk in private.'

'The library will serve,' said the earl. 'Come, Josie, Tommy.'

'*In private*, I said,' growled Barridge.

'Me, sir?' Tommy asked.

'If Josie knows something, there's no doubt that you do too. It's time I got to the bottom of things. Cedric, please will you go up and ask Mr James to join me in the library? Apologise for disturbing him.'

Cedric took the stairs two at a time.

'Gentlemen, apologies for leaving you,' said the earl to his avid guests. 'Please help yourselves to whichever drinks take your fancy and I shall join you shortly.'

So there were Tommy and I in the earl's library yet again. Together with the earl and *Winthrop Barridge* of all people. He was still brazening it out. 'I don't believe a word of it,' he said airily. 'This is an outlandish story. No one would ever believe it. This is clearly some scheme to bend me to your will. It won't work.'

Just then the door opened and Manus came into the library. When he saw old Winthrop, the blood drained from his face. And our father looked as though he'd seen a ghost, which in a way he had.

# Chapter 72

────── ❦ ──────

# Tommy

'A fortune,' said Barridge immediately, 'if you will leave and never come back.'

The words hung in the room for a moment, then Manus said, 'I need no fortune, Father. I want nothing from you.'

'I beg to disagree,' said the earl quickly. 'It's your birthright. By killing you, your father has deprived you of your inheritance. Think again and make sure you ask for what you need. I do not suggest you rob him of his entire fortune but you will not set up a suitable life for yourself on a tutor's salary.'

'I don't know,' whispered Manus. 'What's the appropriate amount in such a situation? How many men accept payment from their fathers to continue pretending to be dead?'

'I cannot say,' said the earl. 'What do you suggest, Barridge?'

Barridge was as white as his son. 'Five thousand pounds,' he said. 'Five thousand to leave England and never use the name of Barridge again.'

'Ten,' suggested the earl amicably.

'Ten, then.'

'And eight hundred for Josie,' the earl added.

'Eight hundred for the girl,' repeated Barridge, like an automaton.

Josie looked at me and her black eyes danced.

'And I trust you will give your miners the pay rise we've discussed and put an end to this strike.'

'Yes.'

'Marvellous. When you have left, I'll tell the other men of your change of heart. They'll be delighted. You'll garner an enormous amount of goodwill – can't put a price on that. I think you'll be pleased in the long run. Now, do you have your chequebook on you? Here's a pen, dear fellow.'

Barridge sank into a chair at the desk and wrote a cheque which the earl inspected then passed to Manus. Manus stood there holding it and not saying a word. Barridge looked at Josie. 'Your name, child? Your surname?'

Josie hesitated. I knew she didn't think of herself as a Westgate any more and she certainly wasn't going to adopt Barridge.

'Green,' I said. 'She will be, soon enough,' I added to the earl and Manus.

Barridge muttered and scribbled a second cheque. 'Then we're done here,' he said, thrusting it at Josie.

'Wait!' exclaimed Manus, trembling. 'There is one more thing I need from you, Father.'

'Devil take you,' swore his father. 'I've given you the money. This is extortion. I could have you arrested.'

'It's nothing material,' said Manus. 'I'll never ask for more money, nor give away the secret, nor cause you any trouble. I'll stay as dead as you could wish, I swear it. Only there is one promise I must secure.'

'What then?'

'I want to see my sisters. I mean, Violet and Ivy, of course. And after I leave, they must be allowed to correspond with me. We must be allowed to maintain a relationship. I believe they will be as obliging and secretive as I in exchange for a chance to know their brother and a little liberty.'

Dark emotions writhed across Barridge's face like snakes. He didn't want his daughters to have any happiness or liberty, you could see it plain. Yet what reason could he give for forbidding it? The hidden, unkind way he ran his household was being brought into the light for all to see. A wicked man, cornered, was an unpleasant thing to see.

'A modest demand,' the earl commented. 'He's let you off lightly, Barridge. I imagine you'll say yes, rather than have me go to the police regarding the resurrection of your first-born?'

'Very well. They may call at Silvermoor on Monday.'

'And write to me thereafter?'

'Very well.'

'Splendid! Now I wish you a safe journey, old fellow.' The

earl rang for Portis. 'Tomorrow you'll notify your men of your decision, then put matters in motion to implement the pay increase. Shall we say effective from the end of September? It wouldn't do to let them call *all* the shots, you know. Must do these things on our terms. Ah Portis, Mr Barridge here is just leaving. Would you show him to his carriage? Goodnight, Barridge. We must dine again soon.'

Winthrop Barridge paused on the library threshold and glowered. 'I curse you, Sedgewick,' he spat in a voice thick with hate. 'I curse you to the utmost realms of hell for all eternity.' His sharp cheekbones cast narrow shadows across his face and his eyes were blacker than Crooked Ash. Again, I thought him a demon, something supernatural and twisted, and I shivered. But the earl just laughed.

By the time Barridge was gone, without a backward glance at either of his children, I was laughing too. I had never loved the earl more. I hoped that when I grew older I might acquire even a tenth of his poise and wit. Josie started laughing too, though Manus still stood like a statue.

'Oh, thank you, sir,' she gasped and held out her hand. The earl hesitated, then shook it. 'Thank you for what you have done for us both tonight. I never expected such a thing.'

'You're welcome. I've recently come to realise that a man has responsibilities to those he fathers out of wedlock as well as to those inside it. Sometimes the correct path is not easy or desirable but in this case it seemed clear. James? Or should I say Barridge? No, you're never to use that name, are you? May I call you Manus?'

Manus nodded.

'Are you all right, my good fellow? Did I run away with myself? Did you wish to say something more to your father?'

'No, I didn't. I just . . . I cannot believe what just happened. All these years I've dreaded laying eyes on him again. I've feared it. And now it's happened and he's gone and I'm *ten thousand pounds* the richer? Sir, I could never have brought such a thing about on my own account. What you've done for me . . . You might so easily have thrown me out when you knew that I'd lied to you, when you knew who I really was.'

'When I realised who you were it gave me only sympathy for you. As for lying to me, well, I beg you don't do it again, but I understand the situation was very unorthodox. I'm only sorry I'll be losing you as Walter's tutor. He thinks the world of you and you're a marvel with him.'

'If it's all right, sir, I'd like to stay a year. I know my father wishes me gone at once but I meant what I said, I shan't cause him any trouble. I'd live here as quietly as I have these last weeks. I'm fond of Walter too and I'm in no haste to leave him. And whatever my future will be, I wish it to involve Tommy and Josie. If it would not be too odd for you, sir, I could stay until Tommy's left school, and then decide.'

'No odder than you pretending to be someone else and me pretending not to know.'

Oh, but this was splendid! One more year at Westonbury and then I would marry Josie and go into business with Manus and my world would be . . . anything I wished it to be.

'Sir, how *did* you know I was me?' asked Manus. 'And why did you not challenge me?'

The earl laughed. 'I was distracted when you arrived here, Manus, enough to believe that you *were* the shopkeeper's cousin, enough not to take the trouble to verify your story. But something kept niggling at me. Several somethings. Your manner, too apologetic and diffident for a tutor of boys. Your appearance, at once very unusual and very familiar. I couldn't place it for weeks. Your close friendship with Tommy and Josie . . . overnight. And then my niece suddenly deciding she must buy the Barridge horse but adamant that *you* must not go to Alderway. That's when the penny dropped. That's when I realised why you looked familiar; it was your father that you reminded me of all along. Only in appearance, thank goodness.

'So I knew there was intrigue and that these two, and Miss Embry, and my niece besides, were somehow mixed up in it. Why didn't I confront you? Two reasons. Firstly I had too much on my mind; I needed no further tangle to preoccupy me. And secondly, I had some sort of instinct that you would be a winning hand if it came to an impasse with your father. I would not have played it like that if I hadn't needed to. But I did. And I think it's all turned out for the best.'

Hadn't it just? I thought of my father and brothers, each

earning a shilling a week more. There would be some ease at last in their little house. Winter would not go so hard on them this year. And when I was out of school I would help even more.

'Now, you two . . .' The earl turned to me and Josie. 'I want to know your part in all of this. But I have neglected guests languishing in two different rooms. I shall go and finish the evening and wrap up the business. But tomorrow I want you to tell me the whole story, if you please. Tommy, are you coming or staying?'

'I'd quite like to stay here, sir. Unless Mr Honeycroft needs me.'

'I'm sure Cedric won't mind. You can make yourselves comfortable in here if you like. Until tomorrow then.'

'Goodnight, sir,' we murmured in unison and the door closed behind him.

Left to our own devices, we looked at each other in wonder. The future, for each and every one of us, suddenly looked very different.

# Epilogue

## Tommy

*Summer 1905*

Eleven months later I returned to the house at Silvermoor. I had passed my final exams with flying colours, coming top of my class. It was a very different year from my first at Westonbury. Being certain of Josie's love, knowing that we would be together when I left school, had transformed everything. I had greater reason than ever to work hard, so that I might become qualified to earn a good living and have something to offer her – she a young lady worth some eight hundred pounds!

On the day of my homecoming I packed my bag and looked around my dormitory for the last time. I shook hands with the masters and several of the boys; there were even two with whom I would keep in touch. I said a sincere thank you to the school – in private, of course. I hadn't always enjoyed Westonbury, but it had given me the education I had always dreamed of and the resources to find a job that would fit my talents and make me happy. I still did not know exactly what it would be, but I knew it would be something wonderful, somewhere wonderful. Josie, Manus and I had written each other many letters over that year, dreaming of the places we might visit.

It seemed no time before my carriage was travelling up that broad avenue at Silvermoor once again. Walter flew out to meet me. He was fifteen now; he'd be working in the mines if he'd been born into a different family. He was starting to look a young man and we shook hands like brothers. His father followed and invited me into his study for port. He congratulated me on my examination results and gave me two hundred pounds. 'To give you a start in whatever you decide to do,' he said. 'I'm proud of you, Tommy.'

That evening, the Honeycrofts and Josie returned from two days in Sheffield, where they had been visiting Honeycroft relatives. Josie fell into my arms as if she hadn't seen me for years.

'Never again,' I murmured as I held her warm, slim body. 'Never again will we be parted, Josie. From now on let all our adventures be together.'

'Together,' she sighed and kissed my neck, making me forget where I was for a while.

A week later, we were married in the small chapel on the Silvermoor estate. It was a fine June day. I was utterly forbidden from even glimpsing Josie before the ceremony, which was at noon, and followed by a picnic luncheon on the lawn. My whole family was there. Ma and Da, all my sisters and even all my brothers. Da had spoken to Bulford and insisted they all have the day off; he was even content that they lose a day's pay. At the end of the previous summer at Silvermoor I had divided the money Cedric had paid me and given half to my father.

'Before you've even finished school,' he said in a mildly suspicious tone. 'Full of surprises, aren't you?' I took it as a thank you.

They filed into the little chapel looking as shabby and wonderful as a favourite old book or a much-loved childhood toy. Ma and my sisters all had new bonnets trimmed in improbable ways – improbable for Grindley that was. They sported satin flowers and glossy ribbons in summer colours: violet, emerald green, butter yellow. Josie had bought four plain, inexpensive bonnets in York and made them over herself. I had never seen my womenfolk look so vain.

My father shook my hand, his face granite, as if this getting married were a grim business.

'You know I'll always be in contact, don't you?' I demanded. 'You know I'll always be a Green?'

'Aye, lad.' He sighed. 'We know it.'

Ma hugged me so that I thought she would never let me go. 'Oh my boy,' she whispered. 'Top of tha class, and now getting married. Oh, I'm so proud I could burst. You look that fine, our Tommy, I never saw such a handsome gent.'

I'd spent the other half of my Cedric wages on a fine grey

suit and it was this I wore, with a green silk tie and a green silk handkerchief in my pocket, for my wedding day. Josie had insisted on the green, saying it matched my eyes. I looked quite well, I thought, but when Josie walked up the daisy-scattered path on Cedric's arm, I wondered what she saw in me. Her fiery hair was poofed and curled fit to rival Miss Coralie's own. It was twined through with cream ribbons and she wore nothing else on her head. Her skin was pale and shining, her dark eyes softly joyful. Her gown was the warm, rich shade of newly churned cream. The fabric was soft and simple; the skirt was straight and fell to the top of her boots. But there were dozens of tiny buttons sewn down her back and the sleeves were threaded with ribbons to match her hair. She wore a dainty diamond pendant in the shape of a daisy – her wedding gift from Coralie.

I felt for her when she paused at the chapel door. I had all my family there – the groom's side was teeming with Greens – whereas Josie had only her sister Martha, and Martha's new husband Edward. I had met Edward several times and he was as right for Martha as Luke Stevens had been wrong. It gave Josie immense peace of mind, as she made plans for our future, to know that Martha was happy. Their brother Bert had wanted to come but had to work that day. Not even Alice came, presumably put out that her red-headed, unpromising half-sister was to be wed on the Silvermoor estate, when she had only managed the church at Arden.

But Josie looked around and smiled. Also on her side sat her brother Manus, her beloved Dulcie, who sat with her gloved hand tucked inside Manus's arm, and of course, Coralie. When Cedric delivered Josie to the front of the chapel he took his seat beside his sister. There were two others on the bride's side of the church: Violet and Ivy Barridge, who had escaped the clutches of their father for the day to see the half-sister, of whom they had heard so much from their brother's letters, get wed.

All the Sedgewicks were there, except for Lady Amelia. She was currently on the continent. The earl had long ago recognised Latimer as his son. Lady Amelia wanted nothing to do with it and now travelled more than six months of the year. There was a new schoolteacher in Grindley, a woman! Latimer had moved to Leeds, a respectful distance from the Sedgewick family, where the earl had arranged a very fine apartment for him and spent one afternoon every month getting to know him. It was said that he did not enjoy those afternoons but was determined to do the right thing. One could only hope that Latimer was happier now.

The ceremony was conducted by Preacher Tawney, who looked bemused in the extreme by the change in my circumstances. I hoped it would not cause him a crisis of faith.

Soon the service was over, and Josie was my wife. It was a glorious moment, iridescent as a bubble. I could have stayed in it forever and yet, when it passed, everything else began. We stepped into the sunshine amid a shower of rice and rose petals. The old bronze bell pealed as if it wanted to carry the good news all the way to York Minster. Friends and family hugged and congratulated us and laughed. All except my little sister Connie, now thirteen, who stood shyly to one side of the throng, looking rather forlorn.

'What's up with you then, our Con?' I whispered, taking her aside.

'Oh Tommy!' she wailed, her eyes welling up, her bottom lip wobbling mightily. 'I'm that happy for you. But you'll go away now, farther than Derby even, and I'll miss you so much! And . . .'

'And what?'

'Well' — she lowered her voice and looked guilty — 'I don't much like Grindley. I don't want to stay washing coal, or be a miner's wife. I want to do something . . . *wonderful*! But Da says it's tomfool nonsense and I've notions.'

I grinned. 'I'm glad to hear you say that,' I told her.

'That's strange. Why?'

'Because Josie and I have had an idea we want to talk to you about. You know that we plan to go away, maybe *far* away, to a world completely different.'

'Yes.'

'And you know we'll be travelling with Manus and we'll all be starting a new life together.'

She sniffed.

'Well, we hoped you might like to come with us.'

She looked at me as if I'd grown two heads.

'We'll understand if you'd prefer to stay. We've no way of knowing what's in store and you're young to leave your parents. But *if* you come, I'll see you get a proper schooling and I'll look after you, you can be sure of that. You'd see the world, my pet. You could do and be anything you want.'

'Even singing?'

'Even singing.'

'Could I have . . . could I have . . . *singing lessons*?' She looked as if she were asking for wings. Which in a way, she was.

'You can.'

'Oh Tommy! I would *love* to come. Only Da would never let me.'

'I've spoken to him. I told him we'd be asking you.'

'And he didn't *kill* you?'

'Not yet.'

'Oh *Tommy*!'

I gave her a squeeze and went back to Josie.

The wedding party was following the earl towards the picnic. Suddenly Josie stopped; I followed her gaze. A silent figure in a dark dress stood outside the railings, watching. Seeing who it was, I made to carry on, thinking to give Josie some privacy, but she caught my hand. 'No, Tommy, come with me.'

So we walked across the grass and found ourselves face to face, though on opposite sides of the railings, with Maggie Westgate.

'Hello, Ma,' said Josie.

Her mother sighed. 'I had to have a look, I suppose,' she said flatly, as if concluding an internal conversation.

'I'm glad to see you,' said Josie. 'Won't you come in? You're welcome to join us for the feast.'

Maggie snorted. 'Nay. It's not for the likes of me in there.'

'It is,' said Josie, oh so gently. 'Celebration is for the likes of anyone, Ma.'

'Please do, Mrs Westgate,' I said. 'We'd be happy to have you.'

But Maggie shook her head. I could feel the rock of impossibility lodged inside her soul. I had known people like her all my life and my heart went out to her for all the barriers that held her, of which the iron railings were the least.

'I know who my father is,' whispered Josie. 'I'm sorry, Ma, I'm so sorry. He's a bad man. I don't blame you for hating me.'

'Oh Josie!' Maggie gasped, as if a lifetime of fury was suddenly too much to hold onto. She seemed to deflate; there wasn't much of her left without it. The stiff, bitter lines dropped from her face and for a moment I couldn't recognise her.

'We're going abroad soon,' Josie continued. 'We don't know where we'll settle yet. I don't suppose you'll want me to write to you but if you ever need me, you can send word by Silvermoor. I want you to know that I'll keep no ill feeling towards you in my heart.'

Josie reached her hand through the railings. It seemed a long moment that she stood like that, then to my astonishment, and Josie's too, no doubt, Maggie took hold of it with her own work-roughened hand, and squeezed.

'Goodbye then,' she said, and turned and walked away.

We stood and watched until she disappeared among the trees.

Hours later, when the festivities, which included fireworks, of course, were done and the guests had gone home, Josie and I sat outside enjoying the summer's evening. After a while Manus came out to join us. He sank onto the ornamental bench beside ours and gave a deep sigh of contentment as he looked up at the lilac sky and the first golden stars. He was hardly recognisable as the ghostly figure I had first seen at Heston. He had a deep tan, his white hair was cut short and fell choppily over his forehead and he had grown a moustache. His eyes gleamed with mischief and his entire air was relaxed and hopeful.

'So then,' he said as he leaned back and stretched. 'I am a man of fortune, boasting impressive experience at tutoring and training horses. You are newly-weds with a thousand pounds between you. Josie has been working in an excellent job for years and is a lady of some culture and refinement. Tommy has a first-class education and the world is his oyster. Are we still to throw in our lot together on some far-flung shore?'

I glanced down at Josie, her face contented in the dusk, her eyes full of dreams. 'We are,' she said.

'God, yes,' I added. 'I've spent all my life in a classroom or a tunnel. Now I want to stretch my legs across some outlandish horizon. I want to live my dreams. I want to live somewhere that's not permanently wrapped about in coal dust.'

'And are you certain you still want to conduct those adventures with me?' asked Manus. 'You're a young couple starting out in life. You might wish to be alone and romantic. For heaven's sake don't feel obligated to take me under your wing; I'm a different man than I was a year ago. I'll be all right.'

'Of course you will,' said Josie, 'but it's what we want. We've all been planning it for so long. You're my brother. You're part of the plan. You'll always be part of the plan. Connie's coming too. We'll have a grand old time.'

Manus smiled. 'Then we might as well add one more to the party,' he said.

'Who?' I asked, though I had a fair idea.

'Dulcie, of course.' Josie sighed happily. 'Yes, Manus. Of course Dulcie must come.'

We fell silent and watched the sky darken to powder blue then indigo and the stars turn cold and white above the woods and lawns of Silvermoor.

'So where shall we go?' asked Josie. 'London? Paris? Rome?'

'Farther,' suggested Manus. 'New York City, or Istanbul.'

'I've been thinking about that too,' I told them, 'and I believe I've thought of just the place.' They looked at me expectantly. There were so many places I wanted to see. But I knew just where we should start out. I had always known. 'How do you feel about India?'

# ACKNOWLEDGEMENTS

First thanks go to my fabulous agent Eugenie Furniss for all her hard work on my behalf and especially, this time, for giving me the seed of inspiration: 'I think someone should write a novel set in the South Yorkshire coalfield,' she said, one day long ago! After several years of mulling and gestation, I came to the same conclusion, and the result is *The House at Silvermoor*. Not only is it a book I'm proud of, but it's given me a new appreciation of what my grandfather Len did for a living, and a renewed respect for his bravery.

This wasn't an easy book to write. It was really hard to be underground so much of the time, albeit only psychically, and there was also A LOT of research to do since the place, period and industry were all new to me at the outset. Huge thanks to Bev and Paul Rogers for our fantastic research week in Yorkshire. Your enthusiasm, support and encouragement were invaluable – I never knew research could be so much fun. Thanks too to *all* my York friends for accompanying me on research trips, for fabulous hospitality and friendship. You're all wonderful. And thanks to the National Coal Mining Museum and to Beamish, the Living Museum of the North, for providing such invaluable resources.

Thank you as always to my Wales and London friends, who persuade me to get up from my desk once in a while and remind me about real life, especially: Rosie Stanbridge, Ludwig Esser, Marjorie and Dale Hawthorne, Donna Piper, Lisa Mears, Lucy Davies, Ann Davies, Patsy Rodgers, Kathryn Taussig, Liane-Louise Smith . . . Knowing you are there makes all the difference.

A special thank you is owed to my group of author friends. The support and friendship of other writers is really special – I've even written an article on it! I really value your empathy and advice. Thanks to the legend that is Twitter, and the general sociability of the publishing industry, it would be impossible to name all the lovely writers who have made a much-appreciated difference to me, but special thanks and love go to: Rebecca John, Lucinda Riley, Gill Paul, Rosanna Ley, Rachel Hore and Louisa Treger for writerly conversations during some trying times and good times too!

Thanks as always to the team at Quercus. It's been five years now and I appreciate every single one of them. Thank you to my editor, Emma Capron, for all your hard work and support. And thank you Lorraine Green for being the best copyeditor *ever*. And to sales, publicity, marketing, rights, digital and all the lovely teams who are part of my publishing experience. You're all brilliant.

Last but not least, thank you to my wonderful parents for cheerleading me through another year and another project. Thank you with all my heart for reading, listening, encouraging and being so invested in what I do for a living. And thank you to my amazing partner Phil who kept me uplifted when Tommy was stuck in the tunnel, and who has transformed everything. I love you all very much.